MW01136068

EXPOSED

Brenna

There are some people in life who know exactly how to push your buttons. For me, it's Rye Peterson. We can't spend more than ten minutes together before we're at each other's throats, which makes working together that much harder. Rye is the bassist for Kill John, the biggest rock band in the world, and I am his publicist. It doesn't help that the man is gorgeous, funny, talented, and...never takes anything seriously. Avoidance is key.

But everything changes when he overhears something he shouldn't: a confession made in a moment of weakness. Now the man I've tried so hard to ignore is offering me the greatest temptation of all—him.

Rye

Brenna James is the one. The one I can't have. The one I can't get out of my mind. Believe me, I've tried; the woman loathes me. I managed well enough—until I heard her say she's as lonely as I am. That she needed to be touched, held, *satisfied*. And I could no longer deny the truth: I wanted to be the one to give her what she craved.

I convinced her that it would just be physical, mutual satisfaction with nothing deeper. But the moment I have her, she becomes my world. I've never given her a good reason to trust me before. Now, I've got to show Brenna that we're so much better together than we ever were apart.

Things are going to get messy. But getting messy with Brenna is what I do best.

AUTHOR NOTE

This book mentions a past instance of an attempted suicide by one of the secondary characters. It is not depicted on the page.

I have tried my best to treat this subject as respectfully and realistically as possible. And while I have consulted with sensitivity readers, and those who have had similar experiences, I am aware that certain points might not resonate the same with everyone. Any mistakes are my own.

Lastly, if you are hurting, please reach out to someone—a friend, a family member, a doctor, or therapist. Reaching out might feel hard but it can make all the difference.

—Love Kristen

EXPOSED

KRISTEN CALLIHAN

Plain Jane Books

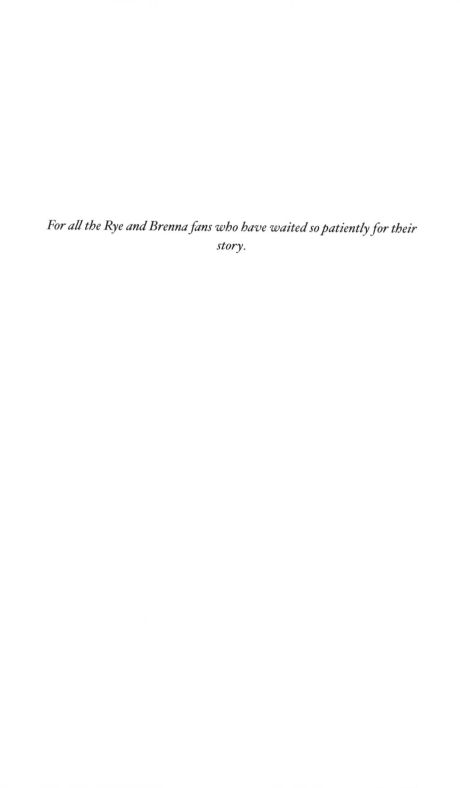

For all the Rye and Brenna fans who have waited so patiently for their story.

Anything worth doing takes a little chaos

— FLEA

CHAPTER ONE

BRENNA

THERE IS a time in a woman's life when her friends start finding their true loves and suddenly everything is a couple's deal, complete with private looks and inside jokes that you're no longer part of, and ugh! Somebody hand me a drink already and get me out of this nightmare.

Not very eloquent, I realize, but that's my general sentiment at the moment.

I mean, who among us hasn't watched the great Adam Sandler bellow "Love Hurts" in *The Wedding Singer* and empathized? Maybe that's just me. God, I hope it isn't just me.

Not that I don't believe in love; I dwell under the blinding light of its shining splendor almost every day. I see the happiness being in love has brought my friends. I'm a believer. But after years of dating, years of searching for that spark and getting only tiny flickers, I'm done waiting.

More to the point, I'm busy.

Even so, I'm in a tetchy funk as I head into my favorite neighborhood bar for a much-needed vodka tonic.

Thankfully, my still-single—and thus not moony-eyed—friend Jules is waiting for me in a booth near the back. It's Thursday night and crowded with young professionals like myself who just want to let loose and perhaps get laid if opportunity strikes. Unfortunately, I'm also done with hookups. They've given me nothing but annoyance and mild regret. The kind you have when you order the dinner special because it sounds fantastic, but it ends up leaving you with raging heartburn.

"Hey," Jules says with a smile. "I've already ordered for us."

After three years of working together, she knows exactly what I like to drink. And I could kiss her right now for saving me from needing to flag someone down. "You are a goddess of the highest order. You know that, right?"

"Of course, I do. You're in a mood, aren't you?" Jules asks as I plop down opposite her.

"I just came back from dinner with Jax, Stella, Sophie, Scottie..." I hold up a finger to ward off her comment. "And Killian and Libby."

Jules's nose wrinkles in sympathy. "Stuck in a lovefest, eh?"

"You know it." And she does. Jules and I both work for Kill John, the best rock band in the world—that's fact, not opinion, if anyone asks. I'm the head of publicity, and Jules is an assistant to Scottie.

Singer-guitarist Killian is my cousin, and he's married to Libby, who is an exceptional singer in her own right. Jax, also singer-guitarist, is now living with his girlfriend, Stella, who handles our charity fundraising efforts. And band manager Scottie is married to the band photographer and social media liaison, Sophie. I love my guys. I love my ladies. All of them are my closest friends. That doesn't mean they don't get on my nerves now and then.

A server drops off our drinks, and I take a long, cooling sip of vodka tonic before sighing in contentment.

Jules toys with the little spear of cranberries in her pink

martini. "How did you end up being the oddball out? Where were Whip and Rye?"

Whip and Rye make up the other two members of Kill John. Whip, the drummer, is a sweetheart but is becoming more and more distant from the rest of us. "Whip is nursing a cold and didn't want to risk anyone else getting sick."

I'd missed hanging out with him, but I have the feeling that, like me, he's weary of all the couple love.

Jules raises an expectant brow. "And Rye?"

Rye. The bass guitarist. The *ass*. The constant thorn in my side.

Rye and I can't spend more than ten minutes together before wanting to kill each other. I guess we both get off on it. It isn't productive, but we haven't found a way to stop.

"Date," I grind out. "If you can call any of his encounters 'dates.'" Which I don't. I don't care who he does or how many he does. I do care, however, about putting sex before our family dinners. Because that's what we all are: a family of our own making. Not that I particularly want Rye in my family. But the rest of my family loves him, so he's part of it, for better or worse. The least he can do is show up.

Scowling, I take a sip of my drink. I'm not going to let him get me worked up when he's not even around. He doesn't get any more space in my head than he's already claimed.

"Dinner was fine, really." My shoulders slump. "I'm just...jealous." God, that stings to say.

Jules leans in, her pretty brown-hazel eyes shining in sympathy. "You want to fall in love."

It feels as though the entire bar holds its breath, which is weird since no one is paying attention to us. Or maybe it's just the way Jules watches me intently. I find myself laughing, the sound full of snark.

"God, no." When she gives me a dubious look, I laugh again, this time more easily. "No, really. It's not that. It's..." I take a deep breath. "I'm jealous of their sex lives."

Jules blinks, her lips twitching. "You're jealous that they're having sex? Because, you gotta know, if you want sex, it's pretty easy to get it around here." She sweeps a slim hand in the direction of the bar. "We're in a virtual buffet of hot singles. Great sex at the ready."

"At the ready" is true enough. Both of us are attractive. Jules, with her sandy-brown skin, high cheekbones, and lush lips, could grace a magazine cover. She's been drawing looks of interest the whole time we've been here.

As for me, I don't know if it's my resting bored face or the fact that I favor pencil skirt suits, sky-high heels, and sleek ponytails, but I tend to attract businesspeople. Arty types don't seem to know what to do with me, which is fairly ironic since I spend much of my life around musicians, producers, and artists. Even so, if I want sex, I can find it easily. Great sex, however, is another story.

"Please tell me you don't actually believe that, Ju-Ju." I stab one of the lemons floating in my drink with a straw. "The great sex part."

"You've never had great sex?" she asks, clearly on the edge of pitying me. Maybe she should.

"You have?" I counter. "I mean, truly great, blow-your-mind, 'gotta have that again and again or you'll die from wanting it' sex?"

At this, Jules stares into her glass then sighs and looks back up at me. "No, damn it. Not like that. I've had good, but not transcendent."

Nodding, I lean forward until we're both half-hunched over our table. "I've had good sex too. But most of the time, the guy has no idea what the hell he's doing. It's all pump and dump. And I'm left unsatisfied."

Her nose wrinkles. "Maybe we should be with women."

I shake my head. "You'd think having the same equipment would give women a leg up, but I've had the same frustrations in that department."

I swear I hear someone choke on their drink behind me. I want to roll my eyes. This is Manhattan, and if a dude can't deal with overhearing a frank conversation, he's not going to make it in this city. Besides, my sexuality isn't something I'll ever be ashamed of. In general, I tend to gravitate toward men, but I also think attraction is a fluid notion, and that, for me, it isn't confined to one gender.

"Some women are just as selfish and clueless as men," I say. "Believe me, there's no golden ticket when it comes to finding great sex."

Jules's eyes go wide. "I don't know if I should be jealous of all your experience or thankful I don't have it, given what you're saying."

I find myself grinning, but it fades quickly. "Definitely don't be jealous."

I'm still alone and still unfulfilled. Actually, it kind of blows to realize I've struck out with two genders.

"I'm serious, though," I say, frowning now. "Whatever the gender, whatever the sexual orientation, we all suffer the same pitfalls and have to weed through the same bullshit when it comes to finding happiness."

"Well." Jules sits back against the booth. "I guess we're doomed, then."

I sit back as well, letting the sounds of the bar move over me. I'm tired, and my feet are aching to be free of the heels I stuffed them into eight hours ago. Not for the first time, I consider no longer wearing them. But they are, in a very real way, defensive weapons, armor against a business that is ruthless.

My aunt Isabella, a famous fashion model, bought me my first pair of heels—black patent leather Manolo Blahnik Mary Jane pumps. She told me then that, whether we like it or not, women in the entertainment industry would always be judged by their appearance, and underestimated, compared to their male counterparts. But put on a pair of killer heels with a sleek suit and the naysayers would be too dazzled to notice you climbing over them. She'd taken me under her wing back then, taught me about fashion, poise, how to handle obnoxious assholes, how to charm people. Mercenary, but I found her lessons to be painfully true.

Over the years, I had to cover myself in a shell of icy perfection. My power is in maintaining the illusion that nothing can get to me, and I accept that as part of doing business. But some days? Some days, I want to crumble. I want...comfort, touch, release.

I should go home and crawl into bed. But I can't shake the restless feeling swelling within me.

I catch Jules's eye, and my shoulders slump. "I know we're not supposed to admit this for fear it might make us sound pathetic or some other bullshit, but I'm horny. Not in a general, I-want-to-have-sex way, but in a deep, irritating, can't-stop-thinking-about-it way. I ache, you know? As in, I go through the day actively hurting for release."

Jules watches me with solemn eyes as if she knows at least a little about that pain.

Shaking my head, I go on. "And, yeah, I can take care of it myself. Hell, I'm so good at it now, it's only a minute or two before I get off. But it isn't the same as feeling someone else's hands on my body, not knowing exactly where they'll touch me next or how. It isn't the same as being mouth-to-mouth, skin-to-skin, sweaty and frantic."

My smile is wry, but my heart hurts. "I'm twenty-eight years old. I am at the top of my profession, have awesome friends, fabulous parties every night if I want to go. I own a kick-ass condo on the Upper East Side and have a shoe closet most women would kill for."

"Truth," Jules says with a laugh.

"I have the world at my fingertips. But I can't fix this problem."

It pisses me off, this weakness, this damn need that won't go away.

Jules licks her lips and hums. "Then go find someone tonight. Take the edge off."

"I've tried that. One-night stands aren't enough." My fingers curl into the leather booth beneath me. "Truly great sex, for me anyway, takes time. More than one night. More importantly, it takes trust. On both sides. We need to trust each other enough to give and take and learn what really works."

"In short," Jules says. "A relationship."

"Except I don't want one." A humorless laugh huffs out of me. "Outside of sex, that is."

The utter bitch of it is, I know I haven't explained my problem properly. Yes, there is this need for sexual release, but it's more. I want that on a deeper level. It's not the daily minutiae of a relationship I crave, but the simple physical connection. I want to be wanted. Craved above all things. Needed with a breathless devotion.

I want to be *seen*, not just as a quick fix—but as something essential. And I want to crave someone too. I want to learn their body, know what sets them off, and what brings them to their knees. To own and be owned. But in admitting that, I'll expose too much of myself, and the hurt of the open wound will be too hard to ignore. "I want the ease and trust of a relationship, but I know I'd utterly fail at a real one right now. Maybe when my life is less about the band...Which it will be never. The band *is* my life."

Purple curls bounce as Jules nods. "Friends with benefits, then. Too bad I don't go for women, because I'd totally offer my services. And I absolutely know what I'm doing." She grins, all saucy and impish.

"Too bad," I tease before growing serious. "Maybe I'll just hire someone."

Again comes that choking sound from behind me. Or maybe I'm just paranoid. But I lean in a little, drawing away from the seat and toward Jules. "Whip is always going on about that, how it's safer, and you can control the situation."

At this, Jules flushes, irritation flashing in her eyes. "Whip is going to end up fronting tabloids. Please tell me you aren't listening to that boy."

"I won't go there. Everything in my life is business. I'm not going to make my sex life another business transaction." I plop back with a sigh. "But it would solve a lot if I did."

We soon finish our drinks, and Jules heads out. "Got an early day with Boss Man."

I love Scottie like a brother, but he makes drill sergeants look like slackers when it comes to work. So far, Jules is the only assistant he's had who has been able to handle his exacting standards without running away in tears.

Before leaving, I head to the bathroom to wash my hands. Standing in front of the sink, cool water running over my wrists, I stare at my reflection. My skin tone has morphed from warm ivory to pasty, the dark auburn of my hair too harsh in contrast. Purple smudges show beneath my eyes despite the fact that I put on concealer. Somewhere along the way, all the polish I so meticulously perfected has hardened into a veneer that's starting to show its cracks.

I can no longer see any trace of the wide-eyed eighteen-year-old who just wanted to fit in somewhere. The girl who begged her cousin to let her be a part of his band, at least on the periphery—because even though she didn't have a glimmer of musical talent, she still wanted to feel the heady rush of excitement that world gave her.

Confessing to Jules had felt good, a purge. But it also made it worse. I gave voice to my problem, sent it out into the night, and, in doing so, I allowed it more strength.

Like it or not, I work in a man's world. Record execs, concert promotors, producers, venue managers, journalists—a good majority of them are male. Over the years, they made certain I was aware that I was in their territory. They tried to make me believe I didn't truly belong. To survive, I had to develop a tough skin and a guarded heart. I had to be perfect, never take an awkward step, never show weakness, vulnerability, or softer emotions. To be seen as needy was to open myself up to the wolves. If it ever got out that cool-headed, take-no-prisoners, Brenna James yearned to be held... I'll never be able to show my face again.

Fuck it. I refuse to be ashamed of my needs. Straightening my back, I reapply my lipstick and leave.

I'm no more than three steps out the bathroom door when I nearly collide with a hard, looming chest, only narrowly stopping short of running into it. "Excuse me, I didn't see you..."

My words trail off in horror as I get a good look at the guy.

Rye Peterson—personal nemesis, general pain in the ass— leans one massive shoulder against the wall as if he's been waiting for me. He's a world-famous rock star, but he doesn't look like one. Tall, broad, with tight muscles and spiky dark-blond hair, he'd easily be mistaken for a football player.

Most people consider him laid-back, the guy who will hand you a beer and make you laugh with a dirty joke. And he is that guy—to everyone else. With me? He's the devil, lying in wait to exploit any sign of weakness. My reaction to Rye may not always be logical but it's definitely visceral.

The blood drains out of my face when he gives me that smile of his, the smug, wide one he uses when he has something on me. The one that says he's going to make me squirm and enjoy every damn minute of it.

But for once his voice isn't teasing; it's dark and deep, almost hard, when he says, "Let's talk."

––––––––

Rye

EVERY MAN HAS A WEAKNESS. Every dog has its day. Those two truths collided in spectacular fashion the second I learned that

Brenna James—my one true weakness—is in desperate need of great sex. She aches for it. Every night.

Goddamn, I'm still hard at the thought. Not just hard—hot, so freaking hot, I'm surprised my skin isn't visibly steaming. It takes true effort to affect a pose of nonchalance and play the part Brenna expects of me—teaser, tormentor, fool.

I'm almost sorry I've unearthed the knowledge that she goes about her days wanting—needing—hands on her skin, a mouth on her clit. Jesus, it's almost too much to handle. Almost.

But dog that I am, this feels like a change in the wind. Her secret is out, and hell if I'm going to ignore it. I hadn't tried to eavesdrop. Okay, that's a lie. The second I'd recognized Brenna's voice behind me, I'd listened in. I'm not proud of it, but the woman has a way of bringing out the juvenile in me. Except hearing her desires and the longing in her voice brought up an emotion I haven't truly experienced when it comes to Brenna —empathy.

Not that Bren would believe me; she thinks I'm a dog when it comes to women. In many ways I *am*—simple things make me happy, and I'm loyal to the people I love. I do not, however, take advantage of women. I just love being with them. So much so that I seek their company as often as I can. But that great, off-the-walls, gotta-have-it sex she's been dreaming about? It's as elusive for me as it is for her.

So, yeah, I empathize.

But when she'd said she was considering hiring someone to give it to her?

Hell. No. Just, no. I can't know this and let it go.

The question is: What to do now that I've cornered Brenna? Over the years, our interactions have become mostly that of pride-based one-upmanship. For reasons I've never wanted to examine too closely, we're constantly trying to prove to one another that we're invulnerable, that we don't care what the other thinks. In short, we lie spectacularly to each other. The fact that I've overheard her confession must be killing her.

She's glaring hate fire up at me, which I know is a defensive measure. When it comes to the two of us, we both come out swinging, so very eager to hide any hint of weakness. God knows what evil deeds are racing behind her amber eyes. Oh, she's definitely thinking about maiming me in creative ways. She's always thinking that. The only difference here is that a tinge of mortification pulls at the corners of her shapely lips, and she's glancing at the floor as if hoping it will open up and swallow her.

Despite what she thinks, I don't relish her discomfort. I don't even like it at the moment. Pushing off from the wall, I take a step in her direction. "I mean it, Bren. I heard what you said..." At this, her nostrils flare, a look of embarrassment flashing over her face. I forge on. "We need to talk."

"No, we really don't."

It's dim in the hallway, the red exit light overhead turning her pale skin magenta and her auburn hair blood red. I can almost imagine her bursting into flames and smiting me with her wrath.

"Yeah, we do. Come on, Bren. You can't expect—"

"Just stop talking." She shoves past me. "I'm not discussing this with you of all people."

"But if you'd just listen—shit! Wait up."

She's fast on those heels, a lithe blade of speed and precision. She weaves through a crowd of guys in suits, and one of them whistles, making some overloud comment about her perky ass. I shoulder-check him as I barrel past, trying to keep up with Brenna.

Outside, she glances back and scowls when she catches sight of me. Her scathing curse and increased speed make me grin. Does she actually expect to shake me?

"You might as well slow down," I say. "I'm walking you home."

She lifts her chin and keeps up her pace. "Go away, pest."

"That would be a no. Safety first, Bren."

"Pfft. I don't need a bodyguard. I could kick *your* ass if I wanted to."

I shouldn't find that hot. But of course, I do. "I have no doubt you're a total badass, babe. But humor me, all right?"

Something in my voice must have gotten through because she relents with an aggrieved sniff and strides onward. The air is cold and crisp, our breath visible in the night. Brenna's thin blouse can't be keeping her warm. But since I know she'd only chuck my sweater into the street if I offered it to her, I shove my hands into my pockets and move to her side.

Now that we're walking out in the open, she can't outdistance me. In those insane heels of hers, Brenna is around five-foot-ten. But I still have several inches on her. Plus, her tight, absolute mind-fuck of a skirt doesn't allow her to lengthen her stride.

She must realize this because she slows—just a little—not enough to concede defeat, but she's no longer half-running. Her heels strike a *click-click, clickety-click* on the pavement. I hear that rhythm in my dreams sometimes. She'll never know it, but that rhythm is the bass line for "Forget You." No one will ever know that but me, though. A man has to keep some things to himself.

"I thought you were on a *date*," she grinds out after a minute.

My lips twitch at the bitterness with which she says "date," but I keep my tone bland. "I was. It ended early at the bar."

This is a lie. There was no date. There hasn't been for a while. But I'm not about to tell her why I couldn't face family dinner tonight.

"Look," she says all brisk business. "Whatever it is you think you heard—"

"Oh, I know what I heard."

"—is none of your business."

"I know that too."

This earns me a fleeting gasp of shock, her amber eyes going wide. Then she huffs as though remembering she needs to stay mad to protect herself. "I cannot believe you eavesdropped on me. You should have said you were there."

I give her a level look. "Tell me right now that if you overheard me in a similar conversation, you wouldn't have listened. Because I call bullshit."

She doesn't say anything for a moment, just walks with that crisp stride. Then a curse breaks free, and she throws up a hand in defeat. "Fine. I would have listened. Doesn't make it right, though."

"Neither of us are angels."

"You most of all."

My smile probably resembles a shark's. Can't be helped. I'm having weird fantasies of eating her up at the moment. "Thank God for that."

"And it doesn't mean you have to bring up what you heard either," she points out with asperity.

"No. But I still want to talk to you." *Please, please, please let me talk to you.*

"No."

"Come on, Bren," I say, softer now. "I'm not going to shame you..." Her snort rings loud and long in the night air. Okay, I deserve that. I've shamed her before, in lots of different ways. Remorse fills me. "I swear I'm not. I'm not going away either. So you might as well hear what I have to say before you slap me upside my head."

Brenna rolls her eyes. "I detest physical violence."

"Uh-huh."

"But for you, I'll make an exception."

A grin erupts. "You'll make it hurt so good, won't you, Berry?"

"Argh!" Despite her exclamation, I see the small smile trying to break out. It feels like a small victory to coax that from her.

I'm still chuckling when we arrive at her building and the doorman opens the door for us.

"Ms. James. Mr. Peterson." He gives us a nod.

"'Sup, Tommy. You got any comment about last night's game?"

Tommy's deadpan expression doesn't change. "None that I'm willing to give, sir."

Saluting him, I step into the lobby and catch Brenna's narrowed gaze.

"How do you know my doorman's name?"

I can practically hear the frantic thoughts running through her head. I've visited many times—not on my own but when she hosts get-togethers and dinners. Certainly not enough to know her night doorman.

Leaning past her, I push the number to her floor. "I saw Tommy at the Garden during a Knicks game and invited him to sit with me."

Killian, Whip, Jax, and I have season tickets on the floor. Not all of us go to every game, and those empty seats are a waste. Stella, Jax's girl, has been running charity raffles and giving tickets to winners. Once a month, we'll also take kids who need a little more joy in their lives—either because they're sick, have mental health issues, or come from broken or disadvantaged homes—to the games. I love those nights and learn something new from those kids every time.

Brenna makes a noise in the back of her throat but doesn't comment as we step into the elevator and ride in silence to her floor. Not speaking isn't a good thing right now. I've been alone in an elevator with Brenna before, but it's never felt this loaded, the air thick with suppressed tension. It's crawling along my skin and plucking at my insides.

She needs "truly great, blow-your-mind, 'gotta have that again and again or you'll die from wanting it'" *sex.*

My skin draws tight. Damn, I want that too. I just didn't realize how much I needed it until Brenna spoke those words. Overheated, I draw in a deep breath. Mistake. Brenna's perfume tickles my nose. She doesn't have a signature scent but wears different ones for different moods. Unfortunately, I know them all. Over the years, I've figured out what mood she's in depending on what fragrance she chooses.

Tonight's scent smells of ripe peaches drenched in honey, dark rum, and good tobacco. In theory, that combination should not work, but in reality, it's pure sex. All I can think of are hedonistic days of lying between a pair of thighs under a Caribbean sun while savoring the luscious taste of slick and swollen...

I cough and stand up straight. *Down, boy.*

Brenna shoots me a look. "Did you just choke on your spit?"

Drool. Lust-induced drool. And thank you for that.

"No. Just a random cough."

"Hmm." Her eyes narrow as she peers up at me. "You're not getting sick, are you?"

"Why?" I lean in—like a fool, because it's never a good idea for me to get too close to Brenna James. "Would you wipe my fevered brow if I were?"

"I'd tell you to go home before you infect me. I can't afford to get sick."

"Now, Berry," I say as the elevator door opens on her floor. "You know perfectly well that, to pick up my germs, we'd have to get much closer than this."

Brenna rolls her eyes, and she's off again—*click-click, clickety-click*. It's the little *clickety-click* that always hooks me. An audible clue that she adds an extra sway to every other step. I'm not going to admit how many times I've watched her walk to figure that bit out.

When we get to her place, she punches in her security code with lightning-fast speed then flings the door open and strides in, leaving me to hustle behind her or have the door shut in my face.

To step inside Brenna's place is to be enveloped by her. It always smells of fresh roses, not overpowering but clean and sweet. The prewar apartment has classic moldings and high ceilings and is decorated in creamy whites and shades of gray with bursts of pink, green, and gold as accents. All very understated luxury. Except for the long empire-style sofa upholstered in leopard-print velvet that sits in the center of her living room—a little visual jolt that thumbs its nose at all that careful coordination and draws the eye with its quirky, glam style. Kind of like Brenna herself.

She rests her pert little butt on the rolled arm of the sofa and crosses her slim legs at the ankle, those killer heels digging into the thick pile carpet. "I'm tired and have a date with Paul Hollywood."

A choking laugh falls out of me. "Paul Hollywood?"

"Yes. He's a judge on *The Great British Baking Show*."

"Oh, I know the show."

Brenna's brow quirks. "You watch it?"

"What's with the shock? I love baked goods. Gotta feed this body to keep it in optimal shape." I rub my abs.

Brenna doesn't take the bait and look. She simply stares, not bothering to conceal her impatience. Thing is, now that I'm here alone with her, my confidence is unraveling like bad reverb. Shit. The silence goes from awkward to stifling. Heart thumping in my ears, skin still hot, I think of how the hell to start.

Brenna sighs. "I didn't—"

"I understand," I blurt out.

She pauses, her amber eyes rounding. "I'm sorry, what?"

All in, Ryland. Go all in. "I understand where you're coming from."

Brenna crosses her arms, protecting herself, blocking me off. "Oh, you do, huh?"

"Well, yeah." I take a step toward her. "I'm a famous guy who loves sex."

"No shit."

"Hey, I'm not trying to hide it. Why shouldn't I—*we*—love sex? Sex is great." Brenna's deadpan expression tells me I'm a sinking ship. I take another slow step closer—no need to put her even more on the defensive by rushing this. "But finding someone to trust? Someone willing to tell me what she truly likes—"

"Oh, no," she cuts in with a choked laugh, shaking her head. "No, no, no. Do not even go there."

I can't stop myself. "You don't know what I'm going to say."

"Unless it's about what to get Scottie for his birthday, I don't want to hear it."

"Easy. Handkerchiefs from Henry Poole." I shrug at Brenna's obvious surprise. "Boring, I know. But Scottie loves those things. And, you're right, that wasn't what I was going to say."

"Rye, no." She holds up a hand. "Just don't."

"You'd rather go to an escort service?" I'm trying hard not to sound panicked at the notion. "Risk all the things that could go seriously wrong with that? Risk your safety?"

Wrong thing to say. Her auburn brows lower. "You *would* focus on that. It's none of your business."

"We established that. But, I'm your friend—"

"We fight all the time."

"Yeah, we fight. And, yeah, you're annoying." She purses her lips in clear irritation, but a flash of acknowledgment makes me fight a smile. Bicker though we may, we know each other well. "I care about you, Bren. If something happened to you, it would tear me up."

The silence that follows is so absolute, the honking from cabs fifteen stories below rings loud and clear. Brenna's obvious shock is another blow. For fuck's sake, did she really think I didn't care? She's Killian's cousin. That alone would make her important to me. But she's also a major part of my life. For better or worse, we've been in each other's pockets since we were headstrong teens.

Despite my best effort to keep quiet, I grumble low in my throat. To my horror, it sounds a lot like hurt. Damn it.

Brenna bites the corner of her bottom lip—something she does when she knows she's stuck her foot in it. Then she sighs. "Of course, I'd care if something bad happened to you."

"Your enthusiasm is overwhelming. Truly."

It's impressive the way she can flip her long ponytail over her shoulder with a slight toss of her chin. I've seen that little move countless times and it never fails to amuse me, even when I know I'm about to get a tongue-lashing.

"I'm not feeling very enthusiastic toward you right now," she says. "However, I'll put your *concern* at ease. I'm not going to hire anyone to take care of my needs. Okay?"

I should be relieved. Instead, I am oddly deflated. Not because I want her to do that, but it weakens the case I've built in my head. "Oh."

Her lips quirk. "I guess you didn't hear that part, huh?"

"Well...uh, no?"

"No?" She *tsks*. "Your eavesdropping powers are sadly lacking, Ryland."

A smile tugs at my lips. "Your voice dipped a few times. It was kind of frustrating. Maybe talk a bit louder next time?"

She snorts but then switches back into her all-business mode. "Now that we've got that settled, you can leave."

I should. I should absolutely turn and walk out her door. And I'd regret it forever. "Nothing is settled until you find what you need."

Red suffuses her cheeks. "Damn it, Rye—"

"I want it to be me," I blurt without any finesse. I breathe deep and say more calmly, "I want to be the one you use."

My words bounce between us in syncopated agitation. For once, Brenna is at a loss for words.

CHAPTER TWO

BRENNA

I KNEW IT WAS COMING. That he was going to offer some ridiculous "solution" to my problem. I knew this. But knowing and experiencing are entirely different shocks to the system.

In both subtle and not-so-subtle ways, Rye has never let me forget that I had a crush on him when the band first got together. Usually, it takes the form of little digs about how irresistible I secretly find him or in remarks about my sex life—the idea being that I'll never have anything better than what I could have with him, if only he wanted me in return.

I gave as good as I got, always making it crystal clear that my love life was intensely satisfying, and that I'd never stoop to wanting Rye again. He responded in kind. Were our interactions mature? No. They'd been forged in our youth, and we'd never been able to break the pattern. But this was too much. He'd gone past light teasing and straight into making my weakness a joke.

It is appalling how hurt I am. I didn't expect that at all. I thought I'd worked past being hurt by him. Unfortunately, Rye

Peterson has never been easy for me to push into the background.

Certainly not now. He stands before me, his beefy arms crossed over his wide chest, thick eyebrows winging up in expectation. Millions view him as Kill John's lovable goofball, a big teddy bear who simply needs the right person to cuddle him into submission. As for me, it's all I can do not to punch his arrogant blunt nose. I won't do it. I still have *some* sense of decorum. But I can't hold my tongue. I can't.

"You asshole," I grind out, lurching up and stalking forward. "I know we've had our moments, but I never thought you'd sink this low."

"Hey," he cuts in with a shocked voice. "Hold on there—"

"No, you hold on." I poke his chest. "This isn't funny."

His mouth falls open. "Wait a minute, you think I'm making a joke here?"

The outrage in his voice gives me pause. "What else am I supposed to think? You overhear me saying I'm..." God, I'm not going to repeat myself. I'm humiliated enough that he heard it the first time. I swallow convulsively, horrified that I might actually cry. "And now you're, what, offering yourself up for the job? And I'm supposed to take that seriously?"

Rye sets his hands low on his hips and cocks his head like he's trying to figure out a puzzle. "Bren, this isn't a joke. I'm completely serious here."

My butt hits the curved arm of the couch, all the blood in my head rushing to my toes. He *can't* be serious. Yes, there had always been a buzz of attraction between us, but we'd both knew it was unwelcome and unwanted. Rye would never fold like this, not after all this time.

But he reads me well and gives a short nod of confirmation. "I'm not trying to yank your chain or belittle you. What I'm offering is real."

I touch my forehead and find it clammy. In truth, I'm reeling. "I need a drink."

Turning my back on him, I march to the kitchen, wobbling on my heels. I *never* wobble. I kick my shoes off before pouring myself a glass of water from the fridge and then take several large gulps.

Rye walks up and leans his forearms on the counter. His expression is completely calm, but his thumb betrays him and taps an agitated rhythm on the marble. He clearly hasn't shaved in a while, and his stubble has moved into beard territory. Over the years, Rye has worn a beard only once—one strange summer when all the guys decided to rock the lumberjack look. That quickly ended when people started sending them beard oil and toy axes.

Rye doesn't look bad, however. Just the opposite; it's hot, different. It changes his face enough that it's as if I'm talking to a new version of Rye. And it throws me off even more.

He bites the inside of his cheek, creating a little dimple, before taking a deep breath and speaking. "Look, I realize this is uncomfortable as fuck. But I'm going to lay my cards on the table. When I first overheard you mention sex, yeah, I started eavesdropping because, yes, I can be an immature shit at times." His smile is wry, and he squeezes the back of his neck. "But then I really listened to what you were saying and... Hell, Bren, I want that too. I know you don't believe me, but I'm tired of moving from partner to partner. I'm tired of feeling..." A deep flush turns his face red. "Alone."

I'm so shocked, a tiny squeak escapes my lips. I'm waiting for him to start laughing, to say he's kidding, but Rye returns my stare without falter. Oh, he's still blushing, his thumb twitches— a telltale nervous tic akin to me messing with my ponytail—but he is not laughing.

It takes me a good minute of intense silence to fully process that Rye has admitted he's lonely. He's never shown me any hint of personal weakness. I haven't either. To expose our underbellies is to open ourselves to taunts. It's just how we are with each other. But now Rye has gone and changed the game. I don't know what to do.

After taking another steadying sip of water, I set the glass down and try to think. "Okay, so you're not messing around with me, and you understand how I feel, but, Rye, to solve the problem by suggesting the two of us..." I can't even finish the sentence without feeling both too hot and too cold. "It's insanity. A total disaster waiting to happen."

"Disaster," Rye mutters under his breath.

"Come on," I insist, feeling slightly frantic. "We're like...like orange juice and toothpaste. Mix us together and we're bound to walk away with a bad taste in our mouths."

He ducks his head, and his fists curl on the counter, making the muscles along his arms bunch. All those lovely muscles working under smooth tattooed skin. At this point in my life, I've met hundreds of men, and none of them have arms as perfectly sculpted as Rye's. Why him? Why does his body catch my eye and hold it like no other?

Oblivious to my gawking, he raises his head and gives me a look of pure, male stubbornness. "Yeah, okay, it could very well be a disaster."

"I said it would be. Not could be." Because it definitely would. Why are we still talking about this? The more we talk, the harder it is to keep certain images at bay. Images I've pushed to the haunted corners of my mind for a decade now. A picture of Rye's naked back rippling with smooth, tight skin and bunching muscles as he works over my body, flashes in my mind, and I blow out a breath. No.

Rye purses his lips. For a second, I wonder if he's debating turning around and leaving. But I'm not that lucky. Instead, he takes a step around the island, his big hand trailing along the marble.

My back tenses as I force myself to remain unmoved. I don't know what his blue eyes see, but he approaches with more caution than usual.

"Do you really think I'd hurt you, Berry?"

Berry. I remember the night he gave me that nickname.

I never wanted to crush on Rye Peterson. Truly, I didn't. When Killian first let me hang out with his new bandmates all those years ago, I thought they were hot. Sitting in on their jam sessions was less about the music—because they weren't very good initially—and more about watching three gorgeous guys (and my cousin, who I knew was hot but refused to think of that way) dance around on stage. To my teenage delight, shirts always came off.

While Whip and John, who soon became Jax to the world, were mighty fine eye candy, only Rye—the big, clueless lug—made my insides flip and my skin heat. He wasn't the most physically beautiful; Scottie, with his black hair, perfect features, and ice blue eyes held that prize. Whip was a close second in looks and first when it came to sheer sweetness.

Rye didn't have the most blatant sex appeal; that was John's role—and I suppose Killian's too, except no, not going there. But there was something elemental about Rye. While the other guys were whipcord lean, Rye was a wall of cut, beefy muscle. The way he beat on his bass guitar, all hot, pounding rhythm, was pure sex to me. Not that I had much experience back then, but he made me feel things—hot, sweaty, fluttery things.

Offstage, Rye's lowbrow humor and quick smiles put me at ease in a way I'd never been with other guys. He was, and still is, the consummate flirt. For a gangly, shy redhead with buck teeth and acne, it was a dream to have an older boy smile at me as though I were the focus of his attention. I knew he did that for every girl. But it felt good to be noticed.

After every gig, Rye would make his way over to me. He'd always ask the same question, "Did that blow you away, kid?"

Kid. I hated that nickname. It made me feel all of twelve.

I'd always answer, "Yeah, Mr. Slap-Happy, it blew me the fuck away."

Rye would snort over the nickname I gave him. But it didn't

bother him. Over the years, he would develop genius finger skills, but in the beginning, slapping the bass was his main way to play, and he knew it. Besides, poking fun at each other was how we interacted.

On my eighteenth birthday, the guys threw me a party and played all night. Sweat-slicked and flushed, Rye tucked away his bass then sought me out. God, I tried my best not to gape at his bare chest, but it was a struggle. Whenever he moved, those glorious muscles shifted and bunched.

"Did that blow you away, Berry?"

I almost didn't register the word because, hello, little brown nipples all tight and right in front of me. Were they as sensitive as mine?

"Berry?" I glanced up, finally, to find him smirking.

"You turn berry pink when you blush."

My happy buzz fizzled. "It's rude to point out a girl's flaws."

The corners of Rye's deep-set eyes crinkled, his brows winging up in that way of his that made him look boyishly pleased. "Blushing isn't a flaw. It's cute. Sexy." And then *he* blushed. A soft wash of red across the tops of his cheeks and along the curve of his ears.

Which is the moment I truly fell for Rye Peterson, the hot, muscled man-boy who blushed just as easily as I did. Not that he stuck around for me to practice any more of my amateur flirting skills; Rye made a hasty exit after that remark and started avoiding me. No, worse, he soon would make it painfully clear that he had no interest in me as anything other than Killian's kid cousin who clung to the fringes of the band like a barnacle.

All for the best. A crush wasn't as important as the job—one that I had to prove over and over to the world that I was the best person for. I did that by maintaining the smooth polish of absolute professionalism. But now? With Rye standing before me with that look? Like he might lean in and take a little taste of me? Those walls are threatening to crack.

I swallow hard. He's too near. I can smell the soap he favors

—Tom Ford's Oud Wood. Spicy and smoky and freaking delicious. Scottie bought it for him one Christmas, and Rye was hooked. I know too much about him. I know that ordinarily, he shaves every two days, not because that's all he needs, but because he's lazy and doesn't mind the thick stubble that will coat his jaw like brown sugar. I know he hates shrimp but loves crab and lobster. He drinks icy cold Coke if it's before three in the afternoon and beer any time someone offers it. I know to stay away from him.

"I don't think you'd hurt me intentionally," I say, weakening. Damn it, his proximity is messing with my head.

He's a foot away now. Close enough that his body heat buffets mine and the sheer physicality of his big strong frame makes me a little light-headed. Yet he doesn't loom. He's just *there,* watching, assessing. "There's always a chance someone might unintentionally hurt you. That isn't enough reason to back away. I never took you for a coward, Bren."

My body snaps to cold attention. "Oh, hell no, Rye. You do not get to play that card." He starts to speak, but I roll over his words with my own. "Do you have any clue in that thick head of yours how many times you've tried to shame me for my sex life?"

His brows practically hit his hairline. "Shame you?"

"Exactly." I poke the air between us for emphasis. "Making snide remarks about me having sex, pointing out how much I have it, when I have it."

"I..." His mouth works as words fail him, and his color drains.

"You weaponized sex against me, and suddenly I'm the coward for not wanting to have sex with *you?*" I laugh without humor. "That takes the cake. Truly."

Rye's skin is the color of old milk. He swallows thickly. "Shit, Bren. I didn't realize—"

"Don't you dare say you didn't know you said those things."

"I'm not going to..." He runs a hand raggedly through his hair. "I just didn't think of it that way. I was giving you shit like I do all the guys."

My snort is long and eloquent.

"I'm serious, Bren." Rye's expression is wide open and earnest. "We all give one another shit for things we know will be a direct hit. Just like you imply I'm a flake because you know it's a sore spot for me."

It's my turn to flinch, because he's right. I do it too. Rye is likely the smartest person I know, but his carefree nature hides a lot of it. Somewhere along the way, the guys started to joke about him being clueless, and it stuck. This is the price we paid for growing up together as a group—we often revert to our most childish selves around one another.

Rye's deep voice cuts through my silent thoughts. "I know it wasn't mature, but I thought it was our thing, trading verbal hits. It never occurred to me that you'd take it as shaming. I always admired your sexuality, and I thought you knew that."

"Oh, please..."

"It's true." His voice grows strong. "You know what you want and go after it. I admire the hell out of that." He winces, rubbing his hair again. "Shit, I feel like a total asshole now that I know it hurt you."

"You didn't hurt me," I mutter. "You pissed me off."

His smile is tentative and lopsided. "Fair enough." The smile dies. "I'm sorry for that, Brenna. Believe that if nothing else."

I stare at him for a long moment. There's no hint of teasing in his steady gaze. He means it. I find myself nodding. "Okay."

He releases a breath. "Okay."

Guilt presses like a heavy hand against my heart. "I don't think you're stupid. You're the smartest one out of all of us."

Rye gives a jerky nod as though he's surprised but doesn't want to show it. "Don't know about that, but thank you."

"It was a horrible thing for me to imply. I'm sorry."

He nods again, and we stare at each other helplessly, neither one of us knowing what to do with this new frontier of mutual apologies.

"Okay. Well, now that we've got that straightened out." I

smooth a strand of hair back. "Let's just agree never to speak of this again."

"Hold on a second." Rye lifts his hands, amusement lighting his eyes. "We agreed that I was a dickhead and am sorry for it."

"And I was a...what's the female equivalent of a dickhead?"

"You don't really expect me to answer that, do you?" He's smiling now. "Because that's bait."

God, I want to smile back. But I hold it together. "We agreed that we were horrible to each other, which merely proves your proposal is ridiculous."

"Ridiculous?" he repeats with a laughing huff. "I wouldn't go that far."

"I would." Damn it, I will not get flustered by the heat that's returned to his gaze. "Clearing the air doesn't create instant trust."

"But you just said you know I'd never hurt you and that I respect you." His expression is so genuinely confused, I have to believe he truly doesn't get it.

I shake my head in exasperation. "Maybe you can easily flip the switch. But I can't. One apology doesn't erase the years of acrimony between us."

"Acrimony is a bit harsh. It was more like light bickering."

My lips purse to keep from laughing. Because he's utterly shameless and annoyingly irresistible. "It doesn't make up for the countless times you let me down over the years. The way you'd brush off interviews I set up—"

"I fucking hate interviews, Bren. Avoiding them as much as possible is about my issues, not to get at you."

"You never take any of my work seriously."

His chin jerks up. "Yes, I do. I know how important you are to this band."

"Which is why you roll your eyes and make cracks about how annoying I am whenever I hand out the weekly schedule?"

"Shit, Bren, all of us do that." His lips quirk with a self-depre-cating smile. "We're rock stars. Thumbing our noses at the establishment is kind of expected. For all intents and purposes, you're our link to the establishment."

Well, he had me there.

He edges closer. "The question is, why do you react with such vehemence when I do it, while the rest of the guys get a pass?"

Because they don't get under my skin the way you do.

He reads the truth in my eyes far too well, and a gleam enters his eyes. "Face it, we react to each other the way we do because we've been trying our damnedest to one-up each other."

He isn't wrong.

His gaze lowers to my lips. "We could meet as equals here. We could...flip that switch."

Was it hot in here? How high had I set the heat?

I push out a breath. "Maybe I'm just not attracted to you."

Oh, such the wrong thing to say. We both know it. His eyes narrow, the corner of his lip curling just enough to taunt. When he talks, his voice is an octave lower, almost a purr. "Is that so?"

He leans in, his head ducking down, closer than he's ever been to me. When I tense, he pauses, his breath ghosting over the sensitive skin of my neck. "I'm not going to kiss you. I'm just...checking something."

He tilts his head, his nose brushing along my jaw. My eyes flutter closed, the urge to lean into him nearly intolerable. The soft touch of his lips on my pulse point makes both our breaths hitch. He sighs heavily, and I shiver.

"Your pulse is racing," he says.

I can't speak. Can't move.

Callused and warm, his big hand finds my smaller limp one. He gently presses my palm into the center of his wide chest. His heart pounds a frantic rhythm that matches my own.

"Feel that? That's just from standing close to you." His voice vibrates against my neck, tickles along my nerve endings. "From me thinking about all the ways I could figure you out, find all the little things that will make you come."

My knees go weak, and I sway. Just once. A small movement. But he notices. His grip tightens a fraction, a rumble sounding in his throat. I take a breath, push back. I haven't fully prepared myself for the heat I see in his eyes, the unapologetic want he's showing me. I've never had it aimed my way. I rest my butt against the counter before I end up on the floor.

"Now you know," he murmurs deep and firm. "I'm physically attracted to you. Always was."

God. He isn't supposed to say these things. We have a silent but very clear deal based on mutual loathing and avoidance.

"This isn't attraction," I manage to get out. "It's agitation."

He hasn't stepped away. He's still so close our chests nearly touch with each unsteady breath we take. I wonder if he can smell the lie I've just told.

Blue eyes the color of well-worn denim spear mine. "It's a promise." The words come down like a hammer. "A promise, Bren, of how fucking good it can be if you just let go of your pride." With that, he steps back, his hands open and facing out as if showing he's got nothing to hide. "Think about it, okay? Just...think about it."

He leaves without a backward glance. And I curse his name for the rest of the night because I don't get a wink of sleep.

Bastard.

CHAPTER THREE

BRENNA

"RYE ISN'T HERE," Sophie says with an exasperated sigh.

The tip of my Jimmy Choo Love pump beats a rapid tattoo on the polished concrete floor of the photo studio. I take a moment to admire them—bright yellow leather with a white pointed tip and an elegant black heel. The other pump is white with a black tip and a yellow heel.

Something in me calms, as it always does when I admire my shoes.

Vain, yes. But for a girl who grew up with nothing, while watching her rich cousin and his friends get everything, the luxury of being able to buy beautiful shoes for myself is something I'll never take for granted. Silly as it may seem, just the knowledge that I can afford these shoes, that I made it to this place through my own hard work, puts everything back into focus. More than any other arsenal in my wardrobe, my shoes have become a talisman of sorts, able to bring me comfort, take away my fears, and soothe my nerves.

So, yes, I stare at my shoes and quietly release the urge to strangle Rye. Because, when he's late for a band photoshoot, we all have to wait. Sophie has a babysitter who's on the clock, and the rest of us have various other appointments we have to attend later. But here we are, sitting around waiting for Rye to get his ass to the studio.

Whip and Jax are playing *Minecraft* in the small lounge we have set up. They're arguing about the architecture of the Fortress of Solitude they're building. Scottie is half on the phone, half watching them and muttering pointers. Killian is on a chair, idly strumming "Stairway to Heaven," which the guys find hilarious. I know there's probably some musician joke in this, but I'm too annoyed to remember it.

"He'll show," I say, silently cursing Rye in my head. I haven't seen him since he dropped the sex bomb on my head last night, and I'm not exactly keen on coming face-to-face with him. Even so, we have work to do, and he needs to get his act together. Not that this is anything new for him. Rye is unreliable. Which is why, when I told him I couldn't fully trust him, I wasn't blowing hot air.

"He hates having his picture taken." Sophie seems more amused than offended. She sets down her camera and runs a hand through her hair. It's nut brown at the roots, lightening into marshmallow white at the tips. "Funny thing is, when I started, it was Killian who was most resistant to photos."

"That's just because he was being an ass." I smile wryly. "Just like Rye."

Sophie shakes her head, sending the pale strands of her hair swaying over her shoulders. "I don't think it's that. With Rye, I mean." She picks up a bottled iced tea and takes a long drink. "Something's going on with him lately."

Everything in me freezes in cold horror as if somehow the entire band, all our friends, know what happened last night. My heart clenches with the fear that the next words out of Sophie's mouth will be to ask me what's up.

But she simply caps her tea and looks thoughtful. "He seems...off."

"Does he?" I hadn't noticed. Which is strangely upsetting, because I should notice. It's my job to notice everything about my boys. Not that I like to think of Rye as "my boy" but... I shake off my wandering thoughts and tap my toe again.

"He used to be larger than life, the first one to stick his face in my camera..." Sophie grins. "Waggling his tongue and saying something wildly inappropriate."

"Inappropriate is kind of his thing," I say dryly.

She shakes her head fondly. "He reminds me of me, so I can't throw stones. We're both like these eager puppies, wanting attention, but when we have it, we don't know what to do with it."

My tapping toe stills. "I hadn't thought of it that way, but you're right."

She hums in agreement. "But now? Rye's gone quiet. Like he's drawing in on himself." Her brown eyes meet mine. "You know?"

I didn't. Not until Sophie pointed it out. An uncomfortable emotion—prickly and itchy, like the weaker cousin of jealousy—fills my insides. Sophie noticed but not me. Deep down, or maybe not so deep, I thought I was the one who paid the most attention to Rye and how he acted.

I don't want to consider why that is. I don't want to think about how he was in my house, asking to be the one that gets to fuck me, and I'd never suspected anything deeper was going on with him.

I make a noise of agreement and act like I'm fine. Everything is fine. But it's not. Everything is off and twisted, and where the hell is Rye, anyway?

My silent scream of frustrated worry cuts short as the elevator dings, and Rye struts into the loft.

"Finally." Killian sets his guitar down.

"Sorry," Rye mutters, not sounding exactly sorry. He's not

looking at anyone but is focused on carrying a large tray of takeout cups in his hand. "This took a little longer than expected."

"This" being the takeout. Instantly, I feel like an ass for cursing him. He sets his messenger bag down then starts handing out drinks. I feel even worse when it's clear he got everyone their favorite.

"With a twist of lemon," Scottie says, impressed but trying not to show it as he sips his Earl Grey.

"Without the lemon, you don't achieve the proper snooty lip pucker," Rye says with a wink.

Whip and Jax snicker. Scottie drinks his tea.

Rye approaches me last. It's a struggle to maintain a neutral facade. It gets more difficult as he draws near. His presence takes away my air. He's just too much. Too big, his body too strong and tight. His voice too deep—not a bass but a low baritone that has a tendency to vibrate along my skin when he's near.

My gaze slides away from his knowing blue eyes, skids along the perfection of his round biceps, and halts on the drink in his large hand. It's wrapped in a thick cloth napkin to keep it warm.

"You see," he says in that low, rumbly voice, speaking only to me. "There's only one coffee shop that makes a truly exceptional flat white, and it's thirty blocks from here."

My gaze flies up to collide with his, shock parting my lips. Months ago, I'd said Nova Coffee was the only place I'd found that makes the perfect flat white—"a truly exceptional one." Rye went thirty blocks out of his way to get me one.

His expression is bland, but there's a small spark in his eyes as he hands me my coffee. A peace offering? An acknowledgment?

Numbly, I take it, still staring back at him. We're far enough from the rest of the group that they can't hear us, but it doesn't shake the sensation of being stuck under a blinding spotlight.

"Got you one of those lemon butter cookies you like as well." Quietly, he slips a small bag into my nerveless grip.

But not covertly enough.

"How come Brenna gets a cookie?" Whip complains.

Rye keeps his gaze on me and raises his voice enough to answer. "She's the one most likely to kick my ass for being late."

"I thought that was Scottie," Jax says, his green eyes impish.

Rye doesn't blink. "He got his twist of lemon."

"Well done, you." Scottie lifts his tea with a small salute. Rye managed to remember that Scottie—the ultra-snob—likes his tea in a ceramic container.

How do you fault an effort like that?

"Is this a bribe?" I ask in a low voice.

That's how.

Rye's expression flickers, the light in his eyes dimming a little. His smile is small and tight. "It's an extended apology. For the shaming thing."

"Oh." Damn it all, this isn't what we do. We bicker. Only he's not playing by our rules. Pressing my lips together, I try to think of something, anything to get us back on familiar ground. But I can't ignore what he's done for me. "Thank you. For the coffee. And the cookie."

The corner of his mouth twitches, and I know he's holding in a laugh at my horribly stilted response. Shifting my weight, I clutch my cookie and try again. "It was nice of you."

"What bothers you more?" he murmurs idly. "Accepting that I might not be a total asshole? Or the possibility that we might start being nice to each other?"

A reluctant laugh bubbles up to the surface, but I hold it in. "Right now, it's a fifty-fifty split."

His mouth curls in a lazy grin. "I hope to afford you more clarity in the future."

The retort dies in my mouth as realization hits. "Did you just quote *Pride and Prejudice*?"

"How many times did you watch that movie on the last tour?"

Too many, apparently. I stand there, dumbfounded and rudderless in this new Rye world.

Rye's attention snags on my parted lips. His lids lower a fraction, and I swear he's closer. Heat blooms under my silk blouse and tickles my skin.

"For the record, if I have to resort to bribery," he whispers. "Then it won't mean anything."

CHAPTER FOUR

RYE

"BALL!"

The warning breaks through my fog just a touch too late, and stars explode behind my lids as I'm pinged in the side of my head by a basketball. "Fuck!"

Laughing, Whip trots over to me. "Dumbass. What the hell are you doing, standing there like a dolt?"

"Standing like a dolt?" I offer, rubbing my head before bending to pick up the ball. I chuck it back to him as Killian and Jax amble over. They're both grinning, loving my pain. Assholes.

"Got good sound out of that head," Jax says.

I flip him the bird.

"You've been staring off into space for half of the game." Killian peers at me. "You high or something?"

"Just not in the mood to play terrible ball with you guys."

Fact is, we pretty much suck at basketball right now. Mainly because Whip is a goof on the court, I'm distracted, my hand fucking hurts, and Jax and Killian keep giving each other advice on what to get their women for Christmas. It's October, fucking October, and they're fretting. I'd pity them, except they're so damn content, I end up envying them instead.

Which blows.

A total disaster waiting to happen.

I wince at the memory of Brenna's declaration. It's not like I wasn't expecting resistance. Or her shock. And she's likely right. We're a disaster now. Adding sex to it would be pouring alcohol onto the flames. But none of that stops me from feeling sucker punched. There's this weird hole of regret and disappointment expanding in my chest. I rub at it as I walk to my water bottle to take a sip.

Whip reaches for his water and eyes me as he drinks. "Seriously, what's going on? You look..." His gaze narrows in assessment. "Spooked."

"Spooked?" I repeat with sarcasm and toss my bottle into my bag.

"Yeah. Like you encountered a floating ghost librarian whose face turned into a skeleton right before she tried to jump you."

Snickering, I shake my head. "*Ghostbusters* really did a number on you."

"Hey." Whip points his bottle at me. "You'd piss your pants if that happened to you."

"Did you piss your pants when watching that scene?"

Rolling his eyes, Whip finishes his water. "Stop prevaricating. What's up?" He's serious now, frowning with worry.

We've always given each other shit. No one is immune. But after Jax tried to take his own life, things changed. We still give each other shit, but we also make very fucking certain no one is truly hurting. Since I know exactly how awful it feels to worry about one of my boys without knowing how to help, I can't evade Whip now.

But I can't tell him the truth either. Brenna will kill me. As in actual murder.

I angle away from Jax and Killian. Neither of them has noticed us talking yet—they're still discussing Christmas—but the fewer people asking me questions, the safer I am.

"I'm not spooked exactly." I shrug, scratching the back of my neck. "I just... Shit, I don't know. It's like my life was going one direction, and there I was cruising along, content, you know?"

He nods but keeps silent.

"And then the thought occurred to me: What if I got off this highway? What if I headed down another road? Even if that road is so curvy, I have no idea where I'll end up." With a self-deprecating laugh, I try again. "Shit, I'm babbling nonsense. Maybe I'm just in a rut."

I've just opened myself wide—shown far more than I'm comfortable with. But this is Whip. Out of all the guys, he's my closest friend. Maybe it's because we provide the rhythm and beats in the band and often collaborate. Or maybe it's because, while Killian and Jax are front and center, taking the lion's share of the spotlight—and all the crap that comes with it—Whip and I are less scrutinized.

We're still famous. Fans will go apeshit if they spot us. But we simply don't experience the same level of frenzy that Killian and Jax do. There's a certain freedom in that. Whip and I have always been able to fade into the background and do our own thing. As a result, we hang out a lot more.

He runs a hand through his black hair, and it stands up in all directions. "We've all changed. Why try to fight it?"

For a tight second, I want to tell him about Brenna. The urge is so great, I can feel the words pushing against my tongue. I swallow them down. Threat of death notwithstanding, it would be a violation of Bren's privacy.

"I'm not fighting it. It's more it finally occurred to me there are things I can't control. Things that affect my peace of mind. And that sucks."

Whip's eyes narrow again. Cold horror bolts down my spine.

He knows this is about Brenna. I know this because we can both read each other like a billboard. It's all there on his smug yet slightly pitying face. My fist clenches, and I give him a quelling look.

That he ignores.

"Man..."

"Don't say it," I cut in.

"I don't know what set you off this time," he goes on as if I haven't spoken.

"Nothing set me off."

He rolls his eyes, but his expression remains troubled. "She's a lost cause. You know that, right?"

His words are a punch in the throat. They spike along my skin with itchy heat and lodge in my chest like a hot, writhing ball. I want to punch back, take him and his truth down a peg. Which isn't like me. Well, anymore. In my youth, I was a hot-headed asshat.

I take a deep breath and let it out slowly. "I *know*."

No use denying or trying to evade anything else. Whip will see right through that bullshit. He eyes me with trepidation, obviously understanding that he's rubbed me raw.

My temper snaps. "Stop looking at me like that. I'm not mooning or whatever the fuck you think. You have no idea what you're talking about this time."

"So tell me."

"Tell you what?" Killian says, suddenly at Whip's side. The guy must walk on cat feet or something. Whip and I both visibly jolt.

"Rye is *not* mooning over Brenna," Whip says solemnly.

He is no longer my best friend.

"Right." Killian nods, playing along. "He never does."

"Fuck you both." I say it without much heat. Getting mad never helps diffuse their nosiness.

Jax ambles over and slings an arm around my neck. "Hey,

now, we all know Rye can be an asshole about non-Brenna topics too. The list is endless." He attempts to put me in a headlock, from which I easily break free.

"Funny." Inside, I'm grateful. Months ago, Jax tried to grill me about Brenna, and I asked him to back off.

"Let's talk about this lumberjack look you've got going." Jax rubs his palm on my cheek, and I swat him away. "What's up with the beard, Rye-Rye?"

"Just felt like growing one." Not the truth, but it's yet another thing I don't want to talk about. When the hell did hanging out with my best friends become something I'd rather avoid? It doesn't sit right with me. But I can't shake the feeling.

"It's definitely a look." Killian eyes my growing beard. "A little scraggly, though."

"Are we going to start giving one another grooming tips now?" I ask while putting my gear into my bag. I need to get out of here. Be alone until I calm down.

"You'd have to actually groom yourself once in a while for me to give you tips, big guy." Killian's smile is wide and easy. He's pretty much relaxed and happy all the time now. Which is great for him; he's getting laid on the regular by someone he loves. Clearly, it works.

Is that what Brenna meant? That she needed to find the kind of contentment Killian and Jax found with their women? Does sex with someone you care about make so much of a difference? On paper, yeah. Of course, I can understand the logic. But I can't make the leap into truly believing it. Sex is physical. I know intuitively that it would be better with Brenna, because I want her more than I've wanted anyone.

Brenna never mentioned love. We don't love each other. But I do care. I've always cared about her. How can I not? Officially, she's the band's public relations manager, but the truth is, she's as much a part of the band as any of us. We've gone from obscurity to fame together. She's witnessed the blood, sweat, and tears

—hell, not witnessed, she's experienced them. Brenna and I can bicker like spoiled brats, but I would do anything for her. All this time, I thought she understood that. Sour regret fills my stomach when I think about how much my actions upset her. I feel like a bonehead, an asshole. I want to make it up to her, to prove I'm one hundred percent on her side.

What if she agrees to give it a try with me and quickly realizes that it's not going to fill the void in her life? What the fuck do I do then? Because Brenna isn't one to keep on with something that's not making her happy. She'll drop me faster than I can zip my pants up. And shit *will* get awkward. Fast.

"You're zoning out again," Whip says near my ear.

The guys are all looking at me with varying levels of amusement.

Shit. I shouldn't have gone out today.

"I'm in a funk. No big deal."

I hate the silence that follows. It presses in on my skin and chokes me.

"Well," Jax finally says, drawing out the word like he's struggling to find a topic that will break the awkward-ass tension I've dropped on them. "Let's play ball, then."

Good. Great. Anything is better than all this talking.

I move to grab the ball at my feet. And it happens. My hand seizes up, curling into a claw as white-hot pain shoots from the tips of my fingers up to my shoulder. I go absolutely rigid. The pain is so intense, I can't move. All I can do is work through it with slow, agonized breaths. No one has seen; it's only been a few seconds. But it feels like an eternity.

Casually, as I can, I grab my bag with my good hand and stand upright. Jesus wept, it hurts. Like a molten poker under my skin. "I'm gonna go." I'm sweating. I know I am. My voice is clipped and tight.

The guys start to protest, but I'm already backing away. *Need to get the fuck out of here. Now.* I feel ill. Dizzy.

Panic attack. Jax has them. He'd empathize. He'd help. He'd ask questions I don't want to answer.

Panting, I jog off the court. My hand is still curled into a painful claw.

Fuck.

Fuck.

Fuck.

By the time I get a cab and collapse in the back of it with a sigh, my head spins with pain and fear. Slowly, with the cautiousness of a ninety-year-old, I stretch my fingers, wincing at the lingering soreness. I move my index finger the wrong way and wince.

As soon as I get home, I'll ice my hand, then follow that with an ointment rub. I could take pain meds, but they don't fix anything, only mask it.

Tears smart my eyes, the city a blur outside the grimy cab window. I'm surrounded by millions of people, and I've never felt more alone. Cold. Empty. And afraid. Because it's not getting better. It's getting worse.

————

Brenna

A SOB RIPS out of me, and I lurch upright in bed, tears rolling down my face. I can't stop crying. Even as I wipe my cheeks and try to calm my breathing, the utter fear and sorrow won't abate. Rocking myself in the dark, I cry and cry until my chest hurts and my eyes swell. I don't need to glance at my phone to know the time. It's always the same when this happens—4:32 a.m., the very moment I got the call from Killian telling me about Jax, how we almost lost him.

From that moment on, I have had episodes when stressed, crying jags that tear me out of sleep and leave me decimated. I hate them, but they won't stop. With a shaky sigh, I flop back on my bed and curl my knees to my chest. I'm freezing cold, from the inside out. The heavy duvet doesn't help. Nothing will. I'm alone and terrified of some unnamed thing that lives inside me.

Other people have experienced deep, personal losses in their lives. I haven't, not really. Not the death of someone I love with all my heart. And I do love Jax. He's a brother to me. I didn't lose him, but it was close. Too close. It shattered something in me. I hate that I can't control this. No matter how many times I tell myself everything is okay now, I can't actually feel it. Nights like this, when it all comes crashing back in, are the worst.

I'm so cold, so empty. Scared. I'm scared. Because I am alone, and I don't want to be. Not right now. I want arms to hold me tight, the warmth of another body pressing into me. But there isn't anyone I want in my bed with me either. There's the rub. I want something that doesn't exist.

Before, I'd have called Jax, just to hear his voice. Sweet man that he is, he'll always answer the phone. He never asks why I am calling; somehow, he knows. He simply says, "I'm here, Bren. I'm still here." That's enough for me. I'll tell him I love him and hang up. We never speak of it, never tell the others. But now, Jax has Stella. I can't call him and wake her too. Besides, I need to cut the cord.

Doesn't make the emptiness end, though. For a brief, mindless second, I consider calling Killian. He truly is the closest thing I have to a brother. Growing up together, we'd often have sleepovers. We thought nothing of curling up together in bed and talking about our dreams. His were always grand and colorful but focused on music. Mine were generic—my own horse; kissing Justin Timberlake; making Becky Todd, my archenemy at age ten, eat dirt. Killian's dreams came true. I followed along for the ride.

But Killian has someone too. He's curled up with Libby now, telling her his dreams.

Do I even have dreams anymore?

Heaving myself out of bed, I make my way into the kitchen. I know my apartment so well now, I navigate it easily in the dark. Making myself some warm milk with cinnamon and honey and heating a hot water bottle, I stare out the windows to where the city glitters like white diamonds against an indigo sky. It's a sight I've never tired of. But tonight, any excitement I usually feel is gone.

Unbidden, I hear *his* voice in my head. *It's a promise. A promise, Bren, of how fucking good it can be if you just let go of your pride.*

"Jesus." I still can't believe Rye said all that. It's like some bizarre nightmare. Any time one of our friends even joked that Rye and I were hot for each other, Rye would react with such offended dignity that I started to develop a complex—nipped only in the bud by returning his disdain with equal measure.

Unease prickles over my skin. He talks of pride. Pride is the only defense I have to protect myself from him. Pride and vigilance. I never let myself slip with Rye. Never let myself think about him as anything other than... What are we to each other? I don't even know how to define it. He wasn't exactly my enemy, but we certainly weren't friends.

He doesn't even know why I started to hate him. He only thinks he does. The truth is far more complicated and painful.

Unbidden the memory comes to the fore as sharp and cutting as it was when it happened.

"Happy Birthday, Brenna." Lacey, a sound engineer, gives me a lingering smile as I make my way through the party. There's been a spark of interest between us, but I push it aside and keep my responding smile light.

"Thanks."

Disappointment flickers in her gaze, but she simply nods as I keep walking. I feel a little bad about it, but since one disastrous and humiliating band meeting where the guys grilled me about my freaking sex life, I made an ironclad rule not to get involved with anyone on the payroll. Scottie once reminded me of the old adage: Don't shit where you eat.

Gross, but true. Getting entangled with someone you have to work with day in and out isn't a good idea.

I wish the guys took that to heart. One full tour under my belt, and I've already had to deal with tearful encounters with various staff members who fooled around with my bonehead friends. I love them, but they're idiots most of the time. Well, I love three of them. The other one... Nope, I will not think about him.

It isn't easy. Stupid, annoying Rye makes it nearly impossible to ignore him. He's always there, taunting, teasing, all but daring me to try and forget about him. My face flames with familiar irritation. It's my damn birthday party, and here I am thinking yet again about Rye Freaking Peterson. No more! That ship is sunk, landed at the bottom of the ocean, and rusted over. His opinion of me means nothing. Nothing.

I move past well-wishers, people dancing, couples hooking up. I turn a blind eye to the drugs spread out on one table. Jax is chugging a bottle of vodka as a brunette goes down on—fuck, I did not need to see that. I turn from the party and head down a narrow hallway that's been roped off for all but the band. Kill John has rented the entire top floor party space of the hotel for this stop on the tour, knowing they'd have multiple afterpar-ties and my birthday celebration. Scottie insisted on having a quiet place to unwind and several rooms are ours alone.

Frankly, I think he's the only one to take advantage of that, though. The guys have been partying hard and fast. It worries me, sometimes, how they act as if they're invincible. I've already seen enough of the underbelly of this business to know that it will suck you down and spit you out if you're not careful.

"You're beautiful."

I stop in my tracks, my heart leaping wildly in my chest. Rye's voice is unmistakable. And I'm utterly ashamed to admit that, for a hot second, I thought it was directed at me. But no, it came from the open doorway of a small lounge a few feet away. I hear a woman's pleased laugh, and my stomach sours. Ugh. I don't want to witness yet another one of his conquests.

"You are too kind to me, dear boy."

My blood runs ice cold. Because I know that voice too. It's my Aunt Isabella. Alone with Rye the Wonderfuck. What the hell is she doing back here with Rye? I knew she was at the party. Isa is a world-famous supermodel; anytime she enters a room, people notice. We're in Manhattan where she lives, and she came to say hello. But I had lost track of her hours ago.

Her laughter, soft with undeniable flirtation, ripples over the silence, and my insides flip.

With a queasy sense of dread, I edge toward the door, even though my sensible voice is screaming at me to walk away. I'm quiet and slow, and neither of them sees me. But I see far too much. Rye sits in a lazy sprawl against the end of a black leather sofa, his profile to me. There's a flush of red on the back of his neck and a certain tilt to his head that tells me he's been drinking too much. No surprise there; all of the guys have been drinking far too much lately.

The surprise is the way Isa is curled into him, her lithe, toned body practically leaning on his. Oh, God, she's touching his hair, gently teasing the tips as he smiles at her with a stupid, fucking hazy-eyed grin. "Do you really think I'm beautiful?" she asks in soft wonder. "I'm so old."

"You're not old," he murmurs. "Any man would be thankful to have you."

I don't hear the rest of what he says, my ears are ringing too hard. My fingers have turned to ice. Jealousy, disgust, rage, disappointment...it's an oily stew in my gut. I swallow thickly, feeling sick. I watch in mute horror as Rye's words are cut off by my aunt's mouth. He makes a noise of what I can only guess as lust as she wraps herself around him and kisses him like he's...

With a muffled sob, I wrench myself away and rush back down the corridor. I hate him. He has no shame. No honor. He's kissing my aunt, his best friend and bandmate's mom.

The memory tears away like a bandage ripped off too fast. I take a deep breath to clear my head. But the feeling of that day lingers with sticky fingers.

Eventually, I let go of what I saw. The health of the band depended on maintaining the status quo. But it broke my trust in Rye. From that day on, I never let him see my deeper emotions. I never let him in the way I let the others. Now he wants in, deep in. Moreover, he wants my trust. I don't know if I can give him that, no matter how tempted I am.

I grab the milk and hot water bottle and head for my room. I no longer feel empty and sad. But I still feel alone. And unnerved.

CHAPTER FIVE

BRENNA

KILLIAN'S LOFT is filled to capacity, the air humid with the warmth of too many humans and the mingling scents of dozens of perfumes. Usually, these parties are exhausting. But these are our closest friends, fellow musicians, people we've met along the way. No one here is worried about being seen or who they should see. They're just having fun. Sophie, Jax, Libby, and I worked hard to make it that way, only inviting people we knew would get along.

Though Jax is more of a homebody nowadays, he insisted on having a birthday party for Stella. She spent years as a professional friend—yes, there really is such a thing—but never had any true friendships of her own until Jax came into her life. Add a shitty, neglectful father to the mix, and it meant that Stella never had any birthday parties. Jax wants to give that to her.

"She needs to see how much she is loved," he'd said.

I know for a fact Stella understands how much she's loved. Jax shows her every day. My cagey, allergic-to-relationships friend has done a complete turnaround to devoted boyfriend.

On the patio, Jax and Stella dance to The Smiths' "How Soon is Now?" There's an inside story to that, I'm certain. Jax requested the song personally, and they're sharing a look that speaks of intimate connection. Watching them bump and sway, so close they appear as one, both pinches at my chest with undefined longing and makes it swell with happiness for them.

I turn from the scene and head for the bar where Scottie is making drinks. What few people know is that he tended bar in the early days to keep himself fed and make connections for the band. He'd never been a chatty bartender, but people loved him —maybe because of that. Okay, and probably because he looks like a walking cologne ad. Doesn't hurt that he concocts excellent drinks, when so inclined.

He sees me coming and pulls out a bottle of high-end vodka from some hiding place beneath the bar. By the time I lean against the gleaming black marble bar, he's setting out an icy vodka tonic with peels of lime, lemon, and grapefruit twisted together in an artful multicolored swirl.

I take a sip and close my eyes for a second. "Despite what I tell the others, you are my favorite friend."

"Obviously," he says with utter sincerity as he fixes himself a Manhattan with quick and precise moves. Impeccably dressed in a dove-gray bespoke suit and more beautiful than a man has a right to be, he really is something to watch in action. I'm tempted to throw down a tip.

"This is where you say I am your favorite too." I take another sip.

The barest smile curls the corner of his lip. "My dear, there was never any question."

"That's not a real answer, handsome." Truth is, neither of us is very good at playing favorites, although we've tried throughout the years. I settle on a stool with a sigh, and Scottie leans a hip against the bar.

His cool blue eyes study me, and I resist the urge to squirm. "Should I be concerned?"

For a hot moment, I fear he knows about Rye's proposal. But Scottie is the last person Rye would confess to, and if the others knew, they'd have already teased. No, Scottie simply knows me well enough that he's noticed something is off. This is the problem with being too close to a group of people. Pretty soon, I'll be facing a group intervention, and I'll have to run off to Tibet just to get away from all the meddling.

"You needn't," I say with forced lightness.

"Hmmm." His eyes squint as he surveys the party and takes a drink of his cocktail. When he looks my way, worry laces his expression. "Whatever it is, I am here for you."

God. He's going to make me cry. My throat clogs, and I hide my distress behind a long swallow. Vodka shoots into my system and warms it up. "Some problems," I say when I'm certain I won't sound like a frog, "friends cannot fix."

His stern countenance smooths out. "Ah. It's like that, is it?"

"Like what?" I huff out a laugh. "I haven't said anything."

"Of course you have. You see your friends settling down. And now you're thinking about your own love life."

"Oh my God. Stop." How the hell does he do that?

"There's no need to feel ashamed."

"I'm not ashamed."

His black brow quirks. "Your blush tells me otherwise."

Curse my pale hide. "Is this your bartender shtick?"

"Shtick? What do you mean?"

"Ten years of living on and off in New York and you don't know what 'shtick' means," I mutter. "Are you the counseling bartender now?"

His smile is quick and ruthless. "Actually, I was thinking this was more the role of a shadchan."

"A what?" And then it hits me that he's used a Yiddish word —one I don't know. The little shit has been playing me.

Lips twitching, he leans closer. "There's someone I think you should meet."

"Oh, hell." Horror threatens to swallow me whole. "You're matchmaking?"

Scottie winces at my screech. "I wouldn't normally, but I believe you two would hit it off."

"Kill me now," I mutter. "Just kill me and feed my body to the wolves."

"I believe you mean to the hyenas. They prefer carrion."

"Scottie," I grind out. "I'm about ten seconds away from killing *you*."

His eyes gleam with evil mischief. "Make up your mind, Ms. James. Is it you or I who should be murdered?"

An arm brushes against mine. "Why are you guys talking about murder?" Rye asks with an amused laugh.

I'm in hell. Who knew it served such good drinks? Shooting Scottie a glare, I answer Rye. "Doesn't everyone talk about murder at some point?"

"I don't know..." Rye scratches the dark-gold beard on his chin like he's thinking about it, when I know he is not. He gives me a sly smile. "You seem to be inordinately preoccupied with murder."

It's so weird seeing him in the flesh now, I don't know where to look. I aim for somewhere around his ear. "Oh, please."

He shakes his head. "You're always threatening to kill me."

Scottie raises his Manhattan in cheers. "The woman is extraordinarily bloodthirsty."

I huff out a laugh. "First off, everyone wants to kill Rye."

"True," Scottie concedes.

"Hey!" Rye scowls at us.

"And I wouldn't be throwing stones." I point my glass at Scottie. "There are Instagram accounts devoted to the people you have made cry in public."

Rye grins wide. "Didn't you start most of those accounts, Bren?"

I shrug. "If the content is real, does it matter?"

"Good point."

"Your attempts at shaming are wasted on me." Scottie turns to mix another drink. "I enjoy making entitled gits cry."

"It's a form of relaxation for Scottie," Rye agrees with a nod. "Thing is, Brenna loves doing that as well. It's like you two are the evil Wonder Twins. Partners in terrorizing the music world." His gaze bounces between Scottie and me. "So, why does Brenna want to kill you?"

I glance at all available exits. It won't do any good. Rye will find me.

Scottie sets a cocktail before Rye.

"Your cocktail of choice is a Moscow Mule?" I blurt out when Rye gives a smile of thanks and takes a drink. Honestly, these past few years, I rarely see him drink any alcohol other than a beer or a few shots of whatever liquor is on hand.

"It's refreshing." Rye gives me a sidelong look. "And stop trying to change the subject."

Damn it, he's like a tick on a dog's butt.

"Brenna objects to my matchmaking efforts."

Scottie might as well have dropped a stink bomb. Rye's nostrils pinch on an indrawn breath. I hold in a curse and force myself to act natural, knowing I'm doing a shit job of it, knowing Scottie is far too observant.

Rye leans an elbow on the bar top. "Matchmaking isn't your usual style."

I give Rye credit. He's clearly trying to appear unaffected; his smile holds its usual smirk, and his stance stays relaxed. The problem is, if it's clear to me that he's upset, then it's obvious to Scottie. We all know one another too well, which is both a gift and a curse.

Scottie's eyes narrow a fraction, then his expression smooths out. "I loathe the very idea of matchmaking."

"Then why are you doing it?" Rye retorts.

They're both staring at each other like gunslingers in a cheap Western. I want to run away from this nightmare, but I'm pathetically frozen in place.

A sly curve twists Scottie's lips. "I'm a problem solver."

"Oh, God," I moan, unable to help myself. "Make it stop."

Rye eyes me and offers a fake frown of concern. "You got a problem, Bren?"

He knows very well what my problem is: him.

"Need a little loving?"

I glare at his smug face. "Yes. And since Scottie cares, he's going to procure a fine piece of ass for me. Aren't you?"

Scottie's grin is a quick flash of calculated evil. "Of course, love. Let's bring him over so you can have a look."

"What?" Blood rushes to my toes. "Now?"

No, no, no...

"Yes, now." He quirks a black brow. "I told you there was someone I wanted you to meet."

"I thought you meant to give me his number."

"And not be there to intervene if you don't find him acceptable? I don't think so."

Before I can stop him, Scottie turns and hails someone in the crowd.

Rye laughs, though there's an edge to it that prickles along my skin. "This should be interesting."

He sounds like he's gritting his teeth. Good. We can suffer together. I shoot him a quelling look then straighten my shoulders. When there's no escape, the only thing to do is let it ride. I can't imagine who Scottie has in mind; I've vetted the guest list. But there are always a couple of strays invited last minute by one of the guys. I never suspected Scottie would offer an invite; the man basically hates everyone.

Despite the agony of this public matchmaking spectacle playing out in front of Rye, I'm now curious. Who the hell would Scottie like enough to set me up with? Because I know one thing to be true: he would never do this unless he was serious. But I don't turn to see whoever it is that he's called over. Neither does Rye. He watches me from under his lashes. White edges his knuckles as he grips the copper mug of his drink.

In my head, his offer makes a mockery of my outward calm. *I want it to be me. I want to be the one you use.*

Damn it all, I actually feel guilty, as though I'm somehow cheating on him. But I haven't accepted his offer. I don't even know if I'll like Scottie's friend. All I know is that I want to be anywhere but next to Rye right now.

I'm ready to tell him to go away, stop with the disapproving silence, when someone steps up to the bar next to me. And then my mind blanks because, holy hell, he is gorgeous. With dark-blond hair the color of butterscotch, lake-blue eyes, and an easy smile that promises a good time, the guy towers over me. He's built like a boxer, lean but stacked with muscles that strain his shirtsleeves.

"Marshall," Scottie says by way of introduction. "This is my mate Rye Peterson, bassist for Kill John. And this is my better business half, Brenna James, publicist for Kill John."

Marshall reaches out to shake Rye's hand. "Huge fan, man."

"Thanks. Good to meet you." Rye's answering smile is tight. The ropy muscles along his arm shift and bulge when he shakes Marshall's hand, and it hits me like a slap. They look so similar, both in face and form, they could be brothers.

Heat swarms my cheeks, and I glance at Scottie. The bastard is smugly composed. But I know he's done this on purpose, dangling a Rye doppelgänger in front of me like a dare.

Marshall turns toward me and smiles. It's a great smile, warm and friendly, with just enough interest to flatter. "Ms. James, I've wanted to meet you for some time."

"Have you?" My mind sticks on his name. It sounds familiar. And then it hits me. "Marshall Faulkner, from Artists Inc.?"

"The very one."

Wow. Faulkner is one of the top artist managers in Hollywood. His clients are legends. Hell, *he* is a legend.

"I thought you'd be older," I blurt out.

Marshall laughs as I wince.

"God, that was rude. I'm sorry."

Thankfully, he doesn't appear offended but truly amused. "No, no, I get that a lot."

"It was still rude."

He leans against the bar. "Scottie said you were wonderfully blunt. I like that."

I'm painfully aware of Rye staring at me, but I ignore him. "What else has Scottie been telling you?"

Scottie merely grunts. The sound I know to mean: *Fishing, Brenna? How needy.* Yeah, well, my ego needs the occasional stroking. Sue me.

"All good things," Marshall says. "But, really, your work record caught my eye long ago." At this, he glances at Rye. "Kill John is arguably the biggest band in the world right now..."

"No arguing about it," Rye quips. "It is." His voice has dropped about two octaves and is hard as concrete. I have no idea if he realizes this. Right now, there's a wall of humming tension dividing us even though he's standing so close, his arm brushes my shoulder when he reaches for his drink. His proximity to me is far too possessive. And irritating.

"Fair enough," Marshall says easily. He smiles down at me. "Let's just say I'm impressed with your work."

Rye makes a noise under his breath. It's intelligible, but I swear I hear it as "I'll bet." The urge to elbow him is high. Instead, I focus on Marshall. "Likewise."

"I'd love to trade notes." He shakes his head slightly as if he's laughing at himself. "No. That's terrible. It's a party. Here's to not working." He salutes me with his beer bottle, and I raise my glass.

"Hear, hear."

"Let's talk of more pleasant things. Such as, do you care for tacos?"

"Tacos?" I chortle. "Random but, yes, I love a good taco."

Blue eyes crinkle with mirth. "Why, so do I. We have exceptional tacos in LA. But I'm willing to go in search of some here if you'd like to join me."

"A taco hunt?"

"If you're willing?"

Rye lets out a breath, the sound just shy of a snort. "I'm going to get some air. Maybe give Jax a run for his money on the dance floor." Tight lines bracket his mouth as he nods toward Marshall. "Nice meeting you, man."

I don't watch Rye leave, but I feel the separation between us with an intensity that unsettles me to the core. My teeth hurt from the effort of maintaining my smile. I probably look deranged, but Marshall simply eyes me with interest, patiently waiting for me to answer. What had we been talking about?

Tacos. Right. A date.

On paper, Marshall Faulkner is perfect: hot, successful, and slightly dorky. I've admired his work for years and would love to talk to him about it. I even get a pleasant warm tingle in my belly when I look at him. Sure, it's no wild flip, skipped heart-beat, fluttering pulse, can't decide if I want to strangle him or kiss him. But that's a good thing.

So why am I still smiling up at him like a frozen doll? *Snap out of it, girl. This is the first good date prospect you've come across in months. Get on it. Not all great loves start with a bang.*

The sharp spike of my heel hits the floor with a definitive *click*—a trick I cultivated to keep my focus when all else fails. It has the expected effect: I stand a bit straighter, thrusting my boobs out and lifting my chin. Marshall's eyes dilate.

"I'd love to go taco-hunting with you."

"Great. Let's set a date." His smile is warm and inviting. He's a beautifully put-together man. And yet I feel faintly sick to my stomach.

Freaking Rye.

———

Rye

. . .

FUCKING PERFECT. Brenna is making eyes at Mr. LA Charm. Horny, *needy* Brenna. Shit.

I need to let this go. Brenna is lonely. Faulkner, though cheesy as fuck with his "let's hunt for tacos" line, seems like a good guy. Scottie wouldn't throw him in Brenna's path if he wasn't. Maybe he can make her happy.

One thing is certain, if the guy has any brains, he'll make a serious play for Brenna. How could he not? She's smart, has a killer wit, and looks like a wet dream. I nearly swallowed my damn tongue when I saw her poured into a cream-colored dress that hugged her toned body and fluttered around her knees, highlighting her sleek, endless legs.

She's wearing yet another pair of killer heels—rainbow patent-leather with red soles. Rainbows, for fuck's sake. And still, I took one look at those wickedly high heels and instantly wanted them digging into my back.

Fucking Scottie. Matchmaking? Seriously?

Never have I wanted to kick his proper British ass more than I do now. Yeah, he's a bruiser under those damn suits and likes to pit fight for fun, but I'm a grappler; I can take him.

"Everyone knows the best MMA fighters are grapplers," I mutter.

A surprised laugh to my right snaps me out of my fuming haze. A pretty brunette leans against the balcony railing. Tiny tank barely covering her toned belly, tight jeans riding low, and a wide, glossy red smile.

"I don't know if you were talking to me, but I agree." Her wide smile turns seductive, and she tosses a length of silky curls over her shoulder. "Grapplers have the best takedowns. All that sweaty writhing on the floor..."

Like that, it's on. She's looking for a hookup, preferably with one of the band members—because we always get first choice. It's all right there in her body language and eye contact. I've lived this life long enough to know that I could do the bare minimum of mundane flirting, touch her skin—maybe caress her forearm or a fleeting brush along her cheek—to show I'm interested, and I'll be in like Flynn. That's not ego talking; it's experience.

She turns more fully my way and extends a hand. "Hi, I'm Jenni, with an I."

I take her smooth hand in mine. "Hey, Jenni with an *I*. I'm Rye."

My younger self would have done a goofy comeback and said I was Rye with a *Y*, but I think I might gag if I tried that shit right now. My younger self was a dillhole.

"I know." She steps into my space, her lips parting. "I'm a huge fan."

She's beautiful. The fact that she knows a little about mixed martial arts, or is at least willing to humor me, is a plus because I like to at least have some conversation with potential hookups.

I roll my shoulders to ease the tight ache there and give Jenni a practiced smile. "You like bassists, huh?"

This particular game of seduction is as easy as sliding into a pair of well-worn jeans. I haven't had sex in a while. A nice physical release couldn't hurt.

Her finger trails down my biceps. "I like *you*."

She doesn't know me from Adam. But that's okay. It's all part of the game.

I'm so fucking tired of games.

She's stroking my arm now, feeling the definition of my muscles. And I'm utterly numb. No, not numb exactly. All of my nerves seem to be focused along my back. The urge to turn around and see what Brenna and Taco Tuesday are doing rides me hard.

Forget about them. Brenna isn't interested. She thinks I'm a joke and out to humiliate her, and there's nothing I can do to make her see otherwise. *Focus on the hot chick feeling you up.*

"I've been meaning to ask you," Jenni says. "Was that a Moog Modular IIIp you used on 'Walk on Days'?"

My attention yanks back with a jolt. Brows raised, I look at Jenni anew. "It was. How did you know?"

Aside from a few music producers, no one has ever noticed that, much less cared. Even the guys got a glazed look on their faces when I'd set it up and tried to talk about the Moog IIIp's merits.

"I teach history of musicology at NYU." Her smile is wry. "And a class on musical innovations of the twentieth century."

I just got a mental boner. I didn't know that was possible. "I've always wanted to take some of those classes. If only to be in a room with other people who are willing to talk about musicology."

"You don't find that here?" She glances around the terrace that's filled with music industry professionals and artists.

"You'd like to think so, wouldn't you? But no. Not to what my friend Brenna would call the geek level." Damn it, why did I have to mention her? She was almost out of my head.

Jenni leans in, resting her elbow against the ledge, which does great things to her cleavage, I'm not going to lie. "From what I've heard, you could run a class."

Ah. So she knows about my obsession with all things musical. It's not exactly hidden, but most people tend to ignore that part of me for fear I'll drop into lecture mode. The threat is real; I love talking about my favorite subject.

"I'd probably bore your students to death."

The tip of her fingernail travels along the clock tat I have on my inner forearm. "You're kidding, right? They'd be afraid to blink for fear of missing a second."

Nice praise. Why doesn't it do anything for me?

Something soft and feminine slams into my back, and I turn to find Sophie hanging on to me like a limpet. Big brown eyes glossy from too many cocktails peer up at me from over my shoulder. "Hey there, Rye-Rye. Why are you so big?"

Snickering, I wing an arm behind me and scoop her off my back before gently setting her at my side. She leans against me, making herself comfortable. I hold on to her shoulder so she won't stumble. "Three square meals a day and a genetic disposition toward awesomeness," I tell her.

She gives me a dopey grin. "Humble Joe. Reliable Rye. Rye the big man pie."

Yep. She's one drink away from being shitfaced.

"You seen Scottie lately?" I'm guessing no. If he knew she was buzzing, he'd be following her around and glaring at anyone who got too close. He knows she can handle herself, but his wife is his entire world, and bad shit can happen at a party, no matter how well you think you know the guest list.

"He's playing matchmaker," she slurs, as Libby walks over and stands close to her other side.

Libby shoots me a look that says she's keeping an eye on Sophie. But I'm distracted by the whole "matchmaker" bit. Did everyone but me know he was planning to hook Brenna up?

"Isn't it cute?" Sophie says. "Look, it's *so* on."

We all turn in the direction of her stare. Brenna is leaning into Marshall's space, her sweet little tits thrust out like eye candy. He's taking the bait, his eyes more on her chest than her face. My stomach roils, and I finish off the last of my drink. It's gone watery and weak.

"I can't believe that's Marshall Faulkner," Libby says with a dreamy sort of sigh. "I had no idea he was so hot. He knows everyone."

"Even Chris Evans?" Sophie asks with wide eyes.

"Yep." .

All three women sigh then.

"I'd probably drool on Evans if I met him," Libby says. "It wouldn't be pretty."

"You two have men," I remind Sophie and Libby, compelled by loyalty to stick up for my boys. Besides, it beats watching Brenna chat it up with Marshall.

They roll their eyes and scoff in exactly the same tone.

"That doesn't mean we're dead," Libby says with a flip of her honey-blond hair. "Killian is well aware of my Chris crushes. He finds it amusing."

"No one is hotter than Gabriel," Sophie adds. "He can deal."

"The ultimate question. Hemsworth or Evans?" Libby grills her.

Sophie shrugs. "Why not both?"

"I'd be the meat in that sandwich," Jenni adds, choosing now to pipe up. She gives me an assessing glance. "You're a bit of a Hemsworth."

They all look at me. Assessing.

"He's definitely got the big, strapping Hemi-body going," Sophie says without hesitation. Drunk Sophie is good for the ego, I'll say that. But I'm beginning to feel like the meat in their sandwich.

Libby's gaze darts to Jenni then back to me. Her brow wings up, and a slow smile spreads over her lips. Shit.

"I'm sorry," she says, holding out a hand to Jenni. "I didn't introduce myself. I'm Libby."

"I know. I'm a huge fan."

"Oh, shit," Sophie laments loudly. "I'm sorry. This is Jenni. Scottie and I met her at a fundraiser, and we invited her to the party."

"And I'm very glad you did," Jenni says.

I don't miss the way she looks at me when she says it. Neither do the girls. Sophie hums, rubbing her cheek against my arm—she's notoriously cuddly when she's buzzing—and then beams. "Scottie thought you'd hit it off with Rye. I guess he was right."

She drops that awkward bomb, clearly quite pleased with herself, while Libby chokes back a laugh and Jenni blushes—though she doesn't appear embarrassed. No, she's pleased as well. As for myself? I'm beginning to wonder if I've fallen into an episode of *The Twilight Zone*. Scottie's matchmaking for me too? What the actual fuck is going on here?

And what the hell do I say now? An uncomfortable laugh

escapes me, and I rub the side of my neck that still tingles with the urge to turn and watch Brenna. The urge to run away is also high on the list. "You're cute when you're drunk, Soph."

"I'm not drunk," she protests, taking the bait. "I'm simply... cocktail-induced happy."

Libby hums. "Let's go tell Scottie about it, shall we?"

"Oh, let's." Sophie's grin goes lopsided. "He's so pretty. My mom is watching Felix for the weekend. I'm footloose and baby-free. I gonna take my man home and ride him like a wild pony."

With that lovely image in my head, I really don't want to look at my friend at the moment. But I can't help myself; I glance Scottie's way. He's still at the bar but has moved away from Brenna and Marshall. Brenna, who pulls out her phone to take down Marshall's number. It's a kick to the gut to see. Irritation surges just behind that, and I grind my back teeth. What the fuck am I doing? My life was so much better when I remembered that Brenna is a pain in my ass and someone I should give a wide berth. It's stupid to get caught up in this "problem" of hers.

A moment of mindless stupidity. That's all it was. Now it's over.

"We're definitely asking Scottie how he feels about pony rides." Libby takes hold of Sophie's arm and peels her off me. "Nice to meet you, Jenni," she says, as they head inside to torment Scottie.

Leaving me alone with my apparent date for the night.

"Well," Jenni says expansively. "That was...something."

"That's Libby and Sophie for you. The encounter only needed Stella to make it a complete 'embarrass Rye' show."

"I can't believe I met Libby Bell." She's wide-eyed now. "God, she's so talented. I mean, you're all so talented. I'd love to meet the rest of the guys."

Normally, that would be my cue to steer someone away from my guys. But I'm not feeling charitable right now.

"Good thing they're over there." I nod toward the corner of

the terrace where Stella and Jax are cuddled up on a big round lounger. They're talking to Killian and Whip. I don't need to make eye contact to know those fuckers are watching me too. I'm being set up big time, and I'm not amused. "Let me introduce you."

"Oh, I didn't mean you had to..."

I gently take her elbow and guide her to my nosy-ass friends. "No, no, it's my pleasure."

They all do a terrible job at pretending they don't see me coming. I fall into expansive, carefree, good ol' Rye mode.

"Hey, guys. Having fun?" I ask, as Libby, having left Sophie in Scottie's care, returns and sits on Killian's lap.

Killian leans back in his chair, his hand on Libby's hip, and grins. "Sophie told us all of Scottie's favorite intimate positions. In detail. So maybe not fun. But entertained, yeah."

"I'm so giving him shit later," Jax says.

"Oh, hush." Stella pinches his side. "You will not!"

"Yes, he will," Whip, Jax, and I all answer in unison.

"You'll embarrass him," Stella says.

I laugh. "Kind of the point, Stells."

Libby shakes her head. "Yeah, and then we'll all have to deal with extra-evil Scottie. And suddenly we'll be doing a guest appearance on some weird Japanese game show where they throw us in a vat of udon to fight it out for points."

"That's...scarily specific," Jax says.

Libby gives him a speaking look. "Exactly."

Sadly, we're all properly spooked. Because she's not wrong.

"You guys are a trip," Jenni says at my side.

It's my cue to introduce her. Stella is all grace and kindness. Killian and Jax are annoyingly smug. Whip gives me a quick look of sympathy. Couples, man. They lose their damn minds when they fall for someone. Suddenly, they want to pair up the world.

"Jenni works at NYU. Music department..." A movement at the corner of my eye catches my attention. Brenna and Marshall are walking away from the bar. They're swallowed up by the crowd. The conversation around me dissolves into an indistinct buzz.

Jenni's warm arm brushes mine. Beautiful, intelligent, into music, and can hold her own with my friends. She should be perfect for me. But I feel absolutely nothing for this woman. Ordinarily, that wouldn't matter. I'm more than able to have sex without emotion. Truth is, I don't know it any other way.

It's kind of a shock to realize I'm tired of using soulless sex as a quick fix to forget the world. Which is hilarious, given that Brenna wants to use sex to forget her problems and I can't stop thinking about giving it to her.

Damn it. My head is done in. Life was easier when I didn't think too much. But I can't stop thinking.

"I'm sorry." I take a step back. Then another. "I forgot there's something I have to do."

My friends and Jenni all pause. Silence falls over our small circle as they gape at me. I don't give a damn. I keep backing away. "Nice to meet you, Jenni."

I don't turn around and head for the living room. But when I get there, Brenna is gone. And so is Marshall.

CHAPTER SIX

BRENNA

CURLED UP ON MY BIG, soft couch before the TV in my den, I finish up the second French braid in my hair then stretch out and wiggle my sock-covered feet. This is more like it. I love my couch. Nice and deep, squishy down-filled and upholstered in pale pink velvet—it's the kind of thing my parents would have called frivolous and, yes, it cost more than a month's rent on my first apartment. But I worked my ass off to get where I am, and I like my luxuries.

I like being home, frankly. I don't get to be here or by myself enough as it is. After I finally escaped the party, I gave myself a mini spa, taking a nice long shower while wearing a detoxifying clay mask, shaving the essential bits, then slathering on a rich body moisturizer that smells of cookies. It's late as hell, and I should be sleeping. But sleep eludes me these days. Instead, I'm watching old movies and eating my way through a can of Pringles. What can I say? They're my weakness.

I'm happily munching when the bell rings. Given that I have a doorman to keep unwanted visitors away, my hackles rise.

Everyone who knows where I live and would visit me at this hour is still at Stella's birthday party. I'm guessing it's one of my neighbors, needing help or maybe wanting to borrow an egg...at two in the morning. Shit.

The bell rings again, and I make my way to the door, remote clutched in my hand like a bat.

A peek through my peephole has me cursing wildly. Rye glares back at me, obviously aware that I'm peeping. I jerk back from the door then wrench it open. "What are you doing here?"

"You gonna club me with that remote?" He nods toward my hand where I still clutch it tight.

"I just might. It's two in the morning."

A long-suffering sigh leaves him. "Bren, I've spent the past decade staying up till all hours." He raises a brow. "And so have you. It's early for us."

"That might have been true a couple of years ago. The thrill is officially gone now."

His smile is barely there and weary. "Yeah, it is. Can I come in?" The smile dies, and he attempts to peer past my shoulder. "Or do you have company?"

"You thought I might have company, and yet you still showed up?"

That lopsided smile of his turns into a grimace. "No?"

I will not fall for that helpless hound dog look of his. It is *not* cute. "No, you didn't think? Or no, you're not actually here, and I'm hallucinating?"

"As much as I like the idea of you hallucinating about me, I meant no, I didn't know if you had company, but I wanted to make sure anyway."

When I gape back at him, he shifts his feet and eyes my foyer. "Well? Are you going to let me in?"

The petty girl in me really wants to close the door in his face. She'd gain a lot of satisfaction out of that—*checking to see if I had a date in here, indeed.* But I act like a grown-up and open the door wider, stepping aside to give him room. "All right then."

With a nod and a grim set to his mouth, Rye walks past me and waits in the living room while I close the front door. He takes a long look at my pink pajama bottoms and black tank top, swallows audibly, then blinks, but his expression remains blank. The Rye I know would have commented on the pj's. And while he would never point out that I am not wearing a bra, because though he is an ass, he isn't a pig, he keeps his gaze on my face.

At first, I assumed he was here to bug me yet again about my "problem," but he's acting as though he's about to face a firing squad, so now I'm not so sure. Fear that it's about one of our friends starts creeping up my shoulder blades.

"Is something wrong?" I ask.

"Wrong?" He rubs the back of his neck, the action making his biceps pop. A huff of dark amusement leaves him. "I don't know. I'm at your house alone for the second time in...well, ever, about to make a fool out of myself. Again." His arm drops, and he frowns, pinning me with a look. "I don't know if I'd define that as wrong, precisely."

My heartbeat has kicked up at his words. "Well, that's easy to fix. Don't make a fool out of yourself." Before he can answer, I head for the den and my movie. I honestly don't know if I want him to leave or follow.

He follows, those denim eyes solemn and watchful. He doesn't sit when I plop myself down on the couch and curl up in the corner. His gaze drifts to the bent glass coffee table littered with fashion magazines and my snack, and the corner of his mouth quirks. "You put your Pringles in a crystal serving bowl?"

"I like nice things." I snatch up a chip and stuff it into my mouth to hide my sudden case of the fidgets.

He glances around the room, taking in the ice-blue paneled walls, the heavy cream drapes, the wall of bookshelves that frame my giant TV, the gold-framed abstract art in splashes of black and indigo. My whole apartment is an ode to 1930s glamour. It's over-the-top but also comfortable. Rye—with his battered boots, worn jeans, and thick-ass scruff that's now firmly in beard territory—looks completely out of place. Then again, Jax's house is done up so fancy, it might as well be Buckingham Palace, so it's not as though Rye isn't used to it.

Even so, I eye him warily, waiting for further comment on my extravagant tastes. But he merely takes a visible breath and sits on the opposite side of the couch, exhaling as though he's at the end of a very long day and it's the first time he's had a chance to rest.

"You want a drink?" I ask, reaching for my wine.

He eyes it but shakes his head. "Nah, I'm good."

The silence between us grows thick and unwieldy, the sound of me crunching on my chips so loud, it's almost comical. I take a sip of my chardonnay to clear my throat.

"Rye—"

"Thing is," he says at the same time. "I told myself the same all the way over here."

"The same?" I parrot, confused.

He turns his head, and our gazes snag. His is bloodshot and unsure. "To let it go and not make a fool out of myself." The corners of his eyes crinkle. "Again."

"And yet you're here."

"That I am." Rye leans back, letting his head rest on the couch. "Scottie said he saw you leave. Without Mr. Taco."

"Mr. Taco?" I half laugh then glare when it hits me. "Is that what you're calling Marshall? Mature, Rye. Truly."

He scowls down at his big hands. They're callused and battered by years of playing dozens of instruments. "Can you blame me with that line? Let's go taco-hunting? If I said that cheesy shit, you'd laugh me out of the room."

"That would be ridiculous coming from you. You're much more of a hamburgers-and-hot dog-lover."

"I like tacos just fine," he grumbles.

I make a sound of amazed disbelief. "Do you hear yourself right now?"

"Yes." He doesn't appear happy about that. With a noise of

frustration, he turns his body to face mine. The couch feels much smaller because of it. Rye is a big guy: muscles for days, long limbs, and wide shoulders. He takes up space, not just bodily, but with his presence of will. All the restless energy that always seems to simmer just under his skin is now focused completely on me.

My skin tightens, a flush of...something...warms my chest.

"Bren...I...fuck it." He puffs out a harsh breath. "Look, I know we've had this holding pattern of mutual irritation and occasional loathing—"

"Only occasional?" I can't help but tease.

He gives me a quelling look before forging on. "And I know you hate that I overheard your confession. But I did. I can't change that or the fact that it changed *me*." He pokes the center of his chest with his thumb for emphasis. "Because it did, Bren. I can't get it out of my head. God knows I'd love to stop thinking about it, about you."

Same here, buttercup. It's oddly reassuring to know he's struggling as well.

Rye leans in as though he might touch me. But he obviously thinks better of it because his hand drops to his thigh instead. From under his strong brows, his eyes are wide and imploring.

"When Scottie fixed you up with Mr. Cheese Puff Taco, I thought, *Good, great, she might find someone to give her what she wants, maybe even more.* Or at least, I tried to think that." He winces and bites his bottom lip. Dusky red washes over his high cheekbones, surprising the hell out of me because Rye never blushes anymore.

"I tried, Bren. I really did. But I'm going to be honest here. Jealousy hit me over the head hard, and all I wanted to do was go back in there and throw him out on his ass."

With that, he stops and stares at me, clearly embarrassed by his confession, but just as clearly willing me to fully hear him. A gurgle of shock sounds in my throat. Because I heard him loud and clear. And I'm floored. I have never known Rye to be jealous. Of anything. He isn't built that way.

He keeps giving up pieces of himself, knowing that my pride took a big hit when he overheard me. The gesture flutters through me like a breath of warm air, finding its way through the small cracks in my resistance. I find myself relaxing just a bit, my grip on the throw pillow I've pulled on my lap easing.

Rye swallows audibly. His long fingers tap an agitated rhythm on his thigh. "You going on a date with him?"

"I'm supposed to." The reply is automatic and wooden; my brain is still having trouble catching up.

"Supposed to? Does that mean you are?"

I shake myself out of my Rye-induced fog. "Yes. I don't know. I mean, we exchanged numbers so we could make plans, but..."

"But?" He slides just a bit closer.

"I wasn't feeling it," I confess without thinking. He stirs beside me, and I catch the faint scent of perfume, sweetly funky and over-the-top, emanating from him. If I'm not mistaken, it's Montale's Amber Musk. It's never been a favorite. I really don't like it now.

My nostrils flare, and I rear back, hitting the couch arm. "Wait, you were jealous? I must have been imagining things again, because I could have sworn you had some woman hanging on your arm when I left."

He stills, confusion blanking his expression before he slowly smiles. "You noticed that, huh?"

"Oh, please. I wanted to say goodbye to everyone. How am I supposed to miss you cuddled up with the bohemian brunette?" One of a seemingly endless line of beautiful women who'll gaze at Rye as if he is the answer to every hot sex question they've ever asked.

His smug smile grows. "And yet you didn't come to say goodbye. You left." He eases even closer. "Tell me, Bren, were you a wee bit jealous as well?"

"Get over yourself. And stop pretending you were unsettled

by thoughts of me with Marshall when you are...reeking of her."
I wrinkle my nose. "Just go away. You stink."

He gives me a long, considering look, then stands abruptly.
Without another word, he walks out of the room, leaving me to
gape after him. I didn't think he'd actually leave. I should be
relieved. Instead, I'm oddly disappointed. I don't know why,
since I've been trying to push him away from the moment I saw
him through the peephole.

Thing is, I don't hear the front door open or shut. I hear
water running. Refusing to go look for him, I stuff a few more
Pringles in my mouth and take a healthy sip of my wine. It's gone
warm and is almost finished. I itch to get up, top off my glass, or
maybe find Rye. *No. I won't do that.*

I'm reaching for my remote, about to turn my movie back on
in a sad attempt at distraction, when he strides back into the
room in the process of tugging on a brand-new Kill John concert
tee. I'm treated to a glimpse of truly killer abs arrowing down
into low-slung jeans before the shirt settles.

"Good thing you had these promos hanging around," he says.

By "hanging around," he means stacked in my home office.
The guys scoff at me for having so many, but I like to send them
out to various sites and people when needed.

The black shirt stretches tight over Rye's shoulders and
strains around his biceps. Clearly, he needs an extra-large, but I
usually keep only medium and large around.

Hiding my surprise at his return, I smirk. "How's it feel
having Killian on your chest?"

The image we used for this shirt was of Killian, shot from
the back, a guitar in hand, blue and red stage lights shining in
the smoky atmosphere of a club. It was the cover of *Volver*, the
first album the band did when they got back together after their
hiatus.

Rye glances down at his chest and grins. "I noticed you don't
have any awesome Rye Peterson shirts on hand."

"Because there aren't any."

His grin grows cheeky. "We need to remedy that."

"Sure. As soon as you actually commit to a photoshoot, I'll get right on that."

Rye runs a hand through his damp hair and sits back down next to me. "I washed and changed my shirt. Can we please talk now?"

My lips twitch. Damn it, the big oaf is cute when he wants to be. And now he smells like my guest shower gel, fresh and citrusy. That he didn't invade my private bath but used the guest room one is a nice touch. I haven't seen him try this hard in well...ever.

"And before you start in," he adds, "I left the brunette back at the party. I wasn't feeling it."

Using my words against me. I grunt in response, hiding behind the act of eating another chip and staring at the French poodles prancing all over my pink pajama pants. He seems pleased at this and moves a hair closer. Over the years, I've developed the power to gauge exactly where Rye's body is in proximity to mine. It's like a superpower I never wanted.

"I can give you what you need," he says starkly.

I feel that claim like a stroke on my belly, and I lift my gaze to his. He's utterly serious.

"I mean it." He rests a hand on the back of the couch cushions, his fingers an inch away from my bare shoulder. "I might be the only one who can."

"The arrogance," I rasp with a laugh. "You think out of all the people in the world, only *you* can fix my 'little problem.'"

His blunt chin lifts a fraction. "At this moment in time? Yes."

"Oh, God." I laugh again. "How on earth do you figure that?"

"Because I'm here. And I know you, Bren." He says it so emphatically, I go still inside. Rye's gaze moves over my face. "I know you get cold if it's lower than seventy-five degrees out, which is why, when everyone else is sweating, you manage to look cool and professional. I know that you can't wear synthetics because they irritate your skin and you break out in a rash. I know that your calves cramp almost every day at exactly one fifteen in the morning..." He quirks a brow. "Which, by the way, is weird as shit that it's always at that time, but we'll chalk it up to one of the endless mysteries of the body."

I'm outright gaping as he slides an inch closer, and his knee brushes the side of my leg. "I know that you love having your hair touched and stroked, but for some reason you never admit to needing that, much less letting your hair down."

"How the fuck...?"

"Because I *know* you," he says softly, firmly. "I've spent years trying not to learn you, and failing."

Slowly, giving me time to pull away, he reaches out and lightly runs his fingers along my braid. Even though my hair is locked up tight, I feel it, and pleasurable little tingles chase along my scalp and down my spine. I fight the urge to close my eyes and whimper. My heart is trying to beat its way out of my chest, and the room has become too warm. I'm far too aware of my braless state now. My girls aren't big, but my nipples are tight and doing their best to poke their way through my tank.

Rye isn't looking at them, though. His gaze holds mine. "I'm good, Bren. I'll do whatever you want, for as long as you want. I'll make certain you're taken care of, and I won't tell a soul."

Jesus. I can't breathe.

"So selfless," I murmur. "And what do you get out of all of this?"

"You." His fingers stroke my braid. "I get you."

Shit. Licking my dry lips, I try to think of something, anything, to say. But he keeps talking.

"I want to fuck you, Brenna. I want that so badly, I'll do whatever it takes to have you."

"Oh, Jesus." I rub a shaking hand over my sweaty forehead. "I don't know how to handle this one-eighty."

His smile is small but wry. "The attraction between us was always there. You can deny it if you want, but it's true. We've been like two magnets facing south, repelling because we can't do anything else. Then I overheard what you needed, and I flipped north. Toward you."

My head flops back on the couch, and I peer up at him. He's sitting closer to me than he's ever dared. And though I know his face as well as my own, I see the faint lines of age and weariness around his eyes, the small, almost-faded scatter of freckles at the edges of his temples, an old, white, sickle-shaped scar on the crest of his left cheek. They're flaws, but they don't make him any less gorgeous. Only more real.

"For all our differences," he says, "we're very much the same. Neither one of us has the time or the inclination to go looking for a real relationship, but we both need physical release and the pleasure of touch or the isolation of our lives starts getting to us." He's starting to make too much sense, and he clearly knows it. He presses his point before I can say another word. "We both know what's at stake if what we're doing gets out, and we both know exactly what this is going into it."

"Rye..."

"I'm safe, Bren. I swear."

Safe. Ha. He's anything but. Rye is my one weak spot. The person most likely to do the greatest damage if he wanted to. But if he doesn't understand that by now, I'm certainly not exposing my underbelly by telling him.

His voice is melting chocolate, all sinful, rich persuasion. "A kiss. Just that. We kiss and see how it goes." His gaze settles on my mouth, heavy and warm with intent. "One good kiss. If you hate it or it's too weird, I'll fuck off forever."

"You'll fuck off forever with or without the kiss if I say so," I warn, trying to make my voice firm. But it's gooey and weak with temptation. Because, God, I've wondered. So many times, I've wondered what it'd be like to kiss him. And here he is offering.

He smiles then, a quick, brilliant flash. "Of course I will. But let's do it anyway. Let me kiss you, Berry."

I must be losing it, because I think I'm going to let him. God help me.

CHAPTER SEVEN

BRENNA

A KISS. I can do this.

"Okay." I squint at Rye through one partially opened eye. "One kiss."

He huffs out a laugh. "Try not to look too enthused there, Bren."

"Shit." I suck in a breath. "I'm sorry. It's just...It's you. You know?"

He runs his thumb along the scruff of his beard as though he's doing his best to rein in a smile. "I know."

The soft understanding tone of his voice tells me he does know exactly how weird this is. But the way he's looking at me, all that carnal heat barely banked, tells another story entirely. And that's the one I suddenly want to read.

Flushed and frazzled, I turn fully his way, tucking my legs under me on the couch as my shoulder rests against the soft back cushion. "Okay. Kiss me."

Silence falls heavy between us. I feel it pressing into the

thudding center of my chest. Rye's expression is serious, almost solemn as he reaches for me. His big hand, warm and rough, trembles before gently cupping my cheek. My insides jump and flutter, but I manage to keep still.

Or at least I do until he leans in. His lips come within a hairsbreadth of touching mine when a laugh bursts out of me. He pulls back as I dissolve into a helpless ball of nervous, snorting giggles.

"For fuck's sake..." He's trying to sound stern, but he's smiling wryly. "Are you going to be serious?"

"Sorry. Sorry." I clear my throat and wipe my eyes. "I'm good now. Totally."

His brow quirks. "You sure, Berry?"

"Yep." I draw in a quick, deep breath and let it out, tilting my head up to meet his gaze. "I'm good now."

The blunt tip of his thumb caresses a sensitive spot just under the corner of my mouth. "You sure?"

"Completely." My lips twitch. Butterflies wage war in my chest.

He dips his head. Every inch of me feels him closing in, warm, big, blocking out the light, the sound. He smells delicious. His breath tickles my lips. A laugh bursts out of me again.

"I'm sorry!" I'm giggling like a schoolgirl, and just as flustered, my cheeks searing hot. All I can think is, *Rye is about to kiss me. Rye Peterson is going to kiss me. Rye. Kissing. Me.*

He has the uncanny power to send me straight back to adolescence.

Rye moves back just enough to meet my gaze, his bemused and dry. He doesn't say a word, just searches my face, probably looking for signs of another outburst.

My lips wobble on a helpless grin. "I'm sorry. I have the giggles. It's just...it's you."

I am repeating myself. But he doesn't point it out. Ducking my head, I try to get a grip; it's embarrassing as hell to be this flustered in front of him. Hell, it's just a kiss. Amateur hour, really. I shouldn't feel like my heart is trying to bang its way out of my chest over a simple kiss.

"Bren. Look at me."

When I do, he takes my hand in his and presses the tips of my fingers against the side of his neck. His pulse beats hard and fast.

"I know," he whispers. "I know."

Because it means the same to him.

I'm no longer laughing. I can't. He's all around me, hands framing my face, the heat of him warming my skin. The man is his own furnace, always running a bit hotter than anyone else. Being this close to him, with all that intense focus on me, is strangely heady, and I find myself breathing a little faster.

I breathe out, and he breathes in. In. Out. We're exchanging air, both of us quietly shaking. I'm close enough to see the crystal starburst of white lines within the warm blue of his eyes. Then his thick lashes lower, his gaze settling on my mouth.

God. I feel it. Feel the pads of each individual finger pressed against my skin. Feel his shuddery exhale.

"Rye, I—"

His lips capture mine. Heat punches through me, flaring hot between my thighs, pulling tight on my nipples. He kisses me like a man who's been stranded in the dark and just found a source of light, his entire body straining toward mine. Firm lips learn my shape. Soft licks, gentle sucks. I lose my breath, and he gives it back to me in a husky exhale, a small murmur that speaks of hunger. It stokes my own. I nudge closer, my lips parting, pressing.

The stubble of his beard is surprisingly soft and springy. It tickles the edges of my mouth with the smallest of counter-strokes, sensitizing my skin. I feel that tickle at the base of my neck, the undersides of my breasts, dancing up my thighs. It's as if every nerve in my body is tied to my mouth and the way his makes me feel. A whimper escapes because I want more. I want it for hours.

But he's easing away. I haven't even discovered his taste. Just that small sample of his lips on mine.

I find myself chasing that clever mouth. But he holds firm, watching me, eyes bright with desire. Then he huffs out a half laugh, half groan and kisses me again. Deeper, slower, so intense I flare fever-hot. He...handles me. Moving me where he wants, coming at me from different angles as if he needs to try all of them. And then try them again.

And I love it.

God, I'm slipping into a daze, my body throbbing. If I weren't sitting down, I'd have fallen.

I grip the collar of his shirt. My other hand is still pressed against his nape. His pulse strums a frantic rhythm. When I run the tip of my finger along the line of his neck, he grunts and breaks the kiss.

His lips are swollen, the bottom one glossy with our kiss. "That was..." He clears his throat. "It was..."

"Yeah, it was."

Rye thumbs the corner of my mouth. "I knew it would be like that."

I want to say something snarky about his confidence. But given the fact that he's reduced me to this hot and melty creature of need, I can only lick my tender lips and stare back at him.

As if he can't help himself, he ducks his head and skims a kiss along the sensitive curve of my jaw. "Tell me we're doing this."

It's all I can do not to jump on his lap and ride him like a bike. My head feels like it's floating. I'm so damn hot, I can barely form words.

"Rules." I tilt my head back, let him nuzzle the crook of my shoulder. "We need rules."

Rye stops, his nose burrowed in the hollow where my jaw meets my neck. He breathes in deep as though he's scenting me.

His breath gusts out in a warm rush that sends a shiver down my spine. "Give them to me."

What were we talking about? Easing away, I sit back far enough that no part of me is touching any part of him. My head clears a little, but when I meet his eyes, a tremor runs through my belly. The very thing I've been trying for a decade to avoid, to not even think about, has happened.

I kissed him. He kissed me.

And it was so damn good, I'm aching to do it again. This is bad. Really bad.

But I can't find it in myself to pull the brakes. Because he's sitting there looking like a fever dream, that big, tight body laid out like a buffet on my couch, a massive bulge straining the soft contours of his worn jeans. I haven't even let myself touch him. And there's so much to explore.

"No one can know," I blurt out.

His nod is sharp and quick. "At first, sure."

"No, the whole time."

A small frown wrinkles his brow. "Is the idea of being with me so embarrassing?"

My insides soften, and I shake my head. "No. It's not that exactly. It's just...We've become this...sideshow in our friends' lives. I can hear them now, 'Oh, look, they're doing it. Let's take bets on which one kills the other first.'"

Rye snorts eloquently. "They'd be smug as fuck."

"Frankly, I think we've provided them with enough entertainment over the years. They don't get ringside seats for this."

"Not that I object to voyeurism in theory, but it takes on a whole other twist when your best friends are watching you have sex."

"Go ahead, make jokes."

"Who says I'm joking? You think I want Killian judging my technique? Or Scottie? That bossy motherfucker would probably make me repeat my dismount. Thanks, but no."

A soft laugh escapes me, both at his exaggerated expression

of distaste and the very idea of our friends sitting around a bed to watch us. Unfortunately, that only conjures up an image of being in bed with Rye, and I start to flush under my top.

Rye notices. His nostrils flare on an indrawn breath. When he meets my gaze, his is slightly hazy. He swallows hard. "You're right. I don't want or need their commentary. This is ours."

Ours.

Flutters run riot in my belly. I push past the feeling and focus. "You don't have to tell me everything you're thinking. And I certainly won't be telling you. But, when we do talk, there should be total honesty between us. No lies, no evasions."

"I can do that." Rye rests his arm along the back of the couch, his long fingers less than an inch from my shoulder. He appears calm and composed while I'm a twitchy mess, damn it. His chin lifts, a shadow of stubborn willfulness in his eyes. "This means that you have to let me in enough to tell me what you really need."

The bottom falls out of my belly with a soundless *whoosh*.

"I know." It's a thready whisper.

His gaze narrows. "Everything, Bren. What gets you off. Where you like to be touched and where you don't. What you dream about but never had the nerve to ask for." The thick rasp of his voice licks between my legs, and I fight the urge to squeeze them together. "I'll find out one way or another. But it'll go easier if you tell me."

Indeed. I'm tempted to dare him to find out the hard way. Images of him coaxing the truth out of me flash like an illicit peep show through my head. I clear my throat.

"Same goes for you."

He has to swallow twice before answering. "I thought the objective here was your pleasure."

That swallow and the flush of color sweeping over his cheekbones has me leaning forward, power and lust swimming through my veins like warm wine. "Thing you should know about me,

Rye. If my partner isn't pleasured, then I'm not going to be either."

He exhales, and it sounds a lot like "guh." But then he's leaning in too, his lids lowering, his hot blue gaze settling on my lips. "If you touch me, hell, if you just look at me like you're doing now, I'm going to feel good. Really good."

We've drifted back together, not touching but close enough that one shift, one deep breath will bring contact. His voice flows like sticky, hot honey. "I'm so fucking hard for you, it hurts."

My lids flutter closed, and I swallow down a rush of pure heat. "It can't happen tonight."

His gaze snaps to mine. "Why?"

"I have my period." Damn it all.

He doesn't move away. "We can do other things."

I want to do all the things. But I don't want half-measures anymore. And I know if he touches me, I'll be left craving more. "When we start," I tell him. "I want to finish."

His nod is barely perceptible. Slowly, painfully, he backs off. "Then I'm going to go before I give in to begging and pleading." His lips quirk. "Maybe crying."

Despite being horny and turned inside out, a laugh escapes me.

His quick grin is full of wry humor. "I'll go cry in the privacy of my own home."

"Yeah, you do that." I shake my head, smiling despite the sexual tension still bouncing between us.

With a groan, Rye stands. I don't move. If I do, I might give in and tackle him. When he reaches the doorway, he looks back. "When will you be ready for me?"

So very blunt. I expect nothing less from him. "In three days."

I can only be thankful I haven't just started my period, or I'd be tempted to cry as well.

His grip tightens on the doorframe until his knuckles turn white. "Three days, Bren."

We understand each other perfectly.

A pulse throbs low on my neck. "Three days."

And then he's coming for me.

CHAPTER EIGHT

RYE

THREE DAYS. I wasn't lying to Brenna. I think I might cry. My dick is definitely weeping, and I've already stroked it off too many times since I left Brenna yesterday.

Three days.

I don't know if I can do it. I've never been this wound up in my life. The anticipation and impatience coursing through me hasn't been this bad since Kill John's first stadium performance. Even then, I had the guys to suffer alongside me. Now, there's only me. And my damn hand.

My hands cannot take any more physical strain. I shake them out, grumbling under my breath, and climb the stairs up to the editing studio we booked. Mike Ramsay is our mixing engineer for a few tracks, and Danny Evans is our producer on this album. We're going for a slightly smoother, more experimental sound this go-round, and there's been a lot of tinkering on the back end.

While Jax and Killian know their shit, they tend to zone out when it becomes technical or we're having discussions on the minutiae of sound levels, beat speeds, and the like. So they won't show up until the final run-through to give their feedback. Whip and I, on the other hand, love music production and are more involved as a result.

Danny greets me with a wave as I walk in. He's already in the booth, talking to Mike. Danny's arms are flailing around in agitation, which means he's in a mood. I'm not exactly keen to go straight in there. I drop my messenger bag to the side and grab a Coke as Whip walks over to me.

"What's up with Danny?"

Whip fishes a beer out of the mini fridge. "Mike ordered a pizza and brought it into the booth."

Danny hates it when people eat while they work. Bitches about equipment and keys being greased up. He's got a point, but it isn't easy when you're at it all day long. Some people would rather eat and work to get the job done faster.

"So...we're staying out here until they finish killing each other, right?"

Whip grins. "Exactly." He pops the cap off his bottle. "I've been meaning to tell you. ShawnE called me the other night. He's putting together a session next month in Chicago, just for fun, trying new beats out and that sort of shit. He said he'd love if you came along too."

ShawnE started as a hip-hop artist but is now a huge producer as well. Whip and I are fans and friends of his. Pure, creative excitement surges through me. Kill John is my own heart's blood. But if I don't stretch my musical wings now and then, I get stagnant and bored.

It's on the tip of my tongue to say hell yes, when Whip adds, "We'd probably be there for two weeks. We can either stay with Shawn or book a hotel room. I know you like the Langham, but I still think the Peninsula has the edge."

I roll my eyes with good humor. Some days, I can't believe how far we've come. When we were starting Kill John, we sneered at the luxury hotels our parents favored. We wanted to be "real" and "authentic" and stay at shitty dives. Rich kids trying to fit in with struggling artists. Truth is, we'd never known how it felt to be without. We were all born privileged and it showed. We eventually got our heads out of our asses and realized that we are who we are. Nothing would change that. The only thing we could truly do to make a difference is to help others who were less privileged and, hopefully, inspire people through our music.

Not exactly lofty goals, but I'm happy with who I am and what I'm doing.

Deliberating between staying with a billionaire producer or in a five-star hotel suite isn't what gives me pause. It's being gone for two weeks. Two weeks? My dick is about to fall off from need. I can't be away from Brenna that long. I might...hurt something.

God, I'm whipped. And all I've done is kiss her.

"The Langham's suite has a grand piano," I say, distracted and resisting the urge to pull out my phone to just...I don't know, text her. Call her so I can hear her voice. Shit. I'm in so much trouble.

"So, does the Peninsula. And it has an outdoor terrace with a hot tub."

I shake my head and focus on Whip. "What?"

"The suite? At the Peninsula."

"Right. We can play 'What Overpriced Snob Suite Will Rye and Whip Pick?' later. I'm not sure if I can go. Let me think about it."

Lines on his forehead appear as he lifts his brow high. "You need to think about it?"

He doesn't have to say that it's totally out of character for me to hesitate on something like this. I'm not the type to think things through. I act—or react. I've got nothing and no one to hold me back from going wherever I want, whenever I want.

My hands are clammy as I stare at my best friend. Sometimes I think he knows me better than I know myself. Whatever he sees in my expression has him frowning. But he simply shrugs. "Yeah, okay. But you'll need to let him know sooner than later."

I nod, and his frown deepens.

"Rye—"

My phone rings, buzzing in my back pocket. I reach for it so fast the damn thing flies out of my hand and up in the air. I fumble for it in some weird slow-mo flail that has the phone bouncing from hand to hand like a juggler's ball before I finally get a hold of it.

"Yeah," I practically yell into the phone in my urgency to pick up before the call pushes over to voicemail. Because I saw the name on the caller ID.

Brenna.

"Shout much?" she asks with a laugh.

"Sorry." I turn away from a sharp-eyed, smirking Whip. "I almost dropped the phone."

I get up to find a private corner and trip over my bag. "Fuck!"

Whip snickers. "Graceful. Very graceful."

"What the hell is going on?" Brenna asks, still sounding amused.

I glare at my bag and head for an empty sound booth. "I tripped."

"Okay..." She's definitely laughing at me.

I can't blame her. Ordinarily, I'm not clumsy. I don't know what the hell is going on with my body. It's too focused on her and ignoring everything else. Scowling, I plop onto one of the overstuffed leather love seats in the dim booth.

"What's up?" I ask. Aside from my dick, that is. Because he's already getting perky at the sound of her voice. Which is unsettling. I have better control than this. Usually.

She takes an audible breath. "I heard Whip in the background. Can you...ah...talk?"

Brenna being hesitant means she wants to talk about one thing. My heart rate kicks up.

"Yeah, I'm in an empty sound booth."

"Oh, right. You're working on the album." She sounds oddly fluttery.

"Bren. What's up?"

"I thought of a few more rules."

I hate following rules. Hell, I'd been breaking them most of my life. But for this?

"Okay, give them to me."

Maybe I surprised her. I don't know, but there's a small stutter in her voice as though she wasn't expecting my quick agreement. "Ah—right. As of last month, you were STI-free. Have you had sex since then?"

Her directness has me grinning. It isn't as though any of this is a secret. Since Jax ended up with an STI last year, we all decided to be tested more frequently and announce our results to the group as a sort of united front. Weird? Maybe, but it cheers Jax up, so it's worth it.

"No sex since then. I'm still in the clear and good to go."

"Really?" It comes out with a slight squeak of surprise. "You haven't had sex in a month? You?"

More like six months, but who's counting?

"Jesus, Bren, you act like I've gone without for a year."

"I'd say a month in Rye time is equivalent to a year for others."

Snorting, I roll my eyes. Not that she can see it. "I don't know if I should take that as an insult or a compliment." Either way, she's not entirely wrong. I like sex. Scratch that, I *love* sex. But a man needs a break every now and then. And I haven't been feeling it lately.

Until her. Now, yes, a month waiting for her would sure as hell feel like a year.

"And you?" I'm compelled to ask, even though I really don't want to think about her with anyone else. "How long?"

"Long enough," she says tartly. "I'm cleared and have an IUD. But we're using condoms."

"Fine by me. I never go without them."

"Okay. Good. That's settled."

"That's it? Surely, not. I expected a whole list from you."

"Right you are," she says with a smile in her voice. "First off, when we're doing this, we're exclusive. No fooling around with other people."

"That's a given, Bren. If I catch you with anyone else, it's over."

Her laugh is quick and dry. "Yeah, I'm the one to worry about."

Biting my lower lip to keep in a grin, I answer with due gravitas. "I'm glad we agree."

"Anyway... Moving on. No spending the night. We do...what we do, and then we go our separate ways."

"Fine." It isn't as though I'm the cuddling type. I like my own bed. I like waking up alone without any expectations of conversation or commitment.

"Also, we meet at a hotel."

"No."

"No?" Her voice rises delicately. "What do you mean, *no*?"

"First off, the chances of me being spotted constantly booking myself into a hotel in New York are way higher than me slipping into your apartment. Secondly, it's too cold and clinical. I'm fine with us being a secret, but I'm not treating this as some sort of business meeting."

When she makes a noise of protest, I clench my phone. "Bren, you said you wanted something deeper. Sex with intimacy but without the complication of finding a boyfriend." Jesus, I want to give her that. I want it so badly, my abs hurt with unreleased need. "That's not going to happen in a hotel room. I'll go to your place if you don't want to come to mine."

Although, in all honesty, I like the idea of her in my space. She's barely ever there, and when she is, it's for our "family" dinner.

"Fine," she says after a long moment. "My place. One day a week."

"One day a..." I bolt upright. "Hold on. Back that truck up. No way. We need more than a day."

"Rye. We're both extremely busy."

"I'll make time."

"The whole point of me not wanting to search for a real boyfriend is that I don't have time to drop everything just for him." An exasperated sound rings through the phone. "Who was I kidding? This isn't going to work. It's too complicated and—"

"It's not complicated. People say they're busy all the time, but in reality, spend hours doing bullshit. And do not go into a tizzy about that. You know it's true. Last night you were free. Unable, okay. But you had time, right?"

"Tizzy," she mutters. "Yes, I was free."

"Exactly. We'll meet late. Four days a week."

That sounded doable. I'd like more, but...

"Four? No. Two."

"Three."

"Do you want me to drop it down to one?" she warns.

"Now, Berry, you'll only regret it if you do. After all, you haven't sampled what *I* can do."

I swear I hear her breath hitch. Wishful thinking, maybe. I'm not exactly breathing steadily right now. Not with the memory of her sweet mouth and just how fucking good it felt against mine playing through my head like a song.

"Fine...two..."

"Three days, Bren. Take it or leave it."

She sputters at that. "Are you seriously throwing down an ultimatum already?"

Yeah, I'm taking a risk. But some things you fight for. "It won't work the way you want it to if we only see each other two days out of the week."

"Gah. Fine. Fine!"

I grin wide. "Good. Oh, but if we want to fuck around on an off day, we can."

"Rye."

"Bren."

God, I love teasing her. Always have.

"Ass," she grumbles. All cute and flustered. "Agreed. But don't hold your breath."

Relieved, I sink back into the curve of the couch. "I won't remind you of that little proclamation later, sweetheart."

"How magnanimous of you," she says dryly.

"I thought so too." Swallowing a laugh as she growls, I glance out of the booth. Danny, Whip, and Mike are now devouring a pizza together. I guess their spat is over. My stomach rumbles, but I ignore it in favor of Bren. "Now that that's settled, tell me something."

"What?" She sounds wary.

My voice lowers, heat running down my belly and under my balls. "How do you like to be fucked? Soft and slow? Hard and deep? Both?"

Her breath definitely hitches this time. "You just went right there, huh?"

I shift in my seat, itching to touch her. "Stop stalling. Tell me something you've wanted that no one has given you."

"Isn't it your job to figure it out?" she asks in a voice gone soft and breathy.

"Believe me, Berry. I'm going to find all your sweet spots." Hell, I'm sweating. Actually sweating. My foot is tapping out an agitated rhythm. "I'm thinking more along the lines of a fantasy you want acted out."

"Rye..."

"Come on," I whisper. "This is part of the fun."

"Fun is peeling back all my layers for your inspection?"

"Well, yeah." I bite my lower lip, imagining said inspection. "I'll tell you one of mine if you tell me one of yours."

"You first."

I laugh softly. "As if I thought you'd go first."

"So..." she prompts. "What is it? Orgy? Public sex? Another guy?"

"You offering those things?" I ask lightly, knowing she's messing with me.

"I can only be a part of some of those. I don't have the equipment for that last one. But, no, none of those are on the table. Except for maybe the other guy thing. I'd totally watch that."

"I bet you would." I run my hand down my tense thighs. God, she's got me worked up. "Sorry to disappoint you, but I'm a rock star. All of that stuff is old news for me."

"Is it?" She practically squeaks the question.

"Bren, I feel like I've seen and done everything at this point. It's boring now. Empty."

A sigh gusts. "Yeah, I know. So what's left? What's your fantasy?"

"You."

There's a pause.

"Oh, for fuck's sake. I knew you were leading me on..."

"I am completely serious. My fantasy is you." I close my eyes, and somehow that makes it easier to confess. "It doesn't even have to be straight-up sex. I have this one scenario..."

"Tell me." The husky demand cannot be denied.

I lick my lips, my mouth suddenly dry. "We're on the tour bus. All of us sitting around that side table where we have to cram in close." Jesus, just saying that much has me panting, and it isn't even anything dirty. I adjust my grip on the phone, my hand damp with sweat. "You're pushed up next to me in that tight spot by the corner."

"Yeah." She says it like she's picturing the bus, the way the banquette curves, and how, even surrounded by our friends, we'd be half-hidden there.

"Everyone would be talking. Laughing and drinking. And while you did too, my hand would slide under the table, find your lap."

I bite my lip and hold back a groan. "You'd have to hold steady, Berry, pretend you didn't feel me gliding up between your thighs." My breath hitches. "You'd part them for me, wouldn't you, Bren? Part those sleek thighs so my hand could squeeze into that tight, hot spot."

Brenna makes a small noise, and I know she would do it for me. She'd let me in.

I shift in my seat, adjusting my throbbing dick. "From the waist up, you'd be all smiles and jokes. But down below, I'd be running my finger over your damp panties, rubbing that swollen little clit."

I'm a dirty fucking bastard because I love the idea of doing that where anyone could catch us.

"Shit," she whispers, as though she loves the idea too.

I close my eyes, swallowing hard. "I'd get that sweet button all plump and needy. And when you started to squirm..." A grunt breaks free. "That would be bad, Bren. I'd have to give your naughty clit a pinch."

She whimpers, and I nearly jerk in my seat. I want to reach into my jeans and stroke my cock so bad, I have to clutch my knee to concentrate. "But I'd make it better, honey. I'd slip under those panties where you're all slick and slippery. I'd stroke you nice and slow."

"Rye..." It's a breathy request. I feel it down my spine, in my balls.

"They'd think you weren't looking my way because you hated me. That you were gritting your teeth because I pissed you off yet again." Sweat trickles down my spine. "They'd never know I was playing with your sweet pussy."

Brenna gasps. My abs clench tight.

From outside the room comes a burst of laughter. It pulls me back to the present, where the guys are just a glass wall away. I have to end this before I come in my damn pants.

I exhale in a hard rush. "Fuck, Berry. I'm all worked up here."

"Your fault," she croaks with a half-pained laugh.

"You asked for a fantasy. I gave you one." I smile then, but it hurts. Everything hurts now, a sweet, hot ache that leaves me weak. "I have hundreds of them."

"I don't think I can handle more right now," she says wryly.

My smile grows. "Then tell me one thing you want, and I'll let you go."

For now.

She waits a beat, and I'm almost convinced she'll tell me no. But then she draws in a breath. "Okay. Okay...I tell people what to do all day long. Every day."

"You're saying you want to order me around in bed?" I'd be down with that. Frankly, I'm pretty sure I'd be down with anything she suggests.

"No," she says tightly. "You're not getting it. I don't want to be in charge. I want to be taken care of, let someone else take the lead."

A pulse goes through me, and I have to hold very still as an electric tingle sizzles over my skin. I hadn't expected this. Not from Brenna. But she's right; she's always in charge, bossy, even. I imagined her the same in bed. The idea that she'd let me...

"You want me to take you in hand."

It isn't a question. More a statement of awe.

A gurgle sounds, and I picture her blushing raspberry red, the color clashing with her auburn hair. Why did we have this conversation on the phone? I want to be in front of her, watching the emotions playing over her face.

"To be clear," she says in a near squeak, "I'm not into bondage or role-play."

"Eh, that gets boring too."

Another gurgle. But when she speaks, it's back to her crisp, no-nonsense tone. "I'm not talking about some dominant-submissive thing. I just don't want to lead. Or give instruction."

"You want me to take you in hand," I repeat in a low voice.

Another pause.

"Yes," she whispers, shy and rattled.

She's never shy or rattled. An unexpected feeling of protectiveness hits me. Now I'm glad I'm not in front of her, because I'd probably try to hug her, and Brenna would hate that. Instead,

I keep my tone gentle but without any hint of tenderness that might make her more uncomfortable.

"I'll take good care of you, Berry."

It will be my extreme pleasure.

"Okay." It's barely a whisper, yet it licks my skin with searing heat.

Two more days.

I might not make it.

CHAPTER NINE

BRENNA

THINGS TO CONSIDER before agreeing to have sex with your once frenemy: remember that you offered to host the weekly dinner for him and all your friends—your extremely astute and nosey friends. Friends who will know in a heartbeat that there's something going on between Rye and me if I show any outward emotion.

How I'm supposed to get through it without losing it, I still don't know.

Also? I hate cooking. Which is why we're having takeout.

"And how is Kenny on this fine evening?" Killian asks as he snags a container of pork dumplings.

Kenny mans the phone for my favorite Korean barbecue place. Given that I order from his fine establishment every week, we know each other well.

I grab a few short ribs, licking the sweet-spicy sauce off my fingers. "I'm expecting a proposal of marriage any day now. Spoiler alert: I shall accept."

Jax laughs and swipes a chicken wing out from under Whip's

fingers. "Marry the chef, Bren. That's the most direct route to the food."

"Maybe I will." I accept the beer Scottie hands me. "I've always had a fantasy about marrying a chef. Good food for life. And our family dinners will become legend."

Scottie takes the bottle from my hand and pours the beer into a glass with a reproachful look, as though drinking from a bottle is a crime. "As much as I love this takeout, I think I speak for all of us when I say I approve of your plan."

"Or go for a pastry chef," Sophie puts in, waving a rib around for emphasis. "Oh, that would be nice. Do it, Bren. Marry someone who will bake us cakes."

"And bring me brioche in bed," I add with a dreamy sigh.

Rye grunts. He's got his eye on his food, but his broad shoulders are stiff. "Would never work."

So far, I've been able to avoid looking his way. No one will think anything of us ignoring each other. We usually do. Unless we're taking a swipe at each other. I didn't think he'd take a shot at me *now*.

"Oh? And why is that?"

He shrugs, swallowing a drink from his own beer bottle—he'd swatted away Scottie's efforts to get him a glass earlier. "Chefs save their cooking for the restaurant. Get them at home and they just want to shove whatever they can in their mouths and then sleep."

His gaze flicks up and collides with mine. I feel it like a physical punch of heat. "You really think this hypothetical chef husband of yours will want to come off a shift and cook for all of us? I doubt it."

"Rye isn't wrong." Stella's red-gold curls bounce with a nod as she scoops a mound of kimchi. "The chefs I knew were like that." She glances up and realizes that Rye and I are glaring at each other. "Of course, there are always exceptions."

"You're making it sound like I'd only get married to the guy to use him for his cooking," I say to Rye.

He blinks, his expression placid. And annoying. "Isn't that what you just implied?"

My back teeth meet with a click. "Do you honestly think we're being serious here?"

"Sure you weren't." He snorts with a smile. "I can practically see the croissants dancing in your eyes."

I eye a slice of eomuk on my plate. It would make such a nice juicy *thwap* hitting Rye's forehead. "It's called hyperbole, Rye. Maybe try it sometime."

"Hyperbole, huh?" He rubs his chin like he's trying to figure out what the word means, when I know perfectly well that he already does. An evil gleam lights his eyes. "You mean like, this barbecue sauce is so good, I want to lick it off—"

"All right," Scottie cuts in. "If I have to hear your sex fantasies, Rye, I'm liable to lose my dinner. And that is *not* hyperbole."

Rye chuckles and reaches for the carton of dumplings. "Don't worry, Dad. I'm done."

The guys start arguing over how far-reaching Kraftwerk's influence was on modern sound, and I zone out, stewing in my annoyance. Rye is his usual cocky and easygoing self. Laughing in that boisterous way that has the corners of his eyes crinkling and those little half-moon dimples forming on his cheeks.

Under the table, my hand fists the loose folds of my skirt. I feel duped. Yes, we'd agreed to keep this...arrangement a secret, but I hadn't expected him to still antagonize me. It reminds me of all the times he made me feel like a fool. Worse, I feel vulnerable. After years of working to protect myself, the sensation twists in my stomach.

I suck in a breath and push back from the table. Rye's laugh falters, and he glances my way, the motion so quick, I'd have missed it if I weren't hyperaware of him. Damn it. I don't want this awareness, this weakness.

"You okay, Bren?" Libby asks at my side.

"Of course," I say with forced lightness. "Just getting some more beers for the table. Anyone want anything else to drink?"

I'm waved off. They've moved on to whether *Off the Wall* or *Thriller* was Michael Jackson's greatest album.

"You're completely wrong," Rye practically shouts at Whip, his arms animated in his fervor. "*Thriller* is too slick and commercial. It was produced with hits in mind. *Off the Wall* was pure Michael. He got to truly play with his sound for the first time."

Whip snorts long and loud. "I can't believe you, who's endlessly fiddling with sound, are dinging an album for being too perfectly produced."

I walk out of the dining room before I'm subjected to any more. Someday, I'd love to go a week without hearing a word or note of music.

Once I'm in the hall, I sigh with relief. Unlike some of the open-concept apartments my friends live in, my condo is prewar with classically separated rooms. I actually love that feature because it means I can escape into my kitchen and rest against the counter for a quiet moment without everyone seeing me. I take a few calming breaths, determined not to think about Rye anymore.

That's when he walks in.

He stands inside the kitchen, his big body filling the doorway, his blue eyes narrowed on me. My frazzled nerves jump and twitch, and I clench the side of the marble countertop to steady myself.

"What's wrong?" His deep voice stays low so no one will hear us.

A laugh rasps my throat, but I don't find this funny. "Are you serious now, Mr. Hyperbole?"

With a quick glance toward the dining room, he moves farther into the kitchen, his gait stiff and halting like he's trying to restrain himself. I take a breath as he comes within touching distance. He makes a furtive motion, reaching for me but stopping short with a growl of frustration.

"That upset you?" He sounds truly surprised and a little distressed.

I want to push him away. And I want to arch my back so the tips of my breasts are that much closer to the hard expanse of his chest. Shit. I'm so messed up. I hold perfectly still. "Was that really necessary?" I hiss. "Arguing with me about something utterly ridiculous yet again?"

"Of course it was necessary," he hisses back, clearly wanting to raise his voice but trying not to. "I have to act the way I always do with you. Because otherwise they'll see." He flings his arm in the direction of the dining room, color rising over his cheeks. "They'll all know how much I want you. That I'm fucking aching to touch you."

My breath leaves in a *whoosh*, and his comes out in a pant.

"They'll see right through me," he whispers hotly. "I couldn't let them know that, Bren. Not if we want to keep us a secret."

"There is no us."

His eyes flash. "Bullshit."

We're both breathing too hard, sparks snapping and flying between us. It heats my blood. My nipples draw tight and tender. Rye's attention flicks to them. He lets out a harsh breath, and I draw one in.

I don't know who moves first. I don't care. He's stepping up to me, and I'm rising to my toes, my hands clutching his big shoulders to hold on. His mouth is hot, desperate, and oh, so good. Rye cups my cheeks as he angles my head to kiss me deeper. The soft stubble of his beard tickles the sensitive edges of my lips and sends licks of pleasure up the backs of my knees, between my shaking thighs.

I slide my tongue over his, and he whimpers. The helpless, needy sound goes straight to my core. It lights me up, and I arch my back, pressing into the warm wall of his firm chest.

With a grunt, he grabs my ass and hauls me onto the countertop. His mouth never leaves mine as he shoves my thighs apart and steps in between them. Instantly, I wrap my legs around his waist, pulling him closer, needing his warmth, his strength.

"Fuck," he rasps against my mouth. "You taste so good."

I'm not ashamed to admit I mewl in agreement. My hands are in his hair, gripping the short strands. We're eating at each other's mouths. It's messy, frantic. I don't want it to end.

Hot palms slip under my skirt and slide up my thighs. I shiver, and his mouth descends to a sweet spot on my neck. "Need to feel you, Bren. Just once."

The tips of his fingers dance along the edge of my panties. I spread my legs wider, tilt my hips up to give him more room. A tremor goes through Rye at my compliance. It turns into a moan when he slides a finger under the silk and touches my swollen sex.

I jolt against that questing finger. My head is floating away, my belly clenching with delicious heat. I'm on the edge of coming and he's barely touched me. His breath is hot and fast against my neck as he explores me with steady strokes. Weakly, I rest my cheek on his wide shoulder, unable to do anything other than feel.

Dimly, I hear our friends laughing in the other room, the rise and fall of conversation. That I'm hidden away with Rye, his hand in my panties, his mouth sucking my neck, heightens everything. This lust has sharp edges, a painful bite that makes me quake.

He pushes his thick, long finger into me. Deep. Demanding. Perfect. I stifle my scream against the damp hollow of his neck as the orgasm rolls and shudders through me, not ending but building, rising all over again.

"Fuck, yes," he whispers, fucking me with his finger. He knows exactly how to do it, how I like it—a little rough, a little hard, but oh, so thorough. The muscles in his forearm shift and flex with every thrust and pull. "Give it to me, Bren."

Panting, I fist his shirt and strain against him. It's too good. I'm liquid lust now, melting for him.

"You're beautiful." His voice has gone rough yet soft. "So fucking beautiful."

I break with a jolt and a whimper. He stays with me, holding me close as I let out a sigh. Weak and spent, I lean against him in a boneless heap. Sweat slicks my skin. My heart thuds hard against my ribs. A fine shaking takes hold of my limbs, and I can only cling to Rye and wait for the world to stop spinning.

He places a tender kiss on the crook of my neck—the final note of his perfect solo. My eyes flutter closed.

"Oy!" Jax shouts from somewhere in the apartment. "Did you get lost in that kitchen, Bren?"

The sound of his voice zaps through Rye and me like an electric shock.

"Shit." I shove Rye away, the fear of getting caught giving me strength, then call out to Jax. "I'm coming!"

That earns me a strangled but weak laugh from Rye. I almost laugh at the irony too, but I'm busy pushing down my skirt. Rye fumbles back a step then runs his hands through his hair. He looks wrecked. With his hair now standing on end, he also looks a bit wild.

We stare at each other in shock. I expected pleasure from Rye. But not this. Not to utterly lose my mind the second he touched me. I let him finger-fuck me to orgasm in my kitchen. Rye Peterson had his hand in my panties and his tongue in my mouth. It's utterly bizarre. And yet it felt so very right. I wonder if he's as dazed and confused as I am.

Rye swallows hard. "Your ponytail is falling out."

With shaking hands, I fix my hair. "You're all mussed up too."

We avoid each other's gaze as we tidy ourselves.

"You go out first," he says, his voice still rough and cracked.

"Why?" I hop down from the counter. My legs wobble like rubber.

He huffs out a half laugh and gestures to the fat bulge behind his jeans. "I need a moment."

Heat swarms my cheeks, but it's not from embarrassment. I want to free that cock and stroke it. Give him the same pleasure he gave me. From the dark look in his eyes, I'm guessing he reads my expression well.

"Go," he says unsteadily. "Before I forget why hiding this is a good idea."

Damn it, he's right. I hurry to the fridge and grab a few beers. I'm almost out of the kitchen when his voice stops me. "Tonight, Brenna."

Glancing back, I find him watching me with hot eyes. This big, beautiful man who has the power to both rock my world and destroy my peace of mind.

"Tonight," he says again. "I'm yours."

For the first time in my life, not only am I tempted to run toward my ruin, I'm anticipating it.

CHAPTER TEN

RYE

HELL IS a dinner party that never ends. I'm convinced my friends are lingering to fuck with me. I nearly ping a chicken bone at Killian when he pulls out a couple of bottles of wine he brought along and opens one. I don't give a flying pig fuck about his Cabernet Rothschild or whatever the hell it's called.

Scottie, on the other hand, is in raptures. And now everyone has to have a glass.

Killian frowns when I wave him off. "You don't want any?"

Considering I'm about ten seconds away from tossing the bottle out the window? "No."

"But it's a 1982 Château Mouton Rothschild," Stella says. "It's one of the best vintages in the world...Oh, my God, I just said that, didn't I?" She covers her mouth, her blue eyes wide with shock.

Jax laughs, slinging an arm around her shoulders to cuddle her close. Lucky bastard. Able to touch his woman whenever he wants. "What's with the horror, Button?"

Her nose wrinkles, but she leans into him with happy ease.

"I've gone from getting excited about affording a six-pack at the corner mart to gushing over wine that costs, what?"

"About a thousand dollars," Killian says with a wag of his brow. "Are you more horrified now?"

She laughs. "Yes. Now fill my glass so I can glut."

God help me.

I grit my teeth and toy with the label on my empty beer bottle. My entire body is humming. I'm like a tuning fork struck by lust. It's so bad, I find myself twitching every few seconds. All because of *her*.

I can't look her way. If I catch sight of her, I'll end up whimpering. Like I did in the kitchen. I actually whimpered. For the first time in my years of sexual experience, I understand true lust-induced pain. Touching her both inflames it and is the only thing that will make it better.

I shouldn't have followed her into the kitchen. Being alone with her is too great a temptation. It was a mistake putting my hands on her before everyone left. But I'd seen the hurt in her eyes, even though she'd tried to mask it with anger. I know better now. When I'm a shit, she gets hurt. Call me an idiot, but I never knew that. I'd taken her snark and anger at face value, thinking she hated me enough that nothing I did or said really mattered.

The realization has my head spinning. Everything is upside down. The only thing that makes any sense is touching Brenna again.

Her laugh cuts through my thoughts, and my abs clench so tight, they ache. My only recourse is to breathe slowly and steadily. But her scent is all over my hand. I'd forgotten to wash it, forgotten to taste her, which is a damn tragedy. I'm tempted to lift my fingers to my mouth and suck them. But if I did, I'd probably come on the spot, I'm so riled up.

As it is, I don't eat another bite of food. If it isn't Brenna in my mouth, then I don't want it. Thankfully, no one notices. That's the strange thing about being the clown, if you're not talking shit and acting like a fool, people tend to forget about you. I'm not sure if that's comforting or insulting. At the moment, I don't care.

Finally—*finally*—the dinner is over. Somehow, I find myself down on the street, sucking in the crisp night air as my friends pair up and pile into their respective Ubers. I don't remember if I said goodbye to Brenna. Or if she knows that, as soon as it's humanly possible, I'm turning my ass right around and coming for her.

"Did you want to get a beer?" Whip asks.

We're the only ones who haven't arranged for a ride. Mainly because, while the rest of the guys go home to sleep with their women after these dinners, Whip and I usually go looking for hookups or sometimes play a round of pool. Anything to avoid returning to an empty apartment.

"Nah." I roll my tight shoulders and lie my ass off. "I ate too much. I think I'll walk for a bit."

Weirdly, he seems relieved. "Yeah, I'm not feeling it tonight either. I'm going to catch a cab home."

Something about the way his gaze slides to the street and won't meet mine has me paying closer attention. "You all right?"

"Sure." He does the chin lift thing—a tell that means he's lying. "Why wouldn't I be?"

"I don't know," I counter. "Why wouldn't you be?"

Around us, pedestrians flow, cabs honk, and a siren wails in the far distance. Whip and I stare at each other. The thing about Whip is that, out of all of us, he hides himself away the most. He does it so well, no one truly notices they're not getting the real deal but a shadow. But I know him better than anyone. Something is up.

Finally, he lets out a breath and shakes his head. "When you're willing to tell me what's going on with you, then maybe I'll do the same."

A lump of regret fills my throat. We share everything. Always have. But I can't share this, and he knows it.

He makes a move to go, and I say the only thing I can. "It's not my secret to tell."

"As long as you know what you're doing."

I have no fucking clue what I'm doing.

He knows that too because he full-on grins. "Have a good night, then." He turns to go.

"Whip." He still hasn't told me what's up with him.

Whip stops and glances over his shoulder. He's not upset anymore, but the cagey bastard just gives me another enigmatic smile. "I'm not ready to tell either."

With that, he walks away.

"Asshole," I mutter with a chuckle before I realize I'm still standing outside. With another curse, I run back into Brenna's building.

CHAPTER ELEVEN

RYE

THE ELEVATOR RISES, and my thumb beats a bass line onto my thigh. It plays harmony with the insistent *thud-thud-thud* of my heart. I'm horny as fuck and nervous as a stray cat. I start humming "Stray Cat Strut" and get side-eye from an older guy stuck in the elevator with me. I'd forgotten he was there. With his tweed suit and thin, gray mustache, he reminds me of my English grandfather, and I have to fight the compulsion to stand straight, maybe check my shirt for wrinkles.

It's enough to make me laugh at myself under my breath.

"Do yourself a favor," he says with a slight smile. "Don't sing that song to her when you get there."

I snap to attention. The hell? Is he a mind reader?

He shakes his head at my apparent ignorance. "Wore that same expression the first night I slept with my now-wife. Knew it mattered, and that scared the bloody hell out of me." The elevator doors open to his floor. He gives me a small salute. "Good luck."

The doors slide shut again, and I catch sight of myself in the bronze matte-metal panels. I look...hungry, impatient. Scared.

I have to laugh at myself again. Because I *am* freaked. Brenna James has me by the balls, and I don't want her to let go.

The smile is gone by the time I get to the door and she opens it. For a second I just drink her in. She hasn't changed out of the flowing knee-length skirt made of some gauzy violet fabric. I remember the cool kiss of it along the back of my hands as I slid them up her hot, silky thighs. She has on a white top that doesn't hide the fact that she's taken off her bra. The soft knit clings to the small mounds of her breasts, lovingly outlining the hard points of her nipples.

My abs contract painfully as my dick rises. I haven't yet seen her tits. It's a travesty. I've spent countless hours fantasizing about what they look like, how they'd feel against my hands, in my mouth. Years of dreaming, wanting, waiting.

God knows I want her. But it's the look in her pretty hazel eyes, soft with desire yet wide with trepidation, that really gets to me. Elevator guy was right; it's different when it matters. She matters. Of course, she matters. She's been a part of me for so long, I wouldn't know how to function if she were gone.

Going after her shifted the foundations of our shared world. She's right to worry. It is definitely a risk doing this. For the first time in my life, I won't be able to keep emotion out of the equation. Maybe she can; I don't know. But if this goes south, I'll be wrecked.

Maybe she reads the fear in my face because a wrinkle forms between the wings of her brows. "Rye...We don't have to—"

I step into the apartment, closing the door behind me, then cup her cheeks and kiss her slow and easy. She's delicious. Perfect. My heart squeezes in the cage of my chest. It flips over when she sighs into my mouth. I kiss her again. Again.

Soft. Light. Just feeling her lips. They're a revelation.

Letting her go was never an option.

"It's going to be okay," I whisper into her sweet mouth.

As if she's been waiting to hear that, she yields, sagging against me. Her hands slide up my chest, spreading shivers of pleasure in their wake. With a grunt of approval, I lift her in my arms and head for the bedroom. Whatever comment she might have made over me carrying her is lost to my mouth because I can't stop kissing her.

When I get to Brenna's room, I set her down by the bed. A single bedside light is the only illumination. I'm tempted to turn more on. I want to see everything in vivid color. But that might break the spell, so I stay where I am, my fingers trailing along the sides of her neck, touching the curve of her jaw.

For all the assurances I made, all my damn bragging about being good at this, now that I have her here, I don't know what to do. I know how to fuck. I excel at fucking. This isn't fucking. I'm not sure what to call it. But it's definitely *more*.

Brenna stares up at me. Out of her heels, she's much shorter. I'm struck by the difference in our sizes. She's tall for a woman, but I top her by at least a foot. Her slim frame is delicate and fragile compared to mine. My hands feel too big, my body clunky. Shit. I'm half afraid I'll damage her with one wrong move.

"Will you take your hair down?" I ask. She rarely lets it down, to the point that seeing Brenna without her standard ponytail feels like a gift.

Silently holding my gaze, she reaches up and pulls the tie out. Her hair falls over her shoulders and nearly to her waist in a river of deep auburn. My fingers thread through the shining mass, and it slides like silk over my skin.

She closes her eyes, a small sigh escaping. I step closer to massage her scalp, and she tilts her head back with a groan of relief. I kiss the pale arc of her neck. She's wearing that perfume, the one that smells of sun-ripe peaches, dark honey, and rum. Pure sex on her. My tongue flicks the hollow near her shoulder.

Goosebumps rise on her skin. I brush my lips over them. I

need to do this right, take my time to give her the proper attention.

But she takes a step back, her fingers curling around my wrists. "I don't want slow. Or gentle."

It's clear by her tone and the way she's drawing into herself that she needs a certain amount of distance here. Disappointment kicks me in the chest.

"Okay." Thankfully, my voice is steady. "What do you want?"

She exhales in a rush before biting the inside of her cheek. "I want to see you."

God, the anticipatory gleam in her eyes. She wants me naked. A bolt of heat spears my gut. "I can do that."

Ordinarily, I'd reach behind my head and haul my shirt off. But I know she wants a show. Toeing off my boots and socks, I straighten and slowly tug my shirt up by the hem, flexing every damn muscle I've got. I'm suddenly thankful for the hours I put in the gym, the years I've spent dancing, sweating, and strumming on countless hot stages.

Her lips part, and she licks them as I toss the shirt aside. Millions of fans have seen me without a shirt. Yet I've never felt more seen than at this moment.

She focuses on my lower abs. I'm not going to object. Not when her nostrils flare as I pop the button of my jeans and slowly draw down the zip. I push my jeans and underwear off in one go, and my hard cock bobs free.

"God," she whispers.

"You're making me feel like one." My body thrums with need. I palm my dick once to alleviate the ache, but she distracts me, stepping forward and tracing the skull flanked by black angel wings inked across my upper chest.

"I've always wanted to touch you here," she murmurs.

My throat closes. I swallow hard but can't seem to say a damn word.

Her fingertips drift down to my nipple and the silver barbell piercing it. She twists the barbell a little, and I swear I nearly whimper again. As it is, my dick twitches, trying its damnedest to get her attention. But she's fascinated by my piercings.

It's sexy as fuck, the way she plays with me, tweaking and pulling just enough to make me crazed.

"Brenna..." I'm begging. But, holy hell, she's killing me.

She presses her palms into my chest, just holding them there, and no doubt feeling the wild beat of my heart. "I know I said I wanted you to take control. But tonight..."

Without another word, I understand her. She's too nervous. Our first time. It's still a little unreal that we're actually here. "I'll give you whatever you want, Berry."

Amber eyes gleam as they meet mine. "Get on the bed."

Oh, hell.

I do as she commands, reclining on my elbows to watch her. She reaches under her skirt and pulls off her panties. My breath catches, my fingers digging into the comforter. But she doesn't take anything else off and, instead, starts walking toward the bed.

I don't know what to make of it. She isn't getting naked.

"You're just going to use me for a ride, then?" I ask, as she crawls onto the bed and hovers over me. My chest suddenly feels like lead. I'd told her I'd give her anything she needs, but ironically, I never realized I'd need things too.

She pauses, her face inches from mine. I see her hesitation but also her joy. She's happy. "Just this first time." She hesitates again before forging on. "It's a fantasy."

Oh. Well, then. A smile spreads over my lips. "To fuck me while I'm naked and you're fully clothed?"

God, she's cute when she blushes. "Yes. And to do other things."

I don't get to ask what those other things are. She shows me, dipping down to kiss the center of my chest. My breath leaves in a rush.

"God, you're gorgeous." She says it with such breathless appreciation that I'm at a loss for words. I can only smile at her like a dazed fool. I want to touch her, kiss her. But she wants to play with me, and I'm more than willing to let her.

Brenna's lips find my nipple, now stiff from her previous torture. When she draws it into her wet mouth, I make a noise. Not a whimper. Oh, fuck, it is, because she's licking and sucking, and I'm going to fucking lose it.

My head falls back, tremors running down my chest and thighs.

"Bren..."

She smiles against my chest, confident now that she has me where she wants. I can only lie there and take it as she trails kisses down the center of my abs. The silk of her hair skims over my dick, and I hiss. Soft lips brush the swollen head. A light kiss I feel in my toes. It's the only warning I get before she sucks me in deep. A groan tears out of me, and I arch my back.

"Oh, fuck. Jesus. Fuck."

I thrust once into her mouth before I get a hold of myself. But it's too good. She's a damn pro. A dick-sucking goddess. I slump back onto the bed, throwing my forearm over my eyes. I'm gonna come. I can't come, because then she'll stop.

"Brenna."

She hums, her tongue flicking over the sensitive tip, fingers gripping my shaft. White-hot heat licks up my balls. I groan again, biting my lip. She sucks me like I'm candy, like I'm the best thing she's ever tasted. Sweat breaks out over my skin.

"Bren. Have mercy."

Through the curtain of her hair, she looks up at me. The sight of her pink lips stretched wide around the hard shaft of my cock nearly does me in. My abs clench tight.

"Please." Yes, I'm begging.

She releases my dick with a devious, prolonged pop. Then licks her lips.

This woman. She's going to kill me.

I think I fall a little in love when she pulls a condom from the waistband of her skirt. My dick definitely does when she deftly rolls the condom down its throbbing length, finishing with a nice squeeze as if to say, *I'm gonna take care of you now.*

I'm so hot for her, my head is spinning, while my body practically burns with need. My voice is guttural when I find the ability to speak. "Fuck me, Bren."

She grins wide. I love that. Love her confidence. Despite the fact that I'm on edge and panting, I find myself grinning back as she climbs onto the bed and begins to straddle me.

"Lift your skirt," I rasp.

Brenna pauses and meets my eyes.

"I need to see that much. Let me..." I lick my trembling lips. "Let me see that pretty pussy taking my cock."

Knees on either side of my hips, she hovers, and then her fingers gather up the loose folds of her silky skirt. Oh, so slowly, she reveals slim, milk-white thighs, and then... I groan.

She's wet, glistening and plump. Rosy lips peek out, begging for a kiss. Beautiful.

"Is this what you want?" she whispers.

"Yes." A tremor breaks my voice. "I want it so bad."

Her breath catches, and she gives me a sly look from under her lashes. "I'm holding my skirt up. You're going to have to put that big dick in me, buttercup."

We're laughing softly, but I'm hot as a furnace. I've never done this, played with someone in bed. Never laughed and felt both light as air and yet strung tight as a wire. It's her. She makes it different.

Our laughter dies, though, when I take hold of myself and slide the swollen tip over her sex.

Hands shaking, I rub my dick in her wetness. "Ride me, Bren."

She sinks down but doesn't get far because I'm too fucking hard and big to go in easily. The crown of my cock notches into the tight, hot heat of her, and all my practiced finesse dies with a harsh, strangled moan. "Oh, fuck. Look at you stretching to take me. Look at how pretty you are."

With a whimper and a wiggle, she pushes harder, and a little more of my dick slips inside heaven.

"Fuck," I rasp. "*Fuck*. Bren..." My hand flies to her hip, holding her steady, stopping her. Which is crazy because all I want to do is fuck her until I can't move. But I'm too close, already teetering at the edge. My head feels light and hot, as though it might float away.

Panting, she stares down at me, a question clouding her eyes.

"I can't..." I swallow thickly. "I might not make it for long this time. It's been too many years of wanting you."

A small, purely feminine smile curls her lips. "You can take it." Then she takes my hand and sets it on her thigh. Her fingers twine with mine. I clutch them like a lifeline.

Brenna's eyes flutter as she circles her hips on a moan. Teasing me. By the light of the lamp, she's shadows and curves and gleaming skin. God, the way she rocks just a bit, working herself onto me. I count to ten, take deep breaths, and shiver like it's my first time.

Halfway in, her eyes snap open, and her gaze meets mine. Emotion grabs me by the throat, and all I can do is stare up at her, this woman who has tormented me for a decade. This woman who is the most beautiful thing I've ever seen.

The urge to thrust up and fuck into her until I can't see straight rides me so high, I have to breathe through it, my fist winding into the sheets to keep steady. She's looking at me like she's lost. I see myself mirrored in those dark, amber eyes.

I don't know what to say except, "I know."

———

Brenna

. . .

"I KNOW," he says to me. He knows. Does he? I'm not sure *I* know. I can't think properly. His hard cock is halfway inside me. It feels so good, so *present*, that I clench around him.

Rye grits his teeth. Sweat has broken out over his skin—all that smooth, rippling inked skin. Good glory, but he's magnificent without clothes on. Built like a tank but with long, graceful lines. I wanted to lick him all over and stroke him like a big cat for hours. But his cock is even better. Thick, straight, and ruddy with arousal. I made that cock weep for me. I'd felt its meaty girth on my tongue, at the back of my throat.

I might have lingered and made him come, sucked him down, but I felt so empty, I needed more.

"Baby," he says now, voice dancing the line between pleading and demanding. He needs more too.

It's almost too much, this connection. Sex is supposed to be fun, a release. Instead, I'm aching, so hot I can't breathe properly. He's spreading me wide, invading, making himself well and truly known. There's no ignoring a cock like his, or that it's *him*. It's primal and inescapable. That I'm experiencing this with Rye does funny things to my head, makes the room around me blur. All I can feel is him. He's all I can see.

My head lolls to the side as I sway, working myself on his dick. Rye groans deep, his jaw clenching. Nostrils flaring, he puts his big hands on my thighs and thrusts, sliding home.

"Oh, shit," I rasp, filled. Utterly filled.

For a moment we stare at each other, our breaths ragged, him in me, me on him. My lids lower, a warm, buttery sensation fluttering deep in my belly. Then, as if we'd planned it, we begin to move. And it's...

It isn't supposed to be like this the first time. We're supposed to be fumbling along, learning what the other likes by trial and error. He's not supposed to be fucking up into me at the perfect angle, each thrust hitting that pleasure spot so few ever find. We've barely started and already I'm at the edge, my body pulsing.

The worst thing is, it's not solely how he moves; it's his scent—crisp apples, heady pheromone. It's the rough, greedy sounds he makes. It's his body—wide, sturdy shoulders, narrow hips, abs bunching—as he clutches the folds of my skirt with white-knuckled fists. Everything works for me; a perfect storm.

We've been moving as one but not letting our eyes meet. I'm afraid of what he might see if I do. Of what I might see. Triumph? Happiness? Lust? Or maybe nothing. I'd been a coward refusing to take my clothes off, insisting on taking control when I want to relinquish it. The truth should cool the moment, but it doesn't. Whatever has happened between us over the years doesn't erase the fact that this man turns my body on like no other.

He hits that spot again and pleasure punches through me so acute, so good, I whimper, my fingers digging into the rock-hard caps of his shoulders.

Rye lifts his head, and his gaze sears me. His hips work faster, harder, our skin slapping together in a quick rhythm. It's too much. My head is spinning, my body liquid heat. I'm too hot. I hate that clothes are still on my body, keeping my skin from his. But I'm unwilling to let go. Not yet. I work myself on him, grinding my hips against his.

Rye's lips part. "Fuck. Oh, fuck."

He's close. I can feel it in the urgency of his thrusts, in the way his breathing turns into light pants. He's refraining from touching me. Because I told him I wanted to use his body without interference. Because I put that distance between us. But he's looking at me with a plea in his eyes. He doesn't want distance. He's pulled taut as an over-tuned string.

My breath leaves in a rush. "Rye. Please."

Permission.

His nostrils flare. His big, rough hand slides up my sweat-slicked thigh, his thumb finding my soaking clit, and then strums it. He plays my pussy with the effortless authority of the world-class bass player that he is. And all that twisted, hot need, all the pressure building up within me fractures.

My orgasm has edges, cutting in its pleasure. With a cry, I slump against him. "Rye." My body jolts as another surge hits me. "Take over. Please."

With a strangled groan, he flips me onto my back. Thickly muscled arms bracket my shoulders as he kisses me with something like desperation. Or maybe it's me. I'm the one clinging to him, opening my mouth wider to taste more of him. Our kiss turns messy, and his lips slide to my neck, his breath coming in hot bursts. But then he lifts his head and looks down at my top.

"Off," he rasps. "I need this off."

"Yes." I lift my arms, arch my back. I'm burning up. "Please. Please."

He strips my top off with brisk efficiency but then pauses to stare. "Oh, hell," he says thickly. "You're beautiful. So much more than I ever...Shit, Bren."

I like my breasts. I don't need anyone to build me up. But the way he looks at me, his throat working as he swallows, like he needs a moment to soak me in, has my breath hitching. His big hand shakes as it glides up my side to engulf me in its rough-hewn warmth. Lightly, he trails the backs of his fingers over my nipples, playing with both of them as if he can't help himself. A tender smile lifts his lips.

"Sweet little cupcakes," he whispers, then ducks down to draw one swollen, tight nipple into his mouth. I groan at the sensation, arching up, and he sucks me deeper, tongue flickering as his other hand trails down my hip, getting caught up in the fabric of my skirt before finding the length of my thigh.

With strong, clever fingers, he massages me, running his hand down my leg to my calf.

"These legs," he growls against my skin. "These gorgeous legs. Dreamed about these legs..."

His voice trails off on a groan before he hooks my knee over his shoulder. Spread wide for him. Rye gives my nipple one more sweet tug, then he starts to move again. Hard, forceful thrusts. Owning me.

Every weighty impact sets off sparks of heat and pleasure. Frantic, I circle my hips, lift up to meet his thrusts, my hands grabbing at his slippery shoulders, desperate for purchase. I need more. Harder. Deeper. More.

I'm not aware I'm saying it until he groans "fuck, yes" against my lips. He's driving me into the bed, his hips snapping with relentless precision. And it's so good. Too much. We're no longer Brenna and Rye. There is only this pleasure, so big and full, I have to push into it until it takes me.

But he's there, taking control, holding me down just like I need him to.

"Bren." He's begging, needing to know I'm pleased before he can find his release.

"Take it," I pant. "Take it *now*."

He complies, hand grasping my ass to gain purchase, that powerful body working for what it wants. We get a little messy, a little mean about it. My teeth sink into the meaty curve where his shoulder meets his neck, and he groans, curling himself over me as he breaks apart in my arms.

There is nothing—*nothing*—hotter than the sight of Rye Peterson coming. All those times being utterly turned on while watching him sweat on stage, thick muscles straining, lips parted as he throws his head back and loses himself to the music—they were just a prelude to this. Here, in this moment, he is beautiful, vulnerable, his body shuddering on a wordless cry.

It sets me off. My orgasm isn't wild or mindless. It is relief, sweet and pure. It feels so good, so needed, a tear trickles from the corner of my eye.

With a grunt, Rye sags into me, his chest heaving. We're so close, I feel his heart thudding against my breasts, each deep breath of air he draws in. Trembling fingers trace my brow, his parted lips touching my cheek. He's too spent to kiss me; he simply breathes.

Weakly, I wait for the room to stop spinning. My heart is beating too fast. My heart. I don't want to think about it or the way my hands keep straying to his broad back, needing to stroke his flushed skin. He's holding me close, tucked against him, like I'm something precious. I've never been held this way. And I know at this moment it's what I've been truly craving.

Connection.

With Rye.

My chest hitches. Suddenly his comforting weight is too much, the air in the room too close. I want to push him off, get some space.

I don't know if he feels me squirm or it occurs to him that we're clinging to each other like survivors of a storm, but his body tenses and he moves away. His gaze slides over my shoulder before pushing back to meet mine. He gives me a smile. That stupid, "I don't give a fuck about anything" smile that he fobs off on the world. Easygoing Rye is back.

"You want to use the bathroom first?" he asks. So casual. A sham, but, as much as I hate this old facade, I'm also grateful for it. I need an out, and I need it now.

"Sure." I'm utterly naked except for the ridiculous skirt crumpled around my waist. Somehow that makes me feel even more exposed. My movements are stiff and ungainly as I stumble out of bed and into the bathroom.

As soon as I close the door, I lean against it and draw a deep breath. Tears threaten, and I bite back a bitter laugh. My fears have come to fruition. He touched me, and I melted. I fell apart, and he put me back together. Only now, I'm a needy, fragile version of myself.

I want to regret making myself vulnerable. I do. My logical brain does, anyway. My body is screaming for more. It's demanding I get back out there and climb Rye's strong body like a jungle gym.

With shaking hands, I wash off as best I can. I'm not about to take a shower now. I have to get rid of Rye first. Thankfully, my robe is in the bathroom. I slip into its thick, silk-lined protection and tie it tight.

Rye sits at the edge of the bed, the sheets pulled over his lap. The sight of his big, strong body, colorful with ink along his upper chest and arms, makes my knees a little weak. The feel of him still pulses along my skin. I have a suspicion it will remain long after I shower.

He looks up, his denim eyes uncertain and strained at the corners. "I don't know if I should stay or go. We never discussed how many..." He trails off with an audible swallow.

How many times we would fuck each other dizzy.

My body wants that again. It wants to take off this suffocating robe and crawl right back into his arms. It's fairly humming for his touch. This is what I told him I wanted. Not just a quick hookup but something deeper.

Connection.

Be careful of what you wish for, Bren.

Rye gives me no clue what he'd prefer. He's gone quiet, his body language placid. For all I know, he's dying to bolt. I wouldn't blame him one bit. And since I'd rather die than ask him to stay when he wants to go, I say the only thing I can.

"You wore me out." True. And also, not even a little.

A slow smile tugs at the corner of his mouth. "That blow you away, Berry?"

He says it just the same way he did when we were kids after a concert, all confident swagger and drawling arrogance. But there's a glint of nostalgia in his eyes, a flicker of dry humor like he knows I need something to lighten the moment. And it's irresistible.

A bubble of true laughter leaves me.

"Yeah, Ryland," I say with a grin. "That blew me the fuck away."

"Fuck yeah, it did." His smile grows, and I can't help but return it. We grin at each other like robbers after a successful heist. But I don't move. And neither does he.

Shit. I don't know what to do here, which is a first for me. Normally, I know immediately if I want a lover to stay or go. But this is Rye. He has a knack for twisting me up and making me want what I shouldn't.

Rye solves the problem by standing. The sheet slips free, and he's...God. It's unfair how good he looks naked. He holds my gaze, his big dick swaying between his thickly muscled thighs as he walks toward me. My breath grows short as he draws near.

He smells of sex and heat and promise. The pulse at the base of his neck visibly beats, but he simply leans down and gives me a soft kiss before pulling away. "I'll head out in a minute, okay?"

It's definitely a question. I can object if I want to.

I can't meet his eyes. "Okay."

His only reaction is to brush another kiss over my forehead before heading into the bathroom.

It isn't the most awkward post-sex exchange I've had. But it's the most uncomfortable. Because a voice inside me is screaming that I've made a huge mistake.

CHAPTER TWELVE

RYE

I AM CHANGED. I feel it in my bones, in the way the world around me suddenly looks different. Edges are sharper, colors are deeper, smells are stronger. I am aware of the way my body moves through the air, of every ache and twinge gained from losing myself in her. Everything is different.

In the words of "Amazing Grace": "I once was lost, but now am found. Was blind, but now I see."

Yes, I've taken to quoting hymns in my head. That's what Brenna has done to me. It's terrifying. But I'm strangely happy about being terrified.

In short, I'm one messed-up dude.

Laughing, I head for Madison Square Park, where I'm meeting Scottie and Jax at Shake Shack. If they notice my mood, they don't say a word while we wait in line. True, Scottie keeps giving me disapproving looks, but Scottie's go-to expression is disapproving, so I don't think twice about it.

I'm setting my strawberry shake down on the table just at the edge of the park area when Scottie launches his attack.

"You've gone and slept with Brenna, haven't you?"

Pink shake flies over my arm and shirt as my hand reflexively squeezes tight and destroys the cup. "Shit!"

Blandly, Scottie hands me a pack of wet wipes he keeps in his briefcase.

I grab them and mop up the mess before tossing my empty shake cup into the trash. "You did that on purpose."

One, imperious brow lifts. "Made you mess yourself? If only I had such power."

Grunting, I sit on an empty chair. "I'm not ruling it out. And quit talking shit. Someone might hear and think you're serious." Thankfully, the park is fairly empty today. Even so, I have to shut this line of conversation down. Fast.

Unfortunately, Scottie just stares with that gimlet eye he's perfected over the years. "You're evading. It won't work. Did you have to screw Brenna?"

Anger swarms in my gut and tightens my muscles. He makes what Brenna and I did last night sound cheap, sordid. As it is, I'm having a tough time ignoring how we parted. She'd clearly wanted me out before the sweat we'd worked up had even dried. It hurt, but I didn't say a word to make her even more uncomfortable. There was no point. Either she wanted me there, or she didn't. It was her choice. Not mine.

I can only hope that she'll eventually want me for more. Scottie's reproachful expression drives home that everyone appears to be hoping for the opposite.

"Enough." I glance at the line where I know Jax is waiting for his shake. I don't see him, which means he could be lurking anywhere. "Do not say another word."

"I'm not going to tell Jax."

"Tell me what?" Jax asks, popping out of nowhere like Houdini and making me jump. "That Rye and Brenna are bumping uglies?"

I glare at Scottie. "Seriously?"

The man nearly rolls his eyes. "Don't look at me. I didn't tell him. I prefer to keep all your secrets to myself. Much easier to manipulate you sods that way."

Jax frowns. "That's creepy, Scottie." He turns to me as he takes a seat. "He didn't tell. Give me a little credit. I can read you guys like a headline. It was obvious you two are doing the bump and grind. The Humpty Dance. Netflix and chillin'. Etcetera, etcetera."

"You sound like an Urban Dictionary page," I mutter.

"Fine. You are fucking. Is that better?" He grins wide.

"No. And we're not having this conversation."

"Yes, we are," Scottie interjects. "Because it's galactically stupid what you're doing."

"Oh, well if it's *galactically*..." I roll my eyes and steal Jax's shake. Chocolate. Good but no strawberry, damn it. "Listen, you two are imagining things. Brenna and I are not bumping uglies."

"Yes, you are." Jax takes his shake back. "It's completely obvious. Every time she blushes and ignores you, every time you grind your jaw and ignore her, you just make it more so."

"We always ignore each other."

"Not like this. You two fairly hum with sexual tension."

"God help me," I plead to the sky. "Seriously, if you get me out of this nightmare, I'll be a good boy from now on."

Jax snorts. "No god would accept that bargain, Ryland. Best you ask the guy downstairs."

I flip him the finger. Even though he's probably right.

"Jax's poetic phrasing aside," Scottie says. "It's clear something is going on between you two."

"Plus," Jax says. "And this is just a suggestion. If you don't want anyone to know, you probably shouldn't suck face in the kitchen during family dinner night."

Blood drains from my head and rushes to my toes. "Shit. You saw that?"

"That horror is burned on my brain now, thank you very much. Hell, I should get an Oscar for backing out and pretending I saw nothing."

I scrub my hands over my face, the urge to jump up and run riding high. But they'd only hunt me down later. "Fuck. Fuck. *Fuck.*" I lower my hands and glare around the table. "She will kill me if she knows we've even talked about this. Do you get that?"

Scottie makes a sound of affirmation. Jax, however, squirms like he's just realized this. Dumbass.

"More to the point," I go on. "She'll be horrified and humiliated." The truth chafes. But I don't blame her. This conversation is horrifying me too much as it is.

Then something else occurs to me, and I go ice-cold. "Shit, does anyone else know?" Whip knows, of course. But he's nice enough not to say the words out loud, which kind of makes it still a secret. The others, though... "Does Killian know?"

No, he couldn't. If Killian knew, he'd be here, punching me in the face.

"Calm down." Jax leans back to slurp his shake. "No one else knows."

I pin him with a stare. "Not even Stella?"

He waves his shake with an idle hand. "She doesn't count. We're a relationship unit."

"God." I groan and pinch the bridge of my nose where a headache is forming. "Which means Sophie knows too."

Scottie's smile is brief but fond. "No. I love my wife, but that doesn't mean I'm unaware that she has the biggest mouth in all creation."

"You keep things from her?" Jax is aghast.

"Not important things that affect us or our family. But Rye is right to look terrified..."

"I don't think I looked terrified..."

"The whole group knowing Brenna is consorting with him would devastate her."

"Thanks," I grumble. "Glad to know *consorting* with me is so awful."

Jax chuckles and slaps my shoulder with good humor. "Your reputation precedes you."

"You're about to wear that shake home, Johnny Boy."

He takes an extra-long suck of it. Asshole.

Sighing, I reach over and steal Scottie's shake, taking a drink before he can stop me. The man is a low-level germaphobe, so I know he won't want it back. Scottie gives me a repressive glare.

Ordinarily, I wouldn't fuck with him in this way, but he's pissed me off. And I'm thirsty. So, I drink some more of his salted caramel shake before I speak. "You're both wrong, by the way. This thing with Brenna and I just started. And it's complicated."

"Of course, it's complicated," he snaps. "Which is why it's stupid."

"Galactically," I deadpan, slurping on his shake. Figures he'd get something salty.

His glare is glacial. "Quite."

When I say nothing—because he's not entirely wrong— Scottie sighs. "Even you should be able to understand how complicated it will be when this thing goes south, and we're all left dealing with the fallout."

When. Not if. As though the very idea of Brenna sticking with me isn't even worth contemplating.

My teeth grind. "Even me?"

"You're not the brightest penny when it comes to this stuff," Jax says.

I've played the role of the band's unofficial clown. Mainly because I don't like sweating the small stuff, and someone has to lighten the mood. But, until now, I hadn't thought my guys actually believed I was an idiot.

"I have near-perfect recall and an IQ of one-fifty. Try again, asshole."

Jax shakes his head. "I was referring to romantic shit. You want to tell me you know what you're doing there?"

I deflate with a sigh. "Fine. I'm romantically challenged." I point my stolen shake at them. "And we're not talking about this."

"We are," Scottie states emphatically. "Damn it, Rye. You know it's a bad idea to get involved with someone in the group."

They are absolutely killing my post-Brenna-sex high. "You all have women who are part of 'the group' as you call it."

"They weren't part of the group when we started. And they weren't working with the band—"

"Sophie was."

Scottie raises his eyes to the heavens and mutters under his breath before trying again. "She wasn't attached to us at that point. Not in the way you and Brenna are attached."

"We've been a family for over a decade, Rye." Jax's expression is earnest now. "You two get together and then break up and it's like a divorce. We'll all feel it, and it will hurt. A lot."

A small, hard lump of disappointment and resentment sits in my chest. I can't help who I want. I've tried to ignore it, and it never went away. But I'll be damned if I say as much to them.

"Look, I don't want to fight with Bren anymore, all right? But we've been stuck in this...thing. It's like we can't help it. Whenever we're around each other, we react like..."

"Angry alley cats?"

"Vinegar and bicarbonate?"

Jax grins. "Way to science it up, Scottie."

I glare at both of them.

"What I want to know," Jax says, "is why Brenna hates you so much. I know you asked me not to bring it up again, but considering you two are now getting into it, maybe it's no longer an issue."

Slumping in my seat, I eye my two friends. Despite their meddling, I know they care. They wouldn't be here bugging the ever-loving hell out of me if they didn't.

"I don't know how it got so bad. I mean, I know it started when you all insisted on that stupid interview..."

"Not our best hour," Scottie murmurs dourly.

Back when we were about to go on our first world tour, Brenna made a bid to become our official PR manager. She'd been doing PR for us since the beginning, but given that she was eighteen, we had some reservations. Sure, we were only twenty, not much older than her, but she was Killian's little cousin; we wanted her safe and at home. But Brenna wanted her shot, and who were we to stop her? So we decided to go over a few ground rules. All understandable, until the meeting somehow turned into making sure Brenna could contain her obvious crush on me.

What a bunch of asshats we'd been. But I'd been the worst. Embarrassed and more than a little tempted by Brenna, I'd gone into total shithead mode. I wince at the memory, the exchange clear as a bell even now.

"I know you've had a little crush on me, Berry." God, the ego on me.

A lovely shade of raspberry had washed up all the way to the dark red roots of Brenna's hair. "Of all the...I do *not* have a crush on you!"

I could have stopped there, but no, I had to make certain she hated me, thinking back then that it was better that way. Safer. "You really shouldn't. I'm a terrible bet. Total player. No offense, Bren, I like you but you're not my type. At all."

"Likewise," she'd gritted out.

Again, I could have stopped. But the guys had been watching. Killian had laughed, a relieved sound like he knew all along Brenna couldn't have been so foolish. It dug at a sore spot I never knew I had. And I lashed out. Like a jerk.

"I mean the very idea is laughable."

"Laughable?" She'd drawn herself up then, lifting her chin, fire flashing in her amber eyes. It was at that moment I truly saw the Brenna I know today. Cool, confident, and oh so disdainful of me. "Listen here, buttercup, I could twist you around my finger if I so choose. But you're not worth the effort."

She'd been magnificent in her rage. And I'd eaten it up, getting off on it in a way I couldn't explain. We'd gone another few rounds before the guys shut us both up.

I wince at the memory and rub the back of my stiff neck. "It should never have happened that way. She didn't deserve it."

"Hey," Jax protests. "We were just trying to keep her safe."

I sit up a little straighter. "No, man. We should have given her the same space to make mistakes. We all were players, young and stupid. We shouldn't have put her on the spot like that. We didn't have to make it about her and me. Aside from Killian, she could have ended up hooking up with any one of you..." I don't want to think about that. I'll get too pissed and have to hit something.

"Ah, hello?" Jax starts with a laugh. "The only one she had a massive crush on was you."

Hearing him say it aloud has my heart thudding with a weird mix of pleasure and regret. For a brief moment in time, I'd had Brenna's regard. And then I lost it.

"Yeah, well, I killed that crush forever."

"Like I said," Jax mutters. "Not the brightest penny."

"I had to do it. She kept looking at me that way..." Tempting the hell out of me. "Even if I'd wanted...Shit. No. You both know Killian had laid down the law and told us in no uncertain terms to stay the hell away from his cousin."

"He shouldn't have done that," Scottie says. "It wasn't his decision to make."

"No, it wasn't." I pick at the edge of the table where the black enamel is peeling off. "But hooking up with her would have led to hurt feelings and messed with the band."

"You're right about that." Scottie looks at me with something close to hesitation before his expression smooths out. "Brenna and I kissed once."

"What?" Jax and I shout together. Although Jax sounds scandalized while I'm just pissed.

Scottie shrugs. "It was still in the early days when we'd started working closely together. We got drunk and decided to try it." He smiles fondly. The fucker. "A colossal failure. It was like kissing my sister, honestly."

I should feel relief, but my petty side is sticking to the point that Scottie got to sample Brenna's lips before I did.

He catches me scowling and lifts a beleaguered brow. "And we both realized how stupid it was because we both had to continue to work together."

"It's only stupid," Jax says thoughtfully, "if Rye's sleeping with Brenna to scratch an itch. Somehow I don't think that's why."

They both turn their eyes on me. Dissected and left open in front of them, I fight the urge to cross my arms over my chest. When the silence grows, and I can't stand it any longer, I let out a breath. "She's the one that got away."

I clear my throat and give them a belligerent look. "I know we bicker and snipe at each other. Honestly, it's some messed up form of self-defense for me at this point. But you think I don't know the risks in trying to change things? That I haven't tried my hardest to stay the hell away from her all these years, when she's the...Fuck it. She's the *only* woman I've ever wanted to be around for more than a few hours, even when she's hating me.

"So, yeah, I know. I know the risks better than you chuckle-heads. But she's finally let me in. And I'm going to take the chance, for however brief it might be. Even if I crash and burn and don't survive the wreck. Because I can't do anything less and still comfortably breathe."

Birds chirp and cabs blare. And Scottie and Jax sit there with their mouths agape. Then Jax closes his. "Shit. It's like that, huh?"

Understatement of the year.

"Yeah. It's like that."

CHAPTER THIRTEEN

RYE

TRUEACEOFBASS: So. I had this idea. I'd drop by your house, armed w/ Pringles & Diet Cherry Coke (even though it's a disgusting drink) and offer you a foot rub. But, apparently, you're in Atlanta.

Berrylicious: Diet Cherry Coke is delicious. Anyone with true taste knows it.

TrueAceOfBass: It's the devil's juice, Bren. Accept that your tastes have been compromised and let the healing begin.

Berrylicious: Never. In fact, I'm going on a tour of the Coke factory tomorrow. Will demand a crate of DCC.

TrueAceOfBass: You're staying in Atlanta? Scottie is coming home tonight. And how is it that Scottie tells me these things and you don't?

Berrylicious: You're sounding suspiciously parental right now, Peterson.

TrueAceOfBass: If you want to call me Daddy, I'm surprisingly okay with that.

Berrylicious: It's like you never want to have sex with me again.

TrueAceOfBass: Oh, I'm getting some. As soon as you return from Atlanta. Exactly when is that, btw?

Berrylicious: You're pretty sure of yourself, buttercup.

TrueAceOfBass: I was there. You were two moans away from, "Oh, Daddy, please give me more."

Berrylicious: Ugh. That's it. I'm turning off my phone. I have to go take a hot shower and scrub my skin to rid myself of the ick.

TrueAceOfBass: You mean a cold shower because you're hot for me. They don't work, you know. I've tried. Several times since I left you. I'm still dying over here.

TrueAceOfBass: Bren?

TrueAceOfBass: You seriously turned off your phone?

TrueAceOfBass: Bren?

TrueAceOfBass: Damn, it's like that, huh?

When Brenna doesn't answer, I tuck away my phone and bite back a grin. Despite the fact she's tuned me out, the small exchange gave me far too much enjoyment. Still, she did turn off her phone. That can't be good.

"Question." I turn to Jax who's thumbing through my LP collection. "Do women truly frown upon the whole 'call me Daddy' thing?"

Jax pauses, his mouth falling open. "Please, for the love of vinyl, tell me you didn't go there."

"What? I was joking." Mostly. I mean, I'm up for anything Brenna wants to throw my way. I aim to please. But it's not my personal kink.

Jax shakes his head. "I thought you had better game than this."

"I never needed game before now."

"Sadly, I believe that." He should; he's had as many women throw themselves on him over the years. Shit, even more. Our fame was our game.

Jax's expression becomes empathetic. "Engaging with Brenna is master-level tactics, and you're over there in primary school."

A sound of frustration escapes me, and I rub my fingers along my tight scalp. "You know what? We shouldn't be talking about this. Forget I said anything."

"Then you shouldn't have mentioned the daddy thing. Not likely to forget that."

With a groan, I flop back onto my couch. "That was stupid of me to text, wasn't it?"

Jax snickers. "You texted that? Now she has a visible record of that horror for the rest of your lives and will pull it up to torture you with in times of strife." He glances at me with unrepentant glee. "Of which I predict there will be many."

I'd flip him the finger, but I'm too busy pressing my fingers to the hollows of my aching eyes. "Fuck. We really shouldn't be talking about this."

"But you want to talk about it, don't you?" Jax's tone is serious now, and for once he doesn't seem to be on the verge of cracking a joke. It must be killing him to hold back.

My hands fall to my thighs, and I instantly start thrumming a beat. But it doesn't stop the twitchy feeling inside me. "I just...I don't know. I don't want to fuck this up."

"You will, though."

"Thanks, man. Truly." I'd be more upset if I didn't think Jax was sort of right.

He shakes his head. "It's nothing personal. We're guys. We'll fuck things up because we haven't got a clue what to do with our feelings once we start having them for someone." His snort is self-deprecating. "Do you know the amount of asinine word spew that came out of my mouth when I met Stella?"

"I can imagine," I mutter.

But he doesn't hear me. He's on a tear now. "Instead of pulling little dudes aside in health class to tell them it's okay to rub one off—which, no shit, man, we all *know* that—they should be teaching them how to handle relationships. I swear that advice is worth more than gold."

He pins me with serious eyes. "Let me save you some more future grief. If your woman comes to you to complain about some shit going down in her life, she doesn't want you to fix it."

"What's the point of telling me if I can't help find a solution?"

"So you can nod and say, 'Fuck that noise, you're completely in the right, sweetness.' Or, 'I'm sorry, honey, that truly sucks. Would you like a foot rub?'"

"I offered a foot rub." I scratch at my growing beard. I need to shave it. "She ignored that part."

Jax snorts. "Doesn't count if you weird her out with a side of bad flirting."

"She's intrigued. I know it."

"You know dick." He seems pleased by this.

"Maybe you should teach a class now that you're so enlightened."

"Maybe I should. Gather 'round, little dudes, and let Unkie John explain this wonderful concept called 'think before you speak.'"

"Probably best if you don't call yourself 'Unkie John.' That's creepy."

"Whatever you say, Daddy."

"God," I groan, pained. "I shouldn't have gone there."

"Live and learn, my friend." He shrugs. "Nothing is easy when you're falling in love."

Alarm has me sitting up. "Hey now, no one said anything about love. I like Brenna. A lot. I want to try and see where this goes without totally messing it up before it even begins. But love? Don't get me wrong, I'm not opposed to love as a concept. But love is..." Flaying yourself wide open and handing over salt to dump in the wound.

Jax stares at me with a placid expression that says I'm talking too much. I stare back, determined not to squirm or pull at my collar because it is damn hot in this room, and I need to get better window treatments.

The silence grows taut, and I clench my fists.

She bolted. Because I know damn well that's what she did. It's a kick in the teeth, a punch in my needy nuts. I'm not going to think about the region of my heart. That organ is off-limits.

Yes, she bolted. But I can't sweat it. We only promised each other three days out of the week. Asking for more already would be pushing it. So, I won't text her again. I won't think about her or count the minutes that she's gone.

Life goes on. I did fine before I ever knew the silken heat of Brenna James's body. Or the sounds she makes when she comes. Or the way her skin flushes peach...

"Hell," I mutter. "My apartment is too stuffy. You want to go for a run?"

Because my friend is far more astute than he likes to let on, he jumps to his feet and stretches. "Sure. But we're stopping for a shake on the way back."

"Doesn't that defeat the purpose of exercise?"

He lifts a brow. "Is that why we're running?"

Damn it, I need that shake. "Let's go. I'll pay for the shakes."

————

Brenna

"Is it just me, or is this movie really bizarre?" I whisper.

Jules gapes at the massive screen where animated polar bears frolic in the snow. A frown forms between her brows. "They're drinking Coke. I hate it when they make animals eat or drink human food."

"Or make animated food items look cute and dance around." I wrinkle my nose. "I'm supposed to want to eat them later?"

"How about when they eat each other?"

"It's never the type of eating I approve of, sadly."

We both snicker. A mother sitting next to Jules shoots us a

repressive glare while her two-year-old tries to put his fist in his mouth. It's kind of impressive how she can glare so effectively while wearing 3-D glasses, though. It must be a mother thing.

Jules eases closer to me. "When is this over? I want to see old-timey Coke advertisements and try weird drinks like ginger-lime Coke."

"I heard they have a pine nut flavor."

"They do not! Why!"

We get another glare from the mother. Her kid, on the other hand, has taken to kicking the seat in front of him. Hard.

I don't blame him. I want out too. Thankfully we opted not to sit in the moving theater seats for the 4-D experience. I'd probably want to vomit at this point.

"Thank you for coming with me," I murmur to Jules.

When Scottie told me he'd set up a meeting in Atlanta with Al Rasken, one of Kill John's A&R men, to discuss their upcoming record, I'd jumped at the chance to join in. Record labels can be notoriously stingy with the promotion and marketing budget. Kill John is their biggest artist, so we have much more leeway. Even so, a bit of finessing never hurt. The more promotion money I can get for them, the better. At least that's what I told myself was the reason for going.

"Hey, it's a mini vacation from work. I'm not complaining."

She doesn't realize it, but her words hit a weak spot, and I suppress the urge to wriggle. Because we aren't working anymore. There is absolutely no reason for me to *still* be in Atlanta. No legitimate reason, that is.

Days later and I still feel Rye on me. If I close my eyes and let my concentration slip, I'm haunted by the ghost of his scent, salty-sweet lust, citrus and spices. Someone should bottle it; I'd rub that stuff all over my skin at night and sleep in it.

God, I miss him. I miss him! How the hell can that be? We had sex once. I shouldn't be craving him like this. Oh, but I do. Before, I ached for physical touch. It was a nebulous need, strong but not rooted in one specific person. Now, it's *him* I ache for. Damn it.

"Don't you start sighing," Jules says out of the side of her mouth. "This was your idea."

"I slept with Rye." The words burst free without warning.

"What?" Jules squeaks.

"Hush," the mother next to us admonishes.

Jules pinches my arm. "You and Rye? Rye Peterson?"

"What other Rye would I be talking about?" I grump, regretting my loose lips. But I need to tell someone, anyone, and Jules won't judge. She'll tease me a little, but that's to be expected.

"Certainly not the one you insisted you'd like to drop in a vat of boiling oil." She rolls her eyes then glares. "What the hell, Brenna?"

"Ow!" I rub my skin. "Would you quit pinching me?"

"Shhh!"

Jules waves off the irate mother then turns my way. Her oversized 3-D glasses reflect the light of the screen as her lips purse. "Spill it."

"You're going to get us kicked out." I dart an apologetic look at the mother. She's too busy trying to prevent her kid from eating floor candy.

"You dropped this bomb on me here so I couldn't properly freak out, didn't you?" Jules accuses.

She's not wrong. Sighing, I focus on the screen but then close my eyes because I freaking hate 3-D movies. "Remember that night we talked about my little problem?"

"The need for a good fucking?"

Thankfully, Jules whispers that.

"Yes. Rye was there. He overheard."

"Shut the front door," Jules says, part scandalized, part anticipatory.

"He offered..."

"To butter your buns?" she says. Loudly.

"There are children here," the mother hisses.

Jules gives her a level look. "Like he's going to understand that?" She shakes her head and glances at the little boy, who is utterly oblivious to our chatter and is clapping at the screen. "I'm sorry, I assumed you'd be pro-sex. My mistake."

I bite my lip to keep from laughing as Jules turns back to me. "I'll be quiet now so Ms. Buttered Buns here doesn't have a fit. But when this show is done, we're having words."

We shut up until the lights go up, and finally we're let into the museum. As soon as we're free, Jules grabs my elbow and hustles me to a corner where a cherry-cheeked Santa lifts a bottle of Coke high in the air. "All right, now tell me everything." Her eyes are alight and avid with curiosity.

"I don't know..." I hedge, feeling weirdly protective of it now that I've opened my mouth. "It was a moment of weakness."

"Uh-huh. Sure."

"What can I say? He was persuasive."

Jules gives me a get-real face. "He's Rye Peterson. He doesn't need to say a word. Just looking at him is enough. I mean, those arms? That ass?"

"I didn't realize you'd noticed."

"Am I dead?" She pinches my arm again with her quick fingers. "Don't be jealous. I'm not into him. But I can appreciate the package."

"Apparently I do too."

"Of course, you do. It's *Rye*. He's always been your weak spot. Not that I blame you. Few can resist that aw-shucks grin. The beard thing is a surprise. I didn't think it would work for him, but it's like when Chris Evans went from wholesome, cute 'how do you do, ma'am?' Captain America, to 'who's your daddy, you're gonna like the spanking I give you' Cap."

"God, don't say 'Daddy,'" I moan, remembering Rye's stupid texts. Call me Daddy, indeed. The arrogance. Why had that turned me on? If it had been anyone else but Rye, I'd be intrigued...No, that's not true. It turned me on more *because* it was Rye. Which makes me twisted. Totally twisted to get hot at the idea of playing Daddy with Rye freaking Peterson when I've spent the whole of my adult life trying to prove to myself that he has no power over me.

Silence greets me, and I realize what I've said. I wince at the utterly gleeful expression on Jules's face.

"Oh, really?" she drawls.

"There's *no* really."

"I knew he'd be a dirty bird in bed."

I clear my throat and catch a glimpse of grinning Santa. Edging away from him, I roll my stiff shoulders and try again. "We did *not* go there!" Texts don't count. "I just don't want that image in my head." Too late. "But, okay, it was...good. Really good. But it's Rye."

Jules hums thoughtfully under her breath then pins me with a curious stare. "Can I ask you something? You and Rye have always been at each other's throats, and I assumed it was simmering repressed sexual tension—"

"Oh, for crying out—" I shut up, because she lifts a brow as if to say, *Get real, Brenna.* And she isn't entirely wrong. Damn it. With a sigh, I make a motion with my hand for her to continue.

Jules sniffs delicately. "As I was saying, I'm pretty sure we *all* thought that. But how did this animosity between you two start? Where's it coming from?"

Part of me wants to turn tail and run. But I squeeze the bridge of my nose and answer her. "In the beginning, it was a simple case of immaturity and my inability to handle rejection." I tell her about my crush on Rye, the way he effectively squashed it, and the resulting low-key feud. "We started relating to each other by bickering and sniping. But a few years later..."

I grit my teeth. I don't want to remember. I put it aside a while ago. Remembering only pokes a sore spot that I've worked to heal. Remembering only threatens to make me view Rye in a way that will make everything harder. But Jules asked, and maybe it's better to get it out instead of burying it away.

"I saw him doing something he shouldn't."

"What, like a crime?"

"No. He was with a woman—"

"Please don't tell me he hurt her." Horror shimmers in her eyes.

"Jules!" I huff out a weak laugh. "Stop interrupting. No, he didn't do that. I'd have told someone, and he'd have been out of the band in a blink. He was just kissing someone he shouldn't have."

I close my eyes and will away the memory, the utter disappointment and rage I'd felt toward him, knowing that he put his drunken lust over the happiness of his friends.

"I'm not going to say who, because it's been ten years at this point, and it does no good to stir the pot." I give Jules a sad, wane smile. "But it set the tone for how I related to him for so long. I held on to that rage for years, let it feed me when it came to him. But it wasn't healthy, and he never did anything like that again—not that I know of. So, I let it go. Only by then, we'd settled into the pattern of animosity like a pair of favorite shoes."

"Does he know about this?" Jules asks.

"No. I never said a word. I didn't want to hurt the band." I snort. "It's ridiculous, isn't it? I protected him from a blowup, when he deserved everything that he would have gotten."

"Not really," Jules says. "Your job was to protect them. I can see how that would put you in a tough spot."

"And I resented that too. I took it out on Rye, even though he had no clue why I was so pissed."

She peers at me, and I have the urge to squirm. When she talks, her tone holds no judgment, only curiosity. "Despite all that, when he made you this offer, you took it."

"Sometimes, I can't believe it myself." I laugh without humor. My chest hurts, and my head feels as if it's stuffed with wool. "I'd like to think we've both grown. And the truth is...Shit. I like this Rye."

Saying it makes it real. Saying it also lifts a weight I didn't know I'd been carrying.

Jules nods as if understanding. "And you're running scared."

"Scared," I scoff. "I'm not scared." I am, though. I'm terrified of falling.

"Of course not." Jules pats my arm. "That's why we're talking about sex in front of St. Nick instead of you being in New York getting some dick."

"Ugh!" I turn away and start walking through the museum. But I can't outrun my memories.

Ride me, Bren.

He'd been so thick. So hard. So good.

"Shit." With a silent groan, I toss up my hands in defeat. I can lie to myself all day, but it won't change the truth. My body doesn't feel right anymore. Like it's waiting for him. "I ran, all right! I know I ran. But I couldn't face him. I just couldn't, okay?"

Not after he'd taken me apart in the best of ways. He'd taken me apart and then put me back together. I'm this new needy woman who can't stop craving one more touch. I don't know if I like it. But I want it.

Jules is silent for a moment, letting me stride along, my heels clicking double time on the linoleum floor. "Brenna, you are my idol, the woman who told the head of RAI Records that the day he started staring at guys' dicks when he talked to them was the day it would be okay for him to talk to your tits."

I snort at the memory.

Jules smiles fondly. "Do you know how many times I've seen you set down random drunk and disorderly dudes at events without breaking a sweat? Or make power-hungry executives quake in their loafers? You're never fazed. You're a badass in five-inch heels. No one takes advantage of you." Her gaze is serious now. "If I could harness half your confidence, I'd be a happy woman. So, I have to wonder why you're running from the one guy who lights you up."

My steps slow to a halt. Lights me up? As much as I want to, I can't deny that I feel something when I'm around him. Alive. Energized.

"I don't know."

But I do. I'm a sham. I am not cool and collected. Half the time, I'm terrified to take any risks. I'm afraid anything I truly want will get ripped away and I'll be that insecure girl on the outside looking in once more.

When it comes to Rye, he has the power to pull the rug out from under me. When I got physical with him, I only gave him more of that power. That knowledge lies on my skin, making it feel too tight. And yet I cannot lie to myself: I crave more of him.

Jules watches me carefully. Whatever she sees in my face has her tone softening. "I know one thing. You don't let a man like Rye see you sweat. He'll never let that go. Get back to New York and face him head-on."

CHAPTER FOURTEEN

RYE

BERRYLICIOUS: Michael says you haven't answered any texts regarding next week's appearance schedule. What gives?

   TrueAceOfBass: Sorry

   Berrylicious: Sorry? That's it? That's all you have to say to me?

   TrueAceOfBass: This a 16 Candles skit?

   Berrylicious: If you fucking forget my birthday, we're going to have words, Peterson.

   TrueAceOfBass: 8/16 will nvr 4gt

   Berrylicious: Even your texting is bad. Are you drunk?

   TrueAceOfBass: No

   Berrylicious: High?

   TrueAceOfBass: Wish

   Berrylicious: Are you avoiding me? Because I went to Atlanta? Is that it?

   TrueAceOfBass: No ???

   Berrylicious: Damn it, Rye. Will you please be serious?

   TrueAceOfBass: K

The phone rings, and I know I've stretched Brenna's patience too far. With a sigh, I prop the phone on the arm of the couch and hit Accept.

"Seriously, what the hell is going on?" she starts in without pause.

I have to smile a little. She's cute when she's pissed. Not that I'd tell her. She'd kill me if I said so... "You're cute when you're pissed." Shit. Painkillers are not my friend.

A growl rumbles over the phone. "Am I on speaker?"

"Yes." I stare up at the ceiling. My entire right arm throbs from shoulder to fingertips while my left only burns from elbow to thumb. "But no one is around."

"Your voice sounds weird. You're drunk, aren't you?"

"I'm not drunk, Bren. I'm..." *In pain. Freaked out. Scared.* "Tired."

Her snort is elegant and full of disbelief.

"I swear, I'm not drunk." I want to pick up the phone and put a little less distance between us, but I'm afraid to move. Moving tends to suck right now. "I'm sorry I didn't respond to Michael's texts. I must have missed them."

Or, you know, couldn't type. It's been a nightmare responding to the few texts Brenna has sent. And clearly, I haven't done a good job since she thinks I'm drunk—or high. I've been thinking about finding some weed and zoning out. Except weed gives me cottonmouth. Maybe CBD oil would work.

"Rye? Are you even listening?"

Right. Brenna. She sounds as irritated as a cat who's been stroked in the wrong direction.

"You caught me napping." I struggle to sit up and clear my head. My arms scream in protest. The pain shoots down my back and hits my hips. Shit, I feel like an old man. An old man who got hit by a crosstown bus. "I'm a little out of it."

Her silence is so loud, I feel it against my chest. When she finally talks, her voice is crisp.

"Is this how it's going to be now? You acting all weird?"

"Now?" I husk out a laugh. "You always accuse me of acting weird."

She's paranoid about fucking me. Awesome. It's a real ego boost. She can pretend otherwise, but it's a damn fact that *she* ran off to Atlanta to get away from this. From me. I still don't know if I should be grateful or pissed. Both. Definitely both.

"You know what I mean, Rye. Now that we..."

"Bumped uglies? Did the nasty? Knocked boots?"

"Jesus. Have you been watching bad nineties teen movies?"

No, I've been listening to Jax. Same difference, I suppose.

"I was always partial to *American Pie*."

"Yeah, I bet," she grumps, then says with clear trepidation, "What's going on here, Rye?"

Slowly, I flex my left hand. It protests, but I push it. Pain is a part of playing. There were nights when we'd get off stage, dripping with sweat, Killian, Jax, and I mopping blood off our hands because we'd played until our fingertips split and bled. Whip would have to ice his arms to ease swollen muscles.

But this? This isn't just pain. It is weakness. My hands and arms lose all strength with this hideous pain, and I can't fucking play.

What am I if I can't perform music?

I glance at the phone where Brenna is waiting for an answer. "This might surprise you, honey, but not everything is about you."

It comes out pissier than I want. But Brenna is used to that. It's our normal.

She snorts, but it's softer now. "Coming from you, that's rich."

I smile even though I have nothing to laugh about at the moment. "My ego is rather huge. You know what else is?"

"Your head?"

"The head is part of it," I concede lightly, still trying to get my hand to unfurl.

"You're such a child," she says with an aggrieved sigh, but I hear the reluctant amusement behind it.

"But you love me anyway." I meant it as a tease. I've said the same thing many times before. But now, with this *thing* looming between us, we both pause in awkward silence. The thud of my heart sounds overloud in my ear.

Brenna finally rallies. "You wish."

Her standard answer. But the thought strikes a nerve this time and weasels its way into the dark cracks of my mind. I've never been loved like that. My parents love me, sure. But that isn't remotely the same thing. What would it be liked to be loved by someone not required by blood to do it?

Sitting alone in my apartment, which is admittedly too big for one person, I am suddenly hollowed out by loneliness. I've been lonely before. Who hasn't? But this is different. Terrifying, like I'm on the edge of a cliff and the only way out is down. It's cold, empty, humbling. I close my eyes against it, turning my head in the direction of Brenna's voice.

"Bren?"

"What?" The reply is tinged with enough wariness to make me smile.

I wish she was back home. I would ask her to come over, just... hang out. Have pizza with me, watch a movie, have an argument with me, anything. But then she'd see me like this. I don't want her pity. Or anyone's; it would only make everything more real.

But I don't like her current mindset on our situation. She's got it all wrong.

I swallow past the hard lump at the base of my throat. "I need you to believe me when I say this, okay?"

I can practically hear her mind racing. When she answers, she's back to the cool professionalism I know all too well. "Fine. What is it?"

My prickly girl. God, I want to wear down that spiky armor, find out if she's as soft underneath as I suspect. "Whatever does or doesn't happen between us, I'm never going to hold it against you. I swear to God. Okay?"

Another pause. This one stilted. I've surprised her. I can feel it in the air.

Her voice comes so soft it's nearly a whisper. "Okay. I...I won't either. Promise."

"Good." I swallow again, bracing myself for movement. With a silent grunt, I rise to my feet. The room spins for a minute, but I take a breath and let it ride. "Now, I really do feel shitty today. So, I'm gonna go."

"You...What's wrong?"

Could that be concern? Surely not.

"Woke up with a headache that won't quit." It's partly true. I do have a headache, but it's a mere buzzing fly in comparison to my hands.

"One of those?" Brenna knows exactly how bad it can get for me. Everyone in the band does. I'll be laid low, hiding out in a dark room for hours. If it happens before a concert, they'll send in a masseuse, acupuncturist, whoever they can find in the city we're playing.

"Well, then," she says quietly. "I'm sorry I yelled at you. And for being paranoid."

The concession clearly cost her. Sick man that I am, I feel lighter. If anything in my life is consistent, it's Brenna.

"Ah, Berry. I'd take you sniping at me in that bossy-boots tone of yours over silence any day."

"God," she says with a half laugh. "You really are terrible, you know."

The insult is laced with affection, though, and I grab on to it. "But you love me anyway."

I hang up before she can answer, chuckling at the thought of her cursing me. My humor dies quickly as the silence resumes, and with it, the pain in my hands and arms returns to the forefront. I have to move. Get out of here.

Blame it on my weakened condition, but I decide to go to the one place I know I'll find comfort.

———

"RYE BREAD!" My mother spreads her arms in greeting, waiting for me to step into her hug.

I do, and she instantly wraps me up. I'm a good foot taller than she is, and my shoulders are twice as wide as hers, but when she holds me, I feel like a kid again, small and safe.

Closing my eyes, I let my forehead rest on the side of her head. "Hey, Mom."

With a final squeeze, she lets go and then ushers me inside the townhouse that's been the family home for the past forty years. Most people, when they think of townhouses on the Upper West Side, imagine sleek elegance, soaring ceilings, detailed molding, spiral staircases, and triple-height windows with light streaming in.

My mom's house has all of that, sure. But the wide plank floors have been sanded down to the original wood, remaining unpolished and creaking underfoot. The air smells of old pine and plaster and books. Probably because the front room has two walls of built-in bookcases crammed to bursting with books of various sizes and topics.

I have fond memories of curling up on one of the mustard velvet armchairs in front of the ornate onyx fireplace and reading during rainy days. Yes, I was that child, bookish and shy. It wasn't until I hit puberty and got too horny for my own good that I forced myself out of my shell.

Mom leads me down the hall, where framed family photos share space with oil paintings by masters, and into the back of the house. The kitchen looks like something out of Victorian England, with dark-green cabinets, butcher block counters, and a pink AGA stove that warms the entire space.

A long farmhouse table is set up in front of the double-height grid of back windows. The other side of the back room is reserved for Mom's studio.

The scent of oil paint, turpentine, and baking is a comforting blend that I know well.

Mom shoves me into a chair. "Sit. Let me make you some tea."

Early on, when we were becoming friends, Whip, Jax, Killian, Scottie, and I figured out our parents' shared obsession with tea. We all grew up knowing that tea arrived with every visit, to fix every ill, to top off the day, or to close out the night. Jax is still fairly obsessed with making the perfect cuppa. I can take it or leave it, but I'm not about to contradict my mom.

"Your father was here earlier. You just missed him."

My back tenses, and I spread my palms wide on the smooth wood table. "What a shame."

My mother doesn't miss the sarcasm in my voice—not that I was trying too hard to hide it—and she turns to give me a reproachful look. "I've forgiven him. Why can't you?"

Forgive my dad. There's a thought. It isn't as though I haven't tried. But then I'll hear about him cozying up to my mom again, and my eye starts to twitch. I shouldn't be upset. As she said, it's her life. She can make her own choices. Only I was the one who heard her cry in her room every time she caught him cheating. I was there when she walked around the house like a ghost, so deep in her depression from Dad's antics that she forgot to feed herself or me. Eventually, they divorced. But he keeps coming back. And he keeps failing her. They're stuck in an ugly loop, neither of them able to break free.

He isn't a bad guy in all other respects. He started as an investment banker but is now an adjunct professor of finance at Columbia, mainly because he'd wanted to retire but still needs to keep busy now and then. He likes the idea of torturing—that is, teaching—bright and malleable minds.

As for my relationship with Dad, he's always been supportive.

Which makes it harder for me to see him break her heart over and over again.

Mom is still giving me that disappointed look, and I feel small for sticking my nose in their business again. But I can't stay silent, apparently. "I just..." I blow out a breath then start again. "How can you trust him?"

She shrugs. "I don't. But some people are inextricably linked to each other in life. Your father and I are like that. We keep trying."

I want to put my face in my hands and block her out. How the hell can she defend infidelity like this? As soon as I hit puberty and understood exactly how my dad had hurt my mom, I vowed I'd never let anyone have that much power over me. Ever.

But I didn't come here to fight with Mom. I want peace. Quiet. Comfort. So I let out a long breath and roll my stiff shoulders. "I'll try to let it go."

She glances at me, and I get the feeling she'd been expecting an argument.

"Good." A slow smile spreads over her face when I simply meet her gaze with a placid expression. Mom huffs under her breath in wry amusement before heading for the stove. "You could stay for dinner, if you like."

"I have plans for later, unfortunately." It's a lie. I love my mom, and I have the feeling if I hang out in this house for several hours, I won't want to leave.

Pushing aside a teetering stack of art books, then resting my arms on the worn wood table, I watch my mother move around the kitchen. She's tall for a woman, nearly six feet, and sturdy. Over the years, her ash-blond hair has become steel gray, but she wears it now with copper-bronze tips. The thick mass is piled up on her head in a messy bun and glows against the pitch black of her standard turtleneck and pants set.

She reaches for the kettle, exposing the faded black tattoo band about her wrist of stylized stalks of rye—her homage to me. The other tattoo she has is known only to herself, my dad, and anyone else who has seen her naked...and I really don't want to think about that or where it might be.

"You're making a face," she says, scooping loose Assam tea into a pot.

"A face?"

"Mmm. Like you've just smelled something off." She glances my way and her brown eyes light with amusement. "My kitchen smells just fine, I'll have you know. So I can only assume you thought of something that upset you. Is it about your dad—"

"No." I pause. "And I didn't make a face."

"Did too."

Grinning, I shake my head. Hell if I'll tell her just what imagery upset me. I'd probably be subjected to a "sex is a natural expression of the soul" talk. Again. I had enough of those during puberty and am lucky I didn't turn out scarred for life. "Stop fishing."

Mom shrugs and finishes up the tea. She sets the pot, a set of teacups and saucers, milk, and sugar—the whole deal—on a tray and carries it over. Because it isn't proper tea if you half-assed it by fixing your cup at the counter like I did when I was at home.

"Baby boy," she says, handing me a cup. "That hello hug spoke for itself. Something is bothering you."

I wait until she pours my tea and adds milk and sugar to answer. "It's a blue day, that's all."

Blue days. That's how she describes them. When you feel down and can't find your way back to the light.

Her cool hand settles over mine. My mother's hands are beautiful but battered. Rough with red patches, swollen knuckles, and bits of color stuck under short, unpainted nails. But I can't ignore the way her skin seems thinner now, the veins on the back of her hand thicker. "We all have blue days. But, Rye, I know you. What's wrong?"

My throat closes, and I have to take a sip of tea. Warmth slides down my throat and floods my belly. Maybe there is something to the ritual of tea. Shaking my head, I stare down at the cup—a pretty little thing of hand-painted fuchsia flowers and gold edging. "You ever think of how it might be if you couldn't do your art?"

My mother is a world-famous artist, known for her enormous portraits and stylized urban landscapes. She spent her twenties and early thirties in obscurity. Then, when I was five, a local dealer featured her works. She took off, and our life went from quietly wealthy, due to Dad's work, to famously rich, with her doing portraits for royalty and movie stars. But Mom never changed. She is an artist obsessed with her work, through and through.

"Why would you..." She bites her lip as if to physically stop the question. Slowly, she sets her hands on the table and presses them against the wood. Her concerned gaze meets mine. "I'm trying to decide if you'd like the easy answer or the difficult one."

I huff a laugh. "You have to ask?"

A smile creases the corners of her eyes. "You always took the hard path." Lightly, she touches my forearm. The skin there is dark with intricate ink. Most of the tats were first drawn by her. Doodles I'd taken from pieces of paper she left around the house, sketches she did when she was with me. I put them on my skin to honor her, my family, my history.

She traces a hothouse lily in full bloom. "Well, my sweet son, the truth is, my art is the deepest expression of my soul. Without it, I think something inside me would wither and die."

Wither and die. It drops like a stone in my gut, and I swallow twice.

"Are you afraid of losing your music?" Mom asks softly. She's trying pretty damn hard not to show her horror, but I see it lurking in her eyes all the same.

Everything inside me clenches tight and churns. I wrap my sore hands around the teacup, but it's too tiny to provide much warmth. "I'm...I just..." I sit forward, wanting out, wanting to confess everything. "When Jax was sick and having a time of it, we all dissipated."

Mom nods, because she was there. She knows how much it affected me, all the times I came home to sprawl on her couches and read or listen to old music while she painted, anything to get away from the sorrow clogging my chest and eating at my skin.

"Your art," I continue through numb lips, "is solely yours. But I'm part of a group. A cog in a machine."

"You are not a cog!"

I smile weakly at her instant rise to defend her baby. "It's not a bad thing, Ma. I like being part of something." With a sigh, I rub my hair and try to ease the tension riding me. "But sometimes, I can't help thinking about the future. As much as I love my music, I can't picture hauling my seventy-year-old ass on stage like the Stones do."

"Hey!" Mom swats my arm. "Old people can kick ass too, you know."

"I don't mean it like that," I say, laughing. "Or maybe I do. It's exhausting, you know. Getting on that stage and doing what we do. I'm thirty-one in a few months, and already I find it draining."

Mom sniffs, slightly mollified.

"I don't want my entire existence to be dependent on my ability to make music." I lean in, gripping the edge of the table as her eyes widen. "And it is, right now. I either play or I'm...It's like I'm not truly here. I don't..."

Frustrated, I break off and rub my hands over my face.

"You've finally discovered you need more," Mom says.

Hunched over the table, I look at her with a helplessness that has my jaw clenching. But I nod. "When the stage lights go off, when the music stops, what am I? Where do I go?"

God, I hate this. I've been avoiding these very thoughts for years. They've built up like water against a dam, rising and rising. My body breaking down and weakening is the final straw. I can't hide anymore.

Mom sees it. She knows me too well. And her hand grabs mine again. Gently. Does she know I hurt? I don't ask; I can barely hold her gaze as it is.

"I know I said art was the expression of my soul." Mom shakes her head, a wrinkle forming between her brows. "But that's not the entire picture. Art, the soul, it needs to be fed. And I know you'll accuse me of being hokey..."

"Me? Never," I tease weakly.

"But love is what feeds me. Your father, you, the family—although not so much Uncle Jay and Aunt Lydia."

Her nose wrinkles, and I laugh. "Well, they're kind of assholes."

They are pious to the point of extremism and do not approve of Mom's art or my music. Fuck 'em. Mom and I share a look that says exactly that, and she grins before sobering.

"Are you lonely, Rye?"

Shit.

Releasing her hand, I sit back. "I don't know."

"It's okay if you are. There is nothing wrong in wanting to find someone to settle down with."

A choked laugh escapes. "Just the term 'settle down' gives me hives."

I know relationships can work. I also know that when they fail, they fail spectacularly.

Being my mother, she leans in and inspects my arm. "No hives here." She winks. "Stop being a male cliché, bitching about commitment. It's pedestrian."

I pinch the bridge of my nose. "Ma..."

"I'm serious. You need love. You always were a sensitive boy..."

"God."

"You've been part of your band for years. Now they're all pairing off. It's natural for you to want that too."

"Okay." I press my hands to the table and stand. "I'm leaving now. Good talk."

"Chicken shit." She says it with a gleam of evil humor in her eyes.

"Yes. Yes, I am."

I don't think it's unreasonable to be cautious with giving my heart away. I'm not unaware of the benefits. Hell, my friends have transformed in front of my eyes, becoming happy in a way I don't understand, content, satisfied. It can't be all bad. But I've seen the dark side too. I'd never say it, but some days I'm afraid for them. I don't think any of them would recover if their relationships soured.

As for myself, I don't know what would be worse. Turning into my mom and clinging to something toxic and ugly. Or my dad, unable to remain faithful but also unable to give up the safety of a sure thing.

Mom stands and gives me another surprisingly strong hug. I soak it in because I'm her boy, even though I give her lip, and I feel guilty for thinking of her as weak. She's not; she's merely human. Maybe that's the problem. We all think we'll act strong, do the right thing, but the reality of it is harder than it looks.

She leans back and cups my cheek. "I love you, Rye Bread. One day, someone else will love you too."

"You have to love me, Ma. I'm your son. Not everyone finds me as lovable."

A journo once called me Rye the Good-Time Guy. Like a ride in a carnival, I was good for some thrills and fun. I'd get you off, but too much of me would leave your head aching and stomach reeling. I probably shouldn't have slept with her and called it quits before she wrote the interview. Lesson learned and all that. But she wasn't entirely wrong. Everyone sees me that way.

Everyone, it seems, except my mother.

Shaking her head, Mom pats my cheek. "You're too smart to think something so stupid."

CHAPTER FIFTEEN

RYE

I'M FEELING SLIGHTLY low and morose when I get home, but I stop short at the sight greeting me in front of my apartment door. "Bren?"

She's bending down to set something on the floor but snaps upright and whirls around at the sound of my voice. "Oh, it's you."

"Well, I do live here." Shock has me staring. I've never found anyone at my doorstep before.

I live in the Dakota—a New York City icon. Each apartment is like a Gilded Age mansion in miniature. The condo board might be picky as fuck, but the natural light and feel of the space is incredible. Moreover, the gothic building has been home to Lauren Bacall, Judy Garland, and, most infamously, John Lennon. He was murdered outside its doors. It might sound morbid to some, but I choose to remember that he had a life here.

Every time I leave or return to the building, I send up a silent word of acknowledgment to John; I'm pretty sure everyone in the band does this when they visit me.

I'd ask Brenna how she got in, because security is tight, but I don't want to ruin the mystery. The main point is she's here. Here, at my house.

"When did you get back?" I ask, unable to stop staring at her like she's a mirage.

"An hour ago."

A pulse of surprise ripples over my skin. She just got in, and she came straight here.

She's fidgeting now, her legs blocking what she left at my door. I eye it—and, okay, her killer legs too—with interest. Those long legs just might be my undoing: sleek, toned, and lovingly showcased by her tight navy-blue skirt and dainty spiked pink heels. I want those heels digging into my back while I bury myself in her wet heat.

Reflexively, I clear my throat. "What were you doing?"

Brenna's cheeks darken, but she lifts her chin to counteract the blush. "You said you weren't feeling well."

Inwardly, I smile at the accusation in her voice. "I wasn't. I went for a walk to clear my head." I'm not about to admit to running home to Mom. Besides, I *did* walk those six blocks.

"Right." She nods briskly, awkwardly. "Good plan. Fresh air is good."

I have to bite my lip to keep from grinning. "It's the best."

Her eyes narrow at the amusement I've failed to hide.

"Well..." she says tightly. "You're obviously doing all right. I'll go."

"Hold on." I step into her path. "What did you bring me?"

Again, she flushes, her gaze sliding sideways as if she wants to be anywhere but here. But then she gathers herself and grabs her gift off the floor. "Here. It's...for you."

God, she's cute. I can't say that without risking a limb, but she *is,* damn it. Instead, I take what turns out to be a wicker basket by the handles.

"I figured that." I glance down at the gift. A stupid smile spreads wide across my face. "You brought me a goodie hamper?"

I'm fairly reeling. It's just so...cute.

Brenna's nose wrinkles as she visibly squirms in place. I know she wants to flee. Too bad. I'm not letting her get away now.

"There's tea," she says. "Coffee too. In case you're sick of tea. And those ginger biscuits and lemon curd that you seem to like... and, well, shit." She huffs out a laugh taut with embarrassment and gives me an accusatory glare. "It's supposed to make you feel better!"

With my free hand, I reach out and cup her neck to pull her close. "I'm feeling better already."

Then I kiss her.

It's meant to be something light, tender, grateful. Because I am grateful. But the instant my lips touch hers, it's like a shot of adrenaline, surging hot and pure and insistent. I duck my head to get closer; she tastes so good, her lips so soft and yielding that a bolt of lust shoots straight through me.

Her breath hitches, lips trembling against mine. I stumble with her toward the door, one hand grasping the silky cord of her ponytail, the other clutching her gift, our kiss going deeper, messier. She gasps into my mouth, a little puff of air that tickles my lips and inflames my need, and then her arms wrap around my neck, drawing me closer.

I approve. But it isn't enough. It's like I've been walking through the desert only to come upon her unexpectedly. Part of me wonders if she's real. But she is. I feel the difference in me already.

For the first time in days, I can breathe. It's unsettling to realize that the woman who has somehow become my air doesn't want to be, that she only needs me for quick physical comfort. Even so, I'm going to enjoy every second of her while I can.

"Four days, Bren." I lick her lower lip like candy. "Four fucking days away. That was not part of the deal."

She grasps my shirt, tugging, her sweet mouth just as greedy. "Stop lecturing me and get inside."

I smile against her lips. "Bossy."

Blindly, I fumble for my keys. It would go more smoothly if I stopped kissing her, but I can't. It takes me three tries to get the key in, all the while, she's sucking on my tongue, nibbling on my lips. I'm going to lose it.

The door finally opens, swinging wildly as we all but fall into the apartment with only my arm around her waist to keep her upright. I set the hamper on the floor—carefully, because it's her gift to me—and kick the door shut.

Then I'm kissing her again because, damn, she feels so good. She's pure adrenaline, delicious addiction. Sex and candy sliding over my tongue. We stumble along, tripping over some unseen obstacle near the doorway to my room.

"What was that?" she asks, words muffled by my mouth on hers.

"Books." I'm not exactly tidy, and I like to read. Teetering towers of books rise like stalagmites along the apartment floor.

Her chuckle is a delighted feminine purr that tickles my lips. Grinning, I wrap my arms around her slim waist and lift her over the spilled stack of books, backing us into a wall in my room because I need to brace myself before my knees give out.

I want her too much. She gets me too hot. Dragging my mouth away from the temptation of hers, I step back, draw in air. Doesn't work; my body throbs in one big pulse of lust.

Slow. I need to slow this down. Savor her.

Brenna leans against the wall, pink lipstick smudged over kiss-swollen lips, her hair mussed and her perky breasts rising and falling beneath a prim, white silk top. She stares back at me with a dare in her eyes, like she expects each of our encounters to be a tussle, a contest to see who comes out on top.

She doesn't realize she's already won. But I'm not going to disappoint her; I'll give her what she wants, then I'll show her that she's safe. Thinking about all the ways I'll show her has a grin spreading over my mouth.

Her eyes go wide, tender lips parting.

Yeah, honey, it's going to be like that.

And then I'm on her.

———

Brenna

I CAN'T BREATHE. Rye has taken all my air. I don't know how he does it; all I have to do is think about him and my body goes haywire. Down is up and wrong is right. It's unsettling to realize that the man I've spent my entire adult life trying to forget about has so much power over me. My body doesn't give a damn. It's humming with heat and need. I'm slick and hot between my legs, my breasts so sensitive, I feel the drag of silk over my bra with each panting breath I take in an attempt to draw in more air.

Rye looms over me, all hot, hard muscle and intensely focused gaze. He leans in, bracing his forearms on either side of my head—so close, but not close enough. I'm surrounded by his heat and strength, but not an inch of him is touching me.

Lines of strain creep out from the corners of his eyes and shadows lay in smudges beneath them, but a flush of exertion stains the crests of his cheeks. I want to trace that wash of dull red with my fingertips and find out if it feels as hot as it looks. He dips his head and fits his mouth over mine.

This kiss is unnervingly tender but so thorough and decadent, like he's drinking me in, that my knees go weak. God, he feels so good, I just want to open my mouth wider and lick into him, eat up every delicious inch.

He pulls back with a little suck to my lower lip. "You all good now?" His voice is darkly carnal as he nuzzles my mouth again. "Got everything sorted out in Atlanta?"

A shiver races up my thighs, my mind threatening to blank. I know exactly what he's really asking, and I give him the answer he deserves. "Yes."

Rye hums as though he doesn't quite believe me. He nips me again before kissing it better. "Good," he says, voice rough and impatient. "No more randomly disappearing on me?"

My hands slide up to his wide shoulders, and I feel the tremor in those packed muscles. It makes me smile a little, because he's clearly as affected as I am. "No more," I promise.

He gives me a hard, seeking kiss, and then he draws away just enough to meet my gaze. His is hazy with lust. It's a good look on him. He eyes my blouse, and my nipples tighten. The flush on his cheeks spreads to the bridge of his nose, and he bites his bottom lip.

"You attached to this shirt?" he asks almost idly, but I don't miss the way his body tenses, all those glorious muscles drawing up tight. "Or can I buy you another one?"

For a second, I blank, and then it hits me what he wants to do. Bright heat flows over me. Oh, shit. I want that. I want that so badly I can barely form the words. "Do it."

He holds my gaze, the intensity of his almost too much to bear as he reaches up and grasps the edges of my button-down blouse. I stare back at him as, with one efficient move, he rips the shirt wide open, little pearl buttons pinging around us like hail.

My breasts swell against the confinement of my bra, and I suck in a deep breath.

"Pink," Rye murmurs, running the blunt tip of his finger along the scalloped edge of lace. "Pretty. But I know something prettier."

A flick of his finger and the front clasp of my bra snaps open.

"There they are." He eases the cups aside to reveal my bare breasts. "Such pretty little cupcakes." Soft lips brush over my nipple, the tip of his tongue touching it. "So fucking sweet."

He licks me like a cat seeking cream. Once. Twice.

Biting my lip, I arch into the touch.

"You like that, Berry?" His voice is a dark rumble. He licks me again then grins when I whimper. "Good girl."

My stomach quivers, the bristles of his beard tickling my sensitive skin. He kisses the tip of my breast, just enough to make me want more.

"Rye," I whine. Yes, whine. I'm dissolving into need, and it's his fault.

"Be still," he says in that deep, stern tone, affection mixing with something sharper, possessive. "It's my turn now."

Understanding hits with a breath that leaves in a whoosh, and hot prickles race over my skin.

I don't want to be in charge. I want to be taken care of, let someone else take the lead.

You want me to take you in hand.

I'd asked for that. Wanted it in the quiet, needy corners of my soul.

At my silence, Rye looks up at me from under the thick fringe of his lashes. Slowly, while holding my gaze, his tongue slides over my hot nipple. I feel it between my legs, in the tight clench of my stomach. A whimper escapes, and he responds with a deep, sharp suck.

"Shit."

Rye chuckles in pure male satisfaction, releasing my nipple with a decadent pop. His lips touch my wet flesh. "Unzip your skirt."

Not a request.

I shouldn't like it. I *shouldn't*.

My hands tremble, fingers fumbling to comply.

He doesn't watch to see if I do. He's preoccupied with peppering light suckling kisses across my chest, seeking out my poor, neglected other nipple to torment. But the second the skirt slides to the floor to pool at my feet, he hums in satisfaction.

"Good, Bren. That's a good girl."

He kisses me soft and dirty, a lazy lick into my mouth, his thumbs gently rolling my stiff nipples. The combination has me mewling, arching my back to beg for more and harder. And he smiles against my lips, knowing exactly what he's doing to me and loving it. His mouth slides away, and I tilt my head to the side, panting and so hot I am heavy with it.

Hands kneading my breasts, he sinks to his knees, mouth mapping its way down my belly, over the flimsy line of my panties. He pauses between my legs, lips pressed to the wet silk that clings to my aroused flesh, and, oh, God, he inhales, like he's drawing me into his lungs.

A groan tears from him. "I needed this."

Fingers hook into my undies to drag them down my hips. Big hands bracket my thighs, spreading them wide to expose me to his view. Rye's lashes lower, a look of almost exquisite pain flashing across his face. "I needed this so much."

Then his mouth is on me. And I'm the one groaning, my body a live wire. I writhe against the cool, hard wall, my fingers scrambling to clutch at his hair so I can pull him closer, hold him to me.

Oral sex is a skill. Rye has skills. But that isn't what has me on fire, my body rushing toward an incandescent orgasm. It's his unfettered devotion to devouring me, as if I'm his last meal, his first.

When he grunts, a greedy, wet, selfish sound—mouth hot and seeking, fingers biting into my ass—I fall apart, melt right there at the edge of his room. But Rye doesn't let me go. He eases me through it, holds me steady. Hot blue eyes gaze up at me from between the pale columns of my trembling thighs. He nuzzles my swollen clit with the soft bristle of his beard, nibbles on the little aftershocks before all but purring against my sex.

Neither of us speaks for a long moment. Rye runs his hands up and down my legs, feeling their contours, trailing his fingers along the curves of my calves, the backs of my thighs. With a lingering squeeze, he rises.

"Let's get you comfortable, Berry." He tugs me into the shelter of his big body. "Because I'm not nearly done with you."

How had I managed this long without having this? How do I

go on when it's gone? For the first time in my sex life, I'm afraid. Not because I think Rye will hurt me; I trust him implicitly with my care. But because I've lost control.

Control has always been mine, no matter the partner, no matter the situation.

Rye is another story. Hell, he's a whole other genre.

I can't control Rye. I can't control my feelings when I'm with him. I'm on a Tilt-a-Whirl in the dark, terrified the harness might snap.

Rye steps to me, all hard focus and softly smiling mouth.

"I didn't come here for sex," I blurt out.

He pauses, head cocked, that small curve at the corners of his lips remaining. Calm blue eyes search my face, assessing. "Do you want to leave?"

Lord, but his voice is rich with arousal. He doesn't move but stands loose-limbed, a lovely flush of exertion on his cheeks. I want to trace my palms down the thick column of his neck where I know his skin will be like satin over steel. Do I want to leave?

"No."

"Hmm..." His voice dips with quiet amusement as he leans in. Smiling lips brush along the sweet spot under my ear, as those clever fingers ease the blouse and dangling bra from my shoulders. "Do you want a drink?"

He asks the question while taking my hand to help me step out of the pile of clothes surrounding my feet, leaving me in nothing but my petal pink Louboutins.

Rye's gaze slides over me like hot cream. "There you are. *God.* Look at you..." He licks his bottom lip, a man thirsty. "Damn, Bren, you blow my mind."

I've never felt more utterly exposed. I don't believe I'm perfect. But right now, under the admiration of his gaze, I feel close to it. My lips quirk as I rein in a smile and answer his previous question. "No drinks. I'm good."

"Yes, you fucking are." With surprising grace, he steps up

to me, sliding an arm loosely around my waist. His hand spreads wide over the small of my back, the other one clasping mine by his shoulder, and it's almost as though we're about to dance.

The pleasant rumble of his voice touches the shell of my ear. "We can read."

Light punctuated kisses follow a path down my neck, the soft bristles of his beard tickling. I tilt my head to the side with a smile, my eyes closing. "Maybe later."

Rye grumbles low within his wide chest. The tips of his fingers glide down my spine and over the curve of my butt. He draws an idle circle and nuzzles the hollow of my shoulder. I sway into him, my fingers threading through his hair.

Rye pauses, lips just touching my pulse point, hand roaming as though he can't stop feeling my skin. When he speaks, his voice pours out like tumbled rocks. "Do you want to fuck?"

My breath hitches, and I rest my lust-addled head on his broad shoulder. My lips find the tender spot on his neck, loving the way he shivers at the contact. Desire coils low in my belly. Do I want to fuck?

"Yes."

I love the way his big body seems to buckle, just for a beat. Then he grunts, a satisfied sound that sends a swoop of heat through me.

"Good. That was my preference too." He steps back, and with brisk movements, tugs his shirt off.

I don't think I'll ever be immune to the sight of Rye's naked chest and arms. He's too beautiful. Power and grace. The silver barbell piercings in his nipples wink in the lamplight, his pecs twitching as he tosses the shirt aside and then toes off his battered black Converse.

His worn jeans hang low on trim hips, highlighting the lovely valleys of taut external obliques that point to the rude bulge of his cock. I'm so distracted by that edible sight that I almost miss him turning to walk away.

"Where are you going?" I sound far too needy. His fault, though.

Rye pauses, a twinkle in his eyes as though he knows perfectly well what state he's brought me to. "Getting condoms. A stack."

Without thought, my hand whips out to grasp his wrist. He stills, brows lifting in question.

"Rye." I pause. Fingers press against the steady beat of his pulse. "Can we go without?"

His pulse kicks up, but he doesn't pull away. He steps closer. "You want me bare?"

I don't know why I do. It feels like another weakness, another crack. But I want something different with him, some small marker that says it's not just a fleeting arrangement. And I don't want to pause and think about logistics.

My voice isn't steady or very strong when I finally answer. "I want to get messy with you."

Rye's breath leaves in a chuff. His hand slides to the damp nape of my neck, and he rests his forehead against mine. "Oh, honey, we're going to get so messy."

I'm not certain either of us is referring to sex. Doesn't matter. He kisses me slow and seeking, drawing my tongue out to play with little licks and nips.

The roughened pads of his thumbs lightly caress my cheeks when he pulls back. "Turn around."

As though I'm a princess, he guides me to the end of his bed and then bends me over it. My fingers curl around the padded, gray linen footboard, a fierce blush burning my cheeks as I imagine the picture I make: buck-ass naked, legs elongated by my heels, the aroused pout of my sex peeking out like a taunt.

It turns me on so much, I'm surprised there isn't steam wafting off my damn skin. The sensation grows as Rye makes a noise of pure masculine appreciation. "Killing me here, Berry."

The feeling is mutual.

The sound of his zipper lowering sings through the close air and has me tensing in anticipation. I feel him behind me, a wall of heat and intention, but I nearly jump out of my skin when he finally touches me.

He palms my butt, massaging a bit as if to test the firmness. His long middle finger slips between my cheeks and finds the entrance to my ass, and I tense, a quivering mess, my entire attention focused on his touch. He presses there, not breaching, just making me feel it, before he slides away to caress the curve of my hip, back over my cheeks, the touch almost reverential.

"I want to spank this ass," he says idly, darkly.

A little shocked, I toss a look over my shoulder and find him staring back at me with hot eyes.

He rubs me gently. "I've always wanted to see your sweet ass ripple against my palm." A small quirk lifts his lips. "And I think you'll like it."

Cocky bastard.

Rye Peterson spanking me isn't something I thought I would ever allow. Not in my wildest dreams. The mere suggestion should set me off because no way should I be giving Rye that power. Never mind spanking is so not my kink.

And yet the way Rye looks at me with that impish glint in his eyes. The one that says, *Let's play.* The way he bites his lower lip as though he can't wait to take me in hand and give me pleasure...

God. A tremor goes up my thighs, and without another thought, I arch my back a little, lifting my butt into his touch. "Do it."

Rye is a bassist; his hands are, quite frankly, huge. And strong. He knows his strength. He knows how to use those clever hands. A slap rings out, the contact sending prickling sparks of sensation over my ass, between my thighs. Everywhere.

I let out a harsh breath, my head falling forward as I lick my lips. "Shit."

"Okay?"

My breath grows short, the tingling heat on my ass glowing. "That shouldn't feel so good."

"But it does." Not a question. Even so, his warm, questing hand goes still. Waiting.

"Yes. Yes, it fucking does."

Rye makes a noise of amusement. "Beautiful," he murmurs, palming me.

Then he spanks me again, a firm but easy slap. I groan, my body jolting with sensation.

Why does it feel so good? How did he know?

Unnerved, I shoot him another look. "I'm going to return the favor later."

His answering smile is dark sin. "I'm looking forward to it."

One more slap and my knees are wobbling. Rye smooths his hand over my hot flesh before dipping between my legs. His finger slides around my messy sex in an indolent circle. "Look at you, all hot and slippery for me."

He spanks me again. Right on my clit.

I jerk in surprise and pleasure. Because it felt insanely good, that slap. I want it again and again. I don't understand it and try to cover my confusion. "You're pushing it, buttercup."

But there's no conviction in my voice, and he chuckles, pleased as punch with himself. I can't exactly blame him for that. He's playing me like a well-loved song. I tense, anticipating another teasing spank, but Rye doesn't do that.

His big hands settle on my ass and glide up my back. It feels so good, so wonderfully tender, that ripples of sweet pleasure run over my body. Slowly he rubs me, along my sides, over my aching breasts. I fight a sob. I hadn't truly realized how much I needed someone—*him*—to simply stroke my skin. To just touch me.

But he knew. Somehow, he knew. And it devastates me.

Unbidden, a memory rises, of me sitting in a booth, tense and fractious as I confess to Jules.

It isn't the same as feeling someone else's hands on my body, not knowing exactly where they'll touch me next or how.

For a second, I can't draw a breath, and then it returns with a rush of aching affection. He's giving me what I yearned for. My throat closes in on me, and I swallow thickly, the fine weave of his flannel bedding blurring before my eyes.

"Rye." It comes out broken.

He makes a soft noise of acknowledgment, smoothing his hand over the crown of my head and down the long length of my ponytail. Shivers flow over my scalp. He was right; I love having my hair stroked. My lashes flutter. Without warning, he coils the length of my hair around his fist and tugs. Not hard, but enough to fucking rein me in.

My eyes snap open, a gasp escaping me.

"Easy, sweetness." Rye steps closer, and the thick slab of his cock lies heavy on my ass.

Heart thudding, muscles trembling, I blink down at the covers. With one hand, he moves his hard dick along my sex, the thick length sliding over my tender slickness.

The wide head of his cock pauses at my opening, notching just inside. Rye bends over me, blanketing my body with his heat. "You ready for me, Bren?"

I feel him there, searing hot against my sex, spreading me wide to accept him. Just the tip. Just that alone is so good I have to brace myself against the urge to whimper and whine, to push back against him, make him sink into me.

Despite my disquiet and the fact that I'm teetering on the edge, a smile breaks free. And I find my voice, strong and sure. "Fuck me, Rye."

His grip on my hair twitches, but he doesn't move. "Tell me one thing first." Soft lips touch the shell of my ear, his voice dark and resonant. "Who's your Daddy?"

Shock explodes over my skin in a wave of heat. My knees buckle. A breath escapes me—half startled laugh, half groan. Sweet hell, I'm so hot, I can barely breathe. My response is thready, needy. "You. Only you."

He tenses. I'm not sure which one of us is more shocked I

capitulated. But then he's pushing in—slow, steady, making me feel every inch he gains. I'm stretched, filled, taken.

We both pause, him deep within the clasp of my sex. Rye makes a noise that sounds almost pained. He mutters something unintelligible under his breath. And then he moves, rolling his hips in a lazy rhythm.

I can't see him. He has me where he wants me, one hand fisting my ponytail, the other gripping my ass. But I can picture him, the way he is on stage, feet planted, massive thighs bulging as he thrusts his hips, thick-cut arms and muscle-packed chest flexing as he plays.

He feels so good, the push-pull of him, the smooth glide and hard impact. Liquid heat flows through my limbs, my nipples tighten and ache, my clit throbs. As if he knows these pleasure points need attention, Rye grunts, and, with one simple move, tugs me up against the sweat-slicked wall of his chest.

He finds my nipple and tweaks it, while his other hand slides between my legs. I moan as he thrusts up into me, fingers strumming a beat on my sensitive flesh.

"Fuck, Bren," he rasps, his lips at my cheek.

I turn my head, find his mouth with mine. Rye groans, his grip on me tightening. My hands slip behind him to cup his ass—that perfect flexing ass—and he grunts, pumps harder.

We stay like that, locked together, moving in perfect rhythm, everything coiling tighter, getting a little more desperate. Rye moans, thrusts going deep like punctuation.

"Beethoven." The husky whisper escapes his lips. I falter, tripped up by the odd non sequitur. Our gazes collide, his widening.

Fingers still clutching his sweat-slicked ass, I pause, panting. "Beethoven?"

Because there's no denying what he said. Rye's lips twitch. "I'm trying not to come."

We're still moving, slowly fucking, as if both of us are unable to fully stop. And it feels so good, that big, thick dick shoving inside me, that my lashes flutter before I lick my lips and speak. "And Beethoven stops that?"

A wry half smile tilts his lips. "Listing composers in my head helps." His hand slides up my belly. We share the same breath as he pumps into me, and his voice grows rough. "It's barely working. You feel too damn good, Bren. I'm hanging on by a thread."

He sounds so disgruntled by his lack of control that I kiss him softly. "Maybe you should try humming his Fifth Symphony."

There's a pause. Rye stares at me as if he's trying to figure out if I'm being snarky, then his face lights up, a smile pulling wide. Something impish glints in his eyes. In a blink, he pulls out and flips me onto the bed, flat on my back. I yelp in surprise. Then Rye is over me, pushing inside with a sure thrust. A laugh breaks free from me when he starts humming the Fifth.

Then we're both laughing. Fucking and laughing. Rye's strong body bracketing mine, his face burrowed in my neck. God, it lights me up, laughing with him. I breathe him in, soak up his heat, his strength. I never want to leave this moment; I want to live right here in this bubbling contentment of sex and joy.

His deep chuckle reverberates through my bones. Soft lips brush over my pulse and press there like a statement, telling me he's right here with me in this joy. And like that, everything turns unexpectedly tender. It catches us unaware, and Rye's grip changes, deepening with intent. Something in the way he moves makes me melt. There's no other word for this liquid wash of pleasure and heat, or how my body wants to meld with his until there's no space left between us.

I don't know how we go on like this. I can't think straight. There is only him and the need for more. Always more. And maybe I sigh the word. Or maybe he simply feels it.

Rye turns his head slightly, and our gazes tangle.

I'm not prepared.

I never put much stock into the whole idea that gazing into

someone's eyes could truly affect a person. But it does. Those dusky blue eyes reach into me and tug something free.

Without my permission, without warning, I'm coming in long, rolling waves that have me whimpering. He doesn't look away, doesn't stop moving within me.

"Bren." His voice breaks on my name. Then he shudders, quietly coming in the same gasping, wide-eyed way. He clings to me, so much strength, but weakness too, as if I'm taking him apart and he trusts me to put him back together.

The tips of my fingers dig into the hard curve of his butt as we tremble and pant, both of us incapable of more than a few small jerks of the hips before he sags against me, totally spent. Rye lowers his forehead to my temple and exhales in a gusty sigh.

The sound brings a smile to my lips, and I cup the back of his head in a half hug. For a beat of breath, he seems to lean into my touch, but then a new tension takes over his body, as though he's afraid to move any farther and break the spell. But it's already broken because we're both aware now.

Carefully, like he's afraid he might accidentally crush me, Rye eases back just enough to slip free from my body. I miss the fullness of him immediately. He curls up at my side, one long, thick leg lying heavily between mine, a warm hand on my hip.

For a long moment, neither of us says a word. But it's in the air, hovering like a dark cloud: how I'd pushed him out last time, how he'd easily left. I don't know what to do. Should I act as before? Get up and get dressed? For all my fears, I know with certainty that I don't want to go. But what does he expect?

In the heavy silence, Rye's gaze searches mine. His expression gives nothing away. I stare back at him, trying to keep my cool. Then he lifts his hand to gently stroke my damp hair back from my face.

"Stay," he says.

Want tightens my stomach. "I should probably get back to work."

I don't sound too convincing. Something Rye immediately capitalizes on.

His words tumble out, tripping over themselves. "You shouldn't leave with only two orgasms. I can give you more. Or we don't have to fool around. I did promise you a foot rub."

I can't stop myself from tracing the strong line of his brow or cupping his cheek where his beard is springy. His eyes close as if by reflex, but he forces them open and watches me.

"You did promise me that," I say, my voice embarrassingly husky.

A smile lights his eyes. "And there are all those cookies and tea you brought."

I laugh softly. "You're going to make me tea?"

"Sure," he murmurs, his lids lowering. "I'll make you anything you want." But he doesn't get up. He gently nudges my legs farther apart before easing over me and making space for himself. His body is still hot. His dick is hard again, a meaty weight on my inner thigh.

Rye gives me a lazy kiss, slowly delving into my mouth. It steals my breath. Like that, I'm melting again. "You sore?" he whispers.

I am. Wonderfully, achingly sore. Doesn't stop me from flushing hot as he cants his hips and slides his hardness higher. Humming, I rock my swollen clit against his cock just enough to send a tremor through me. "I feel empty."

"Yeah?" His lips part mine, just a little, a soft, suckling kiss. "Can I fuck you again? Nice and slow. I'll be gentle, Bren. So gentle."

The wide tip of his cock is at my entrance, not pushing in, but hot and hard and waiting. I spread my thighs wider, meet his gaze and hold it. "Okay, but I still want that foot rub."

His smile is instant and downright dirty with promise as he pushes slowly, oh, so slowly into my slick, sensitized sex. We both shiver, and his voice comes out like rough sand. "Anything, Berry. Anything."

CHAPTER SIXTEEN

RYE

THE THING about making a deal with the devil is that it's always for something you want so desperately you pretend the inevitable suffering will be worth it. You make a little deal with yourself first, that you'll able to handle anything thrown your way.

I shouldn't liken Brenna to the devil. She's not the one who came up with this deal. I did. I guess that makes me the devil here. Whatever the case, it's becoming harder to pretend I'm fine with things as they are.

Don't get me wrong, I'm mostly in heaven. Because getting to touch Brenna, to see her laugh, to make her moan and sigh, is heaven.

We have fallen into a pattern. We go about our days avoiding each other—or at least I try my best not to text or call her—and then we meet up at night and go at each other like sex-starved animals. Or rather, every Tuesday, Thursday, and Saturday night. Brenna insists on keeping to the three-nights-a-week rule.

And that? Yeah, that is hell.

I don't understand it. I was perfectly fine in a no-sex-with-Brenna world. Not happy, exactly. Who is fully happy with every aspect of their lives? But I was fine. I'd live my days and nights without this fucking clawing need to see her, to breathe the same air. Now, I'm a damn wreck on our off days. I walk around like a zombie, not knowing what to do with myself. A permanent ache has taken up residence in my chest, and my skin feels both too cold and too tight.

That's bad enough. But not as bad as having to publicly pretend that we're still at odds with each other. That I don't care about her.

Every time we are together with any of our friends, it gets worse. Maybe it's just me, but it feels like there's a spotlight on our shoulders now.

Killian slides me another sidelong look, and I hold his gaze. "What?"

He shrugs. "I thought you said you were sick of tea."

At my side, Brenna pulls in a short breath, but otherwise she's completely cool. I, on the other hand, get hot under my shirt, remembering the last time Brenna and I had tea and how that ended with me slowly fucking her for hours.

I level Killian a look. "Then why did you invite me?"

With another shrug, Killian reaches for a macaroon. "I invite everyone. You've never accepted before."

Killian, Brenna, and I are at a small shop that offers high tea every afternoon. I know for a fact that Killian and Brenna like it here because it reminds them of England. Jax and Scottie will join in on occasion. And, yes, upon reflection, it does look weird that I'm here. High tea is not my thing. But it's Monday, and I suffered through not seeing Brenna on Sunday, so I decided to show up.

I'm regretting that. I thought more people would be here. I thought I'd have a bigger buffer between me and Killian's watchful eyes. As it is, he's suspicious, and Brenna's tense as hell.

"I wanted to see what the fuss was all about." I pop a tiny

goat cheese tart in my mouth and munch on it. The food is surprisingly good, and I guess it's filling—if you're a Smurf. "I like it."

Brenna snorts into her teacup. "Oh, come on. You hate it."

"I do not." I grab another tart. "It's...tasty. And there's a lot of variety."

Killian grins. "You make a face every time you pick something up."

"I'm squinting because they're hard to see."

Brenna shakes her head. "Why don't you order a sandwich? I hear they do a mean roast beef."

"I do love roast beef. It's my favorite."

"I know." It's a clear slip of the tongue, and she hides it by helping herself to a slice of lemon cake. But I heard it loud and clear.

She knows my favorite sandwich. Why shouldn't she? We all know one another inside and out. Still, it throws me for a loop. I never thought she paid any real attention to what I was doing over the years. Her style has always been to ignore me as though I'm a blight in the room. At least that's what I thought.

Not looking her way, I grab a scone and eat it.

Brenna makes a pained noise. "You're supposed to break off bites and put them in your mouth one at a time, Ryland."

I love when she says my full name like she's a harried schoolmarm. I swallow down my scone before answering. "That *was* a mouthful."

Her nose wrinkles, as her eyes light with amusement. "You eat like a pig."

"I concede that I can be messy, but that's only because I thoroughly enjoy eating."

Pink washes over her cheeks, and she shoots me a pointed look. I deserve it; I wasn't exactly subtle.

Killian snorts and shakes his head. "Dude, you should know better than to try sex jokes with Brenna. She has no sense of humor for them."

Brenna's spine straightens. "Excuse me? I am not a prude."

"You are with us. At least when it comes to that," he says with a shrug. "You hate it when we talk about sex in front of you." Stupid man. Does he not know his cousin at all?

Brenna nods as if in understanding. "Ah. I see. So you'd like to hear about the last time a man made a meal of me? Because I must say, he completely devoured me, and it was indeed messy."

Oh, hell.

Instantly, my mind flashes to the image of me kneeling on the floor between her spread thighs as I *devoured* her. My cock pushes insistently against my jeans. Despite my discomfort, I grin wide.

Not that Killian notices. He's twisting his lips in a grimace. "Hell, Bren. You're putting me off my tea."

"Am I?" She shrugs delicately. "Funny, I find my appetite increasing."

I can't help it. I pick up a scone. "You want one with clotted cream?"

She catches my gaze and grins. "Yes, please."

We both snicker as Killian throws his napkin on the table with a huff. "Fucking hell. I cannot handle it if you two finally start working together to piss me off."

Brenna's laughter dies a swift death, which kills mine too. Because she looks horrified that Killian might actually be thinking of us in terms of allies. I don't know what to say, but it isn't a great feeling. It's far too close to actual rejection.

I fake a casual shrug and smear a big dollop of cream on the scone. "It's easy enough pissing you off on my own." Calmly I set the scone on Brenna's plate.

"Thank you," she murmurs.

Then the unexpected happens: her fingers drift over my thigh under the table. The touch is fleeting yet distinct. My heart thumps hard in my chest. I'm so aware of her at this point that every time she moves, I catch the scent of her skin and hear the soft hitches in her breath.

Today, her fragrance smells of hot buttered cinnamon-sugar toast and strawberry jam. It makes me want to bury my nose in the crook of her neck and hold her forever.

Unable to help myself, I slowly move my hand up to the back of her chair, hidden from Killian's watchful gaze. The sleek tip of her long ponytail tickles the tops of my fingers. Blandly reaching for another scone with my free hand, I use the moment to trail my fingers along the length of her ponytail.

She shivers delicately, and the downy hairs along the edge of her neck lift. Immediately, I get fully and achingly hard. I want to wrap my fist around that silken length of hair and hold on tight, work my hard cock into her tight, slick heat. I want to pleasure her body, watch her lips part and sigh my name.

As if she knows the direction of my thoughts, Brenna keeps her gaze firmly away from me. "Have you had enough of my sex talk?" she asks Killian.

"Totally," he answers far too easily. Then he grins evilly. "Did I ever tell you about Libby's favorite—"

"Keep going," Brenna cuts in. "I'm certain Libby will want to hear all about you describing her sex life to me."

That shuts him up in a hurry. He hunches over his tea with a surly frown. "It's no fun when you call my bluff."

I chuckle. "She's got your number, man."

He slides me a look filled with aggravation but then smiles. "Always has." Lightning fast, he reaches out and musses Brenna's hair, laughing when she squawks and swats him away. "Aw, come on, cuz, don't be like that."

"Ass," she says, smoothing her hair. But there's a glint of amusement in her eyes.

It hits me how close they are. Sometimes I forget about their connection. Mainly because we're all so close. But as I am currently sneaking around and doing dirty things to Killian's cousin, whom he thinks of as a sister, I'm suddenly feeling a twinge of uncomfortable guilt. Not because I think I need permission from Killian or anything; Brenna is her own person. But I'm lying to him, and he cares deeply about her.

Truth is, I don't like lying to any of them.

Killian takes another sip of tea. "You know I actually invited you—not you"—he glances at me before returning to Brenna—"for a reason."

"Hey," I protest.

Killian's expression turns quelling. "Dude, you couldn't be bothered to show up for the last two band meetings, and you're acting outraged because I didn't expect you here?"

A thick, ugly blackness threatens to close down my throat. I swallow past it. "I told you, I had a headache."

"Twice in one week?" His snort is dubious and annoyed. "And yet you're here now. For the food."

Heat invades my face. Brenna stares at me with a frown, but she doesn't say a word. I've told her I have headaches. I've told them all. Evidently, that's not going to fly. Even so, his implication that I care more about food than I do about the band sets my teeth on edge.

I lean forward, pinning him with a glare. "I didn't say one fucking word when you went AWOL for an entire summer, drinking your ass off and dicking around. Not one fucking word."

Killian hisses, but I speak over him. "Because I knew you needed to tap out for a while. Life is sloppy. Sometimes people can't show. Now, are you going to give me the same courtesy I gave you or pull some diva rock star bullshit?"

Anger sparks in his eyes, and I know he's about to blow. Good. I need to work off my own steam at this point. But then a cool, smooth hand lands on my forearm. I glance down to find Brenna is holding on to both my arm and Killian's.

"Cool it," she says briskly. "You guys hate fighting and will regret what you've said later."

"Call me a diva again and— Ow! Shit, Bren!" Killian rubs his arm where she knuckle-punched it.

"You were being a dick to Rye," she says, shocking the shit out of me and Killian, who gapes. Brenna's gaze narrows on him. "You were. We don't rag on each other for having off days."

Now I feel like an ass. Because there are no headaches. The urge to hide my hands under the table is both childish and ridiculous. I need to confess to the guys at some point, and I'm being a coward about it.

A mulish frown twists Killian's lips, but he nods. "Sorry," he says shortly. "I didn't mean it that way."

Given that I hate apologies even more than I hate fighting with my friends, I can only nod back. "From now on, I'll only call you a diva if you start whining about venues not providing your favorite bottled water."

He grumbles, clearly ready to complain, but Brenna hoots out a laugh. "Yes, thank you! So sick of that. It's just water, dude."

Her smile, aimed at me, is brilliant and impish. And it renders me temporarily speechless, my bones humming as if struck by a tuning fork. She's smiling at me. In public.

It is a small sun upon my skin. The warmth slides right into my chest and fills it up. I should make some joke, say something about Killian's weird water preferences. But I only want to say the truth: I want her. I'm here because I can't stay away.

As if she can see it, her amber eyes darken, and a stillness settles over her. My want of her is a thick cord, pulling tight and vibrating between us. Killian slices right through it with an annoyed noise. "Seriously. You two need to stop ganging up on me. It's unnatural."

I raise my brow. "Unnatural."

"Yeah. As in, you're not supposed to be on the same side." He wrinkles his nose in disgust. "As in, you're oil, and she's water, and never the two shall blend."

The wrongness of his statement scrapes against my nerves. And maybe Brenna can tell I'm about to snap, because her hand finds my knee under the table. Another fleeting touch.

"No need to be terrified," she says to Killian with an eye roll. "Rye and I will be back to tearing out each other's throats soon enough."

No. No. No. I don't want to be shoved in that box again. Never again.

"Now, you were saying something about why you asked me here?" she prompts.

Killian pauses as though he wants to keep complaining about me getting along with Brenna. But then he shakes it off with a roll of his shoulders and slouches in his chair.

"Got a call from dear old dad. His sixtieth is coming up in December." Killian runs a hand through his hair. "He's having a big bash and expects all the family to go."

Brenna winces. "Shit."

"You don't like your uncle?" I ask, because I'd never seen her be anything but nice to Killian's dad.

"I love Uncle Xander." She shares a look with Killian. "My father, on the other hand..."

"They rub together like two junkyard dogs," Killian says grimly. "Can't stand each other, which makes Dad's insistence on Neil coming so..."

"Weird?" Brenna supplies.

"Annoying," Killian says.

Brenna glances my way. "My dad is jealous of Uncle Xander."

"Why?"

Her lashes lower, and she's suddenly interested in tracing the flower pattern on the teacup. "Xander was a billionaire by the time he turned forty-five. Whether my dad admits it or not, it chafes. We moved to the States when I was a baby. As I understand it, Dad did so to get as far away from Uncle Xander as he could. But distance doesn't matter; he's always resented Uncle Xander for having what he doesn't."

"Ah."

"The band is invited too," Killian says offhandedly. "Just thought I'd break the news to Bren first."

"You know I'll go," I tell him, wanting to make it clear I have his back. We might get pissy at each other now and then, but Killian is my boy. I'm always going to be there for him when he needs it.

He gives me a quick look of gratitude, but I don't miss the way Brenna's face tightens. I can't tell if she's displeased that I'm going or simply still upset about the situation in general.

"Well," she says, trying to brighten. "I'll be there. Even if my parents decline. Honestly, I hope they do."

"Not gonna lie," Killian says. "I'm kind of hoping the same."

"Are they that bad?" I ask them, worrying for Bren.

"They stress me out," she says. "And when they're around the rest of the family, it gets awkward."

Funny thing is, I have never met Brenna's parents. How can that be? How did I not realize this before? And I get a bad feeling there's a reason for this that I won't like.

"When is the last time you saw them?" I ask Brenna.

Her nose wrinkles. "A few years ago. They aren't really...social."

Call me paranoid, but it sounds like she means they're dick-heads to her. The urge—the need—to gather her up in a secure hug is nearly overwhelming. I fist my hands in my lap. It's been too long since I've touched her. A day and a half. I miss the feel of her. I miss her taste, her sounds, her breathy laughter when I'm giving her pleasure. According to our agreement, I'm supposed to go about my day after this and not visit her until tomorrow. I can't take another night of waiting.

But I ignore all that and focus on the sadness she can't quite hide.

"They're dicks to you?" I find myself asking. Then I wince, because I really need to think before I speak; she shouldn't have it rubbed in her face.

But she doesn't flinch. Her slim fingers wrap around her teacup, and she meets my eyes. "When I told them I wasn't going to college, but planned to join you guys and help out the band, my parents said it was probably a good idea, given that I wasn't very intelligent and that, by hitching my ride to Killian's talent, at least I'd get somewhere in life."

For a second, I can only blink, numb with shock. Then a slow boil starts up in my gut. By the expression on Killian's face, this is old news to him, but it still hasn't dulled his rage. We share a look that says only too clearly how much we'd like to personally respond to Brenna's crap parents.

I clear my throat of the rage clogging it. "You're the smartest person I know, Bren. And if they can't see that, then they're ignorant fucks."

Her lips quirk, and she glances down at her cup. "Thank you. And believe me, I knew they were full of it, even back then. But it was still...unpleasant to hear."

"Of course it was." Damn it, I want to hug her so badly, it's physically painful to refrain. My hands press into my thighs in agitation.

"If they decide to attend," Killian says in a hard tone, "we'll all run interference, Brenna Bean."

She gives him a slight nudge with her elbow in gratitude. "You don't have to. I'm capable of handling them."

"I know," he says. "You're so capable, it scares me a little. Doesn't mean you have to deal with that crap alone. Because you're not."

They share a look that speaks of a lifetime of watching out for each other. And while I'm so damn glad she's had Killian watching her back, I suddenly feel all the years of being on the outside of her life, looking in. I'm still not fully in her life. My chest clenches, and I resist the urge to rub it.

Killian glances at his watch. "Shit, I've got to go."

That's my cue to go as well. I could stick around, wait for him to leave, but Brenna won't like that. She'll worry Killian would suspect something. Maybe he would. I don't care, but I slowly stand—for her, I'll play this part.

"I'm heading out too." It's pouring rain now, pelting against the glass front of the tea house. I could use a good dousing.

Killian gives Brenna a quick kiss on the cheek then flicks down a wad of cash before Brenna and I can pay. "You need a ride?" he asks her.

"No, I'm good. I'm going to return a few emails before calling a car."

She pointedly doesn't look my way. Fine, then. Message received.

I grab a square of lemon cake for the road.

Killian glances at the window and then back to me. "You want a ride?"

"Nah. There's a shop next door I'm going to." Lie. But I'm getting pretty good at it and made note of the bookstore when I'd arrived. Just in case. I give Brenna a nod. "A pleasure as always, Berry."

"Rye."

That's it. That's all I get. It's part of our act. Doesn't stop the oppressive heaviness that settles on my chest. I take a breath and push out into the rain. I'm instantly soaked and cold to the bone.

———

Brenna

ALONE. Finally.

Even though the shop still hums with conversation and the soft clinks of silverware against china, it's wonderfully quiet at my table. A nice little cocoon of silence.

I pour the remaining dregs of tea into my cup and take a sip. It's gone cold and bitter, but I don't care. I need to do something with my jittery hands.

Shit. I don't want to deal with my parents. I really don't want to deal with them in front of my friends. The potential for humiliation is too great. Not when they try their best to make all those around them equally unhappy, and I am one of their favorite targets. In their eyes, I am a traitor. I went off with spoiled, rich Killian and turned my back on them. I shouldn't let it bother me. Yet one snidely spoken comment from my father and I'm decimated, uncertain, and embarrassed to live within my own skin. I loathe how family can do that to me.

I hate feeling weak, feeling less than. I hate that this insecurity has affected every aspect of my life when I've worked so hard to be strong, independent.

After finishing off the tea, I set the cup down with more force than necessary and collect my stuff. It's still pouring, and I call a car from the service we keep on staff. But my mind drifts to Rye. He surprised me by showing up here.

I can barely look at him when our friends are around now. I'm convinced they'll see everything on my face, the need to touch him, the way my eyes linger on his face, his arms, his broad shoulders. The scent of him, crisply spicy, deeply masculine, is still in the air around me, and all I want to do is breathe it in.

Our official sex-up day is tomorrow. It feels like a year from now. I wanted to leave with him, ask him to take me away somewhere—his bed, mine, didn't matter. Just take me away and make me feel good. Make me feel something other than the gnawing sadness and disappointment that talk of my family churns up.

I'm becoming too attached already. I resent the days we're forced to stay apart. They're a punishment, something I have to grit my teeth and bear.

In other words, it's all a mess now. Killian is clearly suspicious. The fact is, Rye and I are getting along too well for any of our friends not to notice. That they expect us to remain as we were, always at odds, always fighting, irritates me. Are Rye and I not allowed to grow?

Either way, it's a good indication of how they'd react if they found out what we're doing. Which is to say: they'd want to discuss and dissect every angle. They'd either proclaim us married by the end of the year or broken up by Sunday. A cold sweat breaks out at just the thought of them converging on us. No, it's none of their business, and I plan to keep it that way.

Maybe I should feel cheap or small for turning to Rye for physical gratification, but I don't. For the first time in years, I feel...well, not safe...but excited. Life was starting to lose its color, its immediacy. Rye gives that back to me.

God, but he's going to be there for this horrible family reunion party. He'll see my parents in action. He'll see how Uncle Xander treats me like a beloved daughter, while my own dad will do his best to belittle me. He won't miss the way my mother questions my profession, my life choices. And he'll be there with Aunt Isabella...Queasiness runs greasy fingers through my belly. I don't know if I can handle all that heaped on me in one go.

My parents aren't happy people. Never have been—at least as long as I've been around. Thing is, as far as I can tell, they used to be. Before they met each other, that is.

Knowing my mom as I do now, it's hard to imagine, but she worked as a model throughout her teens and early twenties. She never reached the superstar fame of Killian's mom, Isabella; her career mostly focused on runway and catalog work. Even so, she met Isabella during Fashion Week, and they became friends. Enough that she was a bridesmaid at Isabella and Xander's wedding. She took one look at the groom's younger brother, Neil, and that was it for both of them. Instant attraction, the sort of high octane lust that burned hot and bright—and fast.

My parents lost themselves in each other, marrying within a month. Less than a year later, their attraction died a swift death, and they realized they didn't actually like each other as people. Only it was too late; mom was pregnant with me, and neither of them wanted to admit their mistake.

It didn't help that, while Isabella and Xander's careers went supersonic, my parents' careers fizzled. Dad kept betting on the wrong investments, the wrong clients, and mom couldn't secure any more bookings. All they were left with was a little girl neither of them seemed to know what to do with, a small house on Long Island, and a mutual loathing that oddly fueled them. They might have divorced but instead they clung to each other in their misery. And they took me along for the ride. My entire childhood was one long reminder that any misstep or wrong decision I made could result in catastrophe. Work hard but don't dream big. Dreams easily died in the face of reality.

"Best you learn now, Brenna," my father had said in a tone that held years of weariness and failure. "You will never be more than a footnote in those boys' lives. They keep you around because you're cheap labor, not because you're of any real value. Don't waste another year on them. Go to school and live an ordinary life like the rest of us."

As much as I've tried to push those ugly words out of my mind, they had become stuck like tar to my insides, a burning weight. I constantly fight an ugly whisper that asked, what if my parents were right? What if I'll never be more than someone the guys can easily replace?

With a sigh, I roll my stiff shoulders and watch the window for my car. It pulls up, and I head out. I don't have an umbrella, and ice-cold water pounds on my head as soon as I step outside. Today is gearing up to be an utterly shit day. Shivering, I huddle deeper into the collar of my sweater and pick up the pace.

"Bren."

Rye's voice, clear and firm over the downpour, has me halting in my tracks. I turn to find him standing off to the side, soaking wet. It's a good look on him. The front of his white Henley is so wet, it's translucent, showing off the swells of his firm pecs and the hard, little points of his nipples. He must be freezing, but he doesn't move, just stares at me with an imploring look in his eyes.

"What are you doing out here?" I ask over the rain.

He steps close. "Waiting for you."

Heat flares through my numb limbs, waking them up. I bridge the gap between us. "Waiting for me?"

It's a stupid thing to repeat. He was perfectly clear. But I can't help it. No one has ever waited for me.

His hand slowly rises, and he touches a raindrop trickling down my cheek. "I came here for you. Of course, I'm going to wait."

Before I can answer, he puffs out a harsh breath, like he's been holding it in until now, and pulls me into his warmth. He kisses me as though I'm dessert, hungry lips and seeking tongue. Right there on the sidewalk in the pouring rain. And I forget about everything else. Here is where I need to be. I'm no longer empty or listless. I'm alive. My senses fire with hot sparks that crackle along my skin.

I stretch up on my toes to reach him, taste more, feel the strength of his big body against mine.

His skin is cold and wet; his mouth is hot and slick. He fists the back of my sweater, holding me tight. Oh, but his mouth is so soft. Soft and seeking. Decadent.

How does he do this? How does he take me apart with just a kiss? I'm grasping at the back of his neck with cold fingers, all but grinding myself against him. I slide my tongue along his with a heady sigh.

Rye grunts low within his chest, comes at me from one direction, then another, reacquainting himself with all the sensitive spaces of my mouth. I'm dissolving like a sugar cube in hot tea. He tastes of lemon cake and dark nights, and all I want to do is get lost in his flavor.

A loud wolf whistle cuts through the haze enough that we pause, our lips grazing. Held in his arms, I stare up at him. I can't think straight.

Rules. There were rules, weren't there? "Our day isn't until tomorrow."

Rain drips from the ends of his hair, now the color of old bronze coins. His lashes are spiked with wetness, shading his urgent gaze. "We said we could have other days if needed." His grip tightens on my sweater. "And, Bren, I fucking need."

I sway, stopping just short of falling into him again. From behind me comes the two short taps of the horn, and I know it's my driver. The service is well paid to wait, but this is New York in a rainstorm. The driver can't idle forever.

I turn to acknowledge him with a nod but don't let Rye go. My hand slips to the side of his neck where his pulse hammers hard and fast. "Come on, then."

With a flare of his nostrils, he nods and then follows me into the car.

CHAPTER SEVENTEEN

BRENNA

"DON'T TAKE this the wrong way," Rye says. "But you have a shit-ton of products."

He's sitting on the scroll-arm bench before the makeup table in my bathroom, picking his way through my things. Wrapped in a white terry cloth hotel robe I nicked years back that barely fits his big frame, he's a bit like the proverbial bull in the china shop. But his long fingers have the delicate dexterity of a musical artist as he lifts up a perfume bottle and takes an investigative sniff. "Smells better on your skin."

I pause in the act of brushing out my hair and watch him with a small smile. His interest in my things is cute and sends a wash of contentment and peace through me.

We'd screwed our way through my apartment, starting in my foyer when neither of us could wait, the living room couch when his knees started to ache, and eventually headed for my bathroom when I said a hot soak in the tub would do us both well.

My bathroom is my secret oasis, done up in white marble, muted brass hardware, and shades of rich cream. A chandelier of pink crystal flowers hangs over a slipper tub that is perfectly adequate for my size. But we discovered it's a tight fit for the two of us. Despite what hot movie bathtub sex scenes would have people believe, the reality is awkward and uncomfortable when trying it with a man as big and tall as Rye.

After a much more accommodating shower, we settled on the window seat bench to dry off. But then I had to have him again; somewhere out there, some lucky person got a nice view of Rye's sleekly muscled back. And probably my tits. I'm okay with that. Sacrifices must be made in the pursuit of pleasure.

Now relaxed and on a mission to personally investigate all my products, he opens a jar of face mask and wrinkles his nose. "It's purple."

"I noticed."

"What does it do?" A little frown pulls between his brows as he peers at the jar's directions.

I put down my brush and sit on his lap. It's a simple thing to do, but it feels significant, like I'm making a claim. I take the jar from his hand. "In theory, it's supposed to smooth out wrinkles and rejuvenate tired skin."

Rye's arm wraps around my waist, tugging me more firmly against him. "You don't need that. Your skin is perfect." He punctuates the statement with a kiss on my cheek.

Pleasure hums through me. "Maybe that's because I have a shit-ton of products."

A huff of warm breath tickles my neck as he explores the area. "Doubtful. You'd be perfect without it."

I've been complimented before, by lovers, potential lovers, idle passersby. I've never been fully comfortable with it. The insecure part of me forged by childhood disappointments stubbornly holds on and insists people are only pandering. But it's different coming from Rye. His quiet conviction of my so-called perfection skitters and bumps along my skin, trying to find its way into my heart.

I brush a strand of damp hair off his brow. He needs a haircut. And a shave. Rye's eyes meet mine, and I notice the tired lines around his.

"You should try the mask. It might do you some good."

A wry smile tips his mouth. "Are you saying I look like shit?"

"Not like shit. But tired." More than that, in truth.

When I'm with him, he's either hot and urgent with lust or wearing the contentment of a big cat sunning on a rock. I swear, there are times I can all but hear him purr, a deeply satisfied rumble in that wide chest. But there's something under the surface that I can't put my finger on. Something off and pained. I don't want to push, but I can't refrain from tracing one of the lines of fatigue that run across his forehead.

In silence, he watches me, not exactly wary but guarded. The moment pulls thick and tight, and then he breaks it with an easy smile. "So put some on me. Rejuvenate my ravaged skin."

He's evading. But then, so am I. Too much emotion isn't smart. I cannot fall for Rye. Not fully. I won't survive it. I'll tumble around with him for a while, but I have to stay safely on the ledge.

"Let the healing begin." I grab my mask applicator and smear a big dollop of purple cream across his forehead.

He closes his eyes as though I might somehow get the thick paste in them. I fight the urge to kiss the tip of his nose. I seriously need to get a grip. Working faster, I concentrate on the task at hand.

"There!" I sit back and inspect my work. Rye has a nice coat of purple covering his forehead, nose, and cheekbones. "Now just relax."

He frowns, creating purple valleys over his forehead. "It's not going to melt my face off, is it?"

Rolling my eyes, I toss the applicator brush in the sink. "Yes, that's exactly what it does. When we skincare lovers get tired of having faces, we reach for this stuff. Instant Wicked Witch of the West meets water."

His lips purse at my sarcasm.

"And stop *making* faces." I set the timer. "You're cracking the mask."

He exhales in a long-suffering sigh, but I know he's enjoying his "spa" time. His body is loose and relaxed, his hand idly gliding up and down my waist. Humor gleams in his eyes, made bright blue by the surrounding lavender cream.

"You have a bit on your beard." Leaning forward, I rub my thumb over the spot. He catches me with his teeth, gently biting down before letting it go.

"Animal." Laughing, I snatch my hand away.

The mask cracks like a drying riverbed as he grins. With an exaggerated growl, he grasps the back of my neck and hauls me forward. His kiss is greedy and messy.

Squeaking, I push off him. But I'm laughing. I can't help it. Playing with Rye is the kind of fun I rarely allow myself.

He chuckles, totally unrepentant, eyes alight. Shaking my head, I towel off the smudges of purple he left on my face and then tidy his mask. He grins the entire time, his hands roving as though he can't stop himself from touching me. I'm not even sure he's aware he's doing it.

"It's all in your beard now." I rub away a clump. "Honestly, Rye. This beard is out of control."

That has him frowning. "You don't like the beard?"

Leaning back a little, I study his face. The strange thing is that I really do like it. Rye has the kind of strong features and square jaw that hold up well to a beard. Coupled with his dark-blond hair, fierce blue eyes, and dark tats, he reminds me of a marauding Viking. And I love the feel of it against my skin, between my legs, or tickling the corners of my mouth.

I suck in an unsteady breath. "Two weeks ago, I loved it." My thumb touches a scraggly bit that threatens to overtake his lip. "But it desperately needs trimming and grooming."

The frown sinks deeper into his eyes, and he glances away.

"I'm surprised you even have one," I say, pushing for lightness. "I distinctly recall you complaining that you hated beards because they make your face itch."

The thick columns of his thighs tense beneath me. "Felt like a change, is all."

His tone screams, *Back off!* But there's something in his eyes that has me looking closer. It's fear. He's afraid. Rye is never afraid.

"You're usually fastidious when it comes to grooming." Sure, he's been a wild child, drank his way through the first three years of fame, has done a bunch of stuff I don't even want to think about. But Rye is never a slob.

His gaze narrows. "It's just a beard, Bren. Let it go."

Gently, I rub the curve of his neck where it meets his shoulder. "I'm just curious. It isn't like you to be so untidy."

A long, harsh breath leaves him, and he carefully but firmly moves me off his lap. "I'll get rid of the fucking beard, all right?"

"I didn't ask you to get rid of it."

Rye stands, reaching for the washcloth. With brisk movements, he wets it and starts cleaning the mask off his face. "I'm gonna head out," he says when he's finished.

"You're leaving? Because I asked you about your beard?"

"No, because you won't let it go."

I can't believe this. I stare at him in amazement. "It was one freaking question."

"It was more than that."

"Okay, fine. I didn't let it go." I lift a hand in frustration. "Only because I don't understand. You're freaking out because I asked why you don't groom your beard."

He snorts derisively. "What are you, a beard detective?"

"Yes. I have a badge and everything. My unit specializes in unchecked beard growth violations."

His glare is cutting. "Cute."

"I thought so, yes. Now answer the question."

"I don't give a shit about the fucking beard!"

The force of his anger has me stepping back, shock prickling along my skin. "Why the hell are you yelling at me?"

He grimaces. "I didn't mean to shout." With that, he moves past me, shrugging out of the robe and tossing it on the hook by the door.

I gape as he strides away, his beefy butt flexing with each angry step.

"You're seriously leaving?"

"You're the detective. Figure it out."

He's being a dick. I should let him go. But I can't. Not when I've upset him in a way I don't understand.

I follow him into the hall. "Rye."

Gloriously nude, and clearly not giving a fuck, he heads for his clothes. "Shit," he says when he realizes they're still in a wet heap by the door. He reaches for his jeans anyway, snapping them in an attempt to untangle the legs.

"Rye, stop. Don't go like this."

"Look, it's all good." Viciously, he shoves on his wet jeans. "I'll call you later."

Maybe I should back off. He's vibrating with agitation, a dull flush rushing up the back of his neck. But the deep creases in the corners of his eyes and the pinched look around his mouth speak of hurt. I don't know what to do to make it better.

He reaches for his boots but stops short as if stung. "Shit," he shouts, recoiling and spinning away like a trapped animal with nowhere to go. "Fucking shit."

"Rye?" It's a breathless whisper because his rage borders on panic.

A great shuddering sigh escapes him, and he rests his forehead on the wall. His big, clenched fist presses against the wall as though he'd like to punch a hole through the plaster. But he doesn't. The long lines of his back tense as he stands there breathing hard and fast.

Slowly, I move to him. He flinches as soon as I touch him,

but I keep my palm lightly on the small of his quivering back. "Hey," I whisper, soothing this time. "Talk to me."

He doesn't say anything. His eyes are closed tight against me.

Softly I stroke him. "I'm sorry. Okay? You have to know I think you're gorgeous."

A laughing snort escapes, followed by a pained groan. "Shit, Bren. It's not about the beard, okay?"

He takes a breath and then turns to lean against the wall and face me. Red rims his eyes, and he blinks a few times, swallowing hard. "I haven't shaved because I can't."

"You can't shave?" I don't understand at all.

A fair amount of belligerence colors his gaze, but it doesn't seem directed at me. "It's my hands. They...they don't fucking work right." A small click sounds at the back of his throat when he swallows. "I move them a certain way and they seize up into this."

Rye lifts a shaking hand. His fingers are curled into a painful-looking claw, the tendons sticking out in sharp relief. Bleakly he stares at me. "Hands, wrists, forearms...It's fucking agony. And I...I can't play, Bren." His voice cracks. "I can't play."

The truth surges through me in a horrible rush. The way he's been evading texting, the missed band meetings, the wariness that lives on the edges of his smile.

I go ice-cold, all his pain and fear flowing in my veins. My lips part, but I don't know what to say, and he's all but glaring at me as if he's terrified I'll pity him.

Silently, I shake my head, trying to tell him without words that it isn't like that. Never pity. When he tenses further, his body recoiling, I can't stop from reaching for him. My fingers close around his fist. I cradle it in my hands.

Rye barely breathes as he blinks down at me. Gently, I run my fingers over his stiff ones, easing my thumb beneath them to rub his palm. "Rye, honey..."

His chest hitches, and I draw his hand up to kiss his knuckles. He lets me. He seems incapable of doing anything more than watching me carefully massage his hand.

"Have you seen a doctor?" I ask.

Another flinch. He makes a furtive attempt to pull his hand from mine. I don't let go, and he sighs, relenting. "No."

My gaze flicks to his. "Why not?"

Rye tilts his head back and blinks up at the ceiling. "Don't yell at me, all right?"

"All right."

Licking his lips, he meets my eyes. "I'm afraid."

Understanding flows over me. If he goes, it will be real. He might learn the worst. His entire life revolves around his hands.

I lean into him and wrap my arms around his waist. He stiffens for a second but then, with a choked sound, ducks his head and rests his cheek against my temple. I hug him close, smoothing my hands up and down his back.

My lips brush his chest. "You can't go on like this. It's tearing you up."

"I know," he says after a moment. He trembles then seems to fight it.

I kiss him again before stepping back. "Come on. Let's get you out of those jeans and we'll relax."

Rye narrows his eyes. "Don't baby me, Bren. I can't handle your pity."

I'm already pulling down his half-open zipper. "I'm not going to baby you. I'm going to wrap your hands in a heating pad, then I'm going to trim that damn scraggly beard. After that, I might sit on that massive dick of yours and ride it for my pleasure, but we'll have to see if you're still being a grumpy ass."

A reluctant smile lights his eyes and spreads over his face. "Massive, eh?"

"Enormous, even. The best dick ever."

Rye snorts, but he lets me help him out of the wet jeans. "Well, when you put it like that."

It's only when I have him back in my bathroom, one

clenched fist wrapped up and warming, that he catches my free hand with his own. "Brenna." He pauses, his gaze darting over my face with a pained intensity, as though he can't find the right words. Or maybe he has and doesn't know if he should utter them.

Either way, I cup his cheek. Tenderness and a fierce need to protect him turn my voice thick. "I know." I press a soft kiss to the bridge of his nose. "I know."

RYE

EMOTIONALLY DRAINED, I sit on the little bench in Brenna's bathroom. My hands have been tucked into a pair of heated mitts that she uses for her mani-pedi days to get her skin soft—something I find unduly cute. But they work well. She's wrapped me back up in a terry cloth robe that's way too small, gaping at my chest and barely reaching my knees. I'd rather go naked, but she'd primly told me to put my dick away while she's working because it distracts her.

Frankly, I could use a good distraction. Brenna scraped me raw in a way only she can, pushing and prodding at my weakness until there's nowhere to hide. As usual, I lashed out then tried to run. Only this time, she didn't let me. This time, she put her hand on me, asked me to stay. This time, she showed me something I'd never seen before when we fought: her concern. Her care.

Despite telling her I don't need or want her pity, I don't mind her care. Scratch that. I love her care. She does it so well—efficiently putting all her focus into my comfort in that no-nonsense way of hers that leaves no room for self-pity or doubt. And it works. I relax into her hands, letting her do as she pleases.

I had no idea how much I needed to be touched without any

endgame, to be handled like I matter beyond sex. I'm not fooling myself into believing anything has changed in our arrangement. But it's enough to have me thinking things I shouldn't.

Weirdly, confessing to her doesn't make me feel worse. It releases something within me, and with it, I feel lighter, as though maybe the world isn't about to end, that I can face anything as long as she is there to help me pick up the pieces. Part of me wants to run from that, run far and fast. But I don't. Because I'm not a fool. Being here with her as she fusses over me is worth it.

I hold still as she rests a hand on my shoulder and leans in to peer at my face.

"You want me to shave it all off?" she asks. "Or give you a nice trim?"

Up close, I'm struck by her beauty. Brenna's features aren't conventionally pretty. Her beauty is austere, striking. It is the difference between Vivaldi's "Spring" and "Winter." The lilting notes of "Spring" lull you into peaceful compliance, whereas the vibrant tempo of "Winter" stirs the blood and reminds you what it means to be alive. That is Brenna: thrilling, lively, vital.

Her nose is blunt, her face a narrow oval of smooth alabaster skin that glows with good health. Her lips aren't overly full but are well-shaped and candy pink. But it's her eyes, the color of fine whisky in firelight, framed by thick auburn lashes that take my breath away. Wide and clear, and I swear they see further into me than anyone else has. Or maybe it's that I look at them and all rational thought fades. I could spend a lifetime staring into her eyes and it wouldn't be enough.

Now they're crinkling at the corners, the space between them furrowed in concern.

"Rye?"

Right. I'm staring. I clear my throat. "What do you prefer?"

God, she smells good. Fresh from the bath, spicy-sweet like some exotic flower laced with fruit. Stupid, I know. But I can't describe it any other way. It's just fucking good. A drug. I draw in more of her scent as she bites the inside of her lower lip and contemplates.

"You want me to pick?"

"Well, yeah." My mouth quirks. "I'm the one going down on you on the regular, so..."

I freaking love the way she blushes berry red. It rushes up from her neck and washes over her entire face. I know she hates it, so I bite back a smile.

"You just had to get that out there, didn't you?" she says, lips twitching.

I also know she likes to be teased.

"Honey, if you'd let me, I'd create a full internet ad campaign about that."

Brenna's deft fingers run through my beard, sending shivers along my spine. She huffs out a laugh. "How would it go? 'My name is Rye Peterson, and I'm intimately familiar with Brenna James's lady parts'?"

"Lady parts?" I scoff. "More like, 'And I'm the lucky bastard who gets to lick, suck, and fuck Brenna James's delicious peachy pussy.'"

She's the color of a raspberry now. "Oh my God." Another husky laugh. "You're terrible."

Waggling my brows, I grin. "You love it."

"You're also deluded."

"Not about this. I bet you're wet right now."

"Not even a little." A spark of humor lights her eyes, daring me to prove her wrong.

"Liar. You're so wet. You need me to make it better."

"Rye." She laughs.

"Come on, let me see." I reach for her, but the wires of the heating mitts won't let me get far, and she gently bats my hands back down to my lap.

"Behave. I have work to do."

I keep my hands where they are, but it doesn't stop me from nuzzling her neck. She snickers, but then tilts her head ever so slightly to give me more access. I get a lick in before she dodges away, and with a reproving look, opens one of her makeup table drawers.

"Since you've given me a choice, we're keeping the beard." Over her shoulder, she shoots me a saucy look. "I like how it feels on my skin when you lick and suck my pussy."

I groan long and deep and reach for her again.

Laughing, she evades me. "None of that."

"Evil, Bren. Evil."

She pulls out a pink electric shaver. It looks a lot like a beard trimmer. But, you know, pink.

"Why do you have that?" I ask idly, as she selects an attachment.

"To trim my lady bits," she says with sauce. "Now, let's make that raggedy beard nice and tidy—"

"Hold up. You're telling me that's your pussy trimmer?"

"Rye! God, you're crude."

"Bren, we've established you're just as crude."

"Hardly."

"Answer the question."

She sets a hand on her hip and glares. "I already told you what it was. And I'm not calling it a pussy trimmer, if that's what you're after."

"No, no..." My voice is strangled. "I'm just clarifying."

Her eyes narrow. "You're not going to get all weird about this, are you? I promise, I clean it well after every use."

"I'm not going to get weird. I just have a really good visual imagination. And I'm hard as steel right now."

Her gaze darts down, and she sucks in a breath. Like I said, the robe she gave me is too small. My dick stands at eager attention, jutting out between the flaps of the terry cloth. Brenna's gaze turns hazy, and she licks her lips. My horny dick jumps as if trying to flag her down.

"Put that thing away," she murmurs, her breathing uneven.

Something I absolutely love about Brenna? She's a fiend for

my cock. She loves playing with it, sucking it...I'd marry her for that alone. I don't think she'd appreciate that particular motivating factor. But I do. The memories of all the times she's toyed with my body surge to the surface, and I get so hot, I swear I'm a little light-headed.

Grinning wide, I lean back, parting my thighs. Just enough to let the robe slip farther open. "Putting it away is going to be a problem, Berry. It's too hard."

"Rye..." She's attempting to sound stern, but it doesn't work, given that she's still eyeing my hard-on like it's candy.

She has no idea how much her lust turns me on. She couldn't, or she wouldn't torture me so much with it. Or maybe she would. Brenna loves to tease as much as I do. I nudge my hips, lifting my dick a bit higher, my knee rocking with hypnotic slowness. Taunting her, even though my heart is threatening to pound right out of my chest.

"You gonna help me out here, Bren?"

Her lips part, her pink tongue darting out. My cock actually pulses. I swallow a groan. The trimmers hit the counter with a clatter. As though moving through water, Brenna sinks to her knees before me, her clever hand going to the tie of the robe. Cool air hits my hot skin.

Gaze rapt on my dick, she slides a hand up my thigh and gently strokes my hip. Then her free hand, cool and slim, wraps around my aching flesh. She gives it a tug.

"God, Rye, just look at you." Damn if I don't feel her gaze moving over my body with something close to awe. It trips my heart, makes my mouth dry. She licks her lips, greedy, her voice husky. "You're so..."

I don't get the rest. The wet pull of her mouth is on me a second later, and I'm lost.

I'm so fucking lost.

CHAPTER EIGHTEEN

BRENNA

"SPEND THE DAY WITH ME," he'd asked.

Never mind he asked with his mouth between my legs, his newly trimmed beard rubbing oh so gently against my swollen flesh. When I could only answer yes.

And yes.

And, oh, fuck, yes.

I hadn't thought to ask where, how. It hadn't mattered.

So here I am, walking up the steps into the Metropolitan Museum of Art with Rye Peterson at my side. He takes my hand in his. And I don't pull away. His clasp is gentle, the skin on his palm callused and worn. His beautiful, fragile hand.

"This wasn't exactly what I thought you had in mind when you asked me to spend the day with you," I say as we collect our tickets.

Rye stops and carefully presses a little sticker that shows we've paid for entry onto my silk blouse just below the collar. His fingers trail over my shoulder before dropping away. Wry humor glints in his denim-blue eyes. "You thought we'd stay in bed fucking, didn't you?"

A woman glances our way, clearly overhearing, and I step closer to Rye.

"Hush. This is a tourist spot. People will listen here."

His lips quirk. "And you don't want them to know of our special lovin'?"

Narrowing my eyes, I poke his firm abs with my finger. "I'm about to give you a special ass kicking, buttercup."

He grins outright, and his arm snakes around my waist to pull me up against him. "Kinky, Berry." His lips brush over mine. "Stop thinking about sex, we're here to see art."

The nerve. "*I'm* thinking—"

He cuts me off with another light kiss then tugs me along beside him. "I know what you're thinking. And you can use my body later. For now, we're getting our culture on."

Torn between grumbling and laughing, I follow him into the Egyptian wing. The museum has just opened, so it's fairly empty, which is something of a relief. The last time I was here, it was filled with so many people, I nearly lost it. I'm fine with crowds, but I've never seen the point of viewing art when you have to vie for even a small peek of it.

Rye takes my hand again. It's different, being here with him, as though we're on a date. Which is...not what we're supposed to be doing. He was right, I'd expected him to want a day of sex. I'd been prepared for that. I'm not prepared for this, or what doing this even means. But I don't want to think. I just want to be.

We take our time, stopping to peer at tiny scarabs or ancient papyrus scrolls mounted on the walls. The few people we pass barely glance our way. It always amazes me how rarely Rye gets recognized in public. Jax and Killian almost instantly get mobbed, but Rye has a way of blending in, which is amazing given that he's six foot three inches of tightly muscled perfection. I can only conclude it's the ease with which he moves through the world. The man cuts through space like a hot knife into cold pudding. That smooth flow draws me in and has me relaxing my usually crisp stride.

"I love this place," Rye murmurs as we stroll past a massive basalt sarcophagus. "I know it can be packed with tourists, and that's annoying, but when I was younger and my parents were fighting, I'd come here and get lost for hours. Just soak in the art and breathe."

My arm brushes against his as I move closer to him. "I did too."

"What? Really?"

"Yeah. I'd come here on Saturdays. Even filled with people, it was better than being at home." I shrug. "And...shit, this is going to sound stupid."

"I highly doubt that."

"It reminded me of staying with Killian."

Rye's brow furrows, and I know I'm doing a terrible job of explaining. Honestly, I don't even know why I'm telling him this. I hate this particular vulnerability of mine. But I know he won't judge, and sometimes having someone bear witness to your weaknesses makes them easier to manage. I never truly understood the power of that until Rye broke down and admitted his fears about his hands to me. I thought he might break apart, but he leaned on me instead, as though I gave him strength. And he'd gone light with it. Playful and happy once again.

I'd given that to him. Just by listening.

"You've seen how Killian's parents live, right?" I say, easier now. "Beautiful homes filled with light and art. I had a bit of that here."

Rye's expression clears. "I get it."

"I loved staying with Killian. And with my aunt and uncle. They treated me like..." A small laugh escapes. "I was going to say family, but I am family, so that isn't exactly surprising."

The blunt tip of Rye's thumb caresses my knuckles. "They treated you like a daughter."

A heavy, familiar weight settles on my chest, but this time, it's easier to let it go. "Yeah."

He doesn't say anything but leads me into the Sackler Wing, a soaring modern space with its iconic slanted grid window wall overlooking Central Park. Sunlight streams in, and blue sky meets the tree line, now colored with the golds, reds, and oranges of autumn.

The airy gallery houses the Temple of Dendur, two large Egyptian structures which sit on a limestone floor, surrounded on three sides by a wide reflecting pool. Save for a guard, it's quiet and empty—a true rarity.

"It feels as though we're in a church," I whisper, a sense of reverence falling over me.

"I suppose we are, in a way." Rye's hand settles on the small of my back as we walk into the larger temple building, flanked by two thick, fluted columns.

Standing by Rye's side, I study the hieroglyphs someone carved into the stone over a millennia ago then pause with a jolt. "1821? Someone carved graffiti."

Rye leans in, his eyes narrowing. "Son of a bitch, they did. It's all over the place. I can't believe I never noticed it before."

"Maybe because it's usually crammed with people breathing down your neck in here?"

He huffs out a laugh. "Probably. Damn, look at that. One of them was from New York. Dude must have thought he'd left a piece of himself in Egypt for all time. Now it's here." Rye shrugs. "He'll live on in infamy, that's for sure. I guess that's one way to be immortal."

"How does it feel? Knowing that you're going to live on like that too?"

His brow wings up as he turns my way. "In infamy?"

"Rye." I nudge him with a laugh. "No. You. Your music. It's going to live on far after you do."

He steps into my space, running his fingers along my waist as though he can't help himself. His voice lowers to a husky rumble. "I don't know. Sometimes, I think about it, and I feel...empty."

"Empty?" My hands slide over his chest to cup the back of his neck.

He leans into the touch, ducking his head so his cheek brushes mine. "Yeah. Empty. It will hit me that someone might listen to my music when I'm dead and gone, and I feel so fucking empty. Because I know my life will be over, and I wonder if I will ever..." He trails off, swallowing hard.

My fingers toy with the short, silky strands of his hair. "Ever what?"

A gust of breath tickles my neck. "Ever fill it with something more than just music."

We're holding on to each other. Hugging. I'm not even sure how that happened or if I should step away. I close my eyes and sink into it instead. The steady beat of his heart thumps against my chest. His big hand slides along my spine, stroking me.

I could stay like this forever, but I can't ignore what he said. I lean back to meet his gaze. His is troubled. Setting my hand on his cheek, I speak with quiet conviction. "You're more than just your music, Ryland. You always were."

A small jolt goes through him, and his nostrils flare on an indrawn breath. The way he looks at me, with wide, pained eyes, has my heart skittering. Those blue eyes fill with something else, something deep and tender. His hand slips under my hair to my neck. "Bren. What you do to me..."

Then he's kissing me. Slow and soft and so damn good, I forget where we are. I kiss him back, swallow down his moan. My bones melt. I am liquid heat and wanting.

"I love kissing you," he says against my mouth. "I could do it forever."

Forever.

He's devouring me. Slowly taking me apart. I let him do it. I want more.

A polite but pointed throat-clearing catches my attention.

Rye and I separate enough to glance over at a guard who gives us a censorious—if slightly amused—look. Right. Public museum.

Rye's answering smile is not the least bit repentant. He drapes an arm over my shoulders and leads me out of the temple.

We don't speak for a while but simply look at artifacts and artworks.

"I'm having fun," I announce as we enter the Arms and Armor wing.

"You don't have to sound so shocked about it," he teases. "I'm a very fun person to be around."

"Yes, I know," I deadpan. "Except when you're around me."

Rye flinches. And I realize what I just said. "Shit. I didn't mean that." Flustered by my utter boobery, I wave a hand in the air. "I meant before. The way we were before."

Rye sucks the inside of his cheek, as though he's figuring out how to answer. His eyes meet mine, and I'm struck anew by how gorgeous he is. I don't know why it hits me so hard now; maybe it's the pure filtered sunlight that fills the room and illuminates every inch of him. Maybe it's simply that I can't look at Rye and not feel an overwhelming attraction.

He's beautiful in his raw and utterly masculine simplicity. Clean lines, strong bone structure, the dark blond of his hair spiking up in wild disarray. Faint laugh lines grace the corners of his expressive dusky-blue eyes. Even when he's serious, it's as if his natural inclination is toward happiness and any other emotion is just temporary.

"That's why I wanted you to come out with me," he says. "I don't want us to be stuck in the past. We're not those people anymore. We're...new."

"New, huh?"

He nudges me with his shoulder. "New *and* improved."

"Goof."

Grinning, he gives me a swift, affectionate kiss on the cheek. "You need goofy in your life."

"Because I'm so serious?" I say it lightly. He's not telling me anything I haven't heard before or thought of myself.

"You can be, and someone has to brave that death glare of yours to remind you how fun it is to let go."

"I suppose you're the brave someone in this scenario?"

"Of course. Sir Ryland, the noble sex knight. Able to tame the savage Brenna beast one orgasm at a time."

"That is painfully bad."

His eyes twinkle with good cheer. "And yet you're laughing."

"Yeah, at you."

"Good enough. Face it, Bren. You need me."

It hits too close to a tender spot I've been trying to ignore.

Rye, being observant as hell when it comes to me, notices. His happy expression slips away. I've made it awkward again, and I don't know how to fix it. A stupid joke would be obvious, and frankly, insulting to Rye's intelligence. But what can I say? *You're coming to mean too much to me, and I'm not sure I can take that.*

Rye's deep voice breaks the silence. "Can I ask you something?"

I stop beside a group of knights on horseback with lances up and at the ready. "That question never bodes well."

"Probably not." He rubs the back of his neck before turning the full force of his attention on me. "Back when we were having tea with Killian, I said I'd go to his dad's birthday party, and you flinched."

I flinch again, sliding my gaze away. "Did I?"

He's closer now. I can feel him even though he's two feet away. "Bren, come on. It's me you're talking to. You flinched and made a face, the one that says you have to deal with an uncomfortable situation but will try your best not to let it get to you."

It's irksome that he reads me so easily. Worse, I know him well enough to realize he's going to keep at the question until I answer. Hot, itchy panic crawls up my chest.

"Rye. Can we not do this? Let's just go back to having a good time."

"I don't want to pressure you, but it's been bugging me." He stands in front of me, so I have nowhere to run. "Do you not want me to go? Is that it?"

Damn it. I don't want to do this. "Rye..."

He takes my hand. His has gone clammy, and it hits me how hard it is for him to ask. He thinks I don't want him around. I don't, not at my aunt and uncle's house. But not for the reasons he probably assumes.

"Just tell me," he says with that same soft but insistent tone. "If you think I can't be discreet—"

"It's not that."

"Then what? We get along well now. What can it possibly—"

"I saw you," I burst out, my voice ringing in the gallery.

Rye's head jerks at the sound, but his eyes narrow. "Saw me? When? Where?"

Glancing around at the few people in the room, I tug Rye to a smaller alcove. No one appears to have recognized him as a member of Kill John, but I have no desire for our conversation to end up on some social media account.

My heart tries to beat its way up my throat. I swallow hard and face him. "I didn't want to do this. It's history, but you won't let it go, will you?"

His chin kicks up with a stubborn stare. "If whatever the hell is bugging you was actually history, you wouldn't be this upset. And, yeah, I'm not letting it go. Not now, at any rate. What the hell are you talking about, Bren? What did you see me do?"

Letting out a harsh breath, I lick my lips. "With my aunt."

His expression goes blank. "Isabella?"

"Aunt Isabella. Otherwise known to the public simply as Isabella, one of the most beautiful and successful models in the world." As if he doesn't know this.

Cuban American with tanned legs for miles, Isabella was the star of a major lingerie campaign for most of my childhood. One of my first memories of her is when she strode down the catwalk wearing the now-famous bikini made entirely of diamonds and rubies.

Killian had a hell of a time dealing with his schoolmates panting over his mom. As for me, most of my friends didn't know she was my aunt, but if they found out, they wanted to meet her, be her. I'd wanted to be her too, for a time. To this day, she's idolized, adored, pursued.

"It was your twenty-first birthday party," I continue woodenly. "Isabella was in town and popped in to join the party..."

Something clears in his eyes. His lips part, but he doesn't utter a sound. He doesn't have to. I see the guilt starting to stir. The horror of being caught.

A wave of old anger rises within me. "I saw you, Rye. Kissing my aunt. My fucking aunt! Killian's mom—"

He cuts me off with a sharp sound, something close to pain. "Bren—"

"You had your tongue down her throat."

Rye makes another sound, like it's ripped from deep within him, and takes hold of my arm. His grip doesn't hurt but holds me still. I'd been backing away without knowing it. I don't move, don't try to break free. I want to face him now.

"No," he says. "No fucking way are you walking out thinking that's what happened."

A high, humorless laugh breaks from my lips. "I saw it with my own eyes."

He steps into my space, his voice low and urgent. "It's your interpretation of what you saw that's the problem, Bren." He takes a quick, hard breath. "I was drunk off my ass—"

"That's no excuse."

"Would you just listen?" he hisses.

My mouth snaps shut, and I raise a brow, silently prompting him to continue. He grits his teeth then speaks again.

"I was drunk off my ass, and Isabella walked in. We chitchatted in that sloppy, stupid way only the exceptionally drunk can manage. Suddenly she was sitting closer. Too close. It freaked me out, because, yes, she's an extremely beautiful woman, and it was becoming too clear that she was hitting on me."

"What?" It comes out high and shocked. Because I am. Shocked. Shaken.

There's something desperate about Rye's expression. "She was, Bren. She knew it. I knew it. And, trust me, I was painfully aware that she was Killian's mom. Frankly, it scared the hell out of me. I moved to go, and..." He closes his eyes with a wince. "Fuck, she kissed me. I was so fucking shocked—"

Blood drains from my head so quickly, my skin prickles. "Are you telling me that Isabella jumped you?"

He ducks his head until we're almost nose to nose. "That's exactly what I'm saying. You don't have to believe me, but it's the truth. I would never, *never*, do that to Killian." A flush washes over his cheeks. "Loyalty means everything to me, Bren. Killian, the guys, they are my brothers. I would die before I hurt any of them that way."

I stare up at him, searching his gaze. He doesn't flinch, doesn't even blink.

"I thought you knew that much about me, at least," he says in a broken tone.

"Why do you think I was so upset?" I rasp. "It killed something in me to see that."

His eyes narrow to slits. "Why didn't you confront me back then?"

"Because it would hurt the band. Hurt Killian. It was my job to keep you guys going. No matter what."

Rye hasn't let me go. His grip burns through my shirt. "That's why you really hated me all these years, isn't it?"

"I was so disappointed in you," I whisper through numb lips. "I couldn't look at you without seeing it. For so long, I truly hated you for that."

"And yet you let me into your bed." It isn't an accusation. He's surprised. Moreover, he's clearly confused.

"It's been years at this point. And I've seen the way you're always there for the guys." I shrug weakly, my shoulders weighed down. "I knew you were drunk, and I figured maybe it was time to let it go."

His hand slips from my arm. "But you didn't. Not really. It's been oozing between us like sewage."

Dully, I nod, glancing down at my feet. "I don't like to think of it. But when you said you'd be at the party..."

"And Isabella will be there too," he finishes succinctly.

My breath hitches. "I didn't want to remember, Rye."

Rye runs a hand over his jaw. "And now? Do you believe me?"

We're standing close enough to touch, but there's an ocean of history flowing between us now. It would be easy to say he's lying to save his ass. Except I know this man better now. I know he has a core of integrity that is stronger than steel.

I've been quiet too long. He moves, as though to go, and I hold out a hand. "Of course, I believe you."

Pressing his lips together, he stares at me as though he's trying to see if I really mean it. But then he shakes his head and turns away. "You know what exhibit I never remember to visit? The eighteenth-century French and English rooms they have set up—"

"Rye..."

He keeps walking. Not fast, but steady enough that I know he's not going to stop. I have no choice but to follow, my heels clicking loudly on the limestone floors. They say the truth shall set you free. Doesn't feel that way at the moment. It feels like I've sent us back to the beginning.

CHAPTER NINETEEN

RYE

I'M RUNNING AWAY from an argument with Brenna. I promised myself I wouldn't do that anymore. But I can't shake the weight of disappointment and frustration crawling down my throat. I can't joke right now. I can't be the guy who pretends nothing matters.

Brenna's heels click in that familiar pattern of hers. I hear that *clickety-click* in my sleep some nights and wake up smiling. Damn it, why did it have to be her? Out of all the women in the world, the one that thinks I'm dirt is the one I want.

"Rye..." She sounds tentative, remorseful. And even though I want to ignore her, I can't. Never could.

Letting out a breath, I slow my stride so she can catch up. But I can't look at her. Not yet.

We've reached the American wing, another light-filled, glass-covered courtyard. There's a cafe at the far end by the windows, and the scent of stale coffee and warm bread fills the air. I hang a left and step into the relative quiet of a neoclassical interiors gallery.

Brenna follows, and when I stop to stare unseeing at an exhibit, she stands just behind me like she's afraid to face me. The idea sends a wave of exhaustion through my body.

"All this time," I croak, my throat too thick. "You hated me for something that I didn't do."

The air stirs with her sigh. My skin twitches when her hand settles on the back of my arm. "Rye, I'm sorry." With another sigh, she rests her forehead between my shoulder blades. When she slides her arms around my waist, I close my eyes tight.

"It's okay," I get out. "I'd have come to that conclusion if I'd seen the same."

She holds me a bit tighter, her hand spreading wide over my abs. "You would have confronted the person and demanded an explanation."

"I get why you didn't."

Brenna hums in doubt, her fingers pressing into me like she's afraid I'll move away. "I let my feelings for you color my judgment. You weren't exactly my favorite person back then."

"I know."

The movement of her lips against my shirt tickles, and yet it feels so good, I want to lean into her. I hold steady as she talks. "It was so petty, that dislike. You rejected me, and I acted like a spoiled brat, hating you when it was your prerogative not to want me that way."

Surprise whips through me, locking all my muscles tight. I knew that was why she stopped liking me, but never in all these years did I think she'd ever admit to it or be sorry.

Throat thick, I turn in the circle of her arms, sliding my own around her. She stares up at me, her expression almost blank, her slim body so stiff, I know she's bracing herself.

"I wanted you," I say. "Jesus, Bren. I wanted you so badly, it scared the hell out of me."

A wrinkle forms between the auburn wings of her brows. "You don't have to say—"

"I sought you out after every gig, every practice. Why do you think I did that? Because I was attracted to you. I liked you, Berry." My thumb strokes a circle over the small of her back. "I knew you liked me too. But Killian had made it clear he'd kill any guy who got too close, and you were so young..."

"You were young too," she points out, high color coming over her face. "And Killian should have fucked off. He had no right to go all Victorian protector on me."

A small laugh tickles my throat. "No, he didn't. But you're right. We were both young. It would have gone pear-shaped and messed with the band's dynamic. Back then, I wasn't willing to risk that. So I acted like an asshole to make you dislike me. I handled it badly."

"We both did." All the stiffness drains out of her, and she rests her head on my shoulder. But I don't make the mistake of thinking she's okay. A fine tremor runs through her body. I slide my hand up her back and wrap the silky length of her ponytail in my fist, knowing she likes to be held that way. It works, and she melts into me. "I'm sorry I hurt you, Ryland."

Sometimes the guys will say my full name, mostly when they're giving me shit; it's what we do. But when Brenna says Ryland, it feels like a secret between us, like she's pulled back my armor and sees the man beneath all the bullshit. I have no defense against it.

Dipping my head, I press my lips to the crown of her head and breathe her in. "I'm ashamed of that night," I confess heedlessly. "It was my fault."

Her voice is muffled against my chest. "Why would you think that?"

"I gave her the wrong idea. We were talking about nothing in particular, then I said something about how cool it was that she showed up at my birthday party, that I was honored, you know?"

Brenna stays silent, and I swallow audibly. "She laughed it off and said it was nice to be around people who appreciated her, that her husband didn't have time for her."

A sharp sound escapes Brenna, and she stiffens. I'm guessing she didn't know that about her aunt and uncle's relationship. I stroke her back, an automatic gesture because I don't like upsetting her. But my words keep flowing out of me. I can't seem to hold them back. "I was all sloppy drunk, but I remember leaning into her space and saying that she was the most beautiful woman in the world and any man who didn't have time for her was an idiot."

Brenna huffs out a shaky laugh. "You always were a smooth talker."

I don't smile. The past sits too heavily on my shoulders. "I wanted to make her feel better. And I'm not going to lie, Bren. I honestly couldn't understand how your uncle could ignore this beautiful, intelligent woman who loved him."

"There's nothing wrong with any of that, Rye."

"Yeah, well, it was a mistake, because she got a look in her eye, and it hit me that I was inches away from Killian's mom. Your aunt. And...shit. My hand had ended up on her thigh. I didn't even remember doing it. But I'd said those words, touched her...I wasn't thinking. And then suddenly, she was kissing me."

With that, Brenna pulls away. I let her go because I'm not about to hold her against her will. A frown mars the oval of her face.

"It took me too long to react," I blurt out. "My mind went blank. And then I was so fucking horrified. I pushed away, mumbled some excuse, and got the hell out of there." My hand shakes as I run it through my hair and clutch the back of my tight neck. "I threw up all night. I couldn't look Killian in the eye for months."

"It wasn't your fault," Brenna says, quiet now, pensive.

"I should have told him. But I just...couldn't."

The wrinkle between her brows grows, and she turns her head to stare off into the distance. "Some things are better left unsaid."

"Are they? Because that particular act drove a wedge between you and me for nearly a decade."

Her lashes sweep down over her eyes for a brief moment before she faces me, all hard determination. "That's different."

"Maybe. Maybe not."

"It is, because I saw it happen. Killian doesn't know and doesn't need to know. It will only hurt him now."

Tightness pulls at my shoulders, and I roll them. "I buried that night deep within me, because I couldn't stand it—"

"Rye—"

"You don't understand. My dad is a cheater."

At the sound of her indrawn breath, I give her a wry, tired look. "Always was. It hurts my mom and pisses me off. It ruined our family."

"I'm sorry," she says, and I know it's out of sympathy. Surprisingly, the sentiment warms me.

"I am too." I shrug. "Mainly, I'm sorry my mom can't get out of the cycle of forgiving him."

"I wouldn't," she blurts out then pinks. "Forgive someone for cheating on me, I mean."

"No," I agree with a weak smile. "I suspect they'd search for the body and never find it."

Brenna huffs in amusement, but her lips pinch. "You haven't forgiven him either."

Not a question.

"I'm trying. He's a good dad—aside from that. He's always been supportive of me. I think that bothers me most of all, how he can be so good in one aspect of his life and so crap in another."

"I guess we're all flawed in some way or other."

"I don't want to be like him," I spit out.

Brenna considers me for a long moment. "I don't want to be like my parents either."

"I can't be..." Damn my tight shoulders and stiff-ass neck. "I like sex, women, having fun..." *This is coming out well. Fuck.* I clear my throat. "But I'd never be a cheater. Never."

I want her to understand I wouldn't do that to her. Maybe

she's been afraid to trust me in that way. After all, she witnessed my worst moment and came to the worst conclusion.

Pride shaken, I fist my hands and turn away.

"I believe you," she says, softer now. "I should have believed it from the start. But I didn't know you like I do now. You have a sense of honor and loyalty that shines bright, Ryland. I admire it. So much."

Shocked, I wrench around, my mouth falling open.

But she isn't looking my way. With a sigh, she shakes her head ruefully. "I'm guessing we'll simply make our own types of mistakes."

"I don't want us to be a mistake, Bren."

It's her turn to be shocked. She blinks, her pretty mouth falling open. But it's only for a second, then she visibly collects herself, and I'm faced with the woman who smoothly runs our public relations. "We won't. We'll be careful."

Careful. Like I'm a campaign to be managed. Disappointment is a kick to the gut. But she's only playing by the rules we both set down. That's the way Brenna is. She makes a plan and sticks to it. If I want more, I have to spell it out, make demands. Right now, I'm too drained to do anything other than take her hand and give her a reassuring smile, because I know she's drained as well. We've exposed too much of ourselves too quickly.

"Come on. There's a fashion exhibit on high couture that has your name all over it."

"I don't know if I like how much you get me."

Get used to it, sweetheart. I intend to get a lot more.

CHAPTER TWENTY

BRENNA

WORK IS the last place I want to be. It occurs to me that I've begun to resent going to work more and more lately. I thought being with Rye would end this restlessness within me. I thought this hole inside of me was about needing a good sexual release. But it's not.

At least not entirely. Yes, I am sexually satisfied. And, yes, that's great. But it isn't the quick fix I'd been hoping for.

All morning I am bombarded with texts from the guys, texts from Jules and Sophie. Questions about the band. Questions from their record label. Questions from my staff about fan clubs, concert passes, upcoming events. It's all about the band. All the time. But nothing from Rye.

I have to fight the compulsion to pull out my phone and check. I haven't spoken to him since we went to the museum two days ago. It's as though we both needed to pull back and regroup. But he's been on my mind ever since.

God, how could I have gotten things so wrong? On the surface, the whole incident between Rye and my aunt appeared clean-cut. I'm horrified to know how it really happened. But I can't find it in myself to judge my aunt. The whole thing makes me tired now. And unsettled.

It's as if the smooth foundations of my life have a hairline fracture that's slowly spreading out in all directions. I want to fall to my knees, plaster over those cracks and get on with my life. But I can't. I'm changing, my well-ordered plans shifting into something uncontrollable.

It's enough to make me curl up into a ball and hide. It shames me. Who am I to complain about my life?

Rye hasn't complained. Even though his hands, his beautiful, talented, perfect hands are letting him down. I want to seek him out and wrap him in a hug.

He'd hate that. The man has recesses of pride I never considered. His sense of honor is rock-solid. The more I'm with him, the more I learn about him, which in turn makes me want to know more and more. I have to stop thinking about him. Work. I need to work.

Only, I don't want to talk about Kill John. With an ugly start, I realize I could go months without carrying on another Kill John related conversation and be happy.

I set my head in my hands let out a groan.

"Bren?" Michael leans into the office, a small frown of concern wrinkling between his brows. "Your phone is going off nonstop."

Which is unheard of for me.

"I wanted to make sure you were still alive," he says with a wink.

Sighing, I sit back and rub my face. "Just taking a breather."

I don't think he buys it, but he's smart enough not to ask any more questions. The phone rings again. I pick it up and do my job.

"Brenna, babe!" Tim Wilks. Another reporter. Lovely. He starts in on all the things he needs to know about Jax and Stella.

"I'm sorry," I tell Wilks. "But as I've said, Jax is not taking questions about his personal life. If you ask any, don't be surprised if he walks."

And I won't blame Jax one bit, I think silently. Ever since the world got wind of his relationship with Stella—and the fact that she used to be a professional friend, something people find either fascinating or unbelievable—he's made it clear he won't drag her into the harsh light of public scrutiny. Well, any more than she already is.

For as much as people love their heroes, they're exceptionally good at tearing them and their loved ones down if they don't act exactly as expected. Truth is, most rabid fans don't like the idea of the guys pairing off and finding love. Not that they don't want the guys to be happy, but it kills the fantasy that someone out there might eventually snag one of them.

Jax and Killian being off the market is both an endless source of speculation, fascination, and disgruntlement. It is my job to protect them all from the brunt of it.

"I hear you loud and clear," Tim says. "But you have to know his fans keep asking. They deserve to know—"

"Exactly dick about Jax's personal life," I snap.

Silence greets me.

For a moment I just sit there, mouth slightly open as if gaping at my rudeness and stupidity. Rule one in my job is not to lose my cool. Getting defensive or snappish with a reporter only makes them dig in further.

But I can't help myself. I'm tired of fielding the same questions. It's a horrible shock to realize that I'm sick of even saying Jax's name. Blood drains from my face, and I pull in a deep, quiet breath. I feel like the most disloyal friend in the world right now. And a shitty PR manager.

"Send me the questions," I say before Wilks can respond. "I'll have Jax go over them. He has final approval. That's all I can promise."

Wilks grumbles, and I get the hell off the phone with him as fast as possible. My hands are shaking. I need fresh air. Putting my phone on silent—a cardinal sin in Scottie's book—I head for the coffee shop down the street.

"I've worn that frown before," says a masculine voice over my shoulder while I'm standing in line.

Startled out of my pout, I turn and find Marshall Faulkner grinning at me.

"Have you?" I ask wryly.

"Sure," he says easily. "It's the, 'I'm at my wits' end and need to mainline coffee stat' frown."

Laughing, I shake my head in resignation. "Guilty."

His blue eyes crinkle at the corners. "But you're still itching to look at your phone, aren't you?"

"You *are* good."

Marshall shrugs. "It's the curse of the workaholic."

The line moves, and we amble onward. "I don't know," I find myself muttering. "I'm kind of over work at the moment."

As soon as I say the words, I want to take them back. I don't complain about work to outsiders. Ever. But confessing to someone who doesn't know the guys, or the entanglements of my life, feels like a balm. Marshall might not know me, but he does understand PR.

It's clear in the way his expression is both sympathetic and amused. "I've had those days as well."

My turn comes up to order. I place mine and pay before stepping aside and letting him do the same. When he's done, we move to the waiting line.

"Thing is," he continues as though we hadn't paused our conversation, "I usually turn my focus to other projects. How does it work when you only have one client?"

A grimace twists my lips before I can school my features. "It doesn't, sadly. I just...push through."

Marshall nods, and an awkward air falls between us, brought on by my painful honesty and the uncomfortable feeling that I've betrayed Kill John by complaining. It's broken by the arrival of our coffees. It's my cue to go, but I find myself walking out with him as if by silent agreement.

It's one of those perfect New York autumn days where the air is crisp but not too cold and the sun is shining lemon yellow in a lapis sky. We stroll toward Central Park, which is at the end of the block. Tourists are wandering up Fifth Avenue, heading for the Met. We ease past them and go into the park.

"You ever think about taking on more clients?" Marshall asks as we amble down a path.

"I work for Liberty Bell too." A small, wry smile tilts my mouth. "Although that's more of a 'keeping it in the family' kind of thing."

"You all really do think of yourselves as a family, don't you?"

An image flashes through my mind, of Rye kneeling between my spread thighs, his eyes searing with hot need. Cheeks hot, I'm grateful for the cool breeze that cuts across the park. "I suppose we do. Perhaps that's my problem. Family matters are always complicated."

"You're burnt out, aren't you?" He doesn't so much accuse as ask, as if it just hit him and he empathizes.

And I find myself telling the truth.

"I think I am. I'm just not into work these days and that's utterly foreign to me."

Marshall ducks his head as he walks, and I'm struck by how similar in appearance he is to Rye. But where Rye exudes a kind of kinetic vitality, Marshall is more grounded and serious. My body doesn't hum with want when it's next to his, but he does make me comfortable. It's a rare talent, given that I don't let my guard down with anyone.

"I'd been planning to ask you something…" He pauses and glances over at me. "Now I feel like an opportunist."

My stomach tightens just enough to make my steps slow. If he's planning to ask me out, it will be awkward. Before Rye, I'd be all over this man. But I keep my voice light. "Well, now you have me intrigued."

Marshall huffs out a small laugh as if to say, *Well, I tried, albeit not very hard.* "My firm has been looking for top talent to recruit."

"You're looking at Kill John?" The very idea slides like ice inside my stomach.

His laugh is heartier now. "No, I'm looking at you."

I stop in my tracks. "Me?"

Marshall pivots to face me. "You're the talent I'm interested in. The firm is growing leaps and bounds, and our PR division is having trouble keeping up." His expression is kind, persuasive. "We'd be lucky to have someone like you leading it."

He's offering me a job. Surprise prickles over my skin. "And here I thought you were about to ask about going out for tacos," I blurt out. Like an idiot. Because I don't want tacos.

He chuckles and takes a step closer. "I am not opposed to doing that either."

Shit.

Wryly, I shake my head. "Sorry, that just slipped out."

Heat enters his gaze. "I'm not sorry. We can do both."

Even if I weren't doing whatever it is I'm doing with Rye, the idea of going on a date with the man offering me a job doesn't sit right. "I couldn't, not if you're serious about the job offer. It would be a huge conflict of interest for me."

Marshall winces. "God, that was inappropriate of me. I'm usually better than this. Please, accept my apology."

"It's all right. I'm the one who mentioned tacos." I shake my head slightly. "It came out wrong, anyway. I'm seeing someone." Jesus. It's true. I'm in a relationship with Rye. The truth of that hits me in the knees and makes them weak. I brace myself and push on. "Although, I'd love to take you out for tacos as a friend."

A flicker of disappointment darkens Marshall's eyes, but it's gone quickly, and his smile seems genuine. "Ah, well. I suspected someone like you wouldn't be available for long. But my offer about the job remains. In fact, it's stronger than ever. You speak plainly, and I like you."

I can't help laughing. "That's succinct."

He winks, and it is surprisingly not cheesy. "You haven't said anything about the position. Tell me you're thinking about it."

Am I? God. Am I?

Excitement over the prospect of something new to work on bubbles through my veins. But the very thought of considering leaving Kill John feels like the ultimate betrayal. I'm guessing Marshall knows this because he leans in slightly, his expression one I've used on reluctant record executives and promoters over the years. "We're offering an equal partnership position. At least come to LA and hear us out."

Ah, yes, and that's the other thing. The job would be in LA. All the way across the country. It isn't as though the guys don't have homes scattered around the world. Hell, Scottie has more houses than any of us. He's a hoarder that way. But I'm always here, steadfast and loyal in New York. And completely out of sorts.

A lump fills my throat, and I swallow it down.

"No pressure," Marshall says. "I swear. We'll just give you the nickel tour, throw money at you, and beg."

A reluctant laugh escapes me. "No pressure, huh?"

"None whatsoever. You can meet the team, see how we operate. Spend a few days in the sun and find out if it's a good fit."

There's no harm in one visit. It doesn't mean anything.

I tell myself this, and yet my fingers feel like ice when I finally say, "All right. When would you like to do this?"

His smile lights up his face. "Next week?"

"Wow, you're fast."

"I have to be if I want to snare you."

Smooth. But then he is at the top of his game for a reason.

"Good answer. All right, give me the details, and I'll make some arrangements."

"Bren?"

The sound of Rye's voice behind me has my entire body seizing up like I've been caught skipping school. Heart thundering in my chest, I turn to find him behind me. Dressed in black track pants and a Nine Inch Nails T-shirt molded over his broad chest, he's damp with sweat and clearly out for a run. He'd come upon Marshall and me without either of us noticing. Sweet mercy, how much had he heard?

By the pinched look on his face, enough.

"Rye," I get out. "Hey. I didn't see you..."

The cutting glare he gives me all but screams, *Yeah, no shit, Brenna.* He turns his attention to Marshall and gives him a bland smile. "Faulkner, right?"

"Call me Marshall." He extends a hand for Rye to shake.

I almost want to shout a warning not to do it, because the not-so-hidden glint in Rye's eyes says he'd gladly crush Marshall's bones if he could. But he simply does a brief handshake and then lets go before leveling me with another look.

"You're going to LA?"

Not subtle. The very fact that he's asking sends another wash of guilt over my skin. I shove it down. "I am."

Oh, he doesn't like that answer. Not at all. And though I feel like I've been caught doing something I shouldn't, the fact that he's here, standing before me in the sunlight, makes my heart beat faster. I drink him in, wanting to step close, wrap myself around him and hold on. He's clearly pissed, and I should be wary because I don't know how to explain Marshall's offer, but he's also a familiar comfort. One I suddenly need very badly.

I turn a fake, too wide "please don't say anything else about this now" smile on Marshall. "Can I call you later?"

Marshall might be a talent manager, but he's clearly adept enough in public relations to read me well. "Sure thing." His smile is tinged with an apology as if to say he's sorry for any awkwardness he caused. And because it's my job to read people too, I know he's just figured out who I'm seeing.

My cheeks heat again.

"I have a meeting to get to in about twenty minutes," Marshall tells us. "If you'll excuse me."

Rye grunts. I say goodbye in some stilted fashion, but I'm not fully paying attention anymore. Blood rushes through my ears, and my limbs buzz with unaccustomed anxiety.

The second Marshall is out of sight, Rye and I round on each other.

"Rye..."

"You're going to visit that guy in LA?" Rye says at the same time. "What the fuck, Bren?"

He's too close, smelling of hot skin and fresh sweat. And, damn it, that scent is forever associated with fucking him. My body reacts accordingly, pulling tight and achy. I ignore it because what Rye said finally registers.

"Hold the phone," I say. "Are you implying that I'm hooking up with Marshall?"

His brows lower, the muscles along his shoulders bunching. "What am I supposed to think when I hear him talk about snaring you, and you're...giggling like some smitten kitten!"

The last part booms out, startling a pigeon into flight.

I cast a hasty glance around, noting the people watching—and God help us if anyone recognizes Rye and starts recording—then turn and walk away. If Rye wants to follow, he will. If not, screw him.

He follows, easily keeping up with my quick steps.

"I was not giggling," I grind out. "But that's beside the point. Why don't we start with why you think it's okay to have a go at me like some irate, neanderthal boyfriend. Because that is bull-shit, Rye."

"What, am I supposed to grin and bear it? Because *that* is bullshit." He flushes red. "Are you fucking him?

"Are you kidding me? I can't believe you have the nerve to even suggest it. Hell. And to think I was actually happy to see you."

At that he blanches, then takes a step closer to me. But I hold up a hand to ward him off, still too pissed for contact.

"I'm sorry," he says with a rasp. "Okay? I shouldn't have...

fuck. All right, you wouldn't do that. Of course, you wouldn't. But..." He lifts his arms in a helpless gesture then flops them back down, defeated. "Do you want to? Is that it?"

The hurt in Rye's expression levels me. I instantly feel terrible. I know now what cheating means to Rye and how badly it unsettles him. And hadn't I jumped to horrible conclusions about him with Isabella?

"No, Rye. No. Not even a little."

His nod is tight and quick, but the line of his jaw bunches stubbornly.

"I'm with you now," I say. "I promised my fidelity, and I meant it."

He doesn't speak for a moment. Instead, he frowns at his feet. "I saw you with him and... Shit, Bren. You two flirted at Stella's party, now you're making plans to visit him in LA. I reacted. Badly." His gaze collides with mine. "I'm sorry, Berry."

Now that I've calmed, when I view the situation through his eyes, I know that if I were faced with the same set of circumstances, I would flip out. It isn't easy to admit, but I would be jealous. On the heels of that comes the strange dizziness of knowing he's jealous.

He's jealous.

It should turn me off. It doesn't.

With a sigh, I walk over to the trash and chuck my cold coffee. There's an empty bench facing the Bow Bridge, and I head for it, knowing Rye will follow. At the very least, we'll have a little more privacy.

He sits next to me, close enough that I feel his warmth, but not touching.

"He offered me a job, Rye."

I feel the impact my words have on him, the shock, the way it upsets him, and the way he rallies to lock it down. When he speaks, his voice is gravel. "You want to leave us?"

Leave us. Leave *him*.

"No," I whisper. "I don't. But I'm not..."

When I trail off, he speaks again, softly. "You're not happy?"

God, this is horrible. I feel small and petty and disloyal.

"Rye, your music is your passion. It's something that is part of you. But this is a job for me. One that I've always loved and been proud of, but it's still a job. And lately..." I take an unsteady breath. "I feel...tired, uninspired. Off."

He turns my way, his gaze on my face as if he's seeing me anew. "I get it, Bren. The well has gone dry for me before. It isn't fun."

"Maybe that's all it is," I say, keeping my focus on the lake in front of us.

"But maybe it isn't," he says, knowing I'm thinking it. "Maybe a change is what you need?"

He says it tentatively, as though it kills him to voice the truth out loud, but he will accept it because my happiness is important to him. Horrifyingly, tears prickle against my lids, and I have to blink rapidly to clear them.

"Maybe. I don't know."

His big hand engulfs mine. His strong, rough, messed-up hand. He holds on to me like I'm precious, like I matter. He holds on to me as though he knows how much I need it.

The blunt tip of his thumb runs along the sensitive skin of my palm. "How long will you be gone?"

"A few days. I wasn't looking, you know. His offer came out of the blue. Surprised me, really. But his firm is legendary. I couldn't turn down the opportunity to at least take a look."

Rye holds my hand more securely. "Bren. It's okay. You don't have to explain."

I close my mouth abruptly, the lump in my throat growing. Ducking my head, I focus on our intertwined hands. It is surreal to sit on a park bench, holding Rye Peterson's hand, but, in this moment, it feels like the safest place in the world. He's not judging me; he's giving me exactly what I need. He keeps doing that. How will I ever be able to let him go?

"Maybe I have to explain it to myself."

"Yeah, I get that." Somehow, he's moved closer. Our shoulders brush, and I lean into him. I'm not leaning *on* him. I'm just...resting with him for a minute.

Rye's thumb keeps sweeping across my palm, over the tips of my fingers.

"I'm afraid." I close my eyes against the confession.

Rye pauses, his body lifting on a breath. "Of what?"

Don't say it. Don't let yourself fall to weakness.

The words come anyway. "I'm afraid I'll like it there."

His grip tightens, as warm and secure as a hug. "No matter where you go, you will never be alone. Do you understand?"

I'm going to cry. Right here on a park bench with Rye Peterson holding my hand. My throat works as I swallow convulsively. "Yes."

A tender squeeze of my hand is his reply. Two little girls in matching red coats run across the bridge, followed by a harried woman pushing an empty double stroller.

"I have a house in LA," Rye says. "Up in the hills."

"When did you buy that?" Our voices are quiet, easy as though we're not talking about the prospect of me leaving everything I know and love behind.

"Last year. I had it renovated." He turns his head. Lines of strain still bracket his eyes, but they're clear and steady on me. "Stay there. It'll be more comfortable than a hotel."

"I'm used to hotels."

The wide curve of his lips kicks up on one end. "Maybe I just want to know what you think of my house."

His cautious yet excited tone catches my attention.

"What are you not telling me?"

He gives a careless shrug. A breeze picks up the ends of his bronze hair and lifts it back from his brow, and he squints into the sunlight as he looks over the lake. "It's just something I'm working on. I haven't told anyone else about it. You can see it if you stay there."

Another gift. He keeps giving me these pieces of himself. If he isn't careful, I'll soon have all of him.

"I'll stay at your house."

He keeps his gaze on the lake, but he can't hide the pleased glint in his eyes. "Cool."

Without thinking about it, I lean in and give him a quick kiss on his cheek. "Thank you, Ryland."

He inhales swiftly as though not expecting a kiss but then looks down at me. "I want to kiss you," he says, low, urgent.

"Right here on this public bench?" I tease, stalling the moment.

"Yes, ma'am."

The chances of being seen are low, but there's still a chance. We're a few blocks from my office. Rye uses this particular route for running and so does Scottie.

But Rye looks so good, that wide firm mouth of his perfectly framed by his close beard, and he'll taste so good...My breath grows short.

"Kiss me, then," I whisper.

His nostrils flare, then he's cupping my cheek, dipping his head. He kisses me soft and slow but with such depth that I feel it behind my knees, in the empty ache of my sex. My breath catches, and he gives me his with a little nuzzle and suck.

"Do what you've got to in LA," he says against my mouth. "And then come back to me."

———

LATE THAT NIGHT, I pack for my trip, but I can't shake the feeling of wrongness within me. I shouldn't be leaving Rye. He backed my trip with unfailing conviction. It means more to me than he'll know. And yet he's still alone and floundering. No one knows about his hand, his fear, his pain. It isn't right.

I shouldn't be leaving. But I have to try. I have to see if...

With a hard swallow, I bat at my prickling eyes. I have to go.

But that doesn't mean I have to leave him all alone. I pick up my phone and call Scottie.

"Brenna." His voice is warm and slightly amused. Why, I have no idea, since I call him at least twice a day for the most part.

"I'm going to LA for a week on personal business."

Silence follows, and damn it, he *knows*. I have no idea how he does it, but he knows I'm going to see Marshall. Refusing to squirm, I wait out that silence. Scottie likes to draw it out, hoping his victim will roll over and blab away all their secrets.

Not today, Satan!

"All right," he says finally, grumpy because I didn't fold.

"I need you to do something for me, though." My hands have gone ice-cold, and I clutch the phone tighter.

"If it's to water your plants, be warned, I once killed a silk fiddle leaf fig tree. Sophie called it dark sorcery."

"Ha." My throat is dry, and the sound comes out far too rough. I lick my lips and try for cool cynicism. "It's about Rye. He's been evading his PR schedule..." God, I'm the worst betrayer. "And I know he's missing band meetings. And...Check on him, will you?"

If I thought the silence was bad before, it's freaking ominous now. But, to my surprise, Scottie breaks it quickly. "You want me to check on Rye?"

We both know how out of character it is for me to show any concern about Rye.

Cheeks hot, I grip my phone like a lifeline and close my eyes. "We both know something is off with him." *I'm sorry, Rye. I'm so sorry.* But I'm leaving and he's hurting. I can't stomach knowing he's alone with this. "Just...take the guys with you and check on him, all right?"

I know I've shocked the hell out of Scottie. But his voice remains cool as silk. "All right."

Relief sweeps through me. I've betrayed Rye's trust by pushing this, but I can't regret it. Not when I know how much he needs his friends, not when I know he won't ask them for help when they're the only ones who will truly understand what he's facing. Maybe before everything happened with Jax, I could let it go, but now I just can't. I won't ever leave someone I care about in the dark again.

It's how much I'm beginning to care that scares me and makes my reply to Scottie stilted and stumbling. "Okay. Good. Thanks."

I move to hang up when Scottie's voice stops me. "Brenna?"

"Yes?"

He hesitates for a fraction of a second. "Take care."

The worst part is, I'm not certain it's myself he's asking me to take care with.

CHAPTER TWENTY-ONE

RYE

I'M PLAYING "DON'T GET Around Much Anymore" on the piano when they invade. And by "they," I mean Jax, Whip, Killian, and Scottie. The Four Stooges.

"I'm beginning to regret giving you guys the code to my door," I say while I keep playing smooth and easy. It feels good to make music that doesn't hurt.

Jax stops by the baby grand and sings, "'Thought I'd visit the club. Got as far as the door...' Nah, it's like I'm serenading you."

"I'm crushed. Your melodic voice makes me all warm and fuzzy. Maybe something a little livelier? Without lyrics." I play a few lilting bars of the classic Gershwin Jazz piece "Rhapsody in Blue."

He shakes his head. "Doesn't work as well without the full symphony to back you. Not nearly as stirring."

With a dramatic sigh, I move on to "Für Elise," taking it nice and slow, drawing out the notes. It was the first song I'd learned on the piano—at the sweet and innocent age of five. Part of me misses those days. My parents had been over the moon about their musical prodigy.

Music, music, music. It is part of the fabric of my being. Pull it away and I unravel.

Scottie looks me over with a narrowed gaze. "You've groomed yourself at last."

Leave it to Scottie to notice that first. I resist the urge to touch my jaw. But I can't hold back the memory of Brenna's fine blush, like cherry wine spreading across her creamy cheeks when she confessed she liked the feel of my beard against her skin. I spent the rest of the night between her legs to show my appreciation for her taking care of me. Too bad she's on her way to LA. I'd rather be with her right now instead of facing the firing squad glaring down at me.

The memory of Brenna must show on my face because Scottie's eyes narrow. "Looking rather smug about something too."

I shrug, my fingers dancing over the keys. "Not particularly."

"You're well enough to play piano, at least," Jax says.

"Which makes us wonder," Killian puts in, "why the fuck you keep blowing off band meetings?"

I play a few more notes and then trail off. A lump fills my throat, and I spread my hands over the cool keys.

Whip sits on the bench next to me and taps out the beginning of "Chopsticks." He doesn't look up when he speaks. "Why don't we ask Rye what's up before laying into him? It's not like he's ever disappeared on us before." He glances up a Killian with a pointed look.

Killian flushes a ruddy color and glares. But he catches my expression, which I'm trying really hard to keep blank, and his shoulders sag. "Whip's right." He says it so grudgingly that I huff out a laugh. But neither of us is smiling. He stares at me, hard. "Rye, man, what's up?"

"Is this some sort of weird intervention?" I quip, the lump in my throat growing bigger, sharper. The fucker has tips that puncture deep.

"Avoiding it is only going to make it worse," Jax points out.

Given that he knows this better than anyone, I don't make a joke. Even though I'm dying to make a joke, to do anything to put off the inevitable.

A finger twitches, hitting the E-flat. "I...ah...I went to the doctor today."

The words slap down onto the room like a thunderclap, and I know my friends are collectively unsettled. But no one says a thing. So I keep going.

"Been having pain in my hands, wrists—fuck, my whole arms." Goddamn, that lump is getting too big to manage. "They seize up and I can't..." I draw a deep breath. "I can't play sometimes."

Someone makes a strangled sound. Maybe Jax or Killian. I can't tell because I'm staring at the black and white keys of the piano. "Turns out, I have acute tendinitis. Nothing for it but to rest and let it heal."

"Then why the fuck are you playing the piano?" Whip snaps, visibly pale as if he expects my hands to seize up at any second.

"Different angles of motion. Keeps me limber, I guess, and I..." My voice breaks, and I swallow convulsively. "Fuck, Whip, I can't *not* make music. I can't."

A hand comes down on my shoulder and squeezes. It's Killian. A world of sorrow darkens his eyes, and it almost does me in. But then he blinks and smiles tightly. "So you play the piano. You rest. You get better."

Scottie already has his phone out and is typing away. "I'm redoing your schedules. We'll work this out, mate."

They're killing me. It isn't that I didn't expect their kindness; we're best mates, as Scottie likes to say. But the swiftness of it, the way they're instantly all in...even if I'd do the same for them, being on the receiving end of it is a comfort I didn't know I needed.

I sit on the bench, unable to form the proper words of gratitude. "Thank you" doesn't feel adequate.

Whip nudges my other shoulder with his own. "You've always healed fast as fuck. Remember how quickly the bone mended that time you broke your ankle diving off the stage in Edinburgh?"

The guys snicker, and I purse my lips, not wanting to laugh, yet also wanting to so badly my chest hurts. "Thanks for the reminder, William."

"No problem. Although I don't know how anyone could forget." He smiles wide and evil. "It was pathetic. No one wanted to catch you."

Jax starts laughing. "Oh, God, the way that crowd parted."

"Like the Red Sea," Killian says with a snort.

"Oh, look." I lift my hands to flip them off. "I still have the use of my middle fingers. Fancy that."

But they ignore me.

"They're no fools, the Scots," Scottie says dryly. "They bloody well knew a bloke Rye's size would crush a man like a grape when he landed."

"My size?" I repeat incredulously.

"Yeah," Whip confirms. "Mountain-sized."

"More like a sequoia," Killian says, eyeing me.

All at once, Whip, Jax, and Killian call out, "Timber!"

They dissolve into childish laugher, while Scottie looks on with twitching lips. And I find myself chuckling. It feels good, but it doesn't linger. The heaviness is too settled in my chest.

"Maybe..." I clear my throat. "Maybe you should consider finding a replacement for a while."

The suggestion goes over like a lead balloon.

"Rye," Jax says, snagging my attention. His jaw is set. "Hear me now. No one is fucking replacing you."

The lump is back. "And if I don't get better?"

Fuck, that hurts. But there's no guarantee that it won't come back, especially since, if I keep playing bass the same way, I'll be doing the same repetitive movements that got me here. Part of me is falling into an abyss; it's fast and endless. If I weren't sitting on the bench, I'd probably topple over.

There are people with worse problems, worse pain. People fighting for their lives. In the scope of things, my issues are small. Doesn't stop them from feeling big to me.

"Whatever happens, we'll deal with it," Killian says firmly.

"We deal with it together," Whip adds.

Blinking rapidly, I don't say anything for a moment. "Shit." A shuddering breath escapes me. "You guys are going to mess me up."

"There, there." Jax reaches out and musses my hair. "They're only feelings. You'll get used to them."

"The fuck I will," I mutter, moving out of his reach.

"I've ordered pizza." Scottie tucks his phone in his pants pocket and then removes his suit coat. "I assume you have beer."

"You assume correctly."

He nods and heads to the kitchen. "There's a *Supernatural* marathon on. They're starting from the pilot."

Killian groans loudly. "It's like he's a preteen."

Whip, on the other hand, is already jumping onto my couch and reaching for the remote. "Okay, the Star Trek thing is annoying but *Supernatural*, Kills? How can you hate on Dean and Sam?"

Baffled, Killian looks to Jax and me as though seeking help.

Maybe I'm the only one who remembers we offered to watch *Supernatural* with Scottie when he was falling apart over Sophie. It knocks me on my proverbial ass to realize he's trying to return the favor. For a thick moment, I'm so damn grateful for my friends, I can't speak.

Holding up my hands, I affect a casual tone, like I'm not five seconds from bear-hugging all of them. "Hey, it's *Supernatural*. Castiel is my boy."

I head for the couch as Killian gapes in outrage. Jax gives him a slap on the shoulder. "Guess that means you're getting the door when the pizza arrives." He jogs over and flops down next to me while Whip cues up the TV.

Scottie comes in carrying a tray—a freaking tray—with a neat pile of napkins, plates, five pilsner glasses, and five bottles of beer. He sets it down and starts pouring the beer in glasses; I honestly didn't know I had pilsner glasses.

Killian snorts one last time. "Biggest rock band in the world and we're sitting around drinking beers and watching paranormal melodrama."

"Yeah," Whip says, accepting a beer. "Life's pretty fucking grand, ain't it?"

In that moment, I feel as close to normal as I've been in months. There's only one thing missing. And while we're eating pizza and arguing whether Dean's '67 Impala is the best muscle car ever, I slip my hand into my pocket and curl my fingers around my phone. I don't pull it out and text her.

But I want to. I'm aching to. And that's not good. She's already dangerously close to becoming an addiction. Add all these tender, protective feelings she's bringing to the surface, and I'm just asking to have my heart stomped on. I'm not going to become a shadow of my mother, always wanting someone who doesn't want me in the same way. Not going to happen. I refuse to go down that road with Brenna.

The fact that she's considering leaving Kill John hit like a hammer to my chest, cracking it open in a way that's far too exposed. If she leaves, nothing will be the same. And I have this ugly, twisting feeling that she will. That part of her wants to go.

For my own good, I have to keep my distance. Somehow. Some way.

Good luck with that, man. You're already screwed, and you know it.

CHAPTER TWENTY-TWO

BRENNA

"YOU'RE VISITING LA, aren't you?" the woman in the seat next to me asks.

If you fly enough, eventually you'll be seated next to a talker who insists on engaging in conversation no matter how deep your nose is buried in an eBook.

I set my e-reader down. The woman next to me appears to be in her early thirties and sports a tan that, short of using chemical sprays, I'll never hope to achieve.

"How'd you guess?" I ask.

She shrugs, flipping a length of silky blond hair over her shoulder. "You're all *Sex and the City* high fashion—love the boots, by the way." She gives my knee-length floral print boots an appreciative glance. "Whereas if you were from LA, you'd be wearing couture loungewear and sneakers on the plane."

I can't help but smile, given that she's wearing pale pink couture loungewear and pristine Pumas. "I'll have to go shopping for some good loungewear while I'm there."

"I have a boutique on Melrose." She hands me a card that

conveniently appears in her hand. "Stop by, and I'll hook you up."

So, this is a sale. I tuck the card beneath the protective cover of my e-reader. "Thanks…" I move to read again, but she keeps talking.

"You visiting someone? I'm Valerie, by the way."

"Brenna. I'm going for business."

Valerie sighs and takes a sip of a now-watery pink cocktail resting on her seat tray. "I went to New York to visit a guy. Thought he might be the one, you know? The sex was off-the-charts good."

I nod, not wanting to talk about sex but not knowing how to end this conversation without coming off as totally rude. It never fails to amaze me how some strangers will tell you anything about their lives.

"We've been going back and forth, visiting each other for a couple of months. We started talking about maybe picking a coast and making it permanent. But when I got there this time, he was like a totally different person, all distant and cold. He insisted nothing was wrong, it was all good."

Her eyes go wide as if she's imploring me to understand. And I do, because I've heard some version of this story before. I'm beginning to think almost every woman has lived it at least once.

"Last day, he's all, 'hey baby, I'd love to cuddle, but I'm not feeling so good, you think you can run on down to the pharmacy and get me some aspirin?'"

"He told you he had a headache?" I find myself asking in rising outrage.

She nods, her nostrils flaring in remembered annoyance. "And like a sap, I was so sympathetic. Of course, I'd get it for him. Only the fucker insists that I have to go to this one pharmacy twenty blocks away."

"No."

"Yes. Oh, and he wanted soup from a specific deli too."

I turn in my seat, leaning in so Valerie can speak her pain

without being overheard. But she doesn't seem to mind anyone else hearing. In fact, her voice rises. "Took me nearly two hours, and when I got back?" She pauses, lifting her hand as if to say she needs a moment. "That fucking fuckface was kissing some skank goodbye at the door."

"That was..." I struggle. "Fast. And...wow."

Valerie sits back with a huff and toys with the toggle on her hoodie. "He wanted to get caught. I swear, they all want to get caught. It's the easy way out for them."

"I'm sorry." I don't know what else to say. I've seen the wreckage of too many failed relationships, and nothing anyone says seems to take away the pain. This is why I avoid them. Why risk the hurt when the majority of people out there are total assholes?

"I'm sorry I wasted money on these stupid trips," Valerie mutters then snorts bitterly. "Long-distance never works. Never mind, I keep picking the man version of low-budget cling wrap—the ones who claim they'll hold on tight but then slip and slide away the second you relax enough to let go."

I laugh, but a niggle of doubt creeps over my skin. Am I a female version of cheap cellophane? I never try to hold on to a lover. I always find an excuse to let go, get away: they weren't right for me, fatally flawed in some way, I was too busy, I didn't need them. Looking back on my various attempts at relationships, I can't say I missed anyone or regretted ending things. But it still bothers me. Because the fault can't *all* have been with them. Part of the problem has to be with me.

Doesn't it?

Why is it so hard for me to find someone I want to stick to?

Unbidden, Rye's face rises up in my mind. He's full-on smirking, one brow quirked like he thinks I'm full of it. Annoyed, I bat the image away. It doesn't silence his voice in my head, telling me that I can lie to myself all I want, but I'm still running.

I'm not running this time. It's a legitimate trip. A trip to see if I'll take a job that moves me out of his life.

Because Valerie is right; long distance never works. If I give up Kill John, I'll have to give up...God, am I really thinking of quitting my boys? Quitting Rye? I can't. *I cannot.*

Crap. What I cannot do is think about this anymore. I won't be able to function.

"I'm asking for some champagne," I say to Valerie. "Do you want one?"

She perks up. "Sure. Why not?"

By the time the plane lands, and I'm in the back of the town car I hired, I'm fairly buzzed and overly warm—because champagne is evil that way. My head aches, and I hate all the traffic.

New York has horrible traffic. I'm fairly certain it makes most visitors cry in panic. But LA is a different kind of hell. In New York, you can bail and walk, take the subway. Here, you're stuck in the car until you get where you need to go.

The sun is too bright and hot. I have no idea how anyone would voluntarily want to walk down the overly exposed sidewalks. When the car begins to snake up Benedict Canyon, the movement making my stomach roil, I'm cursing LA and wishing I were back in New York.

I swallow thickly, breathing through the pounding pain in my temples. My period is knocking on the door, and I am regretting the timing of this trip already. I should have waited.

The car pulls up in front of a gate that must be twenty feet high, and the driver stops. "Is there someone to buzz you in, miss?"

"I got it." I'm already tapping the code into the app Rye sent me. The gate slides open, and the car makes its way up a long drive that hooks around a sharp bend. Mature olive trees with lacy little silver-green leaves flank the drive and provide both welcome shade and privacy.

The house doesn't appear until we round the bend. Low-slung and L-shaped, it's a massive modern structure of steel, expansive windows, and honed wood.

Finally, the car stops, which is a blessing. I'm not going to make it another minute. I grab my bags, wave the driver off, and head toward the house.

The front door is fifteen feet high and made of wood stained a rich, warm brown. It opens with surprising ease, and I find myself inside the soaring space that's both cool and light filled.

Leaving my bags in the hall, I head toward the back where glimpses of a pool beckons. My heels echo in the silence. It's a beautiful house if you like modern, but I don't see what would cause that secretive little smile that I'd seen in Rye's eyes when he spoke of it.

All of the main rooms face the back of the house with expansive canyon views. It takes me a minute, but I finally figure out how to operate the window walls. They slide back without a sound, opening the house up to the outside courtyard and garden. As soon as I step out, a sweetly scented breeze lifts my hair and kisses my overheated skin.

This is why people deal with the traffic and the ugly sidewalks that stretch for miles without succor. This lovely weather, the gentle rustle of palm trees, and the sweet scent of jasmine and chamomile dancing in the air. I breathe in deep and let it out slowly.

The pool stretches along the side of the house and is flanked by an orderly row of loungers. A pavilion has groups of low-slung couches, a fire pit, and what appears to be an outdoor screening area. There are a few outbuildings, little guest houses if I had to guess. They're well hidden, surrounded by more olive trees and potted lemon trees. Each house has a pretty patio set up.

Again, though it's beautiful, I don't know why this excites Rye. It isn't anything we haven't seen before.

Turning back into the house, I make my way past the living room. Each room is designed for comfort, with slouchy, deep couches and chairs, and inspiration in the form of art on the walls and objects of interest that I recognize from our various trips around the world. Rye is a collector. On our off days, he heads to the markets or small shops in whatever city we're visiting.

My fingers trail over a teak Danish-modern sideboard, drift past a Georgian marble bust of a young girl with one of Rye's baseball caps resting jauntily on her head. And then I find it. Peppered around the lower wings of the L-shaped house are recording studios. Beautifully fitted and comfortable studios.

Knowing my boys as well as I do, this place would be a dream to record in. There's an upstairs and downstairs gourmet kitchen and several expansive bedroom suites. All the amenities of home, coupled with state-of-the-art facilities. One could entertain or hang out while not recording, swim in the pool, exercise in the gym, or sweat it out in the sauna.

Every room, every view is soothing and serene. Inspiring.

Smiling, I reach for my phone and dial.

Rye answers on the second ring. "You get in okay?"

"Just now, yes." I sit in a gray, velvet club chair. "I'm in your house. Or should I call it a recording studio?"

"Both, I guess. What do you think?"

"It's beautiful. I wish we'd had places like this to use with earlier records." Technically, I never need to be at any of those sessions, but it seems that where Kill John goes, I go. I am utterly enfolded in their world.

"That was the idea," he says. "I'm planning to lend it out to friends when we're not using it."

"Not rent it? You'd make a killing."

He chuckles, and the warm sound rolls over me in a hazy wave. I close my eyes and sink into the chair.

"I've been thinking I could produce more, Bren. Make music that way."

His hands.

A lump rises in my throat. "You'd be great at it."

No one knows music the way Rye does. He's already

produced more than half of Kill John's albums, and I honestly don't know why he doesn't do all of them, because the ones he handles are the most popular.

We've been quiet for too long, and Rye clears his throat.

"Thanks." The tentative tone makes me wonder if I've surprised him with the compliment. Then again, I haven't given him very many over the years. Regret lies heavy on my shoulders.

"I mean it, Rye. You have a way with music that's transcendent. Killian and Jax might write the lyrics, but you polish everything up and breathe life into them."

Why hadn't I ever told him? Because we'd always been focused on hating each other.

His breath hitches, and I know I've affected him.

"Thank you," he says with a rasp. Then pauses. "The guys stopped by. They...ah...well, they knew something was up and wouldn't go away until they got it out of me."

"The fiends," I tease softly, like I'm not quietly aching for him. He'd been so alone, when he didn't have to be.

He hums, a bit self-deprecating, before forging on. "I told them about...everything."

I know this. Scottie had texted. But the quiet, almost shy pleasure and relief Rye can't quite hide in his voice pokes at my tenderized heart. He'd needed his guys' support but didn't know how to ask for it. "I'm glad, Rye."

"Yeah, me too. We're working things out."

"Good."

Emotion shouldn't be able to reach through a phone and wrap around a person's heart. But it does. I'm not certain either of us knows how to handle it.

Rye clears his throat, and when he speaks, he's back to his old, playful self. "You meeting with Mr. Taco today or tomorrow?"

I roll my eyes. "Mr. Taco is the worst name ever. It's not even clever."

"It'll grow on you," he insists in a teasing tone. "By the time you meet him, that's all you'll be able to picture."

"Are you trying to sabotage me?" I ask lightly, because I know he isn't really.

But he answers with quiet seriousness. "No, Berry. Never that. I'd wish you luck right now, but you don't need it. And, admittedly, I don't know if I can wish you luck."

"Why?" I whisper, feeling the need to follow his hushed tone.

"Because I don't want you to go."

My breath hitches, the fluttery feeling in my heart threatening to make me say things I shouldn't. "Rye."

"But I will," he says quickly. "Let you go. You deserve to be where you're happy."

He'll let me go. Because I'm not really his. And he's not really mine. I stare blankly at the wall and wonder why everything aches.

"I understand," he says steadily. "And the guys will too."

Right. He wasn't talking about us, but about me and my role with Kill John. My period is definitely knocking on the door, because I'm on the verge of weeping for no particular reason. It occurs to me that the last time I had my period was the first time Rye kissed me. Has it been a month? Before I know it, our time will be over and done, and I have the feeling it will all seem like a strange dream.

I need to get off the phone with him. I'm maudlin and weak-willed right now.

"I've got to go," I say. "The flight wore me out."

"Take the bedroom on the second floor at the end of the hall. I called ahead and had the service make it up for you."

Tears threaten again, damn it.

"Oh, and the house is stocked with food and drinks, so you don't need to worry about that."

I pull in a deep breath and let it out slowly. I'm the one who takes care of things for others. And I take care of myself. Always have. I don't know how to handle this type of simple kindness.

All I know is if I don't get off the phone now, I'll be begging him to join me.

My will is my strength. I can't crumble.

"Thanks, Ryland."

He huffs a laugh and then says the one thing he'd promised not to. "Good luck, Berry."

I almost hate him for that. Almost.

Rye

I GO to Chicago with Whip. Nothing left for me in New York, so why not? It's a nice distraction from all this thinking I've been doing.

Only, and this is a damn annoying problem, I quickly find out that you cannot run away from thinking about certain things. I've spent a lifetime cramming down the bitter disappointment I felt when my dad cheated on Mom. I did a pretty good job of not dwelling on how, as a kid, when he left her, it felt as though he left me too.

Surely, I can spend a few days hanging out with Whip and not let myself think about a certain redhead. And if my chest feels a little too tight, my stomach a bit hollow, that's easy enough to ignore.

"Why the hell did we decide to go to Chicago in November?" I ask, as we leave the warmth of our hired car and step into the frigid air. It's got to be twenty degrees already—and that's not counting the freaking wind that cuts to the bone, which I am most definitely counting.

Whip hunches into the collar of his coat. "Stop being a wimp. If you stayed in New York, you'd still be playing sad songs on the piano."

"At least I wouldn't be freezing." We hustle our ass down an alleyway, flanked on each side by a security guard. "All I'm saying is that we could have gone somewhere warm like—"

"California?" Whip supplies dryly.

I don't dignify that remark with a response. But given that Brenna told everyone she was headed out to LA on "business" and the fact that Whip is smirking, I'd say he's on to us.

We're almost halfway down the alley when a side door opens, releasing warm air that steams in the cold and a wall of thumping bass. A man steps out, his solid frame silhouetted in the light. He catches sight of us and smiles.

"You made it." He clasps Whip's hand and draws him in for a shoulder bump then turns and catches my hand next.

"Tariq, long time," I say when we half hug. The world knows him as ShawnE, but I met him as Tariq and the name is stuck in my head.

"When was it?" he asks. "London, 2016?" There's a gleam in his brown eyes that says he's remembering our mischief.

"Think so." We'd hung out at a private club we're both members of. I have fuzzy memories of getting drunk, willing women on our laps, and doing something downright dirty with a bottle of Creme de Cacao—however, the details of that remain scant. Probably for the best.

With a chuckle, he leads us into the blessed warmth of the hall. Inside, the music surrounds me like a much-needed hug, pounding into my flesh and pumping my heart rate up. A surge of energy follows as Tariq heads down a narrow staircase.

The club is an underground lair, filled with dancers and flashing lights. I only get a glimpse of it through a two-way mirror before we enter a private room. Tariq gets us settled with a couple of beers, and we chat for a while. The club is Tariq's baby, bought after his first album went platinum. He hosts a variety of artists and has made many an up-and-coming DJ famous.

"So," he says to Whip, "you ready, man?"

Whip rolls his shoulders and then bobs his knee in an

agitated rhythm. "Need to let off a little steam."

Tariq chuckles because he knows how it is. Guys like Whip and Tariq have an energy that can only be burned off by creating beats. Tariq raps and Whip plays the drums, but they'll both go out some nights and DJ at a venue for a couple of hours just to recharge their creative wells.

Right now, I get all the highs I need from Kill John. If I want to refill the well, I get it by producing on the side, helping others find the right sound and smoothing out rough tracks. Tonight, however, I'm Whip's wingman.

The door opens, and the club manager pops his head in. "Whip, Rye, how you been?"

"Jay." I give him a wave.

Whip greets him. "My set all right, man?"

Whip likes to do things old school, which means he spins using vinyl. It's an unwieldy process hauling crates of records around then setting everything up. He'd come to the club earlier today to arrange things.

"Good to go." Jay glances at Tariq. "Need a word. You got a minute?"

"I'll be out in a second." Tariq turns to us. "You good to go in thirty?"

"Yep."

When Tariq leaves, I stand and wander around the room. I'm restless in a way that no amount of performing will settle. It's *her.* She's in my blood now. When I'm with her, it's like nothing else. No better high. When I'm not with her?

I am lost.

I'm lost, and she's in LA—thinking about moving there.

Shit.

What the hell am I doing with her?

I stop at a vintage arcade *Donkey Kong* that's in the far corner. The big screen is bright with its glaring, simplistic '80s graphics. "You ever played this?" I ask Whip.

He gets up and ambles over. "Nah. To tell you the truth,

these old games freak me out."

A laugh bursts out of me. "What?"

Whip grimaces. "It's ridiculous, right? But there's something about the twitchy-ass way the characters move that makes my stomach clench."

I can't help it; I laugh again. "Sorry," I say after a moment. "It's just so..."

"Whack?" he supplies with a self-deprecating smile.

"Random. It's random as fuck."

"Yeah, well..." He glances at the game. The intro is playing and Donkey Kong paces—in an admittedly twitchy fashion. Whip scowls and looks away. "Nope. Still drives me bug fuck."

Grinning, I push away from the machine and start pacing again.

"You nervous?" Whip sounds a little surprised. As he should be; we never get stage fright. That's Jax and Libby's specialty.

"No." I'm not. I'm...I don't want to think about it anymore.

But Whip watches me with those ice-blue eyes of his that see far too much. He leans against the couch back, crossing his arms over his chest. "We ever going to talk about this?"

About her. The one person I'm trying to forget for the moment.

I kept it secret. But, fucking hell, Scottie knows, Jax knows. Why can't I talk about this with my closest friend?

With a sigh, I find an armchair—some ultramodern piece made out of metal and leather straps—and flop down. The damn chair groans in an ominous fashion. "She doesn't want anyone to know."

"But I guessed it," Whip fills in. "So you're not really breaking her secret."

A snort escapes. "That's a thin-ass excuse, and we both know it."

"But it's the defense we'll go with if asked."

"Sometimes I forget your mom is a lawyer."

"Try growing up with her. I couldn't get away with shit."

"That's why you're cagey as fuck now." I rub a hand over my face. "All right. I'll talk. Mainly because I'm...Well, shit. I don't know what the hell I am anymore."

In the halting tones of the reluctant and confused, I explain what happened, starting on the night I eavesdropped on her conversation with Jules. I leave out the personal bits and give him the bare bones of the situation.

"Problem is," I say when I finally get to the present situation with her going off to LA and me sitting here twiddling my thumbs, "I can't think straight anymore. I miss her when she's not around. A lot. I hate hiding what we're doing, but I understand why she wants to. At least that's what I tell myself. But in here?" I thump a fist to my chest. "It feels like bullshit, keeping quiet and pretending we are the same as we were before. Because we're not. We're...Shit. That's the other problem. I don't know what the hell we are."

When I finish, Whip sighs. "What made you think getting physical with Brenna without the possibility of any kind of real relationship in the cards was a good idea?"

I stare blankly at him. "My dick?"

He chuffs. "Yeah, I just bet your dick was doing all the thinking."

"To be clear, I'm not regretting the decision, and neither is my dick, because the sex is off-the-charts fantastic—shit, I didn't say that! You did not hear me say that."

Whip laughs and takes a long drink of water. Wiping his mouth with the back of his hand, he looks away, clearly thinking about something. When he turns back to me, his expression is considering. "This arrangement you've got going with Bren isn't working for you, is it?"

The words gut-punch me so hard, I hunch over, pressing the heels of my hands against my tired eyes. "No."

It tastes like betrayal. Like the end. At this moment, I'm not sure what hurt more to say, that my hands were jacked or that I can't continue like this with Brenna and keep my head up.

My body is tense, wired. I close my eyes. The rhythmic thump of bass and the occasional cry of the crowd in the club punctuate the silence in the room.

Whip's voice, soft yet insistent, slides over me. "You gotta end it. I know it seemed like a good idea at the time, but you keep going like this and it will get so twisted, neither of you will come out of it intact."

"I know. I know, all right? I just..." Can't. Not yet. I need more time. More of her. Our official "day" is tomorrow, and I'm going to miss it. My throat closes in on me. "I like her, Whip."

Like is too weak a word. But it's the only one I can say.

"Yeah, I know." His quiet acknowledgment cuts deeper. He pauses. "Bren asked Scottie to check on you."

My heart starts trying to pound its way out of my chest. "What?"

But it's not a question; it's shock.

Whip nods in acknowledgement. "She knew you needed us but were too stubborn to ask for help." His smile is brief but fond. "Probably because she's stubborn about showing her feelings too."

Brenna always had to be tougher than any of us. To her, revealing any hint of emotional weakness meant the possibility of losing everything.

I rub a hand over my tight chest, as Whip lets it all sink in.

"I think you know what you have to do to fix this." Whip and I have a connection deep enough that I understand what he means. Of course, I do, because he's read me too well and knows exactly what I've been thinking. It's not an easy decision to make.

Truth is, the whole thing scares the shit out of me. But a person can only lie to themselves for so long, and I'm no longer willing to play myself a fool.

"It's a risk," I say.

Whip shrugs. "Everything worth having is a risk."

CHAPTER TWENTY-THREE

BRENNA

I AM SERIOUSLY MESSED UP. I acknowledge that much in the privacy of my head. I had a great time with Marshall and his team. Anyone who possesses even a modicum of passion for publicity and marketing would kill or die to work with them. Dream job is an understatement. Yet I couldn't wait to get back to Rye's house, wanting nothing more than to burrow my head under a blanket and forget everything.

I have the period from hell. My body hurts. I'm so bloated, I imagine this is what a tick feels like. All of that, I expect; I live through it every month. The true horror here, the totally twisted part, is that I'm moping and feeling sorry for myself because I can't have sex with Rye for nearly a week.

No, it's not sex that I want right now. And that's not why I miss him. Truth is, my desire to be with Rye has never been solely about physical gratification. That was simply the lie I told to allow myself to get closer to him. Stupid pride has kept me from admitting that he is one of my favorite people—maybe my absolute favorite. When he is near, I hum like a struck tuning fork. Everything is *more* with him.

So why am I here? Why does the prospect of forging a new career path fill me with excitement but also feel like a betrayal?

"Stop it," I mutter while putting on my rattiest but most comfortable nightshirt. "This is a golden opportunity, damn it."

And I'm talking to myself now. Yay.

Muttering, I curl up in bed and pull the covers up high. I have to get a grip. I will not wonder what he's doing now. I do not want to hear the sound of his voice, or to tell him how my day went.

"Ugh." Flipping onto my stomach, I hug a pillow close. It's cool and lumpy, and what I really want to hug is his big, strong body. Which means I'm definitely screwed. "And an idiot." With a huff, I flip onto my back. "An idiot who can't stop talking to herself."

Great.

An idiot who stares at the clock. It's two minutes to midnight. Our witching hour. Only he won't show tonight. He's in Chicago.

Yesterday, he sent me a short video of himself and Whip performing at a club. And though it appears as if all he's doing in the video is fiddling with knobs on a console and dancing along to the beat, I know the level of skill it takes to create music like that on the fly. It's sexy as hell. Pure competency porn.

I suppose it's for the best that we're in different sections of the country. I'd never be able to stay away otherwise.

The thought barely crystalizes when I hear the front door open. Ordinarily, I'd be terrified. But security in the house is topnotch, and there is only one person who would be able to get through it without any problem.

Then again, it could be a killer or evil rapist. Clutching my phone, I sit up and wait, ready to scream bloody murder if I need to. From the way my heart is doing a little happy dance within my chest, I don't think I will.

The sound of footsteps draws closer. I shouldn't be able to identify anyone by the cadence of their step, but I recognize the pattern anyway. The bedroom door pushes open, revealing an all-too-familiar silhouette. A smile threatens to spread over my face. I hold it in ruthlessly.

"Sneaking into a woman's bedroom is a great way to end up in jail," I tell him, fairly proud that I don't sound breathless and giddy.

Rye pauses at the threshold. He's a hulking shadow, his head tilted to the side as though he's studying me. I doubt he sees much; the room is cool shadows and inky darkness. "I was trying not to wake you."

"And that I'd eventually wake up to find a man in my bed? That wouldn't freak me out?"

"Well... Okay, when you put it that way, this wasn't one of my best plans."

I bite back that smile even harder. "It was a horrible plan. Besides, you're too big to tiptoe effectively."

He huffs out a laugh, slowly walking closer. "What did you used to call me? Big oaf?"

"Only when you were treading on my feet and taking up all the room in the travel bus."

With a nearly full moon and sheers covering the windows, there's enough light to see him clearly now. Weariness deepens the natural laugh lines on his face, but he appears happy, his gaze on me.

"All failed attempts to get closer to you, Berry." He says it like a joke. But there's a ring of truth underneath that makes my heartbeat stutter. It begins to pound when he reaches behind his head and casually tugs off his shirt. "I'll do my best to be more careful with you in the future."

"Um." I don't even know what I'm saying. He's slowly stripping, matter-of-fact about it and not in the least bit teasing. It's holding my attention all the same. His belt buckle clinks, a sound that goes straight to my happy bits, and then he's popping the buttons of his jeans.

Pop, pop, pop.

Good God, when did getting undressed become a symphony?

"You're supposed to be in Chicago," I blurt when his jeans hit the floor.

He stands perfectly still, that long, strong body bathed in the ambient light coming in from the windows. For a brief second, I almost pity those who can't see him now, this Greek statue made into living flesh. Hercules on the prowl. My gaze drifts down. No tiny dick of antiquity there. A raging erection stands proud and waiting. I'm so distracted by that particular length of flesh that I almost miss his reply.

"Am I?" he asks.

"Are you what?"

Another soft laugh. "Supposed to be in Chicago. And stop looking at my dick unless you're going to play with it."

A flush hits my cheeks and snaps me out of my lusty fog. "Stop pointing it at me."

His hard-on twitches. He grins. "It's waving in surrender."

I meet his gaze. "What are you doing here?"

"I got a craving for dogs."

"Dogs?"

"Hot dogs, Berry. We'll go get some tomorrow."

"You came all the way out here for a hot dog?" I don't know why I'm questioning him. I should be sending Rye on his way to one of the other bedrooms. But I'm too stupidly happy to tell him the sad truth, that we can't have sex right now.

"They're excellent hot dogs."

"Better than Portillo's?" The guys drag me there any time we go to Chicago, usually with Rye leading the charge.

"Are we really debating hot dogs? Or is this some weird foreplay talk?"

I can't help grinning, but I fall back onto my pillow with a sigh. "Not foreplay."

"Too bad. There's like ten hot dog puns running through my head now."

Rye is in the act of lifting the covers to slide into bed when I stop him. "I have my period, so you might as well go to another room."

His forward momentum is too much for him to stop with any grace, and he ends up settling down next to me. "I know."

"You know?" I turn on my side to face him. "How do you know I'm being tormented by Aunt Flo?"

Rye's smile is quick as a flash of light. "Aunt Flo? Why the hell do you call her...oh, wait. Okay. Yeah, that's a visual I didn't need."

Snickering, I burrow down farther in the bed, hugging a pillow to my belly. "Try living with the bitch."

"Thank you, no." Rye rests his head in his hand and smiles down at me.

The mix of tenderness and contentment in his eyes unnerves me, and I break eye contact, focusing instead on the massive swell of his shoulder muscle. That's a distracting sight too, because I suddenly want to lick his skin. It's safer than dealing with emotions when I'm currently a hormonal mess.

"You never answered my question," I say to his chin. "How do you know?"

When he doesn't speak, I glance up and find him grimacing. "What's that look?" I'm half amused, half horrified. How *does* he know?

Rye scratches the side of his head, sending his thick hair up on end. "I'm trying to figure out how to answer without getting in trouble."

"It had better be fast, or it'll get worse."

"I'd rather tell hot dog jokes."

"I bet you would. No joy, Peterson. Talk."

"Damn it," he mutters under his breath. "Jax warned me never to bring up lady issues to a woman."

"Good advice, given that you both have the delicacy of a bull in a china shop."

"Yeah," he admits then leans in a little. "But, really, Bren, is there a tactful way to talk about Aunt Flo?"

"True. Now, spill it." I tweak his nipple, loving the way he yelps and rubs his chest with a scowl. It's all show, since I didn't pinch that hard. But it's a good show, since I now can't stop staring at his massive pecs. I want to be the one rubbing them.

Down girl. You can't have sex.

"Evil pixie. I have a mind not to answer you."

"Don't make me pinch you again." I wiggle my fingers in emphasis.

"Okay, okay. Put away the pincers." Rye rests on his pillow, bringing his face closer to mine. His gaze slides over my features. It's a lazy perusal as though he's simply enjoying looking at me. When he speaks, his voice is gentle and unhurried. "Let's put aside the fact that I can count, and it's been a month since the last time she was around."

"Ah. Right."

He keeps talking as though I haven't interrupted. "When evil Aunt Flo is about to come knocking at your door, you start switching from coffee regular to mocha lattes. You put your hair in a low, loose braid, which makes me think you get headaches."

Dazed, I nod. "Feels like someone's kicked my skull."

"Poor baby." Rye reaches out slowly. The tips of his fingers trace a small line along my temple then slide into my hair to stroke it. "You start favoring those pretty jersey dresses that skim your long body instead of those sexy tight skirts that hug your fine ass. Sophie once complained to everyone in the room that her womb feels like there's a war being waged inside when she's on the rag, so I'm guessing looser clothes are more comfortable."

"You pay more attention than I thought," I whisper thickly.

The blunt, callused tips of his fingers caress my jaw. "When are you going to believe me? I notice everything about you, Berry."

I'm struck silent, little fissures forming around the edges of my heart. Would it be too much to ask for just one kiss? Probably. *Definitely. I'd want more.*

"Oh," he says as if remembering something. "And you wear that vanilla and caramel cookie scent when dealing with Flo. Until the day it's over, when you switch to celebratory lemon cake perfume. Both of which, by the way, drive me absolutely frantic to take a bite out of you."

I swear I hear a crack inside my chest. "You... You notice my perfume selections?"

The corner of his mouth kicks up just a bit. "Pay attention, angel. I notice. Every. Thing."

Somehow, he's slipped his arm under my neck. His big hand splays wide between my shoulder blades as he eases me against him. I go willingly because it's too good to deny. And though his biceps are nearly the size of my head, and rock hard, he makes a surprisingly comfortable pillow.

A sigh escapes me, and he slowly rubs my back and toys with the ends of my hair. This is definitely cuddle territory. We don't do that, not without sex. But he feels familiar now. Familiar and good. Until he arrived, I'd been restless and unsettled. I can deny it all night long, but his presence, his touch, is what I needed.

"You were surprised when I told you I had my period last month," I point out, still stuck on this whole revelation.

"I was distracted by an overwhelming case of lust and desperation."

"Poor, Rye-Rye." I nuzzle my cheek on the curve of his shoulder. He's warm and solid and massaging my sore spots.

"You hurting?" His husky whisper gusts across the top of my head.

My hand finds his waist where his skin is like heated marble. "Not particularly. I took some painkillers before bed."

"Good." With an earthy sigh, his body relaxes into the bed.

"Damn, this feels nice. That flight took forever. Two freaking stops. Got on in Chicago and, for some reason, the plane went to Atlanta then back out to LA. We were going backwards to get forwards. Where's the sense in that?"

The outrage in his voice has my lips twitching.

"There were no nonstop flights?" Rye isn't terrified of flying the way Scottie is, but he's never liked it and refuses to fly unless it's nonstop.

Rye stills for a breath, the muscles along his chest going tight. "Not any that would get me here tonight."

I tense with him and suddenly we're awkward again. "Tonight?"

He shifts a little as though he might bolt. But Rye is nothing if not stubborn. "It's Tuesday. I get Tuesday."

Because it's our night.

With that, he turns, cocooning me in his arms. Snuggled under the covers, it's our own little world. I'm content in a way I haven't felt since childhood, which is weird since there's nothing particularly chaste about being pressed against over six feet of naked male. And despite the fact that Rye is simply holding me, he's clearly turned on. His erection presses into my belly with an insistent nudge as if to remind me what we're really about. We only touch for sex; that's the rule.

Except we've been slowly tossing all those rules out the window.

"I have my period, Rye." I don't know why I'm repeating myself. I don't want the hugging to end.

But it doesn't matter because Rye isn't budging. He breathes in deeply and nuzzles the side of my head. "I don't care. We're doing this."

"What?" It comes out in a loud squeak. "I'm telling you now, I am not into that."

Rye pulls back enough to meet my gaze. A furrow runs between his eyes. "You don't have to sound so disgusted."

"And you don't have to sound so insulted. I mean, I'm open-minded and all, but it's my body and...and...ick."

"Ick?" He huffs out an offended laugh. "Cuddling is gross to you?"

Blinking in shock, I stare at him. "Cuddling?"

"What did you think I was..." He freezes before a snort of amusement escapes him. "Why, Brenna James, I am shocked. Were you thinking—"

"Never mind what I was thinking," I cut in hastily.

"No, no, I want to hear more about this alternative scenario."

"Never. Mind. Rye."

Chuckling, he pulls me close again. "You're adorable."

I burrow my flaming face in his chest. "I will pinch you."

"I know. You're very fierce." Strong fingers massage my scalp. His touch pauses for a second. "Did you meet with Mr. Taco... Marshall yet?"

I bite back a smile at his slip. At least he's trying to behave. Then my humor fades. "Yes. Yesterday and today."

"Two days in a row," he murmurs in a teasing tone, but there's an underlying tension that he can't hide.

"It's a big company. Lots of people to meet."

Rye keeps playing with my hair, but the movement is stiff, as though he has to work at maintaining the casual touch. "And? What did you think?" He says it so lightly, anyone who doesn't know him well would assume he's excited for me. But I know better. He's trying not to be, but he's worried.

Perversely, that makes me smile again. I touch the hollow of his throat, caressing the little divot there. He smells of stale plane air and warm, earthy Rye; there's no other scent like him. I'd know it in the dark now—rich and deep yet crisp, like fine bittersweet chocolate. People's natural scents don't actually smell like foods or spices, but it's the closest I can think of. He's hot, melted chocolate to my senses.

"Bren?" he whispers, prompting.

I'm stalling. We both know this. My finger trails along his collarbone, and his skin prickles in its wake. "I liked what I saw,"

I whisper back, watching his throat move convulsively on a hard swallow. I stroke the strong line of his neck. "They have so many accounts, actors, studios, musicians, athletes, even a few wineries. I could spread my wings. But I don't know..."

He swallows again then presses his lips to the top of my head. He doesn't kiss me but simply breathes deeply before talking, his voice muffled in my hair. "Never be afraid to fly, Bren. Even if it takes you from all you know."

This man. My lids prickle with heat, the back of my throat clenching. I close my eyes and lean into him, my hand slipping around his neck. "Thank you." When I feel him nod, I speak again. "I hate change. Whenever I think of leaving Kill John it feels like I'll be losing a limb."

"You'll never fully leave us," he says gruffly. "We'll always be there for you."

"I know. It's more that, when I imagine someone else taking over my job, guiding you all...I don't like it. I *hate* it."

A soft laugh rumbles in his chest. "You want it all."

"Shouldn't everybody?"

He laughs again and pulls me closer, until we're pressed against each other. God, but he feels good, like the most perfect pillow—even if he's all muscle. I sigh and try to quiet my brain. But I can't. Because I can't have it all. Change is coming. And I can't fight the truth of that. Rye must feel my tension because he returns to stroking my back in delicious, slow circles.

"Go to sleep, Berry. It's been a long day."

I'd been struggling to sleep for hours, but his softly spoken words, the warmth of his touch, and the steady beat of his heart against my cheek all work to lull me into a state of languid comfort. My lids grow heavy, and my hand spreads wide over the hard swell of his chest. I could stay like this forever. But the girl inside, who's constantly felt she had to prove herself worthy, won't quiet. "You really came all this way just to sleep with me?"

There's a beat of silence before he answers, his voice a whisper with an edge of surprise. "Yeah, I did."

CHAPTER TWENTY-FOUR

RYE

I WAKE with her hair on my face. All that glorious, silky, thick mass cascading over my cheeks, covering my nose. In truth, I'm smothered by it and am in danger of choking. Even so, I grin wide, as I gently brush the auburn strands away. She doesn't wake but snuffles—I would never dare call it a snore—and wiggles her pert butt closer, grinding it against my increasingly interested dick.

I tell my dick to settle down, as we're not getting any for a while. But that is surprisingly okay with me. I'm content with what I have in this moment: Brenna's slim body cuddled up next to mine, the scented warmth of her skin, the utter peace of watching the rays of the sun stretch across the floor while holding her. After days of twitchy tension, I am relaxed.

It's not the first time I've woken up in bed with someone. I've gone on occasional benders with different women, spending a couple of days just fucking. They were mostly hazy memories involving the high of performing, getting drunk, and getting lost in someone else for a while. There's no shame in it. At least not for me. I had a good time with those women, and hopefully gave them one as well.

But those moments weren't anything more than a bit of fun. It didn't mean anything more to me. Or to them. In the back of my mind, there was always the knowledge that they were with me because of who I was, or maybe they just liked how I looked. But they didn't know me. I didn't know them.

I had no idea just sleeping with someone I have a connection with could be this good. It feels like solace. Like true rest. Right here, in the light of the morning, with Brenna James wrapped around me in blissful sleep, the world stops spinning.

I was thirteen years old when I heard the song that made me the man I am today. I had been obsessed with music my entire life; I listened to everything, from Chopin to Chuck Berry, Portishead to Patsy Cline. But it wasn't until that rainy day, curled up on my bed, trying to ignore the sound of my parents fighting about yet another one of my dad's infidelities, that I downloaded "Taste the Pain" by the Red Hot Chili Peppers.

It was a revelation.

I can't even say it's the Peppers' best song or that it's my favorite. But it was the first song I heard of theirs. I sat on my bed, staring up at a hairline crack on my ceiling as the music flowed over me. As Michael Peter Balzary—aka Flea, one of the best damn bass guitar players in the world—absolutely slayed. He didn't simply provide a background rhythm, he dominated the song, owned it. Funktastic beats, hot slides of soul. It worked into my bones, reverberated through my heart.

I can play any instrument put in front of me. It isn't a trick but simply a part of my essential makeup, like the color of my eyes or that I'm left-handed. But lying there that day, alone and confused, I realized the bass guitar offered something I'd been searching for—an outlet where I could bang out beats or strum taut melodies. I could let the rage, the pain, out in a way that would satisfy some critical need within.

For more than half my life, the bass guitar has been my

world, my heart and soul. But I can no longer play it the way I want. Not with the same intensity and carefree joy. The knowledge hurts. It fills me with a gut-wrenching sorrow and choking fear. Change is terrifying when it isn't your choice.

But here, with Brenna's funny little snores buffeting my chest, it hits me with a calm certainty that music isn't the entirety of my heart and soul. It no longer owns me completely. She's there too, in my heart and soul. A touchstone in the darkness of uncertainty.

The truth of that overwhelms me, and I squeeze my eyes closed, press my lips to the top of her warm head, and just breathe. But it doesn't help. There's a hole opening up in my chest, getting wider and wider. Because this isn't real. It's stolen time.

Maybe I'm holding her too close or too tight because she stirs, flipping over to face me then letting out a small sigh as she stretches. I loosen my hold and watch her wake. Her lashes flutter, then her eyes open, revealing true amber irises flecked with gold. And I swear to God, sap that I've become around her, my damn heart clenches.

It takes a moment for her to focus, and I probably shouldn't be lying here, staring, but I can't help myself. She's adorably mussed, soft and sleepy.

Given that I *am* staring, I don't miss her slight confusion at seeing me. Maybe she doesn't fully remember last night, or maybe she simply regrets letting me stay. It's going to be awkward if she's upset I'm here. Then she blinks again, her gaze growing clear. A small smile quirks the corners of her pink lips.

"Hey," she says, her voice sandy with sleep.

Relief is a rush of air through my lungs. With the tip of my finger, I ease a strand of her hair away from her forehead. "Hey."

Her palm is on my chest. I'm not certain she's even aware of it. Her fingers drift over my pecs, stopping to toy with the silver bar piercing my nipple. Pleasure arrows through me, and I feel like purring. Yes, purring; I'd do it if I could.

I lean in, brush my lips over hers. Once. Twice. She sighs again, a soft sound that I feel all along my skin, and I pull back just enough to meet her gaze. "You want breakfast?"

"You making it?" she asks with an expression that is at once hopeful and doubtful.

I laugh lightly. "Of course."

Her nose wrinkles as she peers at me. "You can cook? Because I have never seen it."

"I can scramble eggs, dole out yogurt and fruit." I kiss the tip of her nose, because I need that touch. "I can even blend up one of those health smoothies you seem to like."

"They *are* quick and refreshing."

My lips skim the line of her jaw. "We don't need to be quick today, Berry."

She makes a noise like she's trying not to laugh. Her hand keeps drifting over my chest, along my side. God, she smells good, not flowery or fruity but pure, heady pheromones that work like a drug to my system. I burrow my nose in the warm curve of her neck and breathe deep.

Brenna chuckles then, her fingers threading through my hair. "I'm so tired. I don't want to move."

"So don't." I curl further into her, cuddling close. I've decided: I fucking *love* cuddling. "We make our own rules here."

She's running the tips of her fingers along my scalp. It feels like heaven. "We do, huh?"

"Yep. Here, we're free." A nice fantasy. One I want to make real.

She murmurs something, her touch already slowing. Her body is melding with mine, warm and relaxed. And then we drift, talk of little things, laugh at inside jokes only we know. Like I said, heaven. It occurs to me that I should talk to her about why I'm really here. But I can't. Right now, everything is perfect.

After a while, I make her breakfast then offer to take her on a drive. I keep a matte chrome Harley Fat Boy at the house. At first, I worry that Brenna might want a car, but, when I tell her about the bike, she gives an un-Brenna-like squeal of delight and puts on stellar ass-hugging jeans, a baby blue tee, and a pair of purple wicked-high heels. My tongue is likely hanging out, but it can't be helped; I love dressed-down Brenna.

"Nice shirt," is all I can manage. I'm not lying, though. It has all my favorite qualities: it's small, tight, and on Brenna. The phrase "Earth Girls Are Easy" stretches across her chest. "Jax give you that?"

"How did you guess?" Brenna smiles, as she slips on a brown leather jacket—seriously, the woman always has clothing for every occasion at the ready.

I hand her a helmet. "Remember that Jeff Goldblum kick he went on during our last tour? Do you know how many times I had to see that movie?"

"Ha! I actually like that one. He tried to get me to watch *The Fly*." She makes a face. "Disgusting. I made him turn it off, but I still had nightmares for a week."

"Poor Berry. I'm sorry I wasn't there to comfort you."

She chuckles like she thinks I'm only teasing. But I'm not. I almost want to push it, but once we're on the bike and her thighs are bracketing mine, I forget what we were talking about. The entirety of my concentration goes to Brenna and keeping her safe. Maybe we should use a car.

An impatient pat to my abdomen has me snapping out of it, and I start the bike. For a while, I just drive, soak in the sun, air, and the feel of my girl pressed up against my back. Brenna wraps herself around me like I'm her favorite pillow. I'm cool with that.

Eventually, I head towards downtown and find a place to park.

"So," she says, pulling off her helmet in a move worthy of *Charlie's Angels*. "Where are you taking me?"

I incline my head to the corner building behind me. "The bookstore."

Her eyes light. "You're taking me book shopping?"

"I'll take you anywhere you want to go, but yeah, I thought you'd like it."

"I thought you'd assume I'd want to shop for shoes." She says it lightly, but there's a glint in her eyes that has me grinning wide.

"Babe, I might be ignorant when it comes to relationships, but I'm not a total fool. That statement is bait."

Brenna laughs and shakes her head. "It so was. Good evasion. Let's go look at books."

The place is massive and smells of knowledge and sunlight. Brenna and I stroll along together and split up when we find something that interests us. But we never stray far. I always have her in my periphery, something inside me not wanting to give up the sight of her. It's a strange thing. Brenna and I have been in each other's orbit for over ten years. I know her face as well as my own—better; I look at her face more than mine. But being with her like this makes it all feel new.

She catches my eye and smiles. For the first time in my life, I fully understand those old-timey cartoons where the wolf is struck by love darts and his heart is trying to pound its way out of his chest. I'm pretty sure there's a lovelorn grin on my face, pink hearts dancing around my head. Whatever the case, it's enough to draw Brenna over to me.

Without a word, I take her hand and lead her onward. There's a tunnel made entirely of stacked books that crests over us like a wave. No one is around, and I pull her close. Her lips are soft and welcoming. I fall into her kiss the way I'm falling for her: completely, like a man denied sustenance. She tastes like cherry-sweet sin. I lick into her mouth chasing that flavor, my back hitting the wall. Brenna eats at my mouth with the same fervor, her arms winding their way around my neck.

A snicker from the right has us pulling apart to look. A group of teen girls walk by, giving us wide grins. I don't know if they recognize me or not. I don't care at the moment, because Brenna is still pressed up against me. I turn my attention back to her, my hand drifting to palm her peachy ass.

She smiles, soft, flushed. "Hey."

Those pink hearts are probably circling my head again. "Hey."

Right now would be the perfect time to tell her why I really came all this way. But the words are stuck in my throat. I don't want to ruin this moment.

Tell her.

With surprising gentleness, Brenna brushes my hair back from my brow. Her amber eyes look into mine.

Fucking hell. Tell. Her.

"Apparently there's a vinyl section here," she says in the face of my silence. "Did you know that?"

Shit. Busted.

"Ah, yes? I mean, yes, I did. But I wasn't planning on going there. Today is for you."

Brenna's laugh is husky. "So self-sacrificing."

I'm about to protest, swear my innocence, but she lifts on her toes and kisses my cheek. "Today is for *us*. Come on, buttercup, I want to see this collection."

Yep. I'm a goner.

I grab her hand and all but drag her to my favorite spot in the store. Vinyl records and Brenna. What could be better? She stays with me, browsing LPs, pulling out old favorites for me to look at. Paradise.

I hand her a battered old copy of "Masterpieces by Ellington."

"Duke Ellington wrote his compositions to highlight his musicians' individual styles and talents," I tell her. "I mean, we do that now with Kill John, but for a big band composer back then to say, this isn't about showing off my skills but to elevate the talents of those around me and take the music to its highest level..." I sigh in appreciation. "He made it an all-encompassing visceral experience, a masterpiece of that perfect moment in time."

"You know," she says as I inspect the back of a Shirley Bassey album. "I think my true appreciation of music came from you."

The record almost slips from my fingers. "I...What?"

Brenna leans a hip against the display stand. "I'm serious. You're so passionate about music. The way you'd talk about it, the endless songs you'd have us listen to, the history of it all..." She shakes her head, ponytail swaying, a fond look on her face. "It made me hear it, feel it, in a whole new way. A better way."

All these years, I never knew she was truly listening. I never knew she *liked* what I said.

Amber eyes hold mine. "Music is part of your heart and soul, Rye. Whether you play or not, that will never change. You will always be able to express yourself through it and move people with your love of it."

Hell.

"Bren. You can't say that to me here. Not when you've gone and cut my heart wide open, and all I want to do is kiss you until...Damn it." I expel a harsh breath and rake my hand through my hair to calm down.

She studies me with interest. "Don't stop. Until what?"

"Until you're slick and swollen and begging for my dick."

A laugh breaks from her, but she eyes my mouth like it's ice cream and all she wants to do is lick it. "I wouldn't have to beg. You'd give it to me without hesitation, fast and hard, wouldn't you, big guy?"

Flames of lust burn my skin, as her voice lowers. "All I'd have to do was spread my thighs and show you just how wet—"

"Not fair, Berry." I shove the record back into place. "Not fucking fair." I march her cute little ass out of the store. And she laughs the whole way. I pretend I'm disgruntled, but I'm not. I am so far from *not* it isn't funny.

I distract myself by taking her to one of my favorite hot dog spots. We opt for carryout, and I drive us up into Griffith Park, stopping at a secluded spot so we can eat. There is a bench nearby, but before I can get off the bike, Brenna surprises me and climbs up to straddle my lap.

"Well, hello," I say, my arm instantly going around her waist.

She settles in. "Much more comfortable than a bench." She reaches down and grabs one of the takeout boxes. "You up for eating this way?"

"You think I'd ever turn down a chance to have you in my arms?" I shake my head and help her out by holding the box steady. "Think again, Berry."

The hot dogs are messy; bacon-wrapped and loaded with toppings—Brenna's has corn, cotija, and spicy aioli, while mine is drowning under fries and cheese. But Brenna doesn't hesitate to pick hers up. It's cute as hell the way she holds the unwieldy dog, her nose wrinkling a little as she tries to take a huge bite without spilling. I chuckle as she almost gets there, and then I wipe the little bit of sauce that lands on her chin.

"Good?" I ask.

"So good."

Because it's not polite to stare, I dig into my own dog. We're silent for a bit, eating in the sunshine. Brenna sets the remnants of her hot dog back in the takeout box and grabs some napkins from her lap to clean her hands. I hand her a frosty bottle of her beloved Diet Cherry Coke. After she's had a drink, she sighs with contentment.

"There," I say with the satisfaction of a man who has seen his woman well-fed. "Tell me a taco is better than this."

She dabs at the corner of my mouth with a napkin. "I hate to break your little dream here, buttercup, but this is basically the love child of a hot dog and a taco."

Damn. She's right.

I rally. "But it is still called a hot dog. Thus *better* than a taco."

"A technicality."

"Which is another way of saying I'm right."

"Or that you're not."

Chuckling, I lift what's left of my hot dog to her. "You haven't tried this one."

With a dubious hum that I know she does to tease me, Brenna opens her mouth and dutifully waits for me to feed her. Fuck. I stare, trying not to get turned on.

Her smile is pure evil. "Come on, Rye. Give me a taste of your wiener."

I burst out laughing, even as I get hard as a pike. "Oh, you'll get more than a taste."

She takes a large, snapping bite, and I laugh again as she chews. By the times she's swallowing, she's laughing too, resting her forehead on my shoulder. "All right, you got me," she says straightening, cheeks flushed and eyes alight. "These are excellent hot dogs."

"Better than a taco?"

Hell, why am I pushing this? I shouldn't. It's stupid. Petty as fuck. I'm thinking Brenna might agree because she goes silent. Her expression is thoughtful as she packs up the mess, shoving it all in the boxes lying on our laps. Heart thudding, I hold up the takeout bag for her to put the trash in. Only when I've set it on the ground does she speak.

"Is this really about tacos?"

She knows it's not. My chin lifts, stubbornness rising with it. But then I sigh. "No."

She hums again, her gaze searching mine. I brace for more questions. But, instead, she reaches out and softly runs her fingers through my hair, brushing it back. "Right now, right here, whatever the meal, I'd prefer to have it with you."

My heart knocks hard against my chest. "Bren...You asked Scottie to check up on me." I hadn't meant to say that. But I don't back away from it.

She searches my face in wariness. "You needed your friends."

I need you too.

I cup her cheek. "Thank you."

She touches the edge of my jaw, delicately, like I'm something she needs to handle with care. Physically, I'm the stronger one, but she's breaking through what's left of my armor with ease.

"Rye, you don't ever have to thank me for having your back, because I always will."

Just like that, I'm done for.

I don't know who moves first but we're kissing. And it fills all the empty aching places I didn't know I had. I take it slow, savor her mouth, her flavor, breathe in her soft sighs. My hand wraps around the silky rope of her ponytail as I hold her where I want her, lick the gentle curve of her upper lip, suckle the sweet, plump give of her bottom lip.

I lose time kissing Brenna. But, beneath all the pleasure, I know mine is running out. This arrangement is measured in stolen moments. It isn't real. I need real with Brenna.

Risk.

One that would mean a potential loss, of my pride, of her.

––––––––

Brenna

WITH A GASP, I tear out of sleep and lurch upright. The room sways like a drunken dancer then settles. But my heart doesn't stop thundering within my chest. Cold empty terror and helplessness shake me so hard, I pant, gripping my knees to hold in a sob. No control. No way to keep them safe. To keep myself safe.

A warm, broad hand settles on my back. "Hey," Rye whispers, at my side. "You're all right. It's okay."

The sound of his voice and the heat of his touch grounds me, and I'm finally able to take a deep breath.

"Sorry if I woke you." It comes out weak and thready.

Rye sits up further and rubs a hand over his face as if to wake himself. "It's okay." His eyes glint in the semi-darkness as he looks me over. "You dreaming about Jax?"

I jolt. "How did you know?"

He rests an arm on his bent knee. "It's four thirty-two in the morning. That's when we all found out."

For a moment, I can't speak. A lump swells within my throat. I swallow hard. "Yeah. I didn't realize that you..."

"Remember it so clearly?" he offers wryly.

"No." I squeeze the back of my stiff neck, and instantly his hand slides up to take over, massaging me with calm competency. "No, that you also made note of the time. Does it haunt you too?"

"Not in the same way. But there are days when I'm up for whatever reason, see the time and..." He rolls a massive shoulder like it's too stiff. "It messes me up so badly, I want to cry."

The confession has me leaning into him, and he wraps me up in his arms, holding me close. We're silent for a moment, Rye stroking my hair and me running my hand up and down his chest just to know he's there, solid and alive.

We'd spent the day together, and it was fun, perfect. A moment of peace. And the whole time I struggled to find a way to tell him...But I couldn't. Not when he was so happy. So I swallowed it down, held in the truth as we crawled into bed and cuddled together. I fell asleep listening to the sound of his heartbeat.

But now it's a new day. And all the tension, all the horrible twisting fear of being too close to someone, of feeling too much, is back. My throat feels too tight, and my words come out a rough rasp. "Before that night, I thought we were all invincible. Nothing could hurt us."

"I thought so too," Rye whispers. He heaves a ragged sigh. "I felt like such a self-centered ass for not noticing that John was hurting. Or that we were all just...I don't know, careening into disaster in our own ways."

Because we were all out of control back then. "None of us noticed, Ryland. Not even John. That was the problem."

He nods, but his body remains tight and tense. "I know. I just wish to God that I had."

In the dark, I find his hand. Our fingers thread in a comforting clasp. Over the last year, all of us have spoken about John's depression, and we've tried to talk things out more, voicing our burdens when they become too much to bear. It's helped. But I've never shared any of this with Rye. The comfort of doing so is strangely relieving. He lets me be open without feeling weak.

"I used to call John," I say at last. "When I woke up."

Rye's breath stalls for a second. "Me too."

A soft, brief laugh escapes me. "God, maybe we all did."

"He doesn't seem to mind," Rye says.with a smile in his voice. But he's raw. I can feel it.

"He has Stella now, though." I ease back a little and rest my head on Rye's shoulder. "So I stopped."

"Bren..."

The quiet sorrow in his voice has me speaking over him. "It's okay, you know? I don't need—Killian thinks I need to go on vacation, get away from the band for a while. I think he's right." Shit. I can do this. I *can*. "About the break."

Rye turns my way. I feel the weight of his gaze. Everything is about to change. We both know it. There's only the matter of who goes first.

"We could stay here," he finally says, slowly, like he's forcing the words out. "Take a break."

God, that sounds so...I close my eyes, my fingers digging into the bedding. "Rye—"

"Don't," he blurts out then pauses with a harsh breath. "Don't say anything for a second."

"Okay."

But he doesn't speak. Instead, he throws back the covers and sits on the side of the bed. Rye has a tattoo of sheet music for

"Amazing Grace" inked in black across his shoulders. To those who don't know him, it might seem a strange choice, but he once said music was his grace. It saved him more times than he could count. Of course, he never confided that to me. He told the guys when he returned from the tattoo parlor. I simply was within earshot and overheard.

Because, before we started this, we never really spoke past trading insults or basic verbal exchanges. Yet, somehow, he knows me so very well. And I know him. I know by the tense lines of his back and the way he's staring off, unmoving, that he's not angry. He's upset.

I can handle angry Rye. That's familiar ground. Upset Rye is another story. At some point, his hurts became mine as well. "Rye?"

He sucks in a breath then stands in one fluid motion. "I need to be dressed for this."

"O-okay..." I don't know where this is going, but I know instinctively it won't be easy.

He heads to the clothes he threw on a chair before we went to bed earlier. His movements are easy, tugging on his boxer briefs and jeans, but the bunched hinge of his jaw betrays him. He pulls on his black T-shirt and runs a hand over his stubble. For a moment, he stares down at his bare feet, his hands braced low on his trim hips.

"Why are you standing there like that?" Foreboding settles over me like an itchy blanket. The sensation grows stronger when his lips flatten.

But then he gives me a wry and tired half smile. "For once, I'm trying to follow your advice and think before I speak. I want to choose my words wisely here, Bren."

"Just say it, Rye. Whatever it is, just say it already."

He draws in a breath and then lets it out in a rush. "I can't do this anymore."

Blood drains from my face, as my chest caves in on itself. "You want to end our arrangement?"

"Yeah. I do."

Shock explodes over my skin in hot spikes of pain. I knew it would come to this eventually. It had to. We're in different places in our lives. Even so, I didn't expect this level of hurt. Not the desolation. I went into it with eyes wide open. Only, I thought... I don't know what the hell I thought. Coherent thought escapes me at the moment. But maybe that we would ease out of it gently. And, God, I'm ridiculous because I've been trying to find a way to tell him my news. Yet here I am feeling rejected when he's the one being adult about this. The irony almost makes me laugh. Almost.

Standing—because no way am I having this conversation while curled up on *his* bed—I gather my fractured thoughts. "I understand. I'll go."

Rye makes a furtive move, like he might try to touch me, but then he pauses and grasps the back of his neck. "Shit, honey. I don't want you to go."

"I'm missing something here. You just told me you don't want to see me anymore."

"I meant, I want to cut the crap and actually do this."

My head is still spinning, and I stare at him in confusion. "Do what? You just said you want to end this."

"End the lies, Bren." He takes a step closer. "Not us. I don't want to lie to our friends. I want to be with you for real. A real relationship."

I freeze, this new shock replacing the hurt. There is a small, hopeful voice that says I should run to him with open arms. But then I remember where I am and why I came here. My eyes close with bitter resentment. Why is it that when one part of life finally opens up and becomes clear another will get tangled and complicated?

"I went to Chicago to try and distract myself while you were gone," he says in the face of my silence. "I tried and failed. Because it hit me that where you are is where I want to be."

God. My toes curl into the thick pile of the rug beneath me, as if somehow that will keep me upright. They're the right words. What every woman wants to hear. And yet those words, the sentiment behind them, cut into my air.

Rye sighs, his gaze pained. "It's not just sex. Not for me. I know that was the plan. But the moment I actually put my hands on you, everything changed—"

"Rye." He's breaking my heart. I don't know how to tell him...

"No, just listen." He rounds the bed to stand before me. He's so close, I can smell the scent of his skin, see the spark of earnest need in his eyes. "I'm not playing around. I'm not trying to trick you. I don't want to hide or wait for a certain fucking day just to see you. That is bullshit—"

"I'm taking the job," I cut in, the words bursting past the fist of regret clutching my throat.

Silence rings out for an agonizing moment as we stare at each other. I see him struggle to be happy for me. And that hurts worst of all. He lets out a slow breath. "That's...that's good. I mean, you should follow—" Rye swallows audibly. "But I don't see why we can't still try to be together."

Head throbbing, I press the heel of my hand to my eye. I don't know how to make him understand without hurting him. But I can't lie either. He deserves the truth. Lowering my hand, I hold his gaze, even as mine blurs.

"My whole adult life has been about Kill John. I've lived and breathed your world, your music. I go to sleep thinking about all of you: what I need to do for you the next day, week, month, year. I hear your songs in my head. I dream of Kill John. The band has become my air, my heart and soul. And, for so long, I loved it. Loved that you all gave me the opportunity to lift you up."

His jaw bunches as he nods in understanding. But he doesn't say a word, just stares at me with eyes that are slowly going red at the edges.

I force the words out. "But Kill John no longer fills me up the same way. I find myself resenting that it takes all of my time, my attention. There's a restlessness in me, an emptiness. I thought... I thought sex would fix it. That maybe if I felt that human connection, I'd be okay. And it has. To a point."

Rye licks his lips, and when he talks, his voice crumbles like rust. "It will be better when we're together for real. I'll be here for you, Bren."

My breath shudders. "It's not enough."

He blinks. Such a small movement. And yet it's as though his entire body flinches.

The lump in my throat grows so large it hurts. "I need a clean break."

"You..." His breath hitches. "You don't just want to leave Kill John. You want a break from us. From me."

I don't want to leave him. But I have to. "My entire life is so entwined with all of you—"

"From *me*, Bren. Please don't lump me in with the guys for this. I can't—" He grips the ends of his hair and turns his head as though the sight of me is too painful.

"Of course, I don't think of you the same way as the rest of our friends. But it doesn't change the fact that, if I'm with you, I'm still with Kill John. I'll still think about the band, worry about all of you. I'll still want to cling."

"Shit," he says with a harsh laugh. "I can't win here, can I?"

"Please don't make this harder than it already is."

He cuts me a look. "I didn't think asking for us to be together would be a difficult decision."

"I can't think when I'm with you; I put the rest of my life to the side. I can't keep doing that. I need to think..."

"Think?" His jaw pops. "What is there to think about? You either know or you don't."

"Well, I don't know!" I raise a helpless hand. "I want to be sure. I need time."

His nostrils flare. "Why is this so hard for you? It shouldn't be hard, Bren. This should be easy."

"And the fact that it isn't? Maybe that means something, Rye. Maybe we should take a step back and...and..."

"And what?"

"And evaluate things!"

"It's a relationship, not a marketing plan!"

We're snapping at each other like we used to. I want to cry. And I never cry over relationships. I've been a party of one for my entire adult life; I don't know how to be part of a pair. I've forged myself in iron, unwilling to rely on anyone else, until it became a shield that I can't seem to set aside. But I want to. Part of me wants that so badly. But my whole sense of worth has become the band. If I don't take this chance, I might never know who I am on my own.

"Damn it," he says with a sigh. "I'm sorry. That was out of line."

I shake my head, wanting to reach out for him but knowing it won't help. "It's on me. It wasn't fair of me to have started something with you when I was feeling this way. This is what I was afraid of. Everything is more complicated. And if we got closer, did this for real right now..."

"Yeah, well, don't worry. We never took that step." His gaze narrows as he runs a hand over his chin, the sound of his beard rasping. "Yesterday was a goodbye, wasn't it?"

My heart thumps painfully. "Yes. No. I don't know. I just wanted to enjoy you before—"

"You said goodbye," he answers bluntly.

"I didn't think of it like that," I whisper before huffing out a pained laugh. "I was trying my best not to."

"But now time's up, isn't it? And we want different things."

I can only stare at him, afraid to move forward, afraid to stay where I am.

"It's okay, Bren. I get it. You need this chance to figure shit out. Don't worry about me. You're free and clear to..." His breath hitches, harsh and loud. "You're free."

"Rye—No. Don't. It can be a small break. I'll go to LA, see how I feel—"

"Bren. There's no way in hell I'm going to be the one who holds you back. Not after all we've been through. You're right. We should end this now before it hurts too much."

"Rye—"

"No. There are things I can't do either. I can't do this half-assed anymore. Find yourself. Find that happiness. And...and if you ever..." He smiles weakly, the forced gesture fading fast. He dips his head, swallowing hard, but then seems to give himself a mental shake. When he looks back, his gaze is flat. "You know where I am."

And then he leaves me.

CHAPTER TWENTY-FIVE

RYE

W ELL, that was a disaster.

CHAPTER TWENTY-SIX

BRENNA

WHAT HAVE I DONE?

CHAPTER TWENTY-SEVEN

BRENNA

THE PHONE GOES off in the dark, clanging and vibrating under my head. Jerking awake, I fumble around, trying to grab it. Whoever it is has my personal number, and I've learned never to ignore a call in the dead of night.

"Hello?"

"Brenna?"

The second I hear my mother's voice, I curse inwardly and grind my teeth. "Mom? What's wrong?"

"Why would anything be wrong?" The ever-present censure in her voice scrapes across my nerves. "Why can't your mother call you without something being wrong?"

God, why did I answer the freaking phone?

I rub my eyes and fight a sigh. "Because it's the middle of the night?"

She pauses. "It's eight in the morning, Brenna."

Again with the reproach. The slight *tone* that says I'm a total dumbass.

"I'm in California, Mom. It's...five here." Which might as

well be the middle of the night, as far as I'm concerned.

"Well, how was I supposed to know you're in California? It's not as though you ever tell me about your life."

My life. I almost snort. My life is shit right now. All of my own making. I rub my aching chest and try not to think of Rye. It's been a week now. A week of me making excuses to the rest of the band and hiding out like a coward. I left his house and found an Airbnb. A necessary step. One that still hurts.

"Why do you keep whispering?" Mom demands. "Do you have someone with you?"

As though the idea of me being in bed with someone is something I should hide. But I'm alone. Again. My fault. This time I do snort, a long scathing sound. It's directed more at myself than my mother.

Unable to sit still any longer, I slide out of bed. "No, Mom. There's no one."

Out in the hall, where the windows lack curtains, it's lighter, the sky beyond a steel gray blanket settled over the dark horizon. I take a breath and walk toward the little sitting area at the end of the upstairs hall. The hardwood is cool against my feet.

"Well, that's a relief," she says darkly.

"Is it? I find it a tragedy."

"It would be if you choose someone working in that dreadful music business."

Gritting my teeth, I take a seat on the soft Womb chair by the window. "Why would it even matter, given that I work in the music business?"

I don't know why I'm asking, or why I'm still on the phone. I should hang up. But I can't. I never can. Where my parents are concerned, I am a glutton for punishment.

"You should have something more than that," my mother says with a gentleness that disarms me. "You're so tangled up in all of them. It isn't healthy when your happiness hinges on just one area of living."

I flop back against the chair, my heart beating too hard and fast. Oh, the fucking irony. Hadn't I said the same thing to Rye? Holy hell, have I become her? My throat closes up in a panic. I need to get off the phone.

"Mom—"

"No, I'm serious, Brenna. I worry about you."

I know she does. The problem is, her brand of worrying leaves me feeling belittled and lacking. I'd rather she worry less and trust me more. Then again, I don't trust myself anymore so I can hardly blame her.

I have no idea what I'm doing with my life right now. I need to tell the guys that I'm leaving; I just messed things up with the one person who has even remotely got close to breaking down my walls, and I'm being lectured by my mother who thinks I'm a perpetual fuckup.

You have *fucked things up*...

"You're almost thirty," she goes on with dogged determination. "Most of your school friends are married with children right now and—"

"You were married with a child at my age. And you've more than made it clear, you weren't exactly happy."

My mother sighs, and I wince at the onslaught of guilt. It doesn't matter that she loves to tell me how sorry she was to have married my father—and that she had to because of me—the fact that I was the one to point it out now is a betrayal.

And this is why I don't talk to my mother when I can help it. I cannot win with her. What bothers me the most is that I want to. I want her to see me as competent, a success.

"You're right," she says in the thick silence. "I wasn't happy. I got caught up in lust and sex—"

"God, Mom."

"You're more than old enough to hear this..."

I'll never be old enough to hear this. Honestly, I may be traumatized for life after hearing this.

"And it's important. I thought great sex and strong attraction were enough. But at the end of the day, when the physical wasn't part of the equation, all we had left was bickering and the knowledge that we chose poorly."

"Then why didn't you divorce him?" I snap, exasperated. "Because of me? That's crap."

"At first, yes, because of you. And it isn't crap, Brenna. Sometimes you make sacrifices for your children. But then, when you were older..." She sighs again. "He's what I know. It felt safer. And I don't hate your father."

She just isn't in love with him.

"When you find someone," she goes on, softer now. "Let it be someone...steady. Reliable. A friend. Don't just pick someone simply because they're good in bed."

Blinking rapidly, I look off into the distance where the lemon-yellow sunlight lines the black mountainside. Which one did I have with Rye? Was he right when he said it shouldn't be so hard to know?

Clearing my throat, I turn my attention back to my mother. "Seriously, Mother, why are you talking about all this? What's going on with you?"

It takes a moment for her to answer. "We're going to Xander's party soon."

The dread in her voice matches my own, but I know it's for different reasons.

"Yes," I say, trying to get her to continue with her point.

"You're going to be with your friends, all of those seemingly happy couples, and that can get to you."

It bothers the hell out of me that she knows this, that I even feel the slightest twinge of jealousy when I see my friends coupled up. But none of that will be as hard as facing Rye again. *That* will be agonizing. I let him go. Over a job.

Was it really the job, Bren, or were you running scared?

"Not having your life settled can push you towards making mistakes," she says.

With a sigh, I slump down in my chair and close my eyes. "That's what I'm trying to do."

But talking to my mom has my blood running cold. Because how much of what I fear has to do with the shit she's put in my head over the years?

It's worse when her tone changes to slightly pitying. "I know you don't want to hear it, but I was exactly like you when I was younger. I tied myself to Isabella's group of friends. I thought it would be my whole life. Then your father...well, I thought I'd have what Isa and Xander had with him. Life left me behind, Brenna. Don't be like me. Choose your own path. Be...wise."

I don't want to see myself as my mother. I never have. I've run as far away from her as I could. The idea that I'd inadvertently end up like her horrifies me. I am dizzy and tense.

"Mom..."

"I won't say any more about it."

I press a hand to my face and try to breathe.

"Now then. You know your father has a bad back..."

I stiffen, because I know *this* tone far too well.

"Flying coach doesn't do him any favors."

And here is the real reason she called. A dull ache forms behind my eyes. "I'll send you both first-class tickets today."

Mom is quiet for a moment, as though she's contemplating the offer and wanting to refuse. We both know better, though.

"Thank you," she says finally, like she's only accepting so as not to offend me.

"It's my pleasure." If it will get her off the phone it is.

"Well, I'll leave you to your day then." And like that, she's in a rush to go. I hang up and clutch the phone in the silence of the morning. The sky is light gray now. I should get dressed and start my day, but I'm so tired now I can barely hold my head up.

I let him go. Over a job that no longer holds any excitement for me. Because it means the loss of him.

The dam I've built around my heart creaks, straining to open. I let out a shuddering breath. The dam breaks. I curl over myself and cry.

CHAPTER TWENTY-EIGHT

BRENNA

I FLY into Heathrow on my own. Everyone else had coupled up and gone on earlier flights. Not me. That would mean either being a third wheel or sitting with Whip. And Rye.

I haven't seen him in five weeks. Five freaking weeks.

The first two weeks are on me. Then, right before I returned to New York, Rye went back to Chicago with Whip, and they worked with ShawnE, producing an album for a new artist he's backing.

I could have called or texted, even gone to see Rye. It isn't as though I didn't know where he was staying. But I felt too raw—uncertain. I needed to tell the guys about my decision; Marshall was good with giving me six weeks to settle things on my end. But the words stayed locked in my throat. A bad sign all around.

I took the time to think. Really think.

It wasn't comforting to realize that part of my reaction to his offer stemmed from the fact that I didn't see it coming. I didn't expect him to want something real. I didn't expect him to want it with *me*.

Truth?

I don't think I'm good enough for anyone.

And here's the real horror: this is the complete opposite of what I project to the world. On the outside, I am a confident woman who knows exactly what she wants and how to get it. I don't let anyone fuck with me. As Jules pointed out, I hold my own with the most powerful people in the industry without flinching.

I believe in myself. When it comes to my profession.

When it comes to me?

Apparently, I don't. It took Rye Peterson asking for more to make me see my weakness.

When he returned from Chicago, I made myself scarce. Like a damn chicken. I chastised myself about it every day, but I couldn't find the courage to face him.

Even though we only spent two full nights together, I reach for him in my sleep, my body aches for him when I wake. The ghost of his scent haunts me, because I swear I catch a whiff of it at odd times. And it doesn't matter how many times I wash my sheets, he's still there.

I miss the sound of his voice. I miss his joking manner, the way he forces me to see the world in a different way—not so dire, not so serious. I miss talking to him.

I would have talked to him on Thanksgiving, but he spent it with his mom. Given that my mom sent me a message saying they were going to Florida for Thanksgiving and would see me in England, I spent the day with Scottie, Sophie, Killian, Libby, Jax, Stella, and Whip. And little Felix, who amused himself with flinging whipped sweet potatoes around the table. He managed to ping Scottie's ice-blue silk tie dead center. Fun times, but the absence of Rye was glaring.

It occurs to me that I've *always* noticed his absence. Anytime he's not with the rest of us, the group feels smaller, dimmer. At least for me. And the crazy thing is that this has been true the whole time, even when I convinced myself that he drove me up the wall. Oh, the games we play.

Sighing, I collect my things and disembark the plane. It's the middle of the day, and I've arranged for a car to pick me up at the airport and drive me to Varg Hall in the Cotswolds. It's about an hour and a half of driving, not ideal given that I've been on a plane for seven hours. But it's either get it over with now or rest a day or two in London first. I'd rather get on with it.

Besides, he's there.

I shove the thought away and head out to baggage claim. It's a surprise to see Whip waiting for me. Oh, he has a beanie shoved on his head and is wearing mirrored aviator sunglasses in an attempt to be incognito, but I spot him immediately and head his way.

"What are you doing here?" I ask.

He smiles wide and adopts an affected English accent. "I'm your driver, Lady Brenna. Varg Hall awaits. Let us away posthaste so we may indulge in decadent revelries."

I roll my eyes but smile. "I hired a car. You didn't have to come all this way." I ignore the small—*tiny*—pang that Whip is the one here and not...No. Nope. I'm not thinking about him.

"A hired car?" Whip makes a noise of disdain. "So you can be stuck with a stranger and spend the entire drive with your nose in your phone?"

"You make it sound like that's a bad thing."

"It is." He points to a set of pale pink bags coming around the carousel. "Those are yours, right?"

"I am horrified that you know my luggage."

Whip gives me a sidelong glance. "Custom-made Gucci luggage has a way of making a lasting impression, Bren."

My cheeks warm. "Yeah, well, blame Scottie. They were a gift from him for my twenty-first birthday." The guys took me out drinking, and I got a killer hangover in return. Scottie gave me luggage. Is there any wonder why he's my secret favorite?

Whip chuckles and retrieves the luggage. "I know. You know

what he gave me for my twenty-first? Mutual funds for my retirement years."

I stumble a step. "He did not!"

"Yep," he says cheerfully. "Those fuckers have already made me a ton of money too."

We both laugh and head for the parking lot. Whip leads me to his car, and I halt. "You thought this would be preferable to lounging in the back of a Range Rover?"

"Hey." Whip smooths a hand over the hood of the car. "This baby is a blast to drive."

The "baby" in question is a vintage ruby-red '70s Austin Mini with white racing stripes. It's been lovingly restored. But it's tiny. "I don't think my luggage will even fit."

"It'll fit. My kit fits, so..." He shrugs.

"You brought your drum kit?" I shake my head. "Uncle Xander will love that."

"Not to Varg Hall," he says as if I'm daft. "I dropped it off at my place in London. I'm going to spend some time there after the party."

"Ah." With that, I get into the tiny car. And somehow, Whip manages to fit my bags in the back. The Mini isn't what I expected. It's not just restored but a custom job, with modern cream leather seats, a stereo, and probably dozens of other upgrades under the hood.

Whip confirms this when he gets in and gives the glossy wood grain dashboard a loving pat. "This little sweetie has been soundproofed, given an upgraded suspension and drive train." He starts in on engine specs, and I hold up a hand.

"You're speaking gibberish at this point. Can you simply assure me that you won't drive like a complete maniac?"

He's too quick to grin. "I promise I won't be a *complete* maniac."

I'm in trouble.

Twenty minutes later, we're flying down the M40, and I'm

clutching my seat. "When you're no longer driving, remind me to thank you again for picking me up."

He chuckles. "What, so you can kick my ass? No way. I'm running for it as soon as we park."

"Good idea." I try to relax against the seat and take in the few glimpses of the countryside that we streak past.

Whip turns on the radio, and Ella Fitzgerald croons Christmas songs with her smooth-honey voice.

"God, I love Ella," Whip says wistfully. "If I lived back in her day, I'd have begged for a date."

Chuckling, I turn my body a little in the cramped space to face him. He's almost too tall for the car. While he's not huge like Rye, he's six feet tall, and his seat is pushed all the way back. But he doesn't seem to mind and handles the car with efficiency.

"I have a weakness for women with beautiful voices." Whip flashes a quick, secretive smile. "Don't tell Killian, but the first time I heard Libby sing, I got a mini crush on her."

"No!" Killian would have flipped. Like me, he's a bit of a hothead, though well-intentioned.

"Yep. But she was Killian's girl, so I ignored it."

"Good idea."

Whip nods, his eyes on the road. "Once had a crush on you too."

"What?" I sit up straight, shocked. And a little unnerved.

He huffs a sound of amusement. "Don't freak. It was back when you were eighteen and I was twenty. Lasted about a week, if that."

"Well...that's...Okay, it's a shock but kind of funny too."

Whip shrugs. "You're smart, pretty, and fun. And we hung out all the time. Seems inevitable that feelings might build. I might have tried something, but I knew you were Rye's girl."

He sucker-punched me. Right here in this tiny car. I breathe in sharply, and Whip glances over. "It's true, and you know it."

"Whip." It's a warning.

He ignores it with a stubborn tilt to his chin. "I told him to take the risk."

My skin prickles with heat. "What?" It sounds woolen to my ears. Can't be helped; they've started to ring. It's fairly clear why Whip offered to pick me up today, and I don't know if I can handle talking about Rye with him—or anyone.

He glances at me again. "He didn't rat you out. I guessed. Wasn't hard, considering the way you two have been acting, trying too hard not to look at each other, and failing each time. I figured something was up. Rye freaked, told me to mind my own business. But he was...confused. So we talked."

I turn my head, unable to look at Whip. I can't truly be upset. Whip is Rye's best friend. And hadn't I spilled everything to Jules? Because some things needed to be sorted out with a sympathetic ear. Still, the idea that Rye and Whip had talked about the arrangement...I squirm.

Whip clearly sees that I'm embarrassed, and his voice softens. "I told him some things were worth the risk of losing them. He thought you were worth it."

Shit. I squeeze my eyes shut for a quick, painful second. The absence of Rye doesn't just hurt; it's a void of loneliness opening up in my chest.

"He caught me off guard," I whisper.

"Yeah," Whip says sadly. "He doesn't know how to be subtle."

A broken laugh escapes. "Oh, and you do?"

Whip shakes his head, smiling slightly. "No. That's the point. None of us guys do. We never had to work for anything other than our music. And that was so long ago, we tend to forget. We live in this weirdly insulated world where everything we want is handed to us. It makes us...stupid."

I laugh again, but it's a pained sound.

"Doesn't mean that we don't care," Whip says. "Or that we don't hurt when we fail."

With a sigh, I tilt my head back and stare out of the window. "You're killing me here."

"I'm not trying to make you feel guilty, I swear. I just..." He exhales loudly. "Shit, I don't know. I feel responsible for pushing him. Maybe if I didn't, he would have taken it slowly and..." He trails off with a helpless shrug.

"It's not your fault. Rye's a big boy, capable of making up his own mind." I fight a smile. Damn it, I miss him. My smile fades. "I didn't mean to hurt him. I don't *want* to hurt him."

"I know. And I probably should have kept my mouth shut with you, but he's...Just handle him with care, Bren."

Whip says it kindly, but I'm thoroughly chastised all the same. I also love him with my whole heart in this moment, because he's protecting Rye in a way few people would. Overwhelmed, I lean across the seat and kiss his cheek.

"You're a good guy, William."

He blushes, his pretty face scrunching up. "Okay, okay. But don't go kissing me when we get there. I don't want to deal with Rye trying to kick my ass."

We ride in companionable silence for a while, then chat about our favorite Marvel movies. Whip turns onto a small one-lane road and arrives at a pair of open gates. The drive up to Varg Hall is long and flanked by stately elm trees that have lost their leaves for the winter.

The estate comes into view, and we both let out an appreciative sound.

"Hello, Downton Abbey," I murmur. Though really, it's more of a Pemberley estate.

Varg Hall sits on the crest of a gentle rise. Surrounded by meticulously kept parkland and formal gardens, it's the type of great old English mansion that, aside from national trusts and peers offering up house tours to foot the bills, only extremely wealthy men like my uncle can afford to own and maintain.

Built in the fifteenth century, the original house was remodeled and added onto in the Georgian era and now has graceful neoclassical lines. The old limestone facade gleams golden in the low, slanting winter light, the mullioned windows glimmering like gemstones. It's utterly beautiful.

My parents hate the place.

I bore the brunt of my parents' complaints every time we visited—they never turn down an invitation; they enjoy their misery and like to spread it. And even though they often spend a week here at Varg Hall or one of my uncle's other houses, I'm the one they treat as a traitor for having fun here, for spending summers with Killian instead of staying in Long Island with them.

They arrive tomorrow. I plan to relax while I can—and avoid them as much as possible the rest of the time.

We pull up in front of the wide front stairs, and Paul, my uncle's butler—yes, he has a butler—comes out to greet us.

"Miss Brenna. Lovely to see you again."

"Hello, Paul. How are Louise and the children?"

We exchange pleasantries, and the whole time I try to acclimate myself to the grandeur and wealth surrounding me. I've been coming here since I was a baby, and yet it never truly feels real. Which is saying something, considering I live in a world of pampered and protected rock stars.

I'm offered the opportunity to go up to my room and relax, but if I do that, I'll fall on the bed and sleep for hours. Besides, it would only put off the inevitable. So I follow Whip around the terrace and toward the rear gardens where everyone is having cocktails.

I spot Rye immediately. Mainly because he's lying prone on the lawn, his big body sprawled at an awkward angle, his eyes wide open and unblinking. I'd be alarmed, but everyone is looking on with a smile as a gaggle of small children approach him with caution. I recognize some of them as the kids of Xander and Isabella's various friends.

"Is he dead, then?" one boy asks.

"Poke him," a girl of about six offers.

From his seat on Sophie's lap, little Felix squawks and waves his fist, as if to say, *Do it, mates!*

The brave pair of kids tiptoe closer to Rye, and the girl nudges his ribs with her toe. Rye remains limp.

"He's faking," she says, but she doesn't look certain.

She tries it again.

With a roar, Rye explodes upward, jumping to his feet with impressive speed. The kids squeal and scatter like a flock of birds. Screaming and laughing, they run for it as Rye goes after them, snarling like a bear. That is until he somehow catches sight of me. He halts, spinning more fully around to face me, and stands straight. Our gazes snare and, oh sweet sin, he smiles.

That smile, it's the sun rising over a dark hill. It spreads over his face and lights his eyes.

A warm wave of sparkling happiness fills me, and I am help-less in its wake. All I can do is smile back, my entire body humming with want and anticipation.

We grin at each other like proper fools. That is until the chil-dren regroup and swarm Rye. He goes down in a tumble of tiny limbs and children's happy screams. And all I can think is that resistance is futile.

———

Rye

SHE'S HERE. It's the only coherent thought I have. She's here. The absence of her was a cold fist in my chest all these weeks. Weeks I spent pretending everything was fine, just the same as ever. Weeks lying to myself. Because the whole time, that cold, hard fist in my chest was there, hurting, aching, reminding me that she wasn't around.

In the quiet, still hours of the night, I'd lie in my bed and wonder if it was for the best, ending things early, telling myself how bad it would have truly hurt if I'd stayed longer, pretending that I was okay with keeping things how they were. My insides were shredded. They'd be completely liquidated if I'd grown even more attached.

Still, I can't regret having her for those brief moments in time. She made me realize I can have something more out of life, that it's okay to want more.

But what I truly want is Brenna. And she wants a clean break. How the hell do I act around her now?

The question runs through my head as I extract myself from the pile of small children I'd been playing with in an attempt to distract myself from her inevitable arrival. I sic them on Jax and Killian and make my way to where she's accepting a pink, fizzy gin drink from a passing waiter.

It's cold on the terrace, but they have large braziers set up around the spot and the outdoor fireplace is crackling away. Brenna huddles near it and sips her drink while some guy named Ned that I'd been introduced to an hour ago chats her up. He's an investment banker from London and is wearing the kind of tightly tailored suit those guys seem to favor. I don't like him. Mainly because I've become a jealous fool when it comes to Brenna. Not proud of that, but I can't seem to shake it off.

It's a strange, uncomfortably weakening relief when Bren turns my way and gives me a small smile.

"Hey," we both say at the same time. With the same, awkward hesitation.

Ned must be as smart as he looks because he fucks off fairly quickly. I don't acknowledge him but keep my eyes on Brenna. God, but she's sharp-edged beautiful in this faded watercolor world of mine. She makes my knees weak and my heart ache. And all I can do is stare at her, afraid to blink and find she's gone.

My palms start to sweat, my breath coming in short. This is what she does to me. And, fuck me, but I like it. Well, except for the fact that I seem to have become tongue-tied. I swallow thickly and force my voice to work.

"You cut your hair." It's all I can get out. And it's probably the worst way to start, because she flushes deep pink and touches her hair.

Her nose wrinkles as she lets out a self-deprecating sound. "I spent over an hour in the car with Whip, and he never noticed."

It chafes that Whip picked her up. I wanted to. And yet when I saw him heading for the car, announcing what he was going to do, I hadn't protested, fearing that the last person she'd want to see at the gate was me.

"It looks good." It does. But different. I've only ever seen Brenna's hair in a sleek ponytail or running down her back. But it's now cropped to the tops of her shoulders, the deep-red mass swinging around her face with the slightest movement. It makes her look softer, drawing attention straight to her amber eyes and petal-pink lips.

I want to kiss her so badly that I find myself leaning in but freeze the second I realize what I'm doing. Thankfully, she doesn't seem to notice the slip because she's staring off into the distance. Hell, this is awkward. I hate it. Hate that I've done this to us. A lump settles in the base of my throat.

A waiter comes by with a tray of drinks, and Brenna sets her half-empty glass on the tray then turns to me. "I'm tired as hell."

I guess that's my cue to fuck off like Ned did earlier. It hurts. Shit, it hurts. But I can't force my company on her. But then she takes a small breath. "But if I sleep, I'll be a mess for days." Her gaze, filled with hesitation I've never seen from her, clashes with mine. "You want to go on a walk with me?"

"Yes." Fuck yes.

"All right. Let me change first." She's wearing her trademark heels—these are pale pink—and one of her sexy, tight skirt suits in dark green that reaches her knees. Sleek and gorgeous as always. Every time I see Brenna James, I want to unwrap her like the gift that she is.

But she's not mine anymore.

Fists clenched, I follow her into the house—not that you can really call a place like Varg Hall a house. The main entrance is an enormous double-height space with a black-and-white marble checkerboard floor. Classical statuaries flank the various doorways, and massive portraits of stern Englishmen and women from centuries past hang from the walls. Soaring overhead is a ceiling mural of frolicking angels that is probably the work of some master artist. But I zoned out when we were given the tour years ago.

I wait by the wide staircase, which has been draped in pine garland. The stuff hangs over doorways and snakes around the blood-red marble mantle in the hall fireplace. There's a twelve-foot Christmas tree at either end of the hall: one is decorated in gold and red, the other in silver and blue. It's so festive, I feel like I've fallen into a Christmas card.

I'm humming "Deck the Halls" when Brenna soon returns, dressed in jeans and a thick Irish sweater. She's traded her heels for sturdy walking boots and is in the process of putting a white knit cap on her head. She's so damn adorable, I get a pang in my chest.

A freaking *pang*.

I'm in so much trouble.

I tuck my hands into my jean pockets and fall into step beside her. We keep silent until we're away from the house and on a path that leads to a Greek revival folly set by an idyllic lake. I swear this place is insane. I can't imagine growing up surrounded by this, but it hits me that Brenna spent many summers here.

I try to imagine her as a kid. Did she dream of this life we have now? Had she pictured herself growing old with someone? Melancholy floods me, and my chest aches.

"You were really good with those kids," she says, breaking the silence. Her lips quirk. "Cute, even."

"Cute. What every man wants to hear: he's cute."

Frankly, I'll take the compliment with pleasure, but a guy has to at least pretend he doesn't want to preen with pleasure over being called cute by the girl he's gone for.

She clearly knows I'm faking my disgruntlement. "Adorable? Is that better?"

"Let's stick with cute." I move to the side to let her pass a close pair of boxwood hedges. "I like kids. They're fun. Uncomplicated."

We fall into step together as the path widens once more.

"You obviously relate to them," she says.

A smile pulls at my cheeks. "Is that your way of saying I'm immature? Or simplistic?"

She huffs a sound of dry amusement. "I would never call you simplistic, Rye."

"So immature is still on the table."

We're not teasing each other with the ease we once had. There's a stilted element that strikes an off-key note. But damn if it doesn't still feel good to my battered soul, all the same.

That small, coy smile lingers on her lips. "Fishing for compliments, are we?"

"If I was, I'd be reeling up a boot right about now."

When she actually giggles, I feel it like effervescent bubbles of light within my chest.

Brenna clears her throat. "Fine. How about this? Despite having the body of Ares,"—I stumble a step at her words—"and the musical talent of Apollo, you retain the childlike wonder of... shit, my knowledge of Greek mythology has run dry."

"That's still a lot of Greek," I croak, my cheeks warm.

Her nose wrinkles. "I read a mythology book on the plane. Clearly, the gods stuck in my mind."

"I have no problem being compared to two gods, Berry."

Brenna's head jerks upward at the sound of her nickname. Our gazes collide. And there it is—as strong and hot and insistent as ever—the pull, the need to touch, taste, and hold her.

A fine sweat breaks out along my lower back, and I draw in a steadying breath. She turns away, concentrating on the path, our easy truce falling back to uncomfortable uncertainty. Fisting my hands, I follow her, not knowing how to fix it.

"How was your Thanksgiving?" she asks as we reach the folly.

"All right." *Miserable. I missed you. So much.* "Yours?"

"The usual." Her shrug is almost bored, but her tone is hesitant, as though she's not sure how to start talking to me again. She stops and leans against one of the stone columns to face me. "I had wondered if you were avoiding me all these weeks."

The words punch my core, and I let out a strangled breath. But I can't deny the truth; she'll see right through me. "I was."

She bites her bottom lip and glances away. "I was too."

Yeah, I figured as much.

"I didn't avoid you because I didn't want to see you. I just wanted to give you space and try to make things less awkward." A humorless laugh escapes me. "It still feels awkward, though, doesn't it?"

Her smile is tight. "That's probably unavoidable."

We're silent for a minute, both of us looking at the small lake that's gone silver under a pale winter sky. A light but icy breeze drifts over the water, and Brenna hugs her arms to her chest. I step closer, blocking the wind with my body. I want to wrap my arms around her, but it's not my place to hold her anymore. Maybe it never was.

The thought depresses me.

She hasn't told the guys she's leaving. I've been waiting for it, keeping my mouth shut until she makes the announcement. But nothing. I don't know what to make of it but can't find the courage to ask either.

"I'm sorry," she says, and my head snaps up. Brenna grimaces. "For avoiding you too."

My chest hurts. It fucking *hurts*. I hate this.

"We both did the same thing. Let's just...Hell, I don't know. Not be sorry anymore?"

She smiles a little wider. I miss her smiles.

"All right."

Brenna takes a breath, like she's gearing up to say something important. I know that look. I've seen her wear it when she's about to give the band bad news and doesn't want to be the one to tell it.

Panic swells within me. She's going to apologize for picking her career over me. I can't handle her pity. I can't. I am a fucking coward, but I can't hear the words coming from her lips. I'll hear them forever.

"I shouldn't have pressed for more," I blurt. "It was a mistake."

She blinks as though surprised by my outburst. I wasn't exactly smooth with it. Hell, I practically yelled.

"I shouldn't have pressed," I say again, trying to gentle my tone. "I've got too many things going on in my life for a real relationship anyway."

The words are heavy in my mouth, but necessary if I want to keep any shred of pride.

She nods, still a little stiff. But her shoulders spread like there's a weight lifting—which just sucks for me. I don't want to be relegated back to the sidelines of her life. Doesn't matter anyway. She wants a clean break. So it's inevitable.

"Despite everything," I say past the lump in my throat, "I don't regret what we did."

It isn't technically a lie. If I had to do it all over again, I would still have gone after Brenna. Except, I'd be upfront with what I really wanted: all of her. But life doesn't work that way. Sometimes you only get one chance, and I missed mine.

She turns back to face the lake, and her voice becomes so low, I have to strain to hear it. "I don't regret it either."

CHAPTER TWENTY-NINE

BRENNA

IT WAS A MISTAKE. That's what he said. A mistake to ask for more.

I asked him to come for a walk with me so I could gather up my courage and tell him yes, let's do this. Let's be together. That it doesn't matter where I am or what I'm doing, I still want him.

But I'm too late. Because he regrets his impulse.

My hand shakes as I try to put on a coat of lipstick. Afraid to risk a smear of brick red across my face, I put the lipstick down and sigh. The face in the mirror is unfamiliar, with her shorter hair and wrecked eyes. Will they all see how much I'm dying inside?

He didn't. He looked almost pleased with himself when we parted. As if it will be easy to pretend we didn't lose ourselves in each other for a heady moment in time, that he never asked for more.

I can't blame him. I had more than enough time to say yes. I should have said yes that day in California. I should have crawled over that bed and gone straight into his arms.

But I didn't.

And now I'm too late.

Some things are worth the risk, isn't that what Whip said?

Fuck it, I can't let this go. I'll regret it forever.

Earlier, everyone had gone out "hunting," which really meant they went into the woods to track one another in what Whip happily described as a Highlander—*there can only be one!*—laser tag extravaganza. I was invited to join, but I couldn't bring myself to be part of that "fun." Bruised and remorseful, I stayed in my room.

They're back now; I hear Killian and Jax debate the merits of the Strat vs the Tele as they walk past my bedroom door on their way downstairs.

I can't hide in here any longer. Bracing my shoulders, I head out into the hall. A steady throb pulses from a door two down from mine. Rye. He always stays in the Tartan Room—so named for the dark green and blue plaid wool covering the walls.

Music is an intrinsic part of him. If he's not listening to it, he's creating it—even if it's as simple as tapping out a beat with his fingers. The man knows more about music than anyone I know. He loves it all, from classical to obscure bluegrass albums only a hundred people bought. I cannot think of Rye without hearing a rhythm.

It's early yet, about an hour before dinner. But this is prime nap time for a lot of the house. Rye blasting music isn't the best idea. Besides, we need to talk.

I freeze, my heart slamming against the cage of my ribs.

Get it together. You can do this.

My fingers are ice.

Don't be a wuss. Knock on the fucking door!

I rap on it hard, convinced he won't hear me, but it opens fairly quickly, releasing a surge of music—"Pit Stop" by Lovage. Rye's large frame is backlit by the room's lamplight.

"If you wake up Felix with that music, Sophie is going to—ah!"

Rye grabs hold of my wrist and gently but firmly tugs me into the room, kicking the door shut. He pulls me into his arms and starts dancing. His grin is wide and boyish. "Be bad with me, Bren."

I have things to say. But it's impossible to resist him. He's too good a dancer, moving me with competence that's utterly sexy. The song is bluesy, funky-dirty sex. His thick thigh slides between mine as we bump and grind.

Rye's arm wraps more firmly around my waist, and he spins me. I'm on air, alive and pulsing with the beat, flowing with him. *Flick-bump-sway.* I'm no longer worrying about tomorrow or regretting yesterday. I'm young and free in his arms, laughing breathlessly, feeling the music in my blood and bones.

Then our gazes collide, and everything changes. God, the heat in his. The way he looks at me as though I'm the only thing in his universe. This isn't the look of regret.

Heart pounding, I lift my arms, dip my hips. His thigh hits my sex and everything clenches. I suck in a breath, my breasts brushing his chest. Rye's lids lower. Mouth pursed in concentration, he works me to the pulsing rhythm. *Flick-bump-sway.*

It's too much. He's all around me, the scent of his skin, the firm, warm feel of his body moving with mine. I've missed touching him. I've missed him touching me. And this is all I'm going to get anymore, this parody of sex, a quick dance. No more skin to skin. No more of his mouth, his taste, his touch.

I swallow hard, my step faltering.

Rye frowns, and I swear he's about to pull away. But he simply watches me.

"I remember the first time I heard this song," he says.

"You do?" I'm too flustered to remember anything right now.

Rye spins me again, popping his hips against mine. "It was the 2010 fall tour, at an after-party in Paris." His palm spreads wide on my lower back, bracing me, drawing me closer. "You were wearing black leather pants like you've got on now, a pair of wicked silver heels, and a little beaded top that flashed your cute belly button every so often."

My lips part on a breath, and I can only stare at him.

His smile tilts. "You climbed up on a platform with one of the roadies and danced to this song. I watched you move—all sex and grace and utter perfection—and I wanted you so much, it was a physical ache."

I can't breathe. I can only hold on, my hand cupping the warm column of his neck.

"You're the most beautiful thing I've ever seen," he says, almost lightly, like he's not slicing into my heart. "I've spent my entire adult life either wanting you or wanting to forget you."

Holy shit. I feel his truth like a hot grip along my body and stumble against him.

He pauses. "Did you know?"

My voice trembles. "Yeah. I think I did."

Not so deep down, I *had* known. And I'd been doing the same, wanting him, wanting to forget, knowing he was my weakness and resenting him for it.

Something flickers through his gaze. "But in all that time, I never tried being your friend." He glances away for a second, giving me his tightly drawn profile, before meeting my eyes once again. His are dark and troubled. "I should have tried."

A lump swells in my throat. It hurts. *This* hurts.

He shrugs one big shoulder, smiling tightly, moving me like we're fucking. The combination scrambles what's left of my brain. "Better late than never, huh?"

It's not better!

The words won't come out, and the song ends. He must have just been playing the one, because nothing follows. We stop in the middle of the room, me panting lightly, Rye staring down at me with an expression I can't read, sad maybe. But then he steps away, releasing me.

"Song is over."

I fear I might fall and never get back up.

"Yeah," I rasp.

A mix of regret and hopefulness shines in his eyes. We've hurt each other. Many times. And yet he's been the one who kept me going, a driving force to prove my worth—both to him and to myself. He's the one who told me I could fly, who gave me hope that everything in my life would someday be okay.

"I should have tried harder too, Rye."

His shoulders droop in apparent relief. "We're here now. That counts for something."

"Of course it does."

Rye runs a hand over his beard then smiles. "Friends, then?"

"Always." Because I need him, in whatever way I can have him.

The truth of him—of what he means to me—sweeps through my body in a rush so strong, I brace a hand to my middle. What do I do? Beg, maybe.

"Rye..."

The door opens with the effect of a gunshot. Rye and I both visibly jump. Whip stops in the doorway, cringing as though he knows he interrupted something.

"Sorry," he says. "But your parents are here, Bren, and we're supposed to head into dinner soon. I thought you'd want to prepare."

I glance at Rye and hesitate, but then my shoulders sag. Facing my biggest mistake *and* my parents in one night is too much. I sigh and head for the door. All the preparation in the world won't be enough for what's coming.

CHAPTER THIRTY

RYE

FAMILY DINNER at Varg Hall is a bit different than our normal band family dinners. And by that, I mean it's a formal, uncomfortable trial. With food.

Okay, the food is good. I'll give them that. And there's a lot of it. If you don't mind being served endless courses by waitstaff in black ties. A woman fills my wine glass with Cabernet then slips away just as another waiter sets down a plate of prettily cut rounds of roast beef, dribbled with a glossy brown sauce, which probably has some fancy name, but I could give fuck all about it at the moment.

Not when Brenna sits at my side, her pretty, long neck and graceful shoulders so stiff, it's a wonder she doesn't crack. I don't blame her. Her parents have been complaining about this or that for much of the meal.

Patricia and Neil James are, in a word, killjoys. At a distance, Brenna looks like a younger version of her mom, albeit about four inches taller. They both have the same red-brown hair, the same amber eyes. Patricia's hair is faded, a washed reddish gray like the undercoat of a fox. Frown lines crease her slightly rounder face, and her nose is more snub than Bren's. Brenna has her father, Neil's, height and narrower, longer features. Neil looks like a version of his brother, Xander, gone to seed.

They both wear a perpetually pinched expression, as if they smell something bad. And they're not afraid to speak their mind. As in all the fucking time. With every damn snipe and whine they dole out, Brenna's slim body flinches, the softness of her lips pressing tighter. It breaks my heart, and it's all I can do not to reach under the table and set my hand on her knee. To hold her or say, *Fuck it, let me take you out of here.*

But I know she won't want that. Brenna has pride. She wears it like armor and strides on five-inch heels made of brash confidence and pure guts.

It doesn't stop me from wanting to toss her parents out on their ears. I slide a look Brenna's way, inwardly aching at how even the golden candlelight can't hide the pale cast of her creamy skin.

"I thought tonight was family dinner," Neil says with a wary glance around the table. He's across from me, with his wife at his side.

We're all sitting like good little soldiers around a table that can easily fit twenty. Three enormous antique silver candelabrum march down the center of the table festooned with sugared fruits and evergreen garland. Porcelain vases, filled to bursting with lush red hothouse roses, sit on either end of the table. Candlelight glitters on the celadon and gold china, silver flatware, and cut crystal glasses.

It's all very pretty. For hell.

Xander, who's at the head of the table, glowers at his younger brother over the rim of his wineglass. "I'm not sure what you mean, Neil. Are we not eating?"

I'm fairly certain everyone knows what good old Neil means. But he makes sure he's very clear by pointedly glancing at me,

Whip, Jax, Scottie, Sophie, and Stella. "Looks more like a party for your son's friends than family dinner."

Killian makes a noise like he's about to rip into his uncle, but Libby touches his wrist, and he merely glares.

Xander sets down his glass. "My son's friends *are* family."

"More like another excuse for a photo op," Neil mutters, taking a bite of beef.

"You see any cameras around here, Neil?" Killian grits out.

"No, but the night is young, boy."

I swear, Killian is a second away from lunging down the table to strangle him. I'd approve, if it weren't for the pained flutter of Brenna's lashes as she stares down at her uneaten dinner.

"Tell me, Sophie," Isabella says in an overly bright voice, "how is little Felix handling the time difference?"

Sophie's brown eyes go wide, and I know she's not exactly pleased to be picked out of the herd. But she is a socializing pro and slides easily into a breezy tale about Felix staying up all night and driving Scottie to plead on his knees for his toddler son to give it a rest.

Sophie's grin is wide and infectious as she laughs, remembering the moment. "Gabriel ended up reading Felix *Go the Fuck to Sleep*—"

Patricia's strangled gasp of horror cuts Sophie off. "You read that? To a child?"

Scottie inclines his head her way. His expression could freeze over hell. "Twice, to be precise."

Lips twitching, Jax takes a hasty sip of wine, and I know he's holding on by a thread. We all are.

Patricia's mouth tightens. "It's immoral..."

"Mom," Brenna cuts in, strained. "He's a baby. He doesn't understand the words, just the rhythm of the story."

"That's no excuse." Patricia dabs her lips with her linen napkin. "Then again, look at what he's growing up around."

It sucks all the air from the room. Every single one of us

tensing in a collective breath of anger. For the first time in years, I'm fairly certain Scottie is about to lose his shit.

Brenna leans in, resting her forearms on the table as she gives her mother a bland smile. "Surrounded by people who love and support him? The horror."

"Mind your sarcasm, young lady." Patricia sets her napkin down. "Your father and I did our best to guide you in the right direction. And still you end up here, hanging on the fringes of this degenerate rock band, wearing those ridiculous heels, and sleeping around with God knows what."

What. As though a person whose lifestyle she doesn't approve of or understand is a *thing.* As though Brenna is one by association.

All the color leaches out of her beautiful face, but her eyes spark with fire. She doesn't shout or snap. Her tone is perfectly even when she replies, "If you want to know about my sex life, just ask, Mother."

"Brenna." Neil slaps a hand on the table.

"Father," she replies neutrally.

"Pay her no mind, Neil," Patricia says. "She's only being fresh because I'm right. She's been living off Killian's charity instead of making her own way—"

"Bullshit."

Every head turns my way.

Right. I said that. I can feel Brenna's gaze, shocked and wide on me.

What are you doing? You're supposed to charm the parents of the woman you want in your life, not antagonize them, you moron.

But fuck this. I cannot sit here listening to them systematically tear her down.

Neil sneers. "Pardon?"

"Your daughter is bold, intelligent, and one of the most respected people in the music industry. She's the living heart of this band. She doesn't hang on to us. She holds us up." *You complete and utter dick drizzle.* "And if you can't see how great she is, then you don't deserve her."

Scottie raises his glass. "Hear, hear."

Our friends follow suit, all of them wearing various expressions of fierce protectiveness and simmering rage.

Under the table, a touch, light as butterfly wings, flits along my outer thigh, snagging the whole of my attention. Without looking her way, I let my hand fall beneath the tabletop and find Brenna's. Hers is cold and clammy. Heart clenching, I rest mine on top of her hand, holding it firmly against my thigh where she'll be warm.

"And who are you, again?" Neil studies me as if I've crawled out from under the floorboards.

"The drummer," Patricia says in an undertone that implies, *What else should you expect from such a low creature?*

Whip snickers under his breath, but I know he's far from amused. We share a quick look of perfect understanding. If they weren't Brenna's parents, we'd have marched them out of here an hour ago.

"The bassist, ma'am. I also go by Degenerate Number One."

Jax coughs into his napkin. And Neil reddens.

All right, it was a cheap shot. I need to reel it in for Brenna's sake, no matter how good it feels to knock her shit parents down a peg. She doesn't look my way, but under the table, her fingers spread over my thigh. She rubs me just once, a tiny movement that I feel along the whole of my side.

Patricia flushes a deep berry that's uncomfortably similar to the way Brenna blushes. "I never implied you weren't intelligent, Brenna. Or capable. That is the point. You could do so much better."

Brenna's hand slips away from me, and she rests her fist on the table. "I honestly cannot conceive of anyone better than these people, Mother."

"Willfully stubborn," Neil remarks, taking another bite of his beef. "Blinded by fame and excess. Mark my words, young lady. One day you'll regret it. You'll be alone and—"

"Oh, leave off, Neil," Xander snaps. "Your issue isn't with Brenna or Rye. If you want to have a go at me, wait for after dinner. I'll be more than happy to accommodate you. But you're putting everyone off their roast."

"So superior, Xander. In your Italian loafers, playing country lord of the manor."

"Well, one ought to wear the proper footwear when lording," Xander intones.

I've always liked Xander.

Neil turns redder. "And this farce of a birthday celebration. Just one big, happy family, eh?"

Xander's eyes narrow, and I swear Isabella flinches. Neil sees her discomfort too.

"Tell me," Neil says, getting his teeth into it. "What are we to raise our glasses to? Your birthday or your divorce?"

And that is when Killian loses his shit.

"What the fuck?"

"Goddamn it, Neil," Xander shouts.

Everything falls apart then. Neil and Xander start yelling at each other. Killian turns to his mom, who begins to cry. Chairs are pushed back, the room clearing out in a hurry. And all the while, Brenna sits cool as carved ice, her eyes on the plate before her.

I sit by her side, unwilling to leave. When a door slams, she flinches, blinking as though coming out of a trance.

"Hey," I say softly. "You okay?"

Brenna pulls in an audible breath. Her whisky eyes are over-bright, glimmering at the corners. "Yes. Thank you, though, for saying all that. It was unnecessary but kind."

"Kind? Bren, this is me. You don't have to pretend. If you're hurting, tell me. I'm here."

Her lips purse into a crimson-red line. "Did you see Isabella? She was so upset."

"Yeah, I saw." Frankly, Brenna's dad could do with a good kick in the ass. But I refrain from mentioning that bit.

"I mean, I know their relationship wasn't perfect." Brenna snorts delicately, the sound echoing in the vast, empty room. "Obviously not, if she tried to kiss you."

Wincing, I glance around; it would do no good for that to get out now. But all is quiet, and Brenna keeps talking with methodical woodenness. "But that was years ago, and she always seemed so in love with Uncle Xander."

"Bren, honey, it's hard to tell what goes on between a couple behind closed doors." I shove away thoughts of my own cheating dad as Brenna sighs, a sad, tiny sound.

"I know. And it was naive of me to assume, but I had hoped they worked their issues out. I don't know...I just wanted to believe they were happy."

With another sigh, she pushes back from the table and rises with the stiffness of old straw. I follow, pulling her chair back for her.

"She was so sad, Rye."

"I know, Berry."

"Crazy thing is, she's been more of a mom to me than my own."

My heart cracks at the hollow sadness in Brenna's eyes.

"Bren..." I reach to take her arm, but she shrugs me off.

"No. I can't right now."

Stung, my hand drops. "I'm sorry. I only wanted to..." *Comfort you. Hold you.* "Help."

"You can't. Not with this." Distracted, she glances over her shoulder to where Killian and Isabella have walked off. "I need to be with my family."

Family. And I'm not hers. This isn't news. So why does it hurt so much?

"All right. Maybe we can hang out later—" I bite my lip to shut up. What am I doing? She's stressed and hurting, and I'm making it worse because I selfishly want to be the one to fix things. What had John said before? I can't fix her problems. I can only be there to support her.

"Do what you have to do," I say. "If you need me for anything, I'm here."

There. That was all right, wasn't it?

She visibly sags with weary relief. "Thank you."

Good. This is good. I'm not completely fucking it up.

Brenna slowly heads for the door but pauses just before walking out of the room. "Maybe you were right to be leery of relationships. Maybe love isn't enough to stop people from cheating or breaking apart."

Shit, that's what she's getting out of all this? Now, when I finally understand what it means to truly only want one person, when it's crystal fucking clear that cheating isn't about a flaw in the other person but a flaw within the cheater.

An agitated shard of panic spears my gut.

"No, Brenna," I say with feeling. "No. I was wrong. That's not what love—"

Another door slams, followed by Killian's deep voice mixing with Isabella's contralto as they argue in rapid-fire Spanish.

Brenna's gaze darts their way. "I have to go."

"Bren—"

"We'll talk later, Rye."

She's out of the room before I can reply.

And I'm left with the cold fear that I might never be able to convince her that love isn't what breaks people apart; it's what holds them together.

CHAPTER THIRTY-ONE

BRENNA

IN THE SCOPE OF THINGS, my aunt and uncle getting a divorce isn't the worst that can happen. It's just...that dinner sucked. My parents suck.

Their words, so easily slung, float around within me like sticky bites of sludge, clinging to my heart, worming through my guts. Some people will say words are just air, they aren't real. As though you don't need air to breathe, to live. Words can kill parts of your soul with astonishing ease.

And yet my parents' words, their disdain for me and those in my life, aren't what bother me now.

I head in the direction where I heard Killian and Isabella arguing and find her in the pink parlor, a relatively small and pretty place done up in shades of pale pink. She's curled up at the end of a Regency-era settee covered in ice-pink silk.

As soon as I enter, she stiffens, sitting straighter and pushing a lock of inky hair back from her face. Pride. Poise. No one knows this, but I modeled my style after her. When I was eighteen, she was the classiest woman I'd ever seen. She still is.

She's wearing a vintage Zac Posen sheath in burgundy satin that makes her light-brown skin glow and highlights her flawless figure. Isabella was trained to walk runways, but her effortless grace still manages to make me feel like a clumsy girl in comparison.

When Isabella realizes it's me, she relaxes. "Dinner is always an event at Varg Hall."

I laugh shortly as I sit next to her. "Some more so than others."

"At least we didn't have to suffer through the cheese course."

"There's that." I settle back into the couch, digging the point of one heel into the carpet thread. "Where's Killian?"

"Liberty took him up to their room to relax." She gives me a watery smile. "My son has an explosive temper, followed by a passionate release of feeling."

"Yes," I murmur dryly. "I'm aware."

"He doesn't like change. Or surprises."

I'm more like my cousin than I care to admit. "Few people do."

Isabella shrugs lightly, sending her glossy locks sliding over her slim shoulders. "He blames his father, when it is not that simple."

"I'm sorry about you and Uncle Xander."

The light in Isabella's eyes dims. "It's not so dire as Neil made it out to be. We're having problems, but nothing has been decided." The tiniest of frowns mars the smooth space between her brows. "We would have discussed this with Killian when we were on firmer ground. Unfortunately, Neil overheard something he shouldn't have."

Shame coats my skin with hot hands. "You mean he eavesdropped."

"Yes."

"I'm so...disgusted, Isa. It was wrong what he did."

She studies me for a moment, her dark gaze moving over my face. "It was. But Brenna, what your parents said to you.

They're wrong there too. Completely wrong. Tell me you know this."

Tension rides my shoulders and I roll them, releasing an unfortunate crack. "While everyone was arguing, I started thinking about my parents—coming to a realization, actually. Thing is, I love them, but I don't like them. I could hunt them down, have a knock-down, drag-out fight about their shitty behavior or why they can't accept me for who I am, but it won't change anything." A humorless laugh escapes. "I suspect only years of family therapy would fully eradicate our issues."

"Mija..."

I'm not Isabella's daughter, but the softly uttered term of endearment constricts my chest all the same, and my voice is clogged when I speak. "Frankly, I don't want to talk to them right now. I can't find it in myself to care anymore what they think." I take my aunt's cool hand in mine. "When it comes down to it, I'd rather be here, making sure you're okay."

Her fingers thread through mine and squeeze in acknowledgment. "You are the daughter of my heart. You know that, don't you?"

My eyes mist, and I blink rapidly, leaning into her. "I always wanted you to be my mother."

Isabella makes a sound of distress. "I am here for you, mija. Always."

We're quiet for a few moments, then she breaks the silence. "For a while, I worried that I might have lost your regard."

Her words punch through me, and I jerk back.

Dark eyes, the exact bittersweet shade of Killian's, lock on me. "I hadn't thought of it in many years but seeing Rye with you tonight brought it all back."

I swallow thickly, my heart thudding so loud, I swear she can hear it.

Her gaze turns remorseful. "You were there that night I made a fool of myself with Rye. I saw you run off just as I pulled away."

Shit.

Cheeks flaming, I duck my head, grateful that my new hairstyle allows the wings of my hair to fall over my face. "Isa—"

"No," she cuts in gently. "Let me say this."

It's one thing to discuss it with Rye, but facing Isabella is acutely embarrassing in a way that might be childish, but I can't shake. But it would be even more childish to refuse to listen. Woodenly, I nod.

Her hand falls to the couch and grips the edge. "I had wanted to apologize before."

"You don't have to. It's none of my business."

"I do. And it is. You're my niece, and something I did betrayed your trust in me. That is not a small thing." Isabella sighs. "At the very least, I want to explain."

I manage a small, "Okay."

It takes her a moment to speak, as though she needs to internally gather her thoughts, and when she does, the words come slowly. "I was favored with physical beauty. I never denied this. In truth, I was always thankful for my looks." Her lips curl. "In my youth, my beauty helped get me anything I wanted: men, fame, fortune. How could I not be grateful?"

She shakes her head, glossy hair gleaming, and blinks into the distance. "But as I got older, beauty became the Sword of Damocles hanging over my head. My whole identity was tied up in how I looked, how others looked at me.

"Ah, Brenna, how the world views women..." Her hand clenches, and she frowns down at the thin skin there as if pained. "It's as though we have a sell-by date. Anything past that, and we're suddenly spoiled goods. A model's life is even worse. One line on the face, one pound gained...Our entire worth wrapped up in this outer package." She waves a hand over her form, expression twisting.

When she glances at me, I nod. Of course, I know. Even now, I have to deal with a world that expects a flawless outer shell.

"I thought it wouldn't happen to me," she confides with a

touch of asperity. "It would be different. Then I hit forty, and it was as though I'd become invisible. I was passed over, put out to pasture. Suddenly, I was a 'ma'am.' Suddenly Xander didn't have time for me. I was no longer his golden girl, his beautiful prize."

"Isa," I cut in, compelled to say it. "Xander loves you for more than your looks. I know it."

She sighs. "I know this too. Now. Then?" She bites her bottom lip. "There were things I didn't understand. About aging. It hits you in ways no one spoke of then. The depression, the struggle to rise out of bed. The weight gain, even though you're eating the same as ever. The constant exhaustion. You forget things, you start to wonder if this is all your life will be. You have aches where there were none. Add to that, breasts that have started to sag and periods that go missed..." She shrugs. "It does things to your sense of identity."

Isabella runs her hand through her hair. "This is how I was feeling when I went to that party. Low and sorry for myself. Wanting to experience that excitement of youth once more. I will not claim it as an excuse, but there I was, drunk and lonely, and this gorgeous young man was telling me that I was worth something, that I was beautiful. I forgot who he was, who I was. I took."

The moment crystalizes in my mind's eye, and I see it anew, the way Rye appeared shocked as Isabella reached for him. At my side, Isabella makes a sound of self-disgust.

"It was the worst thing I've done. I took advantage of a young man and dishonored my marriage. Xander and I went to counseling after that."

"Does he..." I lick my dry lips. "Did you tell Xander about what happened?"

"Not that it was Rye. But, yes, I told him I'd kissed another man, and how I regretted it." She sat up straighter, flicking her hair behind her shoulder. "Later, I tried apologizing to Rye, but he was so appalled by my even mentioning it that I gave up." She laughs lightly. "I did not want to cause him more embarrassment."

"Well," I say weakly. "From what he's told me, he doesn't blame you."

"Which means he blames himself," she says darkly. "Dear foolish boy. Perhaps I should try again to speak to him."

"I don't think you'll get a different reaction from him."

Amusement lights her eyes for a moment before she sobers. "You and Rye are together now?"

I hadn't expected that, and it takes me a second to answer. "We're friends."

"Brenna, the way that man looks at you is not that of a friend."

"We barely look at each other."

"And in those non-looks, everything is exposed. He is either in love with you or falling fast."

My fingers clench convulsively on my thighs. Hope and uncertainty make for a fragile pain in my heart. I don't want to acknowledge it. Not when I'm so tender-skinned. "He asked for a relationship. But I panicked. I said I needed time away from him, from the band."

I blink rapidly, a heartbeat stuck in my throat, and pour out the rest of it. "He said it was the right thing to do," I finish. "Ending things, I mean. He wasn't actually ready. He wants to be friends. I have to respect that, don't I? We promised each other honesty, so he has to have meant it."

"Hmm...And you agreed as well." Isabella's eyes hold a world of skepticism. "That you only want to be friends?"

Biting my lip, I look away.

Her tone turns dry. "Maybe neither of you is as honest with your feelings as you believe."

"Maybe. I don't know. It's complicated."

"Mami," she says with affection. "It's simple. Do you want this man as your friend or as your everything?"

A bubble of emotion pops within my chest, and I find myself huffing out a weak laugh. "Well, when you put it like that..."

She grins, leaning into my shoulder for a minute. I smile too, but it quickly fades.

She kisses me on the temple then sets my hand back on my thigh. "It isn't easy to admit when you've been wrong. Especially for stubborn women like us. Then again, letting love in never is."

"I thought loving someone was supposed to be easy."

Isabella shakes her head slowly. "My dear, I was talking about loving yourself. If you don't do that first, you're always going to push away those who try to love you."

CHAPTER THIRTY-TWO

BRENNA

STELLA!!!: Emergency pajama party in the kitchen. 15 min

WhipIt: I don't wear pajamas.

Stella!!!: Well, find some. No one wants to see your bare ass

So-Sophie: I want cocoa or it's a no-go

WhipIt: You can't make that judgment, Stells, without seeing the product first

JaxJax: Whip, you'll be seeing my foot up said ass if you keep flirting with my woman

So-Sophie: See what I did there? Cocoa no-go? Eh? Eh?

Stella!!!: Yes, you're very clever, Soph. Signed: John's "woman"

JaxJax: Is this some sort of feminist thing I messed up?

Stella!!!: If I have to tell you, it doesn't count. And why are you texting me? We're in the same bed

JaxJax: :-*

Killer: Can you all please shut up? It's one in the morning. I'm not in the mood for No-Go Cocoa

So-Sophie: No-Go Cocoa... :D

Stella!!!: You'll have cocoa and like it, Mr.

Killer: No

Stella!!!: Libby

Libs: I'm on it.

Killer: I resent the idea that you women think you can

WhipIt: She took his phone, didn't she?

JaxJax: Count on it. Scottie? I know you're curled around Sophie like she's your woobie, but we'll need confirmation of attendance, because you're evil and no one trusts you not to turn into a snake or something to get away.

MrScott: Sorry, must run. About to dematerialize.

BrennaBean: I'm joining Scottie aboard the mothership, away from you yahoos

Stella!!!: FUNNY. Now get your butts down here. All of you. RYE! I know you're there. I can hear you breathing.

Rye-Rye: I was having the weirdest dream. You all were in it. No. Wait. It was a nightmare. Or should I call it a wakemare since I'm fairly certain I'm awake now, and you're all still texting.

WhipIt: HUR!

So-Sophie: Cocoa, Rye-Rye. You love cocoa

Rye-Rye: I will not be swayed by a mere beverage

Stella!!!: And cookies. Lots of cookies

Rye-Rye: I'll be down in 5

GROANING, I mute my phone, push my head under a pillow, and welcome the muffled silence. I flop onto my back and stare at the lavender silk canopy above my head. When I was a kid, I slept in this bed and called myself Princess Brenna. I wanted a prince to love me. I'm not going to even deny it. I did. And I wanted to be a knight who took on the world and won. I wanted it all.

Along the way, my definition of "all" evolved. It meant relying only on myself, no more risks to my heart. I would go after what I wanted, safe in the knowledge that I'd get it. I'd played it safe because I kept a part of me locked away. And that part of me has slowly withered.

Life is risky now. Uncertain.

I don't know if I'll get what I want. And I don't like that. But I'm done playing it safe.

Muttering, I shove myself upright and push my hair back from my face. Stella and Sophie will march up here and sit on me if I don't get moving. Besides, Stella is the best out of all of us at reading people's needs. And while I selfishly ran and hid away in my room for the night, she's trying to help Killian by having us all there for him. I know my cousin. He'll grump and bitch, but he truly feels better when his friends are around him.

Ashamed that I didn't think of this first, I crawl out of bed and slip on a black long-sleeve shirt and a pair of pink flannel pants with black French poodles dancing across them. It's the closest I have to pj's, and frankly, I'm tired of dressing up. Having stayed here many times and knowing how cold the floors can get, I have a pair of slippers on hand. I put them on and head downstairs.

As in many old English homes, the kitchen is located on the ground floor and away from the main rooms. The corridor is narrow and fairly dim. I'm not going to say I believe in ghosts or anything, but I've never felt any desire to linger in the hallways down here.

Hurrying around the corner, I nearly collide with Rye. His hands automatically grasp my arms to steady me, but he doesn't let go. With the warm light of the kitchen barely touching us, he's a shadowy figure, but I feel every inch of him, even with a foot of space separating us. He's showered, his skin fragrant with the rosemary lemon soap they provide here. It's never smelled so good. I have to restrain myself from burrowing my nose into the center of his chest.

"Bren," he says, pulling me out of my scent-induced lust. "We need to talk."

The dull, almost pained strain in his voice sends alarm skittering down my spine. His expression is serious, hard, even.

"Bren, I—"

Killian's annoyed mutter echoes from down the hall, and I jerk back, knowing he'll round the corner any second.

"Okay. But not here," I whisper, glancing toward the sound of Killian's voice. "Not now." What I have to say isn't for my cousin's ears.

Rye grimaces, his brows knitting. Killian's voice is closer, complaining loudly about cold-ass floors. The familiar gripe makes me smile despite myself. I touch Rye's forearm, trying to reassure him and find it rock-hard with tension. He turns his head, checking the hall.

"Better go," he says, stepping back to put space between us.

Flustered, I slip into the kitchen without another word. I expect Rye to follow, but he doesn't.

Like the rest of the rooms in Varg Hall, the kitchen is super-sized. But with its wide plank, worn-oak floorboards, sage-green cabinetry, lime-washed plaster walls, and the great big masonry fireplace, it's also cozy.

Whip is feeding kindling into the growing fire as I walk past. I ruffle his hair and then take a seat midway down the old pine farm table that stretches like a felled tree in the center of the room. Scottie, who sits opposite me and one chair down, grunts in greeting then sets his phone with the baby monitor app playing on the table. He's wearing ice-blue Dolce & Gabbana silk pajamas.

My lips twitch. "Sophie got you those, didn't she?"

There is a certain model featured in a Dolce & Gabbana perfume ad campaign that could be Scottie's twin. We're never allowed to speak of it or *him*. But Sophie likes living dangerously. That, and she has her man twisted around her clever little fingers.

A dark brow wings up as he sniffs. "Early Christmas present." His steady stare dares me to say anything.

I smile blandly. "I have just the cologne to go with that. Light Blue, I believe it's called."

Jax snickers as he sets a mug of cocoa down before me. His idea of pj's consists of soft gray drawstring pants and a ratty green Henley. Scottie eyes it with annoyance, clearly feeling he's been punked by having to wear actual pajamas.

But before he can complain, Sophie bounds over swathed in matching pj's with an ice-blue silk robe trimmed in white feathers. "Isn't this cute?" She kicks up a silk-clad leg and shows off little white feathered slipper mules with kitten heels. "I feel like some '30s Christmas starlet."

With her platinum-blond bob floating around her face in a silvery cloud and her lips done up in fiery red, she certainly looks the part.

"Love the slippers." Mine are boring flannel, not at all like my usual heels. Not with these drafty floors.

Killian, Libby, and Rye show up together. Killian and Libby are dressed much like Jax, but Rye surprises me. I hadn't gotten a good look at him in the hall. I'm looking now. I can't help it. A white thermal-underwear top stretches over his broad shoulders and packed muscles. Red flannel pants with white cotton fleece leg cuffs hug his lean hips and thick thighs.

"Look who's playing the role of sexy Santa," Sophie says with a grin.

Rye grimaces, a cute flush running over the bridge of his nose. "My mom got them for me."

And I die. I'm pretty sure all the women in the room sigh as one.

Sophie isn't wrong either. With his beard and that outfit, I'm suddenly flush with naughty thoughts of sitting on his lap and telling him what I want for Christmas while slipping my hand down his pants...

Wrapping my fingers tight around my mug, I order myself to calm the hell down. It isn't easy, especially since he takes the seat opposite of me. His gaze settles on me like a hot palm between my breasts, and I meet his eyes. He gives me a searching, slightly uncertain look that I return with a tiny smile as if to say everything is fine. But I don't think he believes it. His jaw bunches, and he moves his attention to Killian, who's taken the seat at the head of the table.

"You all suck," Killian mutters, but his posture is easier now. His dark eyes pin Libby. "I can't believe you stole my phone."

"You liked what I did after I stole it," she drawls, clucking her tongue.

"Lord deliver us all," Scottie pleads to the ceiling.

"Here." Stella plunks a tray down before him. "Have a cookie."

She sets an identical tray at the other end of the table. Aside from shortbread, there's a selection of treats that has Whip, who sits next to me, making noises of delight. "Are those Mexican wedding cookies?"

"We always called them snowballs," Sophie says.

"I thought they were Russian tea cookies." Jax grabs one.

"I call them 'get in my belly' cookies," Stella says. Jax happily pops the cookie into her mouth. She smiles as she chews. "Thanks, baby."

"Sure thing, button. You want another one?"

"Can we stop talking about cookies?" Killian snarls. Okay, he's still in a mood. I don't blame him. Dinner sucked.

Libby gets up and sits on his lap. With a sigh, he wraps his arms around her waist and snuggles her close. "Sorry," he says to all of us.

"It's okay," Stella says gently.

He sighs again, his fingers tracing the line of Libby's waist. "I'm just...fuck. I'm tired of the people in my life keeping important things from me."

A jolt goes through my center, and I hold my gaze deliberately away from Rye.

"I've no right to demand people tell me their secrets," Killian goes on unhappily. "But it's a kick to the teeth when someone drops a bomb on my lap without warning. I'm a grown man. I can handle my parents splitting up, but I thought they would at least talk to me before giving that ammunition to Neil and Patricia, of all people." He glances my way. "No offense, Bren."

"None taken." My ears have started to ring. "They're horrible. I'm so embarrassed."

"Don't be." Rye's firm insistence has me locking gazes with him. He's utterly serious, the muscles on his wide shoulders and thick arms bunching. "That shit is on their shoulders. You aren't them, and you never will be."

I don't want to be like my parents. He knows how deeply I feel this. What he doesn't know is that finally, *finally*, I understand the truth of his words.

I blink in acknowledgment.

"He's right," Killian says with fervor. "You're the best part of them, Brenna Bean."

"Stop," I protest lightly, even though my voice has gone froggy. "You'll make me weepy."

Rye's gaze is a living thing, and I know he's all too aware of how close I am to actually weeping. This is what happens when change is thrust upon the unprepared; there is no time to shore up any defenses, and well-worn armor crumbles like so much rust.

Stella takes the seat to my right, curling up with a mug of cocoa. "None of us are responsible for the shitty actions of our parents. And thank God for that."

I touch her knee in solidarity. Stella's cool fingers brush over mine in response.

Killian runs a hand through his hair, the epic scowl still twisting his features. "Look, I know we all have a right to our private lives, but can we agree to tell each other the big stuff? Can we do that at least? Because it seems to me that we're stronger when we come together, as opposed to going it alone."

Jax taps out an idle rhythm on the table. "I'd like that. Being more open about shit, I mean."

This is somewhat of a surprise, given that he's very private. But Jax has been changing too. His relationship with Stella opened him up in ways none of us predicted.

Rye remains painfully silent while everyone else talks being open and honest. That's my fault too. I forced silence on him, made him keep secrets. I recall with shattering clarity the frustration and pain in the words he spoke in California. *I can't do this anymore. I don't want to lie to our friends.*

Out in the hall, I told him to wait. Wait for a perfect time to talk. Wait until I find my courage.

Wait.

A thick, choking feeling of *wrongness* fills my chest, my throat. Everything about us is wrong now. I can't shake it. It's like my skin is too tight and my insides too full. The pressure bubbles and builds, a force that refuses to be ignored.

"When I went to LA, it was to see Marshall Faulkner about a job," I blurt out.

A log cracks in the fireplace, punctuating the awful silence. I glance around to find my friends gaping at me. Well, everyone except Rye and Scottie. Rye's expression is one of pride tinged with sadness. Scottie simply looks thoughtful.

I swallow thickly. "I've been…flagging with my job, not finding joy in it. And Marshall offered me a position with him at his Los Angeles firm."

Rye's stare is a palpable touch on my skin. He gives me a small, encouraging smile. He doesn't want me to go. But he'll support me every step of the way.

Never be afraid to fly, Bren. Even if it takes you from all you know.

I hear his voice so clearly, remember the way he pressed his lips to my head as he said it, that lingering touch like he was memorizing the moment in case I left him. Heart aching, I tear my gaze from his and look around at my shocked friends who have begun to argue.

"This is your fault." Sophie wags her slim finger under Scottie's nose.

"Mine?" He raises a brow. "How do you figure, darling?"

"You introduced her to stupid Marshall."

"I thought she might fancy a date with him, not run off to live in LA."

Jax makes a noise of annoyance. "Why the hell were you trying to set her up with a tosspot like Faulkner? Who lives in *LA*."

"Los Angeles isn't that far," Libby tries.

"It's far enough if she's quitting."

"I'm not going to take it," I cut in before they get any more worked up.

Another sharp silence falls. This one doubtful. I can all but feel my friends vibrating with uncertainty.

Killian tries to speak, croaks, then tries again. "You can, Bren. If you want. Don't...Don't stay because of guilt or anything. We wouldn't want that for you."

I really do love my cousin.

"I was going to go. But I just can't. Although the idea of juggling more accounts excites me, leaving you guys doesn't." I take a deep breath, pressing my palms on the worn wood table. "So. I'm going to start my own public relations agency. You'll still be my top priority, but I'm going to expand, take on more clients, hire people." The idea expands and my words trip out with growing excitement. "Women, actually. I want to create a safe space in the industry that's run by women for women."

"I love that," Stella says. "Power in numbers and all that."

"I do too," Libby says.

"I'll be disappointed if you don't let me continue to handle your public relations," I tease.

"As if I'd have it any other way," she says with a wink.

"And I was wondering, Stella and Sophie, if you two would consider joining me as partners."

"What?" Sophie claps her hands together. "Really?"

"Seriously?" Stella adds with a smile.

"You guys are excellent at public relations, and you know it.

With Stella's fundraising smarts and Sophie's social media genius, we could kick ass."

"Oh, I am in," Stella says.

Sophie nods, picking up a cookie. "Me too. I mean, I love these guys, but it would be nice to branch out a little."

"Good." I exhale with a small, bubbling laugh. "It'll be fun."

"Fun," Whip repeats, a little dazed, but then leans over and kisses the side of my head, ending with a brotherly muss of my hair. "Whatever floats your boat, Bren."

I swat him away with a smile. I can't look at Rye. I feel him, though. He is etched in my skin.

Killian lets out a breath. "Okay. That's good. Like I said, it's better when we—"

"I'm not finished," I cut in, my heart in my throat. It's pounding so hard, I'm surprised I can speak. Part of me is screaming that I need to shut it. Not say another word. But I have to.

"There's more?" This from an amused but watchful Scottie.

"Yes." Licking my lips, I look straight at my cousin. "Right after Stella's birthday, Rye and I began hooking up."

The room explodes into comments.

"She went there," Jax says in awe. "Just laid it down on the table."

"Holy shit," Stella murmurs.

Killian's color drains then comes back in a rush. He turns to glare at an obviously poleaxed Rye. "What the fuck!"

"Don't you dare get mad at him," I snap, pulling his attention back to me. "It was entirely consensual, and frankly you have no say in either of our personal lives."

He falls back, slumping in his chair. "Shit. You're right. I'm sorry." He does not address this to Rye, and I'm fairly sure Killian is still imagining kicking his ass. Killian's dark eyes remain on me, wry remorse filling them. "I'll try my best not to act like an overprotective brother, because I know no one can protect someone else from getting hurt. It's just...Rye? Seriously?"

At this, Rye makes a noise that might be interpreted as a growl but could also very well be him scoffing. But he doesn't take his eyes from the table.

"Don't make me come over there," I warn Killian.

He holds up a hand in surrender. "I only meant I thought you two hated each other."

"Not the brightest penny in the jar," Whip murmurs, earning a glare.

"Moving on," I say firmly, as though I'm not shaking like a damn leaf on the inside. "I thought, in the spirit of this newfound openness, I'd tell you."

"Finally." Jax lifts his hands in exasperation. "It was a nightmare keeping silent."

"Amen," Whip agrees with feeling.

Killian gapes. "You two knew?"

I gape too. Not because of Whip, but because almost everyone at the table is nodding.

"From the beginning," Scottie deadpans.

"Well, I didn't," Sophie wails. She glares at her husband. "You kept *this* from me. This? Gabriel!"

He gives her a sidelong look, fondness lighting it. "You wouldn't have been able to keep it secret, chatty girl."

Sophie snaps her mouth closed then wrinkles her nose. "It's true. I would have blabbed to all and sundry."

"I can't believe you guys knew," I say, still not quite able to look at Rye. I'm aware of him, though, sitting there, humming with tension, staring at me like he can't quite figure out what the hell I'm doing.

Jax laughs shortly. "Honey, if you're trying to be discreet, you can't be making out in your kitchen during family dinner."

Killian makes a noise of disgusted horror.

But I have to smile. "Caught us, did you?"

Jax glances at Rye, likely gauging how much to say. "Unfortunately. But Rye told me to fuck off with the gossip and leave it alone on pain of death, so..." He trails off with a shrug.

At Jax's admission, Rye's head jerks up, his eyes wide and slightly panicked. Our gazes collide, and I shake my head slightly, trying to tell him it's okay.

I put him in a difficult position with vows of secrecy. I can imagine Rye worrying that everyone would start talking and how it would embarrass me. It's oddly sweet because I know he was protecting my feelings.

Rye sags slightly, but the muscle in his jaw remains bunched. He breaks our gaze first, blinking down at his hands as though he doesn't know where to look or how to deal with my sudden confession.

I'm sorry, Ryland. It had to be done.

Libby's amused voice tugs my attention away from Rye. "I guessed but didn't say anything because I wasn't sure. It was your body language. People fucking..." She gives a stewing Killian a hesitant glance. "Er...having sex, act differently around each other."

"Yeah, it was pretty obvious," Stella says, then smiles at Killian. "Well, to some of us."

I turn to Scottie, because he's far too quiet and way too smug. "How did you know from the beginning, *Gabriel?*"

He gives me a "get real" look. "I knew what would occur the second Rye stormed out of Stella's birthday party."

"Oh, you did, did you?" Arrogant ass. He probably did. He's creepy that way.

"Love, why do you think I set you up with Marshall, who happens to look far too similar to a certain dithering idiot here? I'd had it with all the sexual tension dressed up as antipathy. Thought you both could use a little motivation."

"That's some Machiavellian shit right there," Jax says with a laugh.

For the first time, Rye stirs, shooting a dark glare at Scottie.

"Dickhead. You gave me so much grief about it. And now you're claiming you were matchmaking?"

Scottie doesn't even blink. "More motivational hurdles, mate."

"Bullshit."

Stella hums thoughtfully. "I don't know...I'm still not convinced Scottie didn't set me up with John."

Jax huffs out a disbelieving laugh. "Us? No. You were only pet sitting. He didn't even want you to bother...Fu-ck me." Gaping, he points a cookie at Scottie. "Make that Machiavelli's evil brother."

I have to bite my lip not to smile, because these sorts of machinations are exactly Scottie's style.

Killian lets out an expansive breath. "Right then. Scottie's moonlighting as the manipulative love fairy. And you two are...?" He makes a vague, helpless gesture with his hand, pointing between Rye and me.

Rye stiffens, his jaw bunching. Red tinges his ears, and he stares at the table like it might hold the meaning of life.

I take another bracing breath. "No. Not anymore. We decided to be friends instead."

I don't miss the way Rye flinches, his big hands curling into tight fists. I want to reach out and touch him so badly, my bones ache. But I can't. Not yet.

"Thing is, I don't want that, Rye."

His head jerks up, his skin paling. Wide, pained blue eyes meet mine.

My lip wobbles dangerously, and I blunder on. "I promised I would never lie to you, but I did. I lied when I said I was okay with being friends. I'm not."

His breath is growing uneven, his eyes turning red. But he doesn't blink, barely moves past the working of his jaw. It's so silent, I can hear the frantic beating of my own heart.

"You once thought I was worth the risk—" My voice breaks then finds strength. "You're worth it too. I don't want to just be your friend, Rye. I want...I want to be yours. I want you to be mine. Wherever I land, whatever I'm doing. Because I...I adore you, Ryland Peterson."

He takes a sharp, shuddering breath, the sound loud in the thick silence.

"I'm saying it here, in front of everyone we love, because you deserve that. I forced you to hide our relationship from them, like a dirty secret. When you're...You're the best man I know, and I'd...I'd be honored to be even a small part of your life. Though, you should know, I want everything. If you'll...if you'll have me."

I stop there, hot and flushed and utterly drained.

Rye doesn't say a word. No one does. The only sound is the *snap-pop* of the fire and the rushing of my blood in my ears. Then, abruptly, he stands, knocking back his chair. I stand too; I can't sit and remain passive. Besides, I'm going to run like hell if he tells me it's too late.

His nostrils flare, and then he's stepping up onto the table. He's tall enough to do it with graceful ease. On a mission, he walks across the table, the dishes rattling, gaze locked with mine as he comes. Lightly, he hops down to stand before me.

I tilt my head back to meet his eyes. He searches my face for one long moment, a man uncertain he's heard correctly, but then his mouth trembles. When he finally speaks, his voice is deep, so deep, as though the words are coming from the very core of him.

"I always was."

I can't quite make my mouth work correctly. "Always was what?"

"Yours." Tender hands cup my cheeks. "I've always been yours. And you...You already are my everything. You're my music, Bren."

A sob escapes. "Rye."

That's all he needs. He dips his head and kisses me, a bit frantic, a bit tender, and entirely perfect. It's air, the first true breath I've had. I pull him to me, but he's already there, wrapping me up in his solid warmth, kissing me like I'm his air too.

I'm his music. And he's my wings.

"Aw," says a voice, breaking the silence. "That's an Instagram moment right there."

Rye pulls back enough to shoot Jax a repressive glare. "Excuse us," he says to everyone, then hefts me up into his arms. I wrap my legs around his trim waist as he palms my butt. And then he's kissing me again and walking out of the room.

Faintly, I hear Killian mutter, "And the world was never the same again."

I smile against Rye's lips, joy soaring, because he's right. My world will never be the same.

CHAPTER THIRTY-THREE

RYE

SOMEHOW, I get us to my room. Somehow, I manage to shut the door behind us without dropping her in my clumsy haste. How am I supposed to function properly when my woman is wrapped around me, eating at my mouth like she'll never get another taste?

My woman. Holy shit. She's mine.

Mine.

I press her against the door, my fingers threading through her hair. "If this is a dream, don't wake me up."

She laughs against my lips, a soft exhale of cocoa-laced breath. "No dream, buttercup."

A shot of pure, unfiltered happiness shoots up my spine, and I kiss her deep, my body pressing into hers. She feels so damn good. Warm and real. Delicate.

Fragile.

Shit. I'm too big to be shoving her up against doors without care. Pulling us away from the door, I spin her around to lay her on my bed. She smiles up at me, auburn hair a halo around the oval of her face, as I take off her little fuzzy slippers, tossing them next to mine, before crawling into bed.

I settle over her, my arms bracketing her slim body. Now that I have her here, I can slow down. I can savor this.

There's so much I want to do, touch every inch of her silken skin, breathe her fragrance in deep. Kiss those cherry-sweet lips. But all I can do is stare, my hands clumsy as I cup her cheeks.

"You nearly killed me down there," I croak. "For a second. When I thought..." My chest hitches, and I kiss her again. Just to feel her, to confirm she's real.

When I pull back, Brenna traces one of my brows with the tip of her finger, her expression solemn. "I bumbled through the first half. I'm sorry."

"I'm not. Thank you."

Her lips quirk with an uncertain smile. "You're thanking me for a badly worded public confession?"

"Yes. My heart was broken. You made it whole again."

"Rye." She strokes my cheek. "I'll do my best to be more careful with you in the future."

I said that to her once. When I risked it all and thought I'd lost her. She's giving my words back to me. A slow smile spreads through me. I feel it down to my toes, on the back of my neck, in the pounding center of my chest.

I want to say something, tell her what she means to me, but she's tugging me down, her mouth fitting over mine.

For a long time, we simply kiss, slow and easy, whispering nonsensical things, exchanging small touches just because we can. Lazy contentment steals over me. She's warm and delicious, her mouth a wonder, her body my most covetous dream. If all I had of her was this—lying in her arms, tasting her mouth—I'd take it.

But she's given me everything. The knowledge fills me up, has me threading my fingers into her hair and holding on.

Brenna's gaze is soft as she rubs the scruff of my beard. "What were you going to tell me in the hallway?"

"Oh, that?" My smile is self-deprecating, the heavy desperation of that moment replaced by buoyant satisfaction. "I was going to engage in a little light begging. Tell you that I was a bonehead coward when I said it was a mistake to ask for more." I tug her closer. "It was a lie, Bren. I wanted you. So fucking badly, that I said what I thought you wanted to hear so I could keep you in my life."

"We spent a long time protecting ourselves from each other." She strokes me to gentle the words. "Made us both a little boneheaded."

"Now I want to make a joke about bones," I confess with a laugh. Because it feels so fucking good just to laugh with her.

Her lips purse, but she can't stop the smile. "Of course, you do." The smile breaks free, and her lips press to mine. "You gonna?"

"Going to what?" I ask against her lips, distracted.

She snickers. "Bone me?"

I blink—and then burst out laughing, my body quaking with it. God, I adore this woman. So much, my hands are clumsy as I lift her shirt to free her from it. The sight of her pert, pink-tipped breasts has me groaning low in my throat. "Hello, lovelies, oh, how I've missed you."

She huffs a laugh, as I lean down and kiss each rosy tip with due reverence. But the sound dies as I gently suckle one nipple, and her fingers thread through my hair. "Rye..."

"Yeah?" I rasp, nuzzling under the curve of her breast. She smells so good, feels like satin.

"I've missed you too."

The confession, softly spoken and filled with longing, has my heart clenching tight. With dreamlike slowness, I map the silken dips and lines of her body, drawing off her pants as I go. She opens her legs for me, and I find the heat of her, swollen and slick, and all for me.

I need a taste. She is luscious, melting against my tongue, dripping honey that I lap up with growing fervor. I drown in her flavors, the musky scent of her desire. It feeds my own, and I grind into the bed to ease the ache. I am utterly lost, working her as she comes and comes.

Until she grabs at my hair, tugging with impatience. "Up here," she demands, all dewy pink and panting. Greedy hands pluck at my shirt. Grinning, I help her out, whipping it off, easing down my pants. My dick slaps against my abs, it's so damn hard.

I palm it, squeezing hard to get it under control. But her hands are on me now, running along my shoulders like a balm. I surge up to kiss her, needing those lips, needing to feel her skin pressed to mine. It's been too long. Forever. Fucking agony.

But she's wrapped around me now, easing the pain. Legs locked with mine, her hands stroke my back, grasping my ass. I love it. Love everything about her.

I murmur words of reverence as I cup her cheek, kiss her mouth. Tell her how much I missed her, missed this, how she's the only one I think of, the only one I want. She shivers, moans against my lips.

"There's only you," she whispers. "No one else will do."

Has she any idea what that does to me? My lids prickle, emotion clogging my throat as I ease between her spread thighs. Staring down at her softly smiling face, auburn strands of her hair sticking to her flushed skin, my arms bracketing her slim body, I push into the snug clasp of her and shudder, undone, pleasure flowing down my limbs like liquid heat.

I move slowly, going in deep and holding there for a long moment before pulling back and doing it again. Again. Working myself home, claiming my place, making her moan.

I kiss her mouth, touch her cheeks, the curve of her neck. This is love. I know it now. The utter adulation in our touches, the perfection of it. It is peace and comfort and pleasure all in one.

The knowledge swells between us, reflected in her eyes. And

she touches me with trembling hands, moves with me, taking me just as I take her. In that moment, I know the truth: I am home. After a long journey, I am home.

———

Brenna

THE LITTLE HOUSE in the woods just beyond the lake started life as a gamekeeper's cottage. Like something out of a fairy tale with its thatched roof, eyebrow dormers, and walls of timber and stucco. It had fallen into disrepair until Uncle Xander renovated the place in the 1990s. Now, the floors glow mellow honey and marshmallow-cream walls contrast with the dark old beams stretched over the low ceiling.

As kids, Killian and I used to sneak in here from time to time, pretending to be Hansel and Gretel. Or, in our teen years, to smoke pot and read books, or listen to music while lounging on the overstuffed sofa set up before the river-stone fireplace.

At some point last night, an envelope was thrust under Rye's door, containing a heavy iron key and a note from Killian that read:

FOR THE LOVE of all that's holy (and my freaking ears), please, please, please take the cottage. Love you, Bean (& Rye, I guess).
—Kills

I SUPPOSE Rye and I had gotten a little too loud, and the note was Killian's way of saying he supported our relationship, something I think we both needed to hear. So we happily decamped to the cottage, heading directly for the massive oak tester bed, draped in butter-colored toile that took up nearly the entirety of the bedroom alcove.

Though the house has a fully stocked kitchenette, later the following day, Whip delivered us a lunch basket, smugly speculating that we needed real sustenance in the form of a hot meal.

A grinning Rye thanked his friend at the door then crawled back in bed to feed me bites of savory steak pasties with a buttery crust that melted on the tongue and left little golden flakes on my lips for Rye to lick off.

We devoured lunch, washing it down with cold, hoppy beers, before Rye shoved everything to the side and then spread my legs to have his "dessert." At some point, we drifted off to sleep, but it must not have been for long, because the fire still crackles behind the grate when I wake.

It begins to rain, a steady fall that taps against the windows and turns the outside light weak and gray. Inside, however, is quiet and cozy and beautiful. Cream-colored rag rugs over mellow wood floors, tobacco-velvet club chairs, and the slouchy long couch covered in faded cream-cabbage rose print lend the room a soft and pleasing feel, while emerald-green gourd lamps with deep red shades cast a rosy glow to the room.

Rye is still asleep, his muscled body a sprawl of firm, golden skin and mosaics of colorful ink. One big foot hangs over the edge of the bed, the white sheets twisted around one beefy thigh. Smiling, I run a hand over the back of his spiked hair. In the dim of the alcove, it's the color of old bronze with glints of gold. He grunts in his sleep, turning his head my way. There's not a gentle line on his boldly shaped features, save his lips. Those are wide and soft, the bottom lip plush and utterly biteable.

A light exhalation leaves him, the thick fan of his lashes fluttering with his dreams. I let him be. The poor man more than earned his sleep.

Languid and replete, I lift my arms and stretch out all the delicious little aches and pains that making love to Rye left behind. The room is warm enough that I don't bother with a robe but pad naked to the bathroom.

When I return, I curl up on the end of the bed, watching the fire play over the pale walls, and draw in the faint scent of lavender tingeing the air. I have no idea where it comes from, but it is sweet and clean and soothes me. Every part of this room is created for enjoyment. And all I can think is that I am here, and I am grateful. I love my life and the people in it.

Contentment has me feeling lazy. I revel in it, give myself permission to let go. It's surprisingly easy to do with Rye.

Damn, but the man can put a smile on my face even when he's sleeping less than two feet away. I allow myself that joy too, because I'm done worrying about what I'm supposed to be doing.

Behind me, Rye stirs, uttering an adorably confused grunt, and I know he's awake and most likely rubbing the sleep from his eyes.

I continue to watch the fire and feel his gaze like a warm caress along my back.

"Good sleep?" I ask softly.

He grunts again, a sated beast lounging in his bed.

"Yeah," he says, just as soft. He's silent for a moment. "You okay?"

The sound of his quiet care has me smiling, but I don't turn around. Not yet. A strange sort of peaceful lethargy keeps me in place. "Yes. Just thinking about my parents."

He waits a beat before answering. "They don't deserve you, baby."

Baby. We rarely call each other by those types of names. But the way he says it, gentle and tender, makes me feel wrapped up in his protection. I like it. A lot.

Ducking my head, I pick at the cashmere duvet cover. "I'm okay. Better, actually."

With a light sigh, I tilt my head back and blink up at the ceiling. "I was sitting here, feeling safe and content, and this realization stole over me. For my entire life, I worried about fitting in, felt like I was the outsider when it came to the wealth and success Killian, his parents, and you guys in the band all had."

Rye doesn't say a word, but I know he's ready to reach out if I need it, and the words come easier.

"I'd hear my parents' warnings, all the times they said I wasn't good enough, that I didn't fit in this world, and deep down, I believed it. But the truth is, my parents were the ones who didn't fit. They were the outsiders, not because they weren't good enough, but because they didn't let themselves belong.

"I belong here for the simple reason the people in my life care about me, and this wealth and success is the result of hard work and talent. I fit in because this is the life I made for myself. For years, I ran from anything that threatened to leave me emotionally open. I denied myself true happiness, denied myself *you*. Back in that kitchen, I stopped running, and everything shifted. And...I don't know...it just truly sank in."

Pausing, I smooth my hand over my bare knee, that gentle sense of peace floating over me. "We are who we are, and who we are is pretty great as far as I'm concerned. No one can take that from me without my permission. Not even my parents."

When I finish, Rye doesn't say anything. But I know he's heard and is processing. The bed creaks with his movement, then his voice, thick with sleep but also emotion, reaches over the small space between us.

"I love you."

So simply said, like it's always been true.

It soaks into my skin, fills my heart. Finally, I turn. He reclines on his side, head resting in his hand, looking back at me with that truth shining in his eyes. Strong, pure, gorgeous. Mine.

This man is mine. My friend. My lover. My home. My heart.

"I love you too."

His smile is the dawn. And when he reaches out to tug me against his solid warmth, I go willingly, curling into him and threading my fingers in his messy hair.

The corners of his denim-blue eyes crinkle as he touches my cheek with the blunt tips of his fingers. "We just said we loved each other."

"We did."

The grin turns incandescent. "Say it again, so I can fully soak it up."

"I love you."

"God, that's nice." He kisses me, melting little presses of lips to lips. "One more time."

"I love you, Ryland Peterson."

"Mmm...Just gets better and better." He rolls me back and settles between my legs, his big, firm body a blanket of warmth around me.

I stroke the short strands of his thick hair. "Let me see. Tell me again."

The corners of his eyes crinkle, a look of utter happiness lighting his face. "I love you, Brenna James."

"You're right, it feels really good."

Rye hums and kisses the crook of my neck. "I'll tell you every day, then."

Little shivers of delight race over my skin. "And twice on Sundays?"

"Multiple times every day." He finds the sensitive spot under my ear, his voice dipping. "I'll say it whenever I'm thinking it, which is basically all the time."

I trace the hard curve of his shoulder where his skin is hot and tight. "Let's not go crazy, now."

"You'll love it," he growls against my neck, playfully nipping me.

My smile pulls wide, joy making me giddy. "You're right. I will."

He chuckles, the sound rumbling and infectious. And suddenly I'm laughing too, wrapping myself more firmly around him as he peppers my face with kisses, his big body quaking with humor.

"Why are we laughing?" I ask idly, my hands finding their way back into his hair.

Rye lifts his head and meets my gaze. His entire heart is in his eyes and it is stunningly beautiful.

"Because we're happy, Berry. We're happy."

EPILOGUE

BRENNA

RYE FINDS me by the pool. I'm more of a burner than a tanner, so I wait until the sun is low in the sky to take a swim. I've had a long day, talking to prospective clients, coordinating with my new staff to set the business up—including wooing Jules away from Scottie's employ. I'd feel guilty about that if he hadn't given me his blessing to pursue her.

Now, all I want to do is drink my cocktail and hang out with my man.

When he stops at the end of the double-wide lounger I'm sitting on, I smile up at him. "Hey, buttercup. You done for the day?"

We've set up camp at his LA house. And it's been surprisingly easy, living and sharing workspace together. I took the home office that overlooked the valley below, and Rye mainly spends time in one of the studio spaces. So far, he's produced two albums this spring, and is working with a bunch of other artists for upcoming projects.

"All done." He eases in next to me, his big bulk taking up

most of the space. With a happy sigh, he leans down and kisses me, his hand cupping my cheek in that way of his that says I'm his world. I melt into the touch, humming in pleasure.

When he pulls back, his expression is relaxed and light. A far cry from how he'd been for so many months. The time off from the band had been hard at first; he'd felt like he was abandoning them. But then he started to heal, to expand his creativity with producing, and the tight lines of pain around his mouth and eyes began to ease.

"Want a sip?" I offer him my cocktail glass.

He leans back, crossing one leg over the other, and accepts the drink. "God, I needed this."

Rye runs a hand through his hair, sending the bronze strands on end. Months in the sun have bleached the tips light gold. His free hand finds mine, and he threads our fingers together in a comfortable clasp. He smiles at me, a soft look, as his gaze moves over my face like he's memorizing it. The mellow light of the late afternoon sun turns his eyes sapphire blue. "Needed you too, Berry."

"Well, obviously," I say, as if his words don't make me giddy. We've been together for nearly six months now, and the man still has the power to make my insides flutter with just a look. "You'd be an utter mess without me."

Of course, that goes both ways. I used to think needing someone was a weakness. But life is better, richer, more real with him in it. And I'm not weaker admitting this; I'm stronger.

Rye lifts our linked hands to his mouth and kisses my knuckles. "I would. I'd probably forget to tie my shoes, run into walls and not notice, be a blubbering lonely wreck. I definitely function better on a steady diet of stellar sex."

Rolling my eyes, I reach over him to take my drink back. "Stellar, is it?"

He catches me around my waist and hauls me close, chuckling. "Spectacular." His lips brush the crest of my cheek. I feel that touch deep in my belly. "Perfect. The very best ever."

I sip my drink, suppressing a smile. "No one likes a kiss-ass, Ryland."

Gently, he takes the drink from my hand and sets it on the side table before hugging me close and burrowing his face in the crook of my neck. "Roll over and I'll kiss your ass right now."

I laugh, half-heartedly trying to wiggle away. "No ass for you, big guy."

He grabs said ass and gives it a fond squeeze. "Now, Brenna, you know we both win when you give me this fine ass."

He's not wrong. Flushing, I cup the square line of his smooth jaw. He shaved off his beard about a month into living in LA, not liking how it felt in the warm California sun. "Give me your fine ass in return and we'll talk."

His grin flashes wide. "Done. Now be a good girl and take this off." He plucks at my bikini bottom.

"We can't." I stroke his cheek with my thumb. "I just got a text from Stella. They're going to be here in ten minutes."

We'd seen our friends on and off for months. Stella, Sophie, and Libby have been helping me set up our business. And while Libby isn't a working partner, she's been active in recruiting talent. The plan is for us to work out of both coasts, and we've had lots of FaceTime meetings. But this is the first time everyone is coming to stay with us all at once.

My birthday is tomorrow, and we're all celebrating.

"Fine. I'll claim that ass tonight." Rye flops back with a long-suffering sigh, but his expression is happy. He's missed his boys. A lot. It is no surprise to me that they're planning to work on new material once they get here.

"We'll see." He totally will. I'll make sure of it.

Rye grunts but then sits up straight as though startled. "I forgot something..." With a quick kiss on my cheek, he rolls over and hops up. "Don't move."

"Wasn't planning to." Smiling to myself, I lift my hands over-head and settle down with a sigh. But Rye returns quickly, carrying a black lacquered box big enough to hold a loaf of bread.

He appears almost shy as he hovers by the edge of the lounger. "Your birthday present."

Hauling myself up, I eye him then the box, not having a clue what's in it, but loving that he's brought me a present. He does that a lot now, though mostly with little things: pastries from my favorite shop, fashion magazines he knows I like—the warming lube was really for both of us, but I appreciated it just the same.

"But my birthday isn't until tomorrow."

"I know." Again comes the strange hesitation in his voice, as though he's nervous. Expectation lights his eyes as he hands it to me. "But I wanted to give this to you when we were alone."

I run my hands over the silky, smooth surface.

"Go on." He gestures with his chin to the box. "Open it."

"I'm opening it," I insist, fighting a smile.

He hunkers down next to me, thick thighs stretching his worn jeans. His nearness distracts me for a moment, and I find myself leaning into his warmth to press a kiss on his neck, but the impatient yet amused look in his eyes brings me back to the task.

Lifting the lid, I find the insides swathed in pink tissue paper. It takes me a moment to discover my prize but when I do, my breath goes short. Hands trembling, I lift out a perfect open-toed sandal made of pale pink leather with a slim rose-gold metallic heel. What makes the shoe utterly beautiful is the pair of delicate laser-cut leather angel wings covered in rose-gold glitter and rhinestones poised on the back of the heel as though they might soon flutter and take to the air.

"Oh, my." I know these heels. They are Sophia Webster Evangelines. I've admired them from afar, but they seemed too frivolous, too ethereally pretty, to buy. And yet the fact that Rye bought me the loveliest pair of princess heels I've ever seen has my vision blurring and my heart swelling. "They're perfect," I get out.

His expression fills with tenderness as he runs a finger along my forearm. "Wings, Bren. So you'll never forget how far you can fly."

Oh, hell.

I set the magical heel back into the box, then grab him, hugging him fiercely, my face buried in his neck. "With you in my life, I'll *never* forget how far we *both* can fly, Ryland Peterson."

He squeezes me back in a grip so strong, it almost hurts, before rasping, "I love you too, Brenna James. I love you too."

And that's really all that matters.

ACKNOWLEDGMENTS

Many thanks to editors, Manu Velasco and Christa Desir at Tessera Editorial, proofreaders Christine Yates, and Angie at pinkadotpages, and my beta readers Louisa Edwards, Sam Young, Adriana Anders, and Kati Brown.

A huge thanks to Nina, Mary, Kim, Kelley, and everyone at Valentine PR.

But the biggest thanks goes to the dedicated fans and reviewers who have made this series what it is and have patiently waited for this book. I cannot express how much this means to me.

ALSO BY KRISTEN CALLIHAN

THE GAME ON SERIES
The Hook Up —Book 1
The Friend Zone – Book 2
The Game Plan —Book 3
The Hot Shot — Book 4

VIP SERIES
Idol —Book 1
Managed —Book 2
Fall—Book 3

Cowritten with Samantha Young
Outmatched

With MONTLAKE
Dear Enemy
Make it Sweet

DARKEST LONDON
Firelight
Moonglow
Winterblaze
Shadowdance
Evernight
Soulbound
Forevermore

ABOUT THE AUTHOR

Kristen Callihan is a New York Times, Wall Street Journal, and USA Today bestselling author. She has won a RITA award, and two RT Reviewer's Choice awards. Her novels have garnered starred reviews from Publisher's Weekly and the Library Journal, as well as being awarded top picks by many reviewers. Her debut book FIRELIGHT received RT Magazine's Seal of Excellence, was named a best book of the year by Library Journal, best book of Spring 2012 by Publisher's Weekly, and was named the best romance book of 2012 by ALA RUSA. When she is not writing, she is reading.

To get to know Kristen
www.kristencallihan.com
Kristen.Callihan@aol.com

Made in the USA
Monee, IL
29 June 2021